PENGUIN BOOKS

THE HOUSE ON CALLE SOMBRA

Marga Ortigas has travelled the world as a journalist for three decades, with a career spanning five continents and two of the largest global news networks. After getting her start in the Philippines, she joined CNN in London, working across Europe and covering the war in Iraq from its inception. In 2006, she returned to Manila and the Asia Pacific region, reporting from the frontlines of armed conflict and climate change as senior correspondent for Al Jazeera. Her extensive coverage of the Muslim rebellion in the southern Philippines was recognized by the International Committee of the Red Cross for Humanitarian Reporting.

A British Council Chevening Scholar, Ortigas earned her MA in literature and criticism at the University of Greenwich. She speaks three languages, and is the editor of *I, Migrant*, an online platform which showcases writing from the diaspora, advocating a universal humanity beneath people's differences.

12/3/22

With my best wishes

Marga Ortigas

(Manila)

ADVANCE PRAISE FOR *The House on Calle Sombra*

'Eye of a journalist, prose of a poet, an exotic tale delicately weaving a nation's history with a family's unravelling. A rags-to-riches parable, in an unfamiliar and evocatively recalled landscape, festooning the reader in garlands of uncanny self-realisation.'

—Nic Robertson, International Diplomatic Editor, CNN

'The author's fluid writing style and her ability to capture the nuances of Filipino inter-relationships make this novel a riveting and compelling read. It is storytelling at its best.'

—Cheche Lázaro, acclaimed Philippine broadcaster
and journalism professor

'Marga Ortigas has written a stellar, soaring, gut-crunching multi-generational tale that is certain to set on edge the teeth of Manila's great and good. Like the tunnels in the book, this will take you into a world behind the curtain, revealing the universal truths concealed behind jewels, privilege and power.'

—Sheila Macvicar, Emmy, Peabody and duPont
Award-winning international journalist

'In her first novel, Ortigas takes us on an intimate exploration of the powerful Castillo de Montijo's family history. The novel skilfully weaves together the destiny of the Castillo lineage with the secrets of its past. Thus, unfurling a complex plot where we can trace the origin of the family's fortune deep into the dark pits of its initial motives and ensuing political alliances. Ortigas is as well-measured as she is compelling in depicting the Castillos' 'original sin' as she seamlessly navigates the conceits and schemes of the Filipino elite across the time span of three generations. In *The House on Calle Sombra*, a family's fate is set against the destructive power of systemic violence. In our time, this very type of violence is conspicuously representative of nations where the ruling class along with the structures of governance have grown weaker under the ever-expanding influence of organized crime. Perhaps this is Ortigas' greatest literary achievement, a well-earned balance in her portrayal of that mysterious place where the inner and outer narratives of our lives come to intersect.'

— Javier Sicilia, Award-winning Mexican poet, novelist,
and social activist, founder of the Movement for Peace with Justice
and Dignity against the crime and violence of Mexico's drug war

'*The House on Calle Sombra* is an epic novel that deals with three generations of the Castillo de Montijo family. Like many Filipino families, the family has mixed bloodlines: Spanish, Muslim, surely layers of Malay and Chinese. The chapter headings and some dialogues are done in three languages—English, Spanish, and Filipino— to mirror the country's hybrid cultures. The family's youngest scion is a Tiresias on drugs: a photojournalist covering the Philippines' infamous anti-drug campaign. The epic sweep is told through a brisk prose style and fragmented sentences. At times, these beautiful sentences sound like heartbeats: quick, foretelling the love and doom in these marvellous pages.'

—Danton Remoto, Author of *Riverrun, A Novel*

The House on Calle Sombra

A Parable

Marga Ortigas

PENGUIN BOOKS

An imprint of Penguin Random House

PENGUIN BOOKS

USA | Canada | UK | Ireland | Australia
New Zealand | India | South Africa | China | Southeast Asia

Penguin Books is part of the Penguin Random House group of companies
whose addresses can be found at global.penguinrandomhouse.com

Published by Penguin Random House SEA Pte Ltd
9, Changi South Street 3, Level 08-01,
Singapore 486361

First published in Penguin Books by Penguin Random House SEA 2021

10 9 8 7 6 5 4 3 2

ISBN 9789814954044

Typeset in Adobe Garamond Pro by MAP Systems, Bangalore, India
Printed at Markono Print Media Pte Ltd, Singapore

The painting used on the cover is 'Portion of Siojo Old Haus. San Miguel, Bulacan'
Oil/Acrylic on Canvas (1979) by Philippine artist, Danny Pangan. With permission
from the painting's current owner and the artist's family.

www.penguin.sg

For my mother, **Maritoni,**
who lived her life sharing her love of stories.

Most cultures have multiple words for things that are
important to them,
or prevalent in their societies.
In cold, polar countries, there are numerous words for
ice and snow.
In tropical ones—rice and grain.
Where I'm from, there are countless words
for murder.

Ximena Yrastegui Castillo de Montijo,
International Journalist
TEDx Talk, London, June 2016

Table of Contents

APERTURE

El Adivino y la Gracia | **The Soothsayer and the Yarn** | Ang Manghuhula at ang Kuwentong Kagila-gilalas

From the time he was a child, Federico Luís Castillo de Montijo III was often seen with his mouth hanging open—an inelegant habit ill-suited to his family's social standing.

'That's how you'll catch flies, *niñito*,' his aunt Alma always disapproved.

Undoubtedly, his family would be grateful that no one of consequence saw him in his current state—hog-tied and hauled like cattle. His mouth agape inside the dirty sack that was over his head. No, it would not do for the progenitor's namesake to be so dishevelled.

'*Paré*,' Ricky addressed his hosts in the local dialect, 'how much?'

He always wondered what the price was on his head.

Without warning, he was dropped to the floor. A heavy foot kicked him in the face, and the sudden taste of blood reminded him of the sour offal stew that—at his house—only the maids ever ate.

His stomach turned as the ground beneath him rolled. Pitching, like an earthquake, or the rocking of a crib. He wasn't sure if he was just nauseous or—*Out at sea?*

The roar of crashing waves usurped the ringing in his ears.

'*Banatan mo uli, p're.*'

2

Ricky's eyes fluttered open at the rumbling voice. Just as someone in the darkness began to beat him.

He tried to move his arms to protect his camera. *Where was it?*

Through the wet burlap—and the sting of salt—he thought he saw the lights of Manila's jagged skyline in the distance. The dense city's uneven ridges looked like a frantic pulse on a heart monitor. Too far away to drown him in its usual din.

No honking cars, bustling crowds, or wailing karaoke machines.

'*Tama na!*' An abrupt command to stop the assault.

Then, he began to hear the clicking. Stabbing through the throbbing in his head as it approached.

Click, cluck, click—like a metronome keeping time for an absent score. *Was that the call of a gecko?*

Ricky remembered the legend of the common household lizard. Tiny creepers, skittering everywhere, overlooked. His nanny told him it was a young boy cursed for disobeying his family. Doomed to roam the home yet be apart.

Every day since, across the islands at sunset, repentant reptiles scurried down walls to kiss the ground.

The clicking stopped. And a deep, rough voice—like that of a chain-smoker with too much phlegm—cut into his self-pity. 'This is no way to treat our special guest.'

It was said in English for Ricky's benefit.

Invisible hands held him down as the sack was yanked from his head. He blinked but was still surrounded by darkness.

Sweat streamed into his eyes, and he couldn't find the line between sea and sky.

He opened his mouth, struggling to adjust to the open air.

It was suffocating.

'I hope you had a good trip . . . click, cluck.'

When Ricky dared look up, he saw his reflection by the glint of the moon, distorted on the speaker's electric-green glasses. Lenses so large they covered half the face.

Ricky wet himself.

He was on his knees before the most powerful man in The Islands, an avuncular shyster known as 'Tukô'—the local word for a gecko, the ubiquitous barking lizard.

'So,' the gravel in Tukô's voice rattled ominously, 'you are Federico Castillo de Montijo, the Third?'

Tukô's hair was tinted black, and he dressed in linen. His eyes—day or night—were concealed by those green-tinted glasses. He was always pushing them up his bulbous nose.

On his stubby fingers, he wore gold rings that gleamed in the darkness, and he famously clicked his tongue when he wasn't speaking. Creating a sound that resembled a gecko's call.

No one knew for sure how old he was, but Tukô was swaddled in wrinkles.

His crinkled skin was rich with red and white blotches—psoriasis—a chronic condition that suitably gave him a coat of scales.

Tukô snorted, then barked a little less menacingly. 'You are much smaller than I expected, Federico . . . the Third.'

Ricky knew better than to reply.

'Like some prince . . . the Third,' Tukô repeated with a flourish.

Ricky felt the stars look down on him as hot sea air sliced into his battered skin.

'Do you like my sub, Young Majesty?' Tukô asked proudly. The full moon shone above them like a South Sea pearl in an oyster-shell sky.

Sub? Ricky's jaw dropped when he realized they were on the deck of a small submarine. It seemed to be peeking just over the waves.

Tukô snorted again. 'Yes, I have a baby sub,' he proclaimed, as if reading Ricky's mind. 'Pity you don't have your camera . . . click, cluck. Are you wondering what other tales about me are true?'

The islanders whispered about Tukô's nocturnal activities, but no one ever dared to gather proof.

The old man was said to be a crime lord with his own militia—the biggest dealer of narcotics, weapons, and contraband. Anything that could turn an indecent profit.

And—so it was said—he did what it took to secure his interests.

Including make anyone who got in his way—disappear.

Like everyone on the islands, Ricky heard the rumours but thought them too far-fetched to be true.

Then again, what better con than to hide the truth in plain sight as a lie?

'Don't look so shocked, Federico the Third,' Tukô laughed. 'You should hear the stories around town about Sombra.'

Ricky bristled at the mention of his family's estate.

Tukô was as cold-blooded as any reptile, and he knew how to lurk unnoticed inside your home.

'I need you to do me a favour, Fe-de-ri-co . . . on behalf of your family.'

Ricky knew that meant he was screwed.

No one survived turning down the barking lizard.

* * *

The sun found him along the coast of Manila Bay, washed up like dregs excreted by the city.

Bad trip, man. He hoped the talking gecko was just another drug-fuelled vision.

But taped to his chest—a mobile phone he didn't recognize. It was wrapped in plastic and blinking a small green light.

There was a single text on the cheap Chinese mobile: 'I know wr 2 find U, Federico THE 3rd. Don't let me down.'

Joder—Ricky's head throbbed as he tried to get up—and where the heck was his camera?

Click. Cluck. Click.

He had to get home to Sombra.

PART I

STRUCTURE

Chapter 1

La Casa y el Caballero | **The House and the Gentleman** | Ang Bahay at ang Ginoo

The house stood at the end of a long, cobbled drive lined thick with acacia trees—its leafy marquee of interlocked branches cast a dense network of shadows that moved with the sun.

The manor—better said—was within a sprawling estate on a street named Calle Sombra, off the main avenue in the centre of Manila.

It was far north of the great Po'on Volcano and just south of the river Pasig, which meandered through the capital towards the bay.

The home rose where the tide ebbed.

On marshland that became the business district.

Over the years, skyscrapers sprouted like reeds, gracelessly dwarfing the large estate.

Yet even up-close—from outside—you wouldn't know the mansion was there.

The property was bounded by thick concrete walls so high that two ladders were needed to see over them. But no thief or bird would dare. All along the top, shards of broken glass were embedded in the cement like unrefined gems on a crown.

The walls themselves were camouflaged in ivy. A vertical carpet of dark grey-green.

Dull and unattractive.

The bright bougainvillea and colourful plumeria were saved for the gardens inside. The last thing the owners wanted was to invite onlookers.

Not that the creeping ivy could be seen from the street. Bamboo plants nearly three feet deep stood like sentries along both sides of the wall.

The only thing missing was a sign saying— 'Keep out!'

In the middle of the front wall—nearly twenty feet high—were heavy black gates of fortified metal, which concealed a pedestrian entrance and a small, latched peephole to the street.

It was like a medieval castle.

Exactly as its owner had planned.

* * *

The owner—Federico Julián Castillo—arrived on the islands from Spain in 1937, a penniless orphan fleeing a brewing civil war.

He was eighteen and not interested in dying.

Fortunately, after nearly four centuries, the far-off Philippines were no longer owned by the Spanish Crown. And from what he'd heard, the Americans—the new colonial masters—were more egalitarian.

Without a pedigree or an inheritance, Federico believed—and rightly so—that he'd fare better in the tropics than in the rugged, landlocked region of his birth. Extremadura didn't sound like 'extreme hardship' for nothing.

The voyage over—though hidden in the hold for most of it—was the first he'd seen the ocean.

Federico fell in love with The Islands the moment he crept off the ship and wandered towards the elegant walled city of Intramuros, once the seat of Spain's only colony in Asia.

Like the country he left, Intramuros had ramparts, cobbled streets, and stone churches—but it was adorned by a wealth of wonderfully unfamiliar trees.

There were more fruits than he recognized and unexpectedly numerous shades of green.

The weather was mild, and everywhere he looked, a fiesta of flowers dazzled against the crystal sky. He was determined to learn their names. *Ka-la-chu-chi, gu-ma-me-la, sam-pa-gui-ta.*

Young Federico could not afford to live in the fortified city of Old Manila, but some evenings—after working the docks—he treated himself to a horse-drawn carriage ride through its narrow streets. Blissfully hypnotized by the patter of hooves upon cobblestone and the heady, sweet aroma of tropical plants.

Sometimes, he walked. To bask more fully in the splendour of its parks and plazas. Imagining himself there in a grander time. Pretending he was one of the aristocratic dons.

It was on those walks that Federico Castillo decided he'd do anything to have a house like the Spanish Colonial mansions on Calle Real.

One with a sturdy stone base and breezy top floors. Exquisitely framed by elaborate woodwork and embellished with translucent Capiz shell windows.

It would have a courtyard—*maybe two!*—and a lush garden.

The home of a tropical gentleman.

But Federico's dreams were deferred when he fled to the mountains in 1942.

World War II broke out, and Japan invaded Manila.

* * *

It rained non-stop for almost two weeks. That's also how long they'd been walking.

Mostly, they trekked through the night. By the light of a thousand fireflies and an unseen chorus of geckos. Federico was soothed by the steady, languid sound and the soft flicker of bugs like embers over the jungle. It was all so beautiful—

if not for the war.

Ka Igmé, the guerrilla leader, said they could rest once they got to the next farmhouse.

But there wasn't a farm, or a house, for days.

As morning broke through the clouds, the geckos silenced and the fireflies vanished.

'*Kasama*,' Federico implored in a mix of Tagalog and English, 'I can no longer feel my feet. How about a few minutes by that boulder?'

He didn't want to seem feeble, but they hadn't eaten.

They were also soaked, and he feared collapsing if they trod on.

The last thing Federico wanted was to burden them with having to carry him. It was hard enough convincing them to take him along.

Besides, they hadn't seen a 'Jap' for days.

'All right, Ka Iko,' Igmé acquiesced. 'Five minutes.'

Federico liked that they gave him a nickname. It meant they finally counted him among them.

He was a kasama. A comrade in arms.

Worthy of being addressed as 'Ka'.

When he first joined them a year earlier, the guerrillas didn't know what to make of him and suspected he was a deserting US soldier.

At five feet seven, Federico was taller than the tallest among them. With hair they compared to coconut husk, and eyes they insisted were the colour of dried corn stalks.

He was paler than anyone they knew, and his young face—unlike other Spaniards—was shaved clean.

It felt cooler that way.

And it made him look more trustworthy.

'*Ang Kastilang naiwan*,' the guerrillas teased him.

The forsaken Spaniard.

They mocked Federico until he proved himself. He stole them food when they were starving and hunted field mice when there was no food to steal. Skinning and eviscerating the catch himself before grilling them.

The clincher was when he volunteered to keep watch during the day—after hiking all night through the jungle—so the others could nap in peace.

By the end of his first month with them, they no longer called him Kastila. He became Iko.

More importantly—Ka Iko.

He had just sat down on the rock when they heard it. The unmistakable cry of a young girl.

No, two girls.

Maybe more.

The awful sound pierced through sheet metal rain and the bawling wall of bullfrogs.

Ka Igmé signalled for them to take cover, fearing the Japs were close.

When no one came, he motioned for them to head towards the screams.

There was a small nipa hut on stilts in a clearing surrounded by trees. A Japanese soldier was sitting on the bamboo steps. His eyes were shut, his rifle on his lap.

The 'lookout' was asleep.

Igmé and his men had seen this before.

Inside, a mother and her daughters were being raped.

Without needing to be told, the guerrillas took positions around the hut, approaching stealthily at Ka Igmé's signal.

Federico was never sure what started it, but next thing he knew, there was a loud snap then an exchange of gunfire.

Japanese soldiers ran out of the hut at the melee. Some with their trousers still undone.

There must have been seven or eight of them.

The wailing stopped.

Federico was closest to the hut and set to advance when he felt the tip of a bayonet on his back.

Japanese words he didn't understand were yelled at him.

The other guerrillas retreated.

He didn't have to turn around to know what this meant.

His arms were tied behind him, and after another few hours of hiking, Federico found himself in a Japanese camp. Tired, hungry, and bleeding.

He passed out.

An eternity later, he stirred to a sweet liquid seeping into his mouth and a low whisper in his ear—'*¿De donde es?*'

Spanish? He thought he imagined it as the bewitching tang of an evening jasmine enveloped him.

Dama de noche. Lady of the Night. He'd only recently learnt its name.

The small, fragrant white flowers grew everywhere, and his comrades used them to guard against mosquitoes.

He laboured to open his eyes.

The room was dark, and the light from the gas lamp was on its last flicker.

When he tried, no sound came out of his throat.

He gasped.

'*No se preocupe,*' she addressed him again, formally. '*Os cuidaré,*' assuring him that he'd be well-tended.

Most people in these mountains presumed he was a US soldier turned guerrilla. But not her.

'They think you are American,' she said, as if reading his mind. 'It is better that way. It will keep you alive if they think you are useful.'

He felt a cool wet rag on his forehead.

'I dressed your wounds, but you had a fever.' She dipped the cloth back in a bowl of water. 'It has broken. I've been dripping medicinal tea in your mouth—you will be all right.'

'*¿Quién es?*' he finally managed.

'My name is Fatimah,' she replied. 'Now, English. Speak to me in English.'

'But earlier—' he started.

'Yes, I wanted you to feel at ease. Like you were someplace familiar. It hastens healing,' she offered.

'How did you know?' Federico wondered.

'Even asleep I could tell you lacked the arrogance of an American,' she said lightly.

That made him smile.

'Surely I also lacked the contentiousness of a Spaniard?' he jested back.

She exhaled softly.

'You lacked a great many things while unconscious, caballero, except the potential to be kinder than these bastards.'

A sudden noise encroached on their privacy.

'Hush, don't let them hear you.'

'Fatimah—' a man's clipped voice called into the darkness.

'*Ima ikimasu!*' she yelled back.

She bent over Federico once more and whispered, 'I must go. *Descansa*, rest. I'll return in the morning.'

* * *

With Fatimah's help, Federico slowly regained his strength. The Spanish-speaking Filipina—who apparently also knew Japanese—seemed free to move around the camp and came to see him almost daily.

She brought him meals, tended to his wounds, and made him curative tea from the soldiers' stash of imported monk fruit.

Fatimah called it the 'fruit of immortals' and said it would bless him with a long life, like the ancient monks in China who first grew it.

To Federico, the rare fruit looked like a small, dried melon hiding a tiny coconut. Unexpectedly bitter when raw, but so sickly sweet when boiled that it was actually tart.

When he could stand—which he inevitably could—she introduced him to the camp commander.

As Fatimah instructed, Federico did not let on that he wasn't an American. To the Japanese officer, that meant he could decipher messages intercepted between US soldiers and Filipino guerrillas.

Federico did as he was asked. Sort of. The Japanese failed to realize that even under threat of death, Iko altered the intercepted messages. Keeping his comrades safe from enemy traps.

Several weeks later, as Fatimah came into his hut to set down his dinner: 'When will you tell me why you're here?' Federico dared ask as he breathed in the smell of evening on her skin.

'It's not important,' she offered him a weak smile.

She loosened his ropes so he could eat and promptly rose to leave.

Federico crawled towards a small hole in the thatched wall and watched her walk away under the sheen of the moon. She appeared untouched by gravity.

He had never seen such grace.

Then, as he did every night, Federico heard music coming from the camp's main house, where the commander was staying.

It's where he saw Fatimah go.

When the moon was full—as it was that evening—there were no shadows. No places to hide. But still Federico decided to chance it. He pulled off his restraints and crept the short distance to the Big House.

He found a post behind it from which he could see into a window.

Fatimah was at the piano, playing a soft melody he didn't recognize. The commander stood behind her, appearing to stroke her hair.

When she finished, he leant down and whispered in her ear.

She nodded gently, then began a sweeping ballad about love and devotion that Federico knew from Spain. A heart breaking ode to a small flower that was at once delicate and strong. An anthem for solitude.

His chest tightened.

It was one of his favourites.

After catching his breath, Iko looked at the commander—still standing behind Fatimah with his eyes shut. He seemed to wipe away a tear.

Federico didn't know how long he watched them, but at some point, the Japanese officer moved to the couch and fell asleep.

Three songs later—he counted—Fatimah stood to go.

Iko caught up with her by the water tank.

'You shouldn't be here,' she said, surprised.

'I wanted to see you,' he whispered.

'If they catch you—'

'They won't,' he said with a certainty he didn't feel. 'When you play the piano, they seem to fall asleep.'

'That's the point,' she replied, visibly tired.

He wasn't sure what she meant.

He said nothing.

'*Mira*, Federico,' she started, weary. 'I'm the commander's—friend.'

He kept his eyes on her, trying not to blink.

'*¿Me entiendes?*

He wasn't sure what she wanted him to understand.

Slowly, she led them back towards the darkness of his hut.

'They caught me in San Andrés,' she whispered as they went. 'I was a guerrilla, but the Japs didn't know that. Eventually, Commander Saito realized I was educated. I could read, speak several dialects, and play his favourite Bach sonata on the piano.'

She looked at Federico.

'To him, that made me more useful than the women they took as sex slaves.'

He blinked, remembering the anguished cries often heard in villages overrun by Japanese soldiers. His guerrilla unit freed several such abused women—but not all of them. Not as many as were violated.

'Has he ever—' Federico ventured, dreading the answer.

'No,' came Fatimah's quick reply. 'He seems too—proud—to force himself where he's not wanted,' she continued. 'His men, as we know, are a different story. But because Saito has taken me under his wing, the others won't touch me.'

'Thank God,' Federico exclaimed.

Fatimah exhaled. 'I sometimes wonder where He is in all this,' she clasped her hands together.

'Do you not believe in God?' Federico was surprised. He hadn't met many Filipinos who weren't devout Catholics—if at least nominally.

They stopped walking within feet of his hut.

He noticed that she spun a ring she wore on her right hand as she pondered his question.

'I don't know what I believe,' Fatimah expressed. 'I feel Allah, exalted and sublime, may have turned His back on me a long time ago.'

Allah? Federico was puzzled.

Fatimah looked at him as if he were a child. Her hands stilled.

She smiled.

'Not all—"Filipinos"—as you call us islanders—are Christian,' she told him.

'I didn't know,' he said, truthfully.

'I'm not surprised,' she sighed. 'Even though your people were here for over three centuries, they never colonized *our* islands—which are further south,' she explained. 'Unconquered and unchanged—the people of Mohammed, peace be upon him.'

Federico had never met a Muslim before. Much less a female one.

'Don't worry,' Fatimah said, reading his consternation, 'we're not contagious.'

'No, it's not that,' he stammered. 'It's. . . I, well I . . . never. . .'

She laughed. A little. Softly.

'It's all right, Federico. I understand.' She pointed towards his doorway. 'Now, off with you. Please. They mustn't see us speaking like this, alone—'

'—on a moonlit night, under a clear sky,' he finished.

'Exactly.'

And with that, Fatimah turned away from him and headed towards her quarters.

Chapter 2

La Fortaleza y la Prometida | **The Fortress and the Betrothed** | Ang Kuta at ang Ikakasal

1 Aug. 1968
   Dear Diary,
   Tonight's the night it's official. I waited my entire life—and in two months, I will finally be la Señora de Alejandro Yrastegui—Eeee!!

María de la Almudena Castillo de Montijo was so excited about her upcoming wedding that she couldn't express herself further in words. She slammed her diary shut and gripped it to her chest.

'Alma!' A knock on her door. 'Hurry! The guests are arriving!'

Her sister only knocked when the door was locked.

Alma shoved her diary back in the dresser and thanked God she remembered to bolt the door.

'Hurry!' her sister called again, trying to turn the knob.

'I heard you the first time, Maca!' Alma yelled back. She shut the hidden latch to her secret drawer, then stood at the mirror. Her delicate ivory dress was a picture of innocence.

Not exactly the look she wanted.

Alma removed the bow with the birdcage veil that her mother insisted she clip in her hair.

Too much—she worried—*ay Mami, I don't want him thinking I'm the Virgen María.*

She combed her fingers through her loosened soft curls, then pinched her cheeks once more before applying a thin layer of powder.

From her balcony, she could see the long queue of shiny Cadillacs pulling up the drive. It stretched past the front gates, down Calle Sombra, and on to the main avenue.

As the cars inched towards the porte-cochère, their headlights cut dreamy patterns through the old acacia trees. Beneath the verdant canopy, silhouettes unfurled like lace on the pavement.

Strings of tiny white lights were wrapped around branches and dangled in clusters. Glowing like fireflies against a burnished lilac sky.

The expansive lawns were freshly manicured, the landscaped gardens sighed in bloom, and water danced gaily in the roundabout fountain.

Behind the house, an abundance of fruit trees, pergolas, and trellises punctuated a stylishly turned-out yard. All dappled in bronze by thoughtfully scattered gas lamps.

In the grandest gazebo, a six-person band played standards from Gershwin and Porter.

The large pool was sprinkled with rose petals and floating candles.

To the side, a small private chapel was shrouded in a burst of flame trees. Their red-orange flowers—a luxuriously embroidered shawl over the estate's most sacred hearth.

The geckos were silent, and it hadn't rained, but a soft breeze hummed along with the crickets.

This could only mean good luck. A perfect evening to announce her engagement.

The house itself was at its most elegant.

Like sentries, blazing bamboo torches lined the way through wrought iron bars at the adobe stone entrance towards the inner courtyard and the grand foyer beyond. In the amber glow, the home's sturdy walls of volcanic rock showed robust and regal.

The antique granite cobblestones were polished. And the thick narra floors had been scrubbed for hours with coconut husks—until their ebony surface shone a deep, gleaming red.

The Persian carpets were newly cleaned, and the Chinese furniture was freshly lacquered.

In the portico, a string quartet accompanied the arrival of Manila's crème de la crème.

The chandeliers sparkled. Roasted pigs were on spits. And champagne flowed like a monsoon.

Everyone was in high spirits.

Sombra never looked more beautiful.

On the main landing, two Spanish guitarists rendered a soulful classic about love and a beautiful poppy.

The owner of the house stood in front of them, waiting for his daughter.

'Is he here yet?' Alma called to her father as she descended the tiled stairwell.

For a moment, Don Federico appeared transported by the music.

'Ah, *hija,* yes, of course,' he exclaimed, beaming. 'He was the first to arrive.'

Federico hugged his eldest daughter and kissed her on the forehead.

'Can you blame him? How could he not be excited to be marrying such a jewel?'

He pulled back and took a long look at his beloved Almudena.

They named her—as they did all their daughters—after one of the titles of the Virgin Mary.

Our Lady of Almudena—a designation derived from the Arabic *al-mudaynah*, meaning citadel—was the patroness of Madrid.

Federico believed the Virgin kept not only Spain's capital safe, but also his dearest Alma.

It was time to let her go.

'You look beautiful,' he said proudly. 'Now go find your prometido and greet your guests.'

'*Mi* prometido,' Alma thought dreamily.

Indeed, Andy Yrastegui was her fiancé.

She never felt more fortunate.

* * *

Usually, when Manila's wealthiest people gathered, no one was above criticism and scorn. But not this evening at Sombra.

Every room Alma walked through in her search for Andy was filled with the tinkling of easy laughter. Crystal glasses clinked over animated conversation, and music filtered in from the west salon that was turned into a dance hall.

The combo was playing Chad and Jeremy. She and Andy loved British baroque rock.

In a corner of the grand parlour, under an abacá ceiling fan, Alma spotted Andy's grandmother seated on a rattan throne. She was surrounded by the patriarchs of the oldest, most prominent families. The Spanish sugar barons. The Chinese merchants with Hispanized names. The Basque bankers. The Filipino industrialists. They all bowed to the widowed Doña Constancia.

Even the bishops and the few invited statesmen filtered past. (Naturally, only the most reputable of politicians were invited to the party.)

As head of the highly regarded Yrastegui clan, Doña Constancia was the doyenne of Manila high society.

With her nuptials, María de la Almudena was putting the humble Castillo family from rural Montijo firmly into that circle.

You see, despite Don Federico's hard-earned wealth, Alma and her siblings always felt like outsiders among the islands' Spanish upper class—although they attended the best schools, spoke a respectable number of languages, and learnt their manners. Like all proper families in Manila.

Alma was also sent to Europe to complete her studies.

Educated, refined, and well-spoken, she was as much a lady as she was ever going to be.

But no matter what the Castillo offspring did, they were not *raza pura*.

Not pure-bred.

Their mother—although she'd converted—was always going to be *La Mora*.

The Moor.

A blanket term used derogatorily by Spanish colonizers for anyone of Islamic inclination.

There was no changing the fact that Alma's mother was a native Muslim from the remote—and ostensibly 'savage'—southern islands. Regardless of how cultured 'La Mora' might be.

So, as a mixed-race mestiza whose family was not among the established Old Rich, Alma felt she had to work harder at being the right sort of girl for Andy. She was terribly mindful not to put a foot wrong or call attention to herself.

After all, her prometido was from a long line of upright insulares— pure-bred Spaniards who were born on the islands.

Esteemed and irreproachable, the Yrasteguis had been industry titans since the 1800s. With commercial interests that stretched from the colonies in the Pacific and the Caribbean to the Americas and their Basque homeland on the border between Spain and France.

They were in shipping, construction, cigar-making, and alcohol production.

They had fruit farms, rubber plantations, and sugar mills.

They also pioneered coffee and cacao farming on the islands.

If there was anything innovative and lucrative, the Yrasteguis were likely behind it.

They even boasted a marquesa—yes, an actual marchioness—in their family tree.

That she hooked the noble-blooded golden boy was Alma's ultimate seal of approval. Surely, she would no longer feel like an interloper.

Elegant and beautiful, Almudena Castillo always came across as effortlessly polished—it perfectly masked the steely 'unladylike' resolve that brought her to this moment.

She was smart. She was strong. She was determined.

She was also very much in love.

'Alma!' Andy called out when he saw her across the hall.

Mi prometido, her heart fluttered as he walked briskly to meet her.

He was even more handsome than usual in his tailored suit.

His fair skin glimmered with a touch of copper from playing pelota in the morning sun. His big round eyes shone like the moon against a midnight sky. He was tall, but not too tall, and just broad enough to make her feel safe when they embraced.

It's going to be a good life, thought Alma.

She took quick steps to his side, unable to keep the smile off her face.

'Come meet Senator Rosales,' her fiancé said, kissing her lightly on the cheek. 'He's one of Papá's oldest friends.'

Alma was uneasy about people who made it their business to be so—*public*—but she supposed any politicians the Yrasteguis mixed with would be acceptable. Likely from proper families and not as crass as that upstart Rodríguez who won the presidency three years earlier. She doubted he would've succeeded without American support. The charmless plebeian wasn't even from the city!

When Andy Yrastegui put his hand on the curve of her back, Alma banished further thought of politics.

He led her to a portly and otherwise inconspicuous man holding court by the piano.

The senator stopped serenading those around him to wave at the handsome young couple as they approached.

The crowd parted.

It was going to be a good life.

* * *

'Have you seen Freddie?' Don Federico asked Macarena, his rather timid middle child, as she approached him in the north salon. He worried about his young son who was just expelled from school. It was the third time. They were running out of Catholic institutes to put him in.

'No Papá, I haven't seen him since the ambassador got here,' Maca replied, handing her father his whisky. 'Shall I go find him?' she offered, eager to please.

'Yes, hija. *Por favor*,' Federico was grateful. Cardinal Simón Giménez, Manila's Archbishop, had arrived, and he wanted Freddie introduced. If anyone could get a Catholic school to accept the troublesome boy, it would be the cardinal.

He wished Macarena luck as she went off to find her brother. Searching for someone in the house was never easy.

Sometimes, Don Federico felt there were too many rooms in Sombra. Too many corners and hallways. He lost count.

But he never said this to his wife.

For starters, he was certain there was no need for two large basements—which she had built as bomb shelters. They were serviced by a system of pre-existing, wartime underground tunnels.

There were also narrow corridors that criss-crossed covertly between floors, accessed by hidden wall panels that slipped open as portals.

It was planned like that around a grid of courtyards so there was always an escape from 'the enemy'.

There hadn't been a war in over twenty years.

Yet each time Federico's companies made a profit, his wife expanded the house—the manor—and built more places to hide.

One of the secret doors was in the wall behind Covadonga. Don Federico's youngest daughter was on a plush settee beneath a row of ancestral portraits. All dark suits and thick moustaches. As imposingly European as imaginable.

Not relations of theirs, of course. Though no one knew that.

Federico acquired the paintings from a young Filipino artist he met in Intramuros.

By coincidence, Cova resembled one of the images—she was the most European-looking of Federico's children. With dark fiery hair and glistening corn-husk eyes.

She may not have been the brightest of the lot but was the most playful and charming.

At only sixteen, Covadonga Castillo was being touted as the highlight of her season's debutante ball—which was still two years away. A multitude of suitors was already gathered at her feet. More boys than the less outgoing Macarena entertained.

Federico watched the young lads talk over each other to keep Cova's attention.

He raised his glass and winked when he caught his baby girl's eye.

Leaving her to enjoy herself, Federico moved on to circulate among the guests like a practiced host. His wife—undoubtedly—would be somewhere in the background making sure things ran smoothly.

In one corner, he toasted to the Mendozas' new publication, *The Philippine Sentinel.*

In another, he lauded the expanded fleet of the De la Torres' Filipino National Airlines.

The Fontanillas were launching a television station. The Laredos were building cinemas. And the Ronquillos were extending the nation's power grid.

Going by the guests at his daughter's engagement, it was clear that Manila was firmly back on its feet despite the War's devastation.

The US—although still interfering in island politics—was no longer colonial master. And the peso was nearly at par with the dollar.

After four centuries of colonization, and only twenty years of independence, that wasn't so bad.

Fact: The Islands' economy was booming, and El Señor Don Federico Castillo of Montijo, Spain was among those to most benefit.

Not only had he become a successful exporter of abacá, or Manila hemp, he was also the capital city's most trusted developer.

There was nothing quite as profitable as land in an emerging country.

* * *

Freddie Castillo was leading 'his boys' through the brightly lit fruit trees in the yard, past the family chapel to the gardener's shack behind it that he knew was cloaked in darkness.

'Did you bring the smokes, paré?' the fourteen-year-old asked Melchor, the chauffer of his father's golf partner.

'*¡Sí, señor!* Got it from Mang Eloy's this morning,' the driver affirmed, quickly handing over the cigarettes. 'You order, I comply.'

'Stop it, Chor. You know you don't need to speak to me like that,' Freddie replied, annoyed.

'Only teasing,' Melchor placated. He was only a few years older than the young Señorito Castillo, and they became fast friends at the golf club.

While his boss Don Ramón was on the green with Don Federico, Melchor was at Mang Eloy's Convenience Store—by the drivers' shed—with the other chauffeurs.

They passed time with the storekeeper's son and an otherwise bored Freddie, who was always there skipping school. They smoked, tried some beer, and played *pusoy*—Filipino poker.

They planned to do the same at the engagement party.

'*Coño*,' Freddie cursed under his breath. 'It's locked.'

He tried the door to the shed again.

'I left this open earlier,' he tucked his flashlight under one arm and put the weight of his slim frame against the wooden door.

Eventually, it gave way.

'¡Joder!' Freddie exclaimed. 'What are you doing?'

Up against a wall, lit by a low candle, was his eighteen-year-old sister, Macarena—with young Tomás García's hand inside her dress. He was fondling her breast.

Freddie pointed his flashlight to see Maca's lips swollen pink from kissing.

Caught by surprise, she awkwardly yanked her hands out of her companion's trousers.

Freddie erupted in laughter. The group of lads behind him tried to peer into the shed.

'Oh boy, you've really done it this time,' he sniggered. Zipping his light between the interrupted couple.

'Excuse me,' Tomás mumbled, doing up his trousers as he pushed past the gawking boys at the doorway and ran from the shack.

'Shut up, Freddie,' Maca said through gritted teeth. 'You better not tell the family.'

'What? That you were making out with Tito Hernán's driver?' Freddie guffawed.

'What?' Maca hurriedly shut the door on Freddie's nosy gang.

'What—what?' Freddie repeated.

'What do you mean "driver"?' she lowered her voice.

'Who did you think that was?' Freddie laughed.

'One of Andy's friends or something. He's so well-dressed,' his sister replied.

'Maca, how have you not noticed that staff are dressed for parties?'

'*¿Como?*' she asked again, hoping his answer would change.

'Tomás works for the Etxebarrias from Malate,' Freddie elaborated. 'Tito Hernán, their dad, is a member of Papá's golf club. I hang out with Tomás sometimes at Mang Eloy's store. Nice guy.' Freddie snickered. 'Obviously, you think so, too.'

'*Cállate,*' Maca muttered, embarrassed. Shut up.

She really thought she'd scored one of Andy's socialite friends. Tomás looked so dashing in his suit when she stumbled upon him in the garden. She was searching for Freddie but found Tomás instead. He was kind and respectful.

And he told her she looked beautiful.

Next thing she knew, she wanted his lips on her and her hands on him. Alma and Cova weren't the only ones who could hook a boy.

'Please stop laughing,' she begged her younger brother. 'Or I'm going to tell Papá you were out here to smoke and gamble again.' She spotted the playing cards and cigarette packet in his hand. 'Isn't that what got you kicked out of—is it three—schools now?'

'Okay, okay,' he said, trying to catch his breath. 'Truce,' he offered, switching off his flashlight.

'I'll make up some story for the boys—they'll believe whatever I say. Don't tell Papá I was with them, and I won't tell him you were practicing your gear shifts on Tomás' *pititing*!' He laughed again at the thought of it, sounding like a choking animal.

'*Vale, ¡basta!*' She agreed, humiliated.

Her brother reached out to shake her hand, then pulled back not wanting to touch where Tomás' 'gear stick' was.

'I hate you,' Maca said.

It was the first of many secret pacts between brother and sister.

Chapter 3

El Circulo | **The Circle** | Ang Pangkat

'It's your turn, Ricky.'

He shut his mouth abruptly, suddenly self-conscious that he was breathing through it.

'Ricky?'

He hated this. How many more times did he need to introduce himself to these same people? As if they didn't already know who he was. It was 2010—he was often trending on social media.

'I'm Ricky Castillo'—they looked bored—'it's the fortieth day of my incarceration.' He paused. Nothing. Not even a chuckle from the drunk deb in the corner.

The therapist sighed. 'Ay, Ricky. A little dramatic, no?'

He smirked. 'I am here against my will, Doc. So that makes me a prisoner—no?'

He believed he trumped her.

She smiled.

He hated when she smiled.

It made him feel—*stupid*.

'Come on, Ricky,' she remained hopeful. 'We'll wait until you're ready.'

Empty faces stared at him in silence. A few he recognized from parties. Possibly.

He took a breath to buy himself time.

He picked at a cuticle.

Then gnawed on a calloused finger.

She nodded, encouraging him to start.

Shit.

'Fine. I'm Ricky Castillo and I'm a meth head.' He wore his shame like a shield of scorn.

'Aren't you all supposed to say "hello Ricky" now?' He scanned the room, petulant and weary.

Silence.

He cocked an eyebrow at the woman sitting across him.

'Go on, Ricky,' she invited with a steady smile.

He sighed. This was not what he planned to be doing on a weekend. Sitting in a 'sharing circle' at the House of Good Graces.

Joder. *Fuck.*

He glared at the doctor.

Who wasn't actually a doctor. But that's how she was addressed because it was more flattering than just being 'counsellor'.

On the islands, such flattery was imperative.

She was still smiling at him, nodding her encouragement.

He groaned.

Silence.

'We're here with you, Ricky.'

He hated how she always said his name. As if reminding him who he was in case he forgot.

He squeezed his eyes shut and took another deep breath. Wishing he had a cigarette.

Wishing he had a gram. Or a rock of crystal meth still stashed away.

*Where the f*ck is my camera?* His mind wandered, anxious about his last assignment. Had he sent in the photos?

His sharing circle gaped like zombies.

'You're turning thirty-three soon, yes?' the counsellor prompted in his direction.

Silence.

'Or was it thirty-four?'

Like she cared. His own family never bothered to remember. Except for his useless sister Pili who sent him postcards from wherever she happened to be traipsing.

He glared at the counsellor across him, focusing his anger.

'I'm sorry your family wasn't able to join us today.'

He shrugged his shoulders and picked at another cuticle.

It was Sunday, the only day visitors were allowed. His parents hadn't come to see him in weeks.

He wasn't surprised.

'Would you like to tell us how you're doing, Ricky?' Again, the ever-encouraging—*maddening*—counsellor.

He'd had enough. This was a waste of time. He knew from experience. It was not his first time in 'lock-up'.

He sighed.

She went on, 'Still having those nightmares?'

He blinked—and saw a flash of lizard green.

He wet himself.

Chapter 4

La Guerra y la Guerrera | **The War and the Warrior** | Ang Digmaan at ang Mandirigma

This was not what Fatimah expected of the evening. Her sharp bolo raised over the man brought up alongside her.

'Put it down, Fatimah,' the frightened, wide-eyed man was on his knees. 'Please, put it down.'

'You shouldn't sneak up on someone like that,' she said, her breathing laboured. 'Especially not in a jungle—in the middle of a war.'

She lowered the knife.

She waited to sheathe it.

'Why are you here?' she challenged. 'How did you find me?'

'You were not the only one taught to read the jungle. I've been on your trail for years,' the man explained, rising from the ground. 'Since you left home.'

'Left?' she said angrily. 'Don't you mean since I "had to" leave?'

'Fatimah,' he wiped his palms on his ragged trousers, 'what other choice was there?'

'Choice?' she repeated, incredulous. 'What choice was I given?'

'You know better than to expect that,' he stated. 'You should be grateful.'

31

'Get out of here, Adil,' she told him, returning the knife to its scabbard. 'Leave before the Japs find you, and you end up dead.'

'Is that a threat?' he goaded.

'I won't be drawn into this discussion,' Fatimah turned to go.

'Wait! Please,' his tone softened. 'He is ill.'

'What does that have to do with me?' she asked, stoically. 'You know how to make the healing tea—or have the Chinese traders stopped bringing in monk fruit?'

'He wanted to see you before—' Adil could not finish the sentence.

'We said our goodbyes before the war,' she replied, hoping to hide the crack in her armour.

'Timah,' a calm voice called from behind a curtain of liana vines. He'd gone to find food and heard her anxiety from a distance.

'Is everything okay?'

'Yes, Iko. Stay back,' she cautioned.

He didn't listen.

'Who is this?' Federico asked, stepping forward.

'Adil,' came the brusque reply from the wide-eyed man with protruding ears. 'Her brother.'

The unexpected interception surprised Federico. He and Fatimah were careful to stay unseen since they escaped the Japanese camp a few weeks earlier.

A visiting officer tried to rape her while Commander Saito slept.

That night—as always—Iko watched Fatimah walk to her quarters from the Big House. He saw the officer follow her moments later.

By the time he freed himself from his restraints and got to her, Fatimah was underneath the officer's corpse. She'd taken his knife while he tried to undress her and slit his throat.

They'd been on the run ever since, helped by her many contacts in the underground network.

Only then did Federico discover that Fatimah was spying for the guerrillas from Saito's inner circle. She found ways to send them details about weapons and troop movements.

It kept the Japanese from stabilizing their hold on the province.

With her gone, the resistance was compromised. But there was no way she could return to Saito after killing an officer.

'Come home, Fatimah,' Adil pleaded.

'Never,' she pronounced.

She turned to Federico and saw the confusion in his eyes.

'Adil's not staying, Iko,' she said icily. 'Don't bother apportioning a piece for him of whatever animal you found for dinner.'

She looked back at her brother and waited for him to move.

No one spoke.

Federico regarded one and then the other, finally seeing a slight resemblance. They had the same dark golden skin, big round eyes, and pert, upturned nose.

Both stood with their heads high and their shoulders back.

Glaring at each other.

Still, no one spoke.

'I will go . . . clean this,' Federico moved a short distance away to disembowel his catch. Wondering why Fatimah—in their many months together at the Japanese camp—never mentioned her family.

He certainly didn't know about a brother.

How did the man find them? How far away was their island in the south?

He had a million questions but knew better than to ask. Fatimah would tell him what she wanted him to know, when she wanted him to know it.

That's if she wanted him to know anything at all.

What Iko knew for certain was that she was learned and smart. Pragmatic and stubborn.

She was stronger than she appeared and braver than he ever felt.

She ate anything he found for them and could walk for hours without a sip of water.

She also knew a lot about classical music, literature, and religion. But she never said much about her own preferences or beliefs.

Federico was nearly done scraping innards when he heard familiar footsteps approach through the brush.

'Don't,' she said before he even turned.

'I didn't—'

'Yes, but don't,' she repeated as she sat across him, ending any possible conversation about the unexpected company.

Federico finished preparing the meat, and they ate it raw in silence. Encircled by a mantilla of fireflies.

The next morning, he awoke to Fatimah sharpening her bolo on a stone.

'I'm sorry,' he said, looking up at the sun. 'I must have overslept.'

'Don't worry,' she replied. 'I couldn't sleep anyway so I covered your shift.'

'You must be too tired now to hike,' Federico was about to suggest they stay put.

'Not at all. We must keep moving. And I need to keep my mind on more important matters.'

They were heading north to Cabanatuan from Los Baños, which was south of Manila.

It would've taken less time had they crossed a nearby lake on a flatboat—but Fatimah refused. Insisting there was enough to fear during a war without voluntarily going into 'treacherous waters'.

She would say nothing more on the subject.

So—avoiding all bodies of water—they wove around the occupied capital city through the jungles. Bringing a singular message to the various guerrilla groups along the way: the Americans were finally returning to help them. The end of the war was near.

Fatimah walked ahead, clearing a path with her bolo.

'How did you learn to wield that knife so well?' Federico asked, after a seemingly interminable silence.

'My father,' she said softly. 'A rite of passage.'

For a few moments, Fatimah seemed elsewhere.

There was no sound other than the soft crunch of their feet on the underbrush.

'Our ancestors were milder people,' she said, breaking the silence. 'But Father insisted Adil and I learn to defend ourselves from infidels who kept trying to take our land.'

She turned to Iko and smiled gently. 'We wouldn't have had to if people like yours kept to themselves.'

He laughed.

'Now where's the fun in that?' he remarked, in jest.

She smiled.

Another few minutes of silence.

'I'm glad we're hiking this jungle together,' he offered.

'Wouldn't you rather be sipping sherry in Spain?' she asked, as he slapped a mosquito on his neck.

'No,' came his unequivocal answer.

'Besides, Europe is also at war,' he reminded her, scratching the bright red bite mark. 'Seems the whole world is falling apart.'

'It's men,' Fatimah said, without irony. 'Their insecurity—and this conceited need to possess.'

She dared him to disagree.

When he said nothing, she went on: 'Women are driven by different needs.'

'Like what?' he asked, enthralled yet again by her opinions.

'I think we have spoken enough on this matter,' Fatimah concluded.

'I don't believe so,' Federico countered.

'Well, I have the knife,' she said jovially, 'and I say we change the topic.'

He chuckled again, turning slightly red.

Fatimah still wasn't sure what to make of him. The gentle Spaniard. He was the only man she'd met who didn't seem to want something from her.

'How much longer do you think until the village?' he asked. Changing the topic.

'We should be there by nightfall,' she replied. 'At least, I believe so.'

She was right.

* * *

Fatimah and Federico were put up by different families when they got to the village—a small cluster of bamboo shacks with thatched roofs and vegetable plots.

They were given handwoven dried grass to sleep on in huts of their own. The *banig* mats itched—but were more comfortable than the wet jungle floor.

It was their first night apart in days.

After settling in, Ka Timah and Ka Iko joined the other guerrillas for a meal.

Over a low fire, they ate boiled vegetables and exchanged battle stories.

Ka Tining—a horribly undernourished and nervous fellow—shared news of the Juramentados, Muslim warriors who swore a religious oath to fight to the death. They were beheading enemy soldiers in the southernmost islands.

Where Fatimah was from.

The Japanese were said to be so terrified that they slept offshore on their ships, hoping to evade being slaughtered.

'I heard they're slicing off Japs' ears and trading them in to American guerrillas for bullets,' Ka Tining exclaimed.

'And money,' Ka Romy piped in. 'Despite their claim, those Juramentados aren't being "devout"—they'll fight anyone as long as it turns a profit. Typical Moro.'

It fascinated Federico that Islanders used the Spanish word for Moor to mean the local Muslim tribes.

'They've killed Americans, too,' Ka Domeng stated.

'And fellow Filipinos,' Ka Luis threw in. 'Those Moros don't consider us compatriots—we're all "enemies" as far as they're concerned.'

'Can you blame them?' Domeng again. 'Look at us—"Filipinos"— so splintered we don't even have a unified guerrilla force. We're all fighting independently, for our own pieces of land. Just as we always have.'

'Because we are islands, Domeng,' Tining defended. 'How else could we do it?'

Domeng shook his head.

'It was always easy for colonizers to turn our native tribes against one another,' Domeng began, 'Moro or not. Our own divisions— and greed—helped invaders stay in power. Look at bastards like Emigdio Maglupit from the north and that Eliseo Salazar from the eastern islands—they're getting rich colluding with Japs against our comrades. Everyone's out for themselves. I'm telling you—without the colonizers, we wouldn't even be a country.'

A heated argument broke out in a variety of different dialects Federico did not understand. It drowned out the wailing of geckos.

Ka Iko never had a family, but he imagined nothing sadder than brothers turning on one another.

As the discussion raged, no one around the campfire paid the new arrivals any mind.

Or realized that Fatimah was Muslim.

Federico expected her to comment, but she subtly shook her head and signalled that he stay silent.

She was used to this. Used to her people being misunderstood. Used to feeling like an outsider.

Used to being invisible.

Men usually didn't see her unless they wanted something.

Fatimah knew better than to speak when the men around her were already angry.

And drunk.

Eventually, the conversation progressed to the central Visayan islands, where there was also pushback against the Japanese.

The men remarked that the resistance was so strong in the Visayas that the American liberators were choosing one of its islands for their landing.

Fatimah was not surprised. Many of the Visayan guerrilla leaders were women. Tenacious, unyielding, and fearless.

'I don't know what I would do when this war is over,' Tining confessed. 'Do you?'

That evening, gathered around a small fire, a ragtag group of fighters let themselves ponder life after liberation. After three years of war, they dared to dream.

Federico realized he no longer knew what peace was like.

Or how evenings smelled without jasmine and the sweetness of boiled monk fruit stolen from the Japs.

Fatimah sat beside him sharpening her knife.

He couldn't blame her for constantly having her guard up. Every sound in the darkness could be treacherous. The dying crackle of a fire might be a twig underfoot of the enemy. A gecko's croak could be a cry of pain. The murmur of insects or the absence of chirping birds—everything—a sign of potential danger.

It was no way to live.

As the men resumed their chatter, Fatimah's eyes remained on her metal blade. The light from the fire cast a soft veil of shadows on her face.

Federico hated to admit it, but there was a part of him that wasn't looking forward to the end of the war.

Chapter 5

Las Protestas y la del Medio | **The Protests and the Middle Child** | Ang Protesta at ang Gitnang Anak

María de la Macarena Castillo de Montijo just wanted it to end.

She was weak, she was starving, and her head ached from the tear gas.

This time, she thought she might truly vomit. Her throat was constricted, and it was hard to breathe.

The twenty-one-year-old's body ached from running on the hard pavement, and she barely escaped the police's truncheon.

Her heart was racing.

She wasn't built for this.

Macarena Castillo joined the student protests because it made her feel important. Relevant. But she didn't realize how difficult it would be.

She just had to get through this final year at university.

She dropped the placard she was carrying. 'Down with Rodríguez!'—it read.

'Who do I think I am?' she wondered. Briefly.

Struggling not to puke, Maca fled from the fracas into one of the school buildings.

She found an open classroom and crouched beneath a table. Staying as still as she could.

It was early 1971, and the country was fraying.

Debt was rising, the peso was falling. Inflation was uncontrollable, and unemployment was up. She heard it repeated throughout the campus like a call to arms.

People were angry.

There was a communist insurgency, and Muslim minority groups were rebelling.

There was uncertainty, anxiety, and rampant crime.

The once-idealized—US-backed—president proved more fascist than democratic. His relatives were in positions of power, and his cronies played pass-the-parcel with industries.

Not that this affected Macarena Castillo.

Her father, Don Federico, remained in control of his businesses— and the Castillos de Montijo stayed insulated and apolitical.

For the most part.

Like the highest of the upper crust, their silence on matters of state projected the illusion of being 'above' it. Polite society didn't sully itself with such menial concerns.

At least not publicly. That was uncouth and vulgar.

The truth was—the elite knew how to protect their interests. And they weren't about to criticize those with the power to make life difficult or take things away from them.

Macarena could have happily remained politically disengaged— but she knew she wasn't as smart as her older sister, or as beautiful as the younger one.

So, she hoped that by making herself the 'useful one' she would gain favour with her parents.

She hadn't thought it through very well.

They tried to hide it, but she knew Papá liked Alma best, and Mami—for all her rigidity and sternness—doted on Freddie, no matter how many times he put them through the ringer.

Just last month, Maca heard he got young Nena pregnant. Not that anyone confirmed it.

Nena's parents—*Manang* Lydia and *Mang* Tining—had worked for the Castillos since the 1940s. Sometime after the Great War.

Nena and her brother, Tino, were also reared at Sombra. They were like the cousins the Castillo de Montijo siblings didn't have.

Maca knew that Freddie and Nena spent a lot of time together. But she never imagined that might lead to a baby. Out of wedlock— *¡que horror!*

Not that Freddie would marry the helps' daughter. Imagine that, the servants as his in-laws? Besides, he was still in school.

Actually, Maca wasn't sure there was a baby. Neither her parents nor Freddie spoke of it.

Nena was just gone one day—like Tino before her—and neither was mentioned again. Not even by Manang Lydia or Mang Tining.

Freddie sulked for a few weeks, and then no more.

Last Maca knew, some new chick named Luísa was 'shifting' Freddie's gears.

* * *

Another loud rumble outside the window. The empty classroom shook, and it felt like the world itself was collapsing around her.

Still crouched beneath a table, Maca abruptly remembered she had more crucial concerns than her brother's sexual proclivities.

She curled herself tighter into a ball as tanks rolled past. The earlier explosion still rang in her ears, and she shut her eyes against the lingering sting of tear gas.

There were screams as police broke up the rally, and then a stampede.

She kept her eyes closed.

'It's over,' one of her classmates rushed in, breathless. 'They're leaving.'

Maca's eyes shot open, and she hurriedly unfurled herself. Straightening her shoulders as she rose from beneath the table.

'How many this time?' she asked, employing her most caring 'in-charge' voice.

'Not sure yet, but I counted around fifteen?' her winded classmate surmised.

Macarena Castillo wasn't actually in charge, but she positioned herself as the student leader's confidante. Close enough to the top without having to bear the responsibilities.

'I think they took Nita and Bobby,' another gasping schoolmate tumbled in.

'Goddam Amá Ipé,' muttered another young man as he collapsed into a chair.

Fact: Felipe 'Ipé' Rodríguez was on his second four-year term as the islands' president.

(After waging a violent and fraudulent campaign.) Unacknowledged fact.

Evidently, Ipé Rodríguez wasn't a fan of civil liberties.

Each time students protested, police detained them. Even if they rallied within their own university campus.

Another fact: President Rodríguez insisted on being called 'Amá', which meant 'father' in the local language.

He believed it made him sound benevolent.

The young activists were regrouping in the classroom.

'You know it's just a matter of time before "our dear Amá" declares martial law.'

The student who said this was wiping blood off his face. His shirt was ripped and dripping in sweat.

Maca was grateful she wasn't in a similar state.

'I heard that, too,' chimed another student. 'For the "good of the country"—apparently.'

One of them had a small transistor radio switched on.

Amá was speaking. Yet another public address about the danger The Islands was in. Falling into rebel hands and all that. Marxists on one side, militant Muslims on the other.

'Blame everyone else for the people's suffering,' the owner of the radio said. 'Isn't that always the play?'

'We have proof that they are making bombs and plotting assassinations,' Amá bleated on over the airwaves. 'They have infiltrated our universities and are corrupting our youth!'

Maca read as much in the papers, but her school friends said that didn't mean it was true.

The dailies—her school friends contended—printed everything Amá said as fact because if they didn't, he would sequester the publications.

Maca's parents were friends with the Mendozas who owned *The Sentinel*, but she never asked them if this was true.

What Maca knew for certain was that many of her friends— some of the brightest people on campus—were taken by police from the rallies.

They were detained indefinitely, and often—tortured.

A growing number were never seen again.

'Are you coming to the station to find them?' one of her friends asked.

'I . . . I think it's best if I don't—it might take attention away from the cause.' Maca said, only half-ashamed.

Actually, she was never willing to go to the authorities. She was afraid—and she was a Castillo de Montijo.

If her parents found out how 'involved' she was, they'd move her to a different school.

Maca liked where she was just fine.

She was proud to be the only one of her siblings to attend the big, secular, state university.

Proud to be a legitimate rebel with a respectable cause. (So long as she didn't get too close to the police.)

Bottom line: She finally stood out among her peers.

This was better than that finishing school she attended in Spain.

At National-U, she got to hang out with folk heroes—student leaders who took her to cool underground meetings where big ideas about 'human rights' and 'socialism' were discussed.

It was an entirely new experience for Macarena Castillo.

Eye-opening.

Dangerous. And exciting.

At twenty-one, she was still too naïve to realize that her family was part of the 'unjust social foundation' against which her friends were protesting.

Maca truly believed she was one of them, doing what she could to fix the country's ills.

She attended meetings. She went to rallies. And then, she went home.

All her classes at National-U reverberated with talk of disenfranchised farmers and the plight of the poor, but it was difficult to commiserate with poverty when she returned to Sombra at the end of the day.

After every political rally, Maca went home feeling a guilt she did not understand.

Behind those walls, tucked in those manicured gardens, Sombra was an island. A well-appointed fortress that protected them from the rest of the ugly world.

And for that, she was shamelessly grateful.

* * *

By this time, Alma and Andy Yrastegui were away from the politics and intrigue of Manila. Sent by his family to Negros in the central islands, to oversee their sugar plantations.

The golden couple only returned to the capital for visits every few months.

Cova, as expected, was the belle of her debutante ball. Featured in every society magazine and newspaper—although she preferred to keep to herself.

—and her hundred or so suitors, Maca scoffed. *That girl's untouched by anything that affects the masses.*

Maca was certain the frivolous Covadonga would be the next one wed to the 'right' prometido.

Another grandiose wedding to further entrench the Castillo de Montijo family among the upper echelons of Manila society.

As if Alma hadn't already done that when she married an Yrastegui!

Maca understood that marrying into that Old Rich clan gave the self-made Castillos an otherwise unattainable layer of respectability.

Even their mother admitted she hadn't been called La Mora—The Moor—in years.

Every weekend since, the ladies of Manila played mah-jong with Mami in one of Sombra's garden verandas.

While they gossiped over Chinese game tiles, Papá mixed his famous sangría and prepared paella or fabada in the outdoor kitchen.

His golf friends lazed by the pool and played gin rummy in the gazebo.

Saturdays at Sombra became a fixed date on the social calendar. Along with Tuesdays at Unión Española for the Basque racquetball game jai alai, and lunch at Polo Club on Sundays.

All that ended abruptly one August evening in 1971. A bomb exploded at an opposition political rally. Dozens of people were killed.

Maca was at home.

'I told you we must always be ready for war,' Doña Fatimah said to her husband that night as they lounged in the salon before dinner.

'This is not a war, *mi amor*,' Don Federico repeated, softly. 'This turmoil will pass. Society is simply working out its kinks.'

'Kinks?' Maca jumped in. 'People are starving, Papá! That awful man is robbing the country blind and using state forces like a private army. I heard some of his ministers are so unprincipled they collaborated with the Japs during the War—'

A knowing look passed between her parents. Maca didn't notice.

'Ay, hija,' Federico gave his daughter a sad smile. 'You should focus on school and not concern yourself with such matters.'

'But it does concern me!' Macarena was exasperated. 'It concerns us all. Shouldn't we learn from the past?'

She stared at her father, indignant. 'My classmates are in jail, Papá—tortured by our own government. Some are missing!'

'We don't know what truly goes on behind closed doors, hija,' Federico said evenly. 'Let's be thankful we are all well—our family is very fortunate. We must keep our noses clean. Stay out of trouble and we'll be fine. Stop worrying about those other matters, Macarena.'

She was dumbstruck.

'There's enough to worry about at home,' her mother added, sharply.

Her father was gentler: 'Why don't you help your brother plan the *bautizo*?'

'What bautizo?' Maca was perplexed. Her seventeen-year-old brother was already baptized—why would he need another christening?

'Luísa is pregnant,' Federico shared, placidly. 'She and Freddie were married civilly last week, and she's giving birth soon.'

This was the first Macarena heard of it.

Her extracurricular activities did keep her busy, but she couldn't believe no one told her about her own brother's wedding. Even if it was just a quiet civil ceremony and not the massive church extravaganza expected for Federico Castillo Jr.

At least he didn't marry the helps' daughter—Maca thought, relieved. And he was wed before anyone found out about the child!

She couldn't believe that Freddie hadn't told her. It was unlike him.

Maca looked at their mother, who was suddenly very interested in the television.

A commercial was on.

Doña Fatimah said nothing.

Just then, Freddie walked into the salon.

'Papá,' he started, 'can Mang Tining follow me in your Volvo? We'll need two cars to pick up the rest of Luísa's things.'

Macarena turned to him questioningly.

'*Hola, hermana*,' Freddie smiled at his sister. 'I got hitched!'

'Yes. . .' she stammered. 'I just—heard.'

Their mother remained unblinking on the settee. Another advert was on the television.

'You're moving her—here?' Macarena smiled politely.

'Of course! Where else will the wife of Federico José Castillo de Montijo Jr live?' Freddie replied with aplomb.

Macarena glanced at their father. He was looking at them, but his face revealed nothing.

Their mother was still pretending to be riveted by imported canned meat on the TV.

She gathered that this was again a Castillo family moment when no one spoke their mind.

'Well,' Macarena mustered, 'I can't wait to meet her.'

'She's got super big tits now,' Freddie sniggered.

'Freddie,' their father finally spoke. 'Don't be rude.'

'Sorry, Papá,' he said, seeming chastised.

Freddie winked at his sister then turned on his heels.

'I'll be back by dinner!' he called out, sauntering towards the door.

After Freddie left, Doña Fatimah no longer found the television so captivating.

'I still say he didn't have to buy the cow when he was getting the milk for free.'

'Fatimah!' Federico exclaimed, indicating their daughter was still in the room. 'It's what he wanted.'

'No, Iko. It's what he thinks is expected of him. Luísa is not going to disappear, and there can't be an illegitimate child besmirching our "good name"—'

Federico signalled for Macarena to leave.

'But Papá—'

'Your mother and I need to talk, hija. Go get started on arrangements for the baptism. Please.'

* * *

Macarena knew how vital their family's 'good name' was. Her father worked hard to establish it.

From what she understood, when the War ended, Federico and his pregnant wife made money recycling weapons and selling debris.

Then, through some man at the port who introduced him to another man, Federico fell into transactions that paid him large commissions.

Among others, he connected buyers with producers of abacá fibres. Then, he began cultivating his own plantations.

Ultimately, he fell into real estate. Developing war-ravaged grasslands and marshes.

Some people said Federico was also involved in salvage digs for Japanese war gold.

Macarena never saw signs of the rumoured treasure—and she never thought to ask.

Whatever the source, Federico eventually had enough money to start a construction firm. Becoming the favoured builder of the post-war city.

The Man behind the new Manila.

Unsurprisingly, everyone liked the soft-spoken Spaniard. Trusting that his deals were sound and fair.

After years of unfettered success, Federico Castillo was larger than life. Myths were spun effortlessly around him.

Ka Iko battled the Japanese single-handedly—he defended an entire village from being burned down and saved a hundred resistance fighters on his own, including Mang Tining—he rescued Fatimah from abduction—and was used as a living blood donor while a guerrilla medic performed emergency surgery on an American general.

There were also stories about why he left Spain for the islands.

The most prevalent was that he emigrated to reallocate his family's fortune—thus avoiding sequestration by the Spanish dictator.

None of the stories were true, of course—but no one corrected them.

It served Castillo de Montijo Enterprises to silently back the lore that became their foundation.

People even augmented his name, which made him sound more—imperial.

The legend of El Señor Don Federico Julián Castillo de Montijo was born.

That's—Mr Federico Julián Castillo from Montijo. His name and place of birth. Literally.

Did you know he was descended from the Marquesa of Cáceres? They owned vineyards and castles in Extremadura.

Another story.

On a wall in one of Sombra's many patios, there was a large mosaic of the Castillo family crest. It was composed of colourful Spanish tiles framed by wrought iron.

In the centre of a golden shield, there was a castle—*un castillo*.

Beneath the insignia, an inscription: '*La Familia Primero: Unida y Protegida.*'

Family First: United and Protected.

Spain's King Carlos I designed it for the clan in the 1500s, after their forefather—with his bare hands—saved the said king from assassination.

Or so the story went.

Macarena didn't know where the coat of arms came from.

And she never thought to ask.

Chapter 6

El Embarazo y el Parto | **The Pregnancy and the Birth** | Ang Pagbubuntis at ang Panganganak

Luísa Acosta felt like a prisoner at Sombra.

A fat one.

She gently put her hand on her stomach and hoped she wasn't as big as she felt.

She wasn't. For being six months pregnant, her stomach barely made a bump beneath her dressing gown.

The first baby came without much fuss, but this time, the doctor confined her to bed because of what he deemed—'possible complications'.

Luísa didn't really understand what that meant, but her husband Freddie said she should mind the doctor.

Freddie dropped out of school so he could earn their keep.

Not that he needed to.

He worked so hard that he couldn't stay home to keep Luísa company during the pregnancy.

Although he reassured her that he wanted to.

After two years of marriage and one child, Freddie Castillo's pregnant-again young wife spent most of her days alone in her room.

Yes, nineteen-year-old Luísa Acosta de Castillo—who wasn't even invited to be a debutante at the society ball—had a room to herself in Sombra.

It was on the second floor, at the back of the manor, on the eastern side. She got a great view of the sunrise from her bed.

Freddie said she would get more rest in a room of her own. That way, she wouldn't be bothered by his comings and goings at all hours of the night.

He was very thoughtful, her Freddie. Most of his business deals were done at night, you see. Despite the government curfew, he seemed able to move around Manila.

It got lonely for Luísa, but her thoughtful husband gave her a new TV—*in colour!*—to keep her entertained. Very few people had that in 1973.

Luísa had the colour TV on most of the time. Even past midnight, when what few channels there were signed off for the day.

Frankly, there wasn't much to watch since Amá Rodríguez declared martial law the year before. He shut down most of the stations to protect something called 'the public interest'.

But Luísa was hooked on these historical Chinese dramas that were on the government channels every afternoon. The costumes were beautiful, the men were gallant, and the palaces— breathtaking. The women—so delicate-looking and graceful—were always strong.

Luísa longed to visit brilliantly coloured China.

It seemed a gentler, more magnificent world than her own.

Beneath its grandeur, Sombra wasn't quite what she expected.

Neither were the Castillos.

* * *

Federico José Castillo de Montijo Jr—also known as Freddie—was supposed to be Luísa Acosta's ticket to high society and the good life.

The Acostas were not exactly poor, but their wealth had nothing on the Castillos'.

Like everyone else, Luísa grew up hearing stories about Freddie's father, the great Don Federico Sr. His aristocratic Spanish lineage, the Japanese gold, and the glitzy soirees.

But with military police on city streets and the nightly curfew, there weren't as many socials at Sombra as there used to be.

Which was not what Luísa bargained for when she became Mrs Freddie Castillo.

She definitely didn't expect to be bound to her room. Regardless of how large and lavish it was.

But besides doctor's orders, Luísa knew that her room was the safest place for her at Sombra. The only space she was sure not to encounter her mother-in-law.

Freddie's father was always polite and gracious, but his mother—*that unrefined Mora*—still acted as if she didn't exist. *Can you imagine?*

Everything Luísa heard about Moros was true: they were crude, uncivilized, and hostile.

Her mother-in-law most certainly was. She was awful. Cold and mean.

Not that La Mora said horrible things to Luísa. It was that she never said anything at all.

Ever.

Which was worse.

It was like that woman was always geared for battle and silence was her ultimate weapon.

It hurt Luísa more than words ever could.

She tried to speak to Freddie about it, but he just laughed, insisting she imagined it.

His mother—he said—was 'the best'.

She and Freddie named their first child after that unpleasant Muslim woman.

Fátima Lourdes Castillo de Montijo y Acosta. Spelled the correct Christian way—Fátima without the 'h'. Born shortly after her teenaged parents were wed.

An adorable little girl with porcelain skin, a shock of curly hair, and big brown eyes.

Little Fáti—as they called her—was turning two. The apple of her father's eye.

Just as well considering how Luísa worked to snag him.

All the girls wanted Freddie Castillo Jr. The swarthy, lanky, mischievous mestizo with handsome Eurasian features and deep pockets.

Or rather, his father's deep pockets.

So, Luísa made sure she was available to Freddie more than anyone else was.

She came when he called. Smoked what he smoked, drank what he drank, and wore what he wanted her to wear.

Most importantly, Luísa's Catholic school upbringing didn't deter her from spreading her legs for him in ways that would have made her a star attraction at the circus.

That she got pregnant was a bonus—Freddie married her much earlier than she planned.

'*Pasok*!' Luísa responded to the expected knock on her door. Come in.

It was a daily ritual. In the half-hour news break between her Chinese shows, the nanny brought her Little Fáti.

Not that Luísa requested the child—but she didn't want to give her mother-in-law a reason to question her maternal instincts.

'I will return after the news,' the nanny said, tousling Fáti's hair before leaving the room.

Dammit—thought Luísa. Again she wasn't addressed as señorita.

I will return—se-ño-ri-ta.

Even the servants in this house disrespected her.

The only person who didn't was Cova, the youngest of Freddie's sisters. Maybe because the girl was rarely home. *Lucky cow.*

The truth was—Luísa wasn't too upset by how she was treated. She was finally a Castillo de Montijo, and the rest of Manila could just suck it.

She did—and Freddie enjoyed it. At least, in the beginning.

Luísa wondered why he no longer came to her for oral ministrations.

'*Ven aqui*, Fáti,' she cooed, summoning her daughter to distract herself from potential marital concerns.

The child refused to approach. Heading, instead, for the toys in the corner.

Truthfully, Luísa didn't mind.

While her daughter sat down to play, she flipped through one of the Spanish celebrity magazines on her nightstand. Freddie brought them the last time he came to see her.

Was it three days ago?

Luísa reminded herself she shouldn't complain. She lived in Sombra, with a view of the sunrise and a colour TV.

Not to mention her enterprising rich husband was making them richer by the day.

She was also carrying her second Castillo de Montijo baby. Another grandchild for Don Federico.

A larger portion of the inheritance.

Freddie's eldest sister Alma Yrastegui had two little girls of her own, but they didn't live in Manila. Besides, they had enough of a fortune from their father's illustrious clan.

So—as far as Luísa was concerned—Alma's children didn't count.

Another bonus: Luísa was certain her new baby was going to be a boy. She felt it. The third Federico Castillo de Montijo.

She caressed the small protrusion in her belly.

This baby would be the namesake of the legend himself. No grandchild would be more important.

And she, María Luísa Acosta y Cruz, would be his mother.

She'd be a better one than that vicious Mora.

She glanced towards the corner to see what was keeping her daughter busy. The little one had been quiet for some time.

'*¡Dios mío!*' Luísa gasped. My God.

Little Fátima was gone.

* * *

She awoke with a start. Clammy and sweating. Her shriek ringing in the small, hot room that was their home.

'You're all right, Fatimah. You're all right.' Federico's voice soothed in the darkness.

It was night. There were no windows and the air hung heavy.

They were no longer in the jungle, but they never felt more isolated.

Federico leaned across the thin wooden board that was their bed and put his arms around his new wife.

Maybe tonight she'd share her nightmare.

He kissed her softly, hoping her cry didn't wake the neighbours again. Though he knew that was unlikely in a space so cramped.

It was 1945 and the War just ended. The Americans were back in charge of the islands.

The young couple rented a room in one of the few blocks left somewhat standing in once-splendid Manila. Not too far from where Iko found work on a construction site.

Or rather, a *re*-construction site. Which was what the entire city— if it could even be called that—resembled.

After the War, all that remained of Federico's beloved capital was a wasteland of rubble and sorrow. The Walled City—and everything around it—was decimated in the final battle before the Japanese surrendered.

Manila was unrecognizable to the young couple when they returned from the jungle.

Every day, Iko came home from work tired and heavy-hearted, but he knew nights like this were even more taxing on Fatimah.

He was a good husband. And he'd make her understand she was not alone.

'I've got you, Timah,' he reassured. 'I've got you.'

Fatimah fought it, but her tears came anyway.

Iko wanted to cool her down with a drink of water, but there wasn't much of anything in Manila that soon after its liberation. No running water, no electricity, and food was hard to come by. He certainly couldn't find monk fruit to brew the tea that always consoled her.

'Please stay calm, mi amor,' he whispered low in her ear. 'It's not good for the baby.'

Their first child was due any day.

Iko held his pregnant wife close and hummed a lullaby.

He wished he knew how to banish her demons.

* * *

Luísa knew she had to get up and look for her daughter.

She could summon the nanny by pressing the buzzer near her bed, but she didn't know how to explain the child's absence.

What a nightmare.

The bedroom door was heavy, so Luísa would have heard it open. And surely the child couldn't turn the knob herself.

So how did Little Fáti vanish?

How would she explain this to her husband?

Delicately pregnant, Luísa tried not to panic.

She lifted herself carefully off the bed and walked towards the Persian carpet she last saw her daughter on.

As she neared, the missing child stumbled back into the room from what appeared to be a crack in the wall.

Only—it wasn't exactly a crack.

A gap? A crevice?

Luísa didn't know what she was looking at. It seemed the wall itself was ajar.

She looked the child over to make sure she was fine.

No blood, no marks, no tears. Small doll still clutched firmly in her tiny hand.

A knock on the door.

It opened before Luísa could speak.

'*Naku!*' the nanny cried as she entered. 'Why are you out of bed, señorita?'

The scheduled interruption surprised Luísa. Nonetheless, she was pleased that the help finally addressed her with the respect befitting her stature as a mistress of the house.

Señorita.

'You can take her now,' Luísa commanded. Ignoring both the question she was asked and the sudden ache in her stomach.

She stood still and hoped the nanny didn't notice the opening in the wall.

When she was alone again, Luísa braved the pain and peered into the darkness on the other side.

* * *

'I still see their faces,' Fatimah stammered into Iko's shirt.

'Whose faces?' her new husband held her close as they sat on their narrow bed.

This was the most she'd ever said after a nightmare.

On previous nights, Fatimah just pulled the thin blanket around her and lay back down.

Maybe if prodded slowly, she'd feel safe enough to tell him more.

He stroked her back.

He stopped trying to soothe her with a lullaby a few nights earlier, when he realized that he always wound up humming his favourite song. The Spanish ballad about the fragile flower.

She used to play it on the piano at the Japanese camp. Apparently, it was also the commander's favourite.

Iko worried it might agitate her further.

He kissed her forehead.

'Whose faces, mi amor?' he asked, again.

She looked up at him for a second, then shut her eyes. Trapped in a labyrinthian darkness.

'They're after me,' she said as tears rolled down her face. 'They're after me.'

'They' clearly terrorized her dreams.

As Iko had come to expect, Timah clasped her hands together and twisted the ring on her right middle finger. It was a thick braid of silver and gold with a piece of ivory at the centre. She seemed to touch it whenever she was troubled.

Federico first noticed it at the camp.

Perhaps Timah was worried the Japanese wanted retribution? For killing the officer who tried to rape her.

'They're gone, Timah,' Iko reassured. 'The Japanese are gone.'

She said nothing.

'You were defending yourself,' he continued.

'No. . . no. . .' she stammered, twisting the ring again. 'Not the Japanese.'

She looked at Iko anxiously. There was only love in his eyes.

She was still not used to it.

'The other boys,' she said, finally. 'The other boys.'

Federico had never seen her so shaken. He tightened his hold and waited.

'T-t-tarek. . .' she sputtered, burying her face in her hands. 'I killed—Tarek.'

Fatimah sobbed inconsolably.

It was the first time Federico heard that name. Was the boy connected to the ring she wore?

Suddenly, Fatimah turned to him terrified. Her breathing—ragged.

Iko felt the wetness spread beneath them.

Amid her nightmare, their first child was on its way.

* * *

When her eyes adjusted, Luísa walked into the hidden corridor behind her bedroom wall.

There were dim streaks of light just visible through cracks at intervals of several feet.

She tried to push a few of the wooden panels, hoping they might open.

A sharp agony pierced her stomach.

She kept going.

On her third attempt, one of the hidden doorways unlatched.

Luísa peered in carefully, not sure what was on the other side.

It was a room she hadn't seen before.

At the far end was a large bed, neatly made. Books sat atop a nightstand as if just set down.

Closer to her, by the open panel, was a sturdy rolltop desk with a lamp on it.

Paintings of faraway places hung on the walls, and several fine silk rugs were scattered on the floor.

There was a musty smell of dust in the air. The particles visible in the slits of light from the loosely shuttered windows. Like the grey and white dots on the television after midnight.

She sneezed. Another quick stab at her belly.

As cautiously as she could, Luísa walked across the room to its main door. It was locked from outside.

She smiled. Feeling both naughty and empowered. Certain she discovered a family secret.

'Finally!' she thought, gleeful. She knew there was more to the close-knit Castillos than people realized. There were too many silences at Sombra to not have things hiding in the shadows.

She immediately set out to explore the room.

In the desk's deep drawers, there were photos tucked tidily into albums. Young boys in school uniforms. In groups, wearing shorts at the beach. Carrying tennis rackets. In dark suits, dancing with polished young girls.

The subject in most photos was a broad-shouldered young man with thick, dark hair and deep-set eyes. He was well-dressed and held his head high.

In the close-ups, Luísa noticed the sparkle in his light eyes framed by long delicate lashes.

His smile was as captivating as a humid June afternoon.

Sticky and sweet.

Dios mio, gasped Luísa, *this is the handsomest man I have ever seen.*

She took a deep breath—as if the air was heavy—and sneezed again.

Puñeta. Another shooting pain. *Dammit.*

She continued to meticulously comb through the photos.

The boy's gaze at the camera—intense. Like a movie star's.

Luísa imagined he was looking at her.

He was like that actor in her favourite movie *Breakfast at Tiffany's.* Fresh-faced and clean-shaven. With a clear complexion, chiselled features, and a tall, thin nose.

Luísa tried to find a resemblance to her husband, Freddie, but there was none.

Freddie's shoulders drooped. His dark eyes were shifty, and he kept trying to grow a beard to hide his weak chin.

So much for 'foxy'—Luísa thought of the husband she suddenly found wanting.

She turned over every photo hoping for information on the subject's identity.

Behind each image, there was only a date and a location.

Baguio, 1958. Cebu, 1956. Roma, 1960. Madrid, 1962.

Nothing was dated past 1965. Eight years back.

By that timeline, Luísa surmised the young man who dominated the pictures must since be in his late twenties.

She nearly swooned when she picked up another photograph.

In it, the boy wore a black leather jacket, light-coloured trousers neatly folded over chukka boots, and dark glasses. He was leaning against a small red car with its top down. His arms were crossed on his chest.

Behind him, a rugged coastline curved around a majestic drop into the ocean.

Luísa turned the photo over.

Big Sur, 1965.

The boy looked—*happy*.

A deep golden glow began to creep into the room as the sun set outside. The approaching darkness seemed to make it harder to breathe.

Clasping her chest, Luísa peeked through the shutters to see if she could tell which part of Sombra she was in.

Her suspicion was right.

This was the room at the end of her wing. Behind the locked door that no one in the house talked about. She had once asked Freddie about it—he changed the topic.

Suddenly, a noise in the hall outside.

It was Freddie. Speaking to one of his sisters. Most likely Maca. Those two were always huddled together in conversation.

Luísa quickly put the photo she was holding into the pocket of her robe. Feeling like a spy in one of those wartime movies.

She returned everything else to its place and hurried back to her room through the hidden passage.

Her husband was finally coming to see her. *Could this day get any better?*

Luísa was giddy with excitement. She would ask Freddie about the locked room again. She might even offer to suck him off.

Luísa didn't have to wait long for her husband. He doubled back to her room when he heard the thud. She'd collapsed as soon as she closed the secret wall panel.

As the evening gecko began its call, Freddie burst in and rushed his wife to hospital.

They all thought Federico III was making his entrance.

They were wrong.

Chapter 7

El Cumpleaños | **The Birthday** | Ang Kaarawan

Ricky hated the solo sessions in the colourless office even more than the sharing circles in an equally sallow hall. At least in group therapy, there were other losers to take the doc's attention.

'Anything new in your journal you want to discuss?'

Seriously? After seeing him daily, he wondered how this woman still didn't get that he wasn't a 'talker'.

It's the reason he took photos for a living—he didn't need words to point and shoot a camera.

'Oh, this came for you, I think,' the counsellor-doctor handed him a postcard from her folder.

It was addressed to 'WhoEva U. R. Castillo' and signed 'WerEva I. M. C'.

It seemed his younger sister, Pili, was in Ibiza.

He flicked the postcard on to a side table.

'How wonderful that she remembered your birthday.'

He didn't tell the doc that Pili just liked to gloat. She was living it up in the Balearic Islands while he languished in this prison.

'Why does she call you that?' the counsellor smiled, hoping to prompt happy memories.

He plucked at his cuticle. And looked out the window.

The sun was high, and the Good Graces lawn sparkled emerald and gold.

'I'm not supposed to be Federico the Third.'

The counsellor's face gave nothing away.

'There was a baby before me,' he gnawed on his finger, 'died at birth or something.'

'I see.'

'We—my sisters and I—think it was a boy,' he paused, 'but we're not sure.'

The counsellor watched him stare out at the garden in the sunshine.

'They don't talk about it,' he meant his parents. 'I mean, it's just another thing we never talk about.'

His parents. *Dear God, what a joke.* They barely even spoke to each other.

As he expected, neither of them came for his birthday. At least his mother bothered to call with a greeting.

He'd rather have heard from Aba, his grandmother. He wondered if she knew he let them down. Again.

A cloud appeared over the garden.

'When can I get my camera back?' he turned to the counsellor, impatient. 'See it as a present for my birthday.'

'I'm sorry, Ricky'—she sounded sincere—'but I think the police are holding on to it until the investigation is done.'

For a brief—*glorious*—moment, he didn't know what she meant.

Then he blinked— and it all came rushing back.

FML.

Chapter 8

La Madre y el Trato | **The Mother and the Deal** | Ang Ina at ang Kasunduan

'I love you, Timah,' Federico repeated as he sat up in bed. 'Please talk to me.'

Every night, like clockwork, his wife awoke distraught.

Every night, she said little. If anything at all.

The baby cooed, and Fatimah rose to take him from his crib. It was the only other piece of furniture in their sparse dwelling.

Iko watched her by the moonlight streaming through the window.

They had moved to a larger room when he got a pay rise. He hoped the window would help his wife feel—less trapped.

She held the baby tight—breathing in air perfumed by the jasmine outside—whispering prayers into his ear.

Fatimah became Catholic on the same day she was wed, just so she could be with Federico.

Manila was in chaos after the War, so the priest baptized, confirmed, and got her wed in one go. Years' worth of religious training condensed to a day.

She dropped the 'h' and chose 'Fátima' as her Christian name. It was on all her legal documents from then on.

The absence of that last letter spelled the difference between being a child of Mohammed and a Catholic devotee of the Virgin Mary.

Fatima(h) reinvented herself in that one day of rituals. Hoping God/Allah would respond to a change of name.

Since then, she held on to faith like a lifeline.

Almost as much as she held on to the braided ring she still wore on her middle finger.

'They won't take him, Iko,' she said to her husband. 'God help me, I won't let them take him.'

She was desperate, and Federico still didn't know what she meant.

For much of that night, his wife tossed and turned before waking up startled. She was muttering a sequence of 'noes' in her sleep like a mantra. Her arms struggling against an invisible tormentor.

'Was it him again?' Iko asked her gently. 'Was it—Tarek?'

Tears streamed down her face as she clutched their child. Their dark-haired, fair-skinned, little Julián.

They'd been married over a year, and Federico still didn't know who Tarek was.

'Can you tell me about him?' he chanced, again.

Fatimah buried her face in baby Julián's chest and shook her head.

Iko stopped asking.

Every night thereafter, he tried a different way to show her she was safe with him.

He kept a gas lamp burning as she slept.

He sang lullabies while she cradled the baby.

He held her close.

Every night, he reassured her of his love.

He came home from work with more food than they could afford.

He stocked water to last them until morning.

He stayed silent while she wept.

Iko was quarrying a stone forged in fire.

Every night, bit by bit, she let him in.

* * *

Fatimah was fifteen when it happened. A few years before the Japanese war.

Her father, Khaled, was just named a chief—a *datu*—of the Suhkmil tribe.

As was customary, all Muslim tribes in the southern islands sent their chiefs to extend salutations. Even the American colonizers from occupied towns came to pay their respects.

Fatimah was proud of her father.

She was proud to be Suhkmil. They were peaceful and devout, diligent and enterprising.

There were those who said the seafaring Suhkmil were so enterprising that they pillaged trade ships in the open waters.

But Fatimah did not believe such nonsense.

Her father—an educated man who was friends with Arab scholars and Chinese merchants—said pirates and other troublemakers had no place in civilized society. Regardless of their tribe.

The American occupiers hoped the new datu's temperance would unite any feuding clans and make them less troublesome.

Fatimah believed her father could do anything.

When tradition dictated she stay home, he insisted she attend school with her brother. Even if the best schools on the island were run by the occupiers.

Education—Datu Khaled said—was 'the path to advancement', the only inheritance worth leaving one's children.

He encouraged all members of his tribe to get an education. From secular schools, from madrasas, from each other.

That afternoon, on her way home from school, Fatimah went off the main road and towards the waterfall. Summer was near, and the heat was unbearable.

Her brother, Adil, stayed behind to work on his English. He wasn't as good at languages as his younger sister.

While walking, Fatimah liked to recite verses by the seventeenth century poet Lope de Vega. She loved how his florid Spanish words played on her tongue. Rolling and tapping a complex rhythm. Like bamboo poles beating time in traditional *singkil* dances.

'Fa-fa-fa-ti-mah, *la fe-a*!'

The taunt cut through the woodland around her. In a creole that sounded like crude Castilian.

It shattered her contentment.

She spotted some boys laughing in the distance. The trunks of the jackfruit trees not wide enough to hide them.

Not that the boys were even trying to hide.

'Fatimah—fea!'

It was her schoolmate Tarek and his friends. They were not of her tribe.

These boys were so arrogant they thought they owned the province.

They fancied themselves brave and bold—Fatimah thought them bullies. Nothing but belligerent buffoons.

Her mother told her to avoid them.

'Mangih kaw dagbus!' Tarek yelled in another native tongue.

Fatimah was used to him calling her ugly. In the only two languages he spoke.

He did so whenever she was in earshot.

'Mangih kaw dagbus! Fea—fea!'

She didn't let him see it upset her.

Another thing her mother told her—*Never let them see you cry.*

A Suhkmil woman didn't reveal her weaknesses. She never exposed her emotions.

If they don't know what you're thinking, they won't know how to hurt you.

Or so she was taught.

Fatimah kept walking. She knew the boy would soon get bored and move on.

The teasing stopped before she got to the falls. *Alhamdullilah.*

Thank God.

She undressed swiftly, laying her neatly folded *tadjung* wrap on a dry rock.

There was nothing Fatimah enjoyed more than bathing alone in the cool water pooled at the base of the falls. It's where she felt freest.

She swam—she soaked—she rinsed her hair.

And she didn't have to worry about undertows, tidal waves, or pirates.

When the shadows began to shift on the rocks, Fatimah knew it was time to head home. It would be dark soon and the fireflies would come out of hiding.

She heard a rustle when she stepped out of the pool.

Her arms went up to hide her breasts. The tadjung wrap was too far to reach.

'Who's there?' she called out, adjusting herself to cover her private areas.

A twig snapped.

Someone was trying to be stealthy. But not very good at it.

Fatimah turned and quickly spotted Tarek. Faster than he could do up his trousers. 'What in the name of—'

The boy didn't have time to run off, and his—*club*—was too stiff to be hidden.

Fatimah had not seen one before.

'D'you like it?' Tarek asked when he noticed her staring. She was so shocked she didn't realize she was still undressed.

He let his trousers drop and pulled his shirt up under his arms.

'Touch it, Suhkmilul,' he commanded pejoratively. His tribe was used to barking orders at the Suhkmil.

'Not a chance.' Fatimah said, disgusted. She turned to get her clothes.

Pulling on his 'club', Tarek stepped out of his trousers and followed her.

'Watch, Fatimah, I'll show you what happens—'

She got dressed. Ignoring him.

He stopped a few paces behind her. She heard him groan.

She also heard his hand moving more rapidly over his member.

'Finish me off, Suhkmilul,' he snarled. 'You did this to me!'

She started to walk away when he grabbed her tadjung and tried to rip it off.

They grappled.

He threw her to the ground and climbed on top, groping where he could. Her breasts. Her thighs. Her groin.

They scrambled violently on the woodland floor.

She screamed.

He tried to slap her silent.

In the skirmish, she picked up a fallen branch and hit him.

Bloodied and stunned, his hold on her weakened. Enough for her to push him away.

She ran.

He grabbed his trousers and chased her. All the while striving to get them on.

'Don't you tell anyone, Suhkmilul!'

Fatimah fled with Tarek close at her heels.

'Tarek!'

She stopped. The voice came from the other side of the grove.

'Tarek, where are you? It's almost time for prayers!'

It was Tarek's brother, Hatif.

Nowhere to hide, Fatimah looked back and froze.

A few metres away, Tarek was face down on the ground with his trousers at his feet. Blood—pooling under his head.

Hatif spotted them before she could move.

'Tarek!' he cried, running over.

He fell to his knees by his older brother. Trying to shake him awake.

'What happened, Fatimah?' Hatif's voice trembled. 'What happened?'

She was so terrified she didn't know what to say.

'Fatimah?!' Hatif was frantic. 'What did you do?'

She didn't know what to say.

The muezzin's call to evening prayer began. His deep wail permeating the woodlands from the mosque.

Fatimah tightened the ripped tadjung around her and ran home.

* * *

Word spread across the villages before the next day's sunrise prayers.

Datu Khaled's daughter killed Datu Rahim's son.

It would reignite the blood feud between their clans.

To prevent that, her father was at Datu Rahim's all night. Returning home just as the servants laid out the midday meal.

'This is the only way to keep the peace, my child,' Datu Khaled explained. 'You must marry Hatif.'

'No, Father, please,' Fatimah begged, 'that isn't fair.' She turned to her mother for support.

Her parents shared a look.

It unsettled Fatimah further.

'I did nothing wrong,' she again expressed. 'Don't you believe me?'

Her anguish crushed her parents.

Finally, voice quivering, her mother, Safiyah, spoke.

'Of course we believe you, *anak*. Of course we do, dear child.'

Safiyah glanced at her grief-stricken husband.

'But you must do this to appease Datu Rahim and his kin,' she reiterated. 'It's the only way to protect our family.'

'You know how this is, Fatimah,' Khaled said evenly, his face ashen. 'We have enough to worry about with the Americans still trying to annex our lands. We don't need more feuds amongst ourselves.'

Fatimah said nothing, trying to comprehend how she ended up as currency in a political transaction.

'It's a matter of honour,' her father spoke again. 'Datu Rahim asked for this. If we do not comply, make no mistake, they will kill us all.'

'It is your duty, beloved daughter,' Safiyah echoed. 'We must keep the peace.'

Anger surged within her, quashing her powerlessness. It took her by surprise.

'A life for a life, right?' Fatimah spat out. 'So, *my* life for his? That is what's—honourable?'

The world was spinning out. Nothing made sense.

She fell to her knees. Despondent.

'But I didn't kill him, Father. I didn't—'

Datu Khaled could not bear to see his daughter this way.

'Hatif said—' he stopped and cleared his throat.

'Hatif said,' he started again, 'that he saw you having—relations—with his brother. That Tarek's trousers were—'

Khaled couldn't finish the sentence from the horror of the thought.

'No!' Fatimah cried out. 'No, Father, that's not what happened.'

Heartsick, Datu Khaled left the room.

'Hush, child,' her mother soothed, embracing the pained young girl. 'Not so loud. The servants might hear.'

Fatimah did not understand. Surely, if people knew, they would realize she did nothing wrong. Exactly as she told her mother the instant she got home the day before.

> *She told her about Tarek and his trousers—and the rod between his legs that stood by itself and frightened and disgusted her.*
>
> *She told her mother how the boy kept pulling on it, insisting that she hold it.*
>
> *She told her mother she refused and fled.*
>
> *How he chased her and pushed her to the ground.*
>
> *How he touched her in places she never let anyone see.*
>
> *She told her mother how she screamed and struck him and ran away again.*
>
> *How he got up and chased her again —and then, he went silent.*

She told her mother everything, and Safiyah believed her.

Most likely—her mother said—the boy tripped on his trousers and hit his head.

But ultimately that changed nothing.

Datu Rahim's son was still dead. Found on Suhkmil land with Fatimah seen over the boy's half-naked—dishonoured—body.

It didn't matter that he trespassed. It didn't matter that he violated her.

It didn't matter what *she* said.

> *'Boys will do what they will,' her mother told her on the night of the assault.*
>
> *She took a cloth and wiped the blood off Fatimah's face.*
>
> *'They are—boys. Few of them are as kind as your father.'*

Safiyah was heart broken for her daughter, but she had to make the girl tough.

She had to make her understand how things worked.

> *'There is a bucket of water in the kitchen,' Safiyah said stoically that evening. 'Go wash yourself before the men return from the mosque. Don't let anyone see you. And get rid of that soiled tadjung.'*

Fatimah did not move.

'We must prevent another cycle of feuding,' Safiyah explained. *'You must never speak of this again.'*

Fatimah stayed by her mother's side, clenching her ripped wrap-around.

She did not understand.

'I will speak to your father when he gets home,' Safiyah was decisive. *'He will go to Datu Rahim and find a way to come to an agreement.'*

Safiyah hoped for the best.

'And you, anak,' she wiped her daughter's tear-streaked face, *'must obey. Understand?'* She was resolute. *'You must be a good daughter—and obey.'*

Fatimah knew things would never be the same.

'Don't worry, my dearest,' Safiyah stroked her child's dishevelled hair. *'It will be all right,'* she reassured, *not quite believing it herself.*

The morning after, they were again in the sacred space between mother and daughter.

'Hatif is a good boy, anak,' Safiyah consoled her beloved child. 'More prudent than his brother. He will make a fine husband.'

'But I do not love him, Mother,' Fatimah said, softly.

'That will come,' Safiyah promised, 'in time. You will see.'

She forced a smile hoping to comfort the weeping Fatimah.

'For now, this is what we must do. Bind our tribes instead of dividing them. You are strong, my beloved girl—please do as your father has asked.'

* * *

Fatimah disappeared with her dowry a few days before the wedding. It was the only way to save them all.

One night, while it rained, she fled the village, heading north. As far north as she could go. Across bridges and islands. Past mosques, until she reached churches.

Somewhere without tribes or blood feuds.

Or so she thought.

She went with her parents' tacit blessing. Her father gave her his plaited ring for protection.

Not even her brother, Adil, was aware she was leaving.

This gave credence to her parents' claim that she ran away.

After several days of professing to search, Datu Khaled officially disowned her. It was the honourable thing to do. She had, after all, 'disgraced' them.

This way, they were all victims of one child's selfish sinfulness, and retribution for Tarek's death would not be taken against their clan.

It was Fatimah's idea.

It broke Khaled's heart.

It broke Safiyah.

They set their daughter free and told her not to look back.

'Trust no one,' her mother whispered when they hugged her goodbye.

Released into the darkness, Fatimah secured her armour and set off.

Chapter 9

La Tiquismiquis y el Idilio | **The Fusspot and the Idyll** | Ang Mabusisi at ang Panandaliang Ginhawa

Something was different. She didn't know what exactly, but she could tell.

And Almudena Castillo de Montijo de Yrastegui always trusted her intuition. It was never wrong.

She put the binoculars down and called for her husband.

'What now, my dear sweet Alma?' Andy indulged her, as always.

Alma was not amused.

As always.

It wasn't the first time she summoned him to this corner of their manor's wrap-around veranda, which also featured her bonsai collection.

It was on the second floor and overlooked the sugar plantation. Not all five-hundred hectares of the hacienda, of course, but a small portion that she considered most interesting.

'I'm telling you, Alejandro—something is going on there,' Alma insisted.

Andy Yrastegui smiled at his wife. She was serious when she used full names.

These days—he noticed—she was increasingly paranoid. Making more frequent stops by her bonsais.

And it wasn't to water her plants or enjoy the view—which was blocked by a rather robust mango tree.

Andy tried to encourage his wife to use the spacious veranda for more social practices. Like inviting people over for afternoon snacks. Or hosting mah-jong parties as her mother did at Sombra.

But after five years on the small, sugar-plantation-covered island of Negros, Alma Castillo had few friends besides her miniature plants.

As did their two young daughters, whom Alma kept mostly at home.

'You can't trust anyone,' she often told her husband. 'Only immediate family. If that.'

She jested.

Or so he hoped.

It was 1976, and The Islands languished under martial law.

Andy stopped counting how many years had passed since 'a friend of the president' was charged with managing the sugar industry. Some self-made businessman named Eliseo Salazar.

He single-handedly controlled everything—funding, trade deals, supplies, prices. Even product transport.

Andy hadn't heard of him before martial law.

But since then, this Salazar character was everywhere. Aside from being trade ~~overlord~~ secretary, he was also national security adviser.

Not the most conducive atmosphere for business, but Andy managed.

Fact: Andy struggled.

As did other sugar barons in the country.

Global prices were down, and Secretary Salazar was making new arrangements with foreign buyers—in secret.

Andy's plantation manager was barely able to balance their books. And he warned that soon, they wouldn't be able to pay their farm hands.

Elsewhere in the world, it was all carefree love and wild abandon, but not in Negros. Andy worried the government monopoly would ruin them.

But he kept that to himself.

Just as he kept to himself that he noticed his wife becoming more rigid and suspicious than the country's dicta— *pardon*—he meant—president.

With everything else going on, Andy couldn't understand why the farm hands were the latest in Alma's crosshairs.

'They gather under that kamias tree every afternoon, at this same time,' she said warily. 'You can't tell me they're using the leaves as some sort of remedy for heat rash or snacking on the fruit—kamias is so sour—and really, they're just standing there—talking.'

Andy didn't know how she could see past the tree obstructing the view from the veranda.

'I can see them through the leaves,' Alma explained as if reading his mind. 'And the sugar cane may be tall on the ground, but I can still make out those people in that clearing near the water tank. I'm telling you I don't trust that new foreman—what's his name?'

Alma raised the binoculars and again looked past the mango tree towards the offending workers.

'I think it was—Dodong? Maybe Totong? Anyway, they're entitled to their breaks, *cariño*—it's the one thing this government hasn't banned,' Andy reminded his beloved. 'And I'm about to take mine,' he kissed her. 'Bertín is coming to get me for golf.'

'Are you kidding?' Alma lowered the binoculars, incensed. 'Your hacienda is falling apart and you're off to golf with your delinquent friends?'

She didn't understand how her well-bred, foreign-schooled husband suffered these simple-minded parochial folks. They were nothing like their friends in Manila. Not only did people in Negros speak a different dialect, the Spanish upper crust on the island also had their own distinct levels of ascension.

Which was why Alma kept to her plants. She wasn't about to waste time figuring out how to navigate another tedious social landscape.

Fortunately for her, the mystique around her husband's family was the same across the islands. So, people in Negros overlooked the peculiarities of the young Señora de Yrastegui.

Andy sighed.

'Cariño, *relájate*. You're working yourself up again, for no reason.'

He gently took the binoculars from her and put it on the table. Then, he took her hands in his and clasped them together.

'The workers aren't plotting anything, my love. And my friends are not delinquents,' he said lovingly. 'Like ours, their plantations run so well, they don't need to be micromanaged. Besides, with the dicta—I mean—the *president's* people handling the ins and outs of the trade, we've got time on our hands.'

That was one way to put it.

He hugged his scowling wife and kissed her loudly on the mouth.

He knew that always dissipated some of her misplaced anger.

'*Anímate*, cheer up. Want to come along? The wives will be sipping iced tea by the pool and getting their nails done.'

Alma rolled her eyes. 'I would rather stick knitting needles up my nose.'

Andy laughed. 'Okay, okay, okay!'

He had to hand it to her, her excuses got more creative every time.

'Maybe another day?' he squeezed her tighter as Bertín's jeep pulled up the gravel drive.

'I'll be home by dinner, cariño.' Andy rushed to get his clubs.

'Love you!' he yelled as he ran out the back door.

* * *

9 Sept. 1976

Diary, he isn't taking me seriously. I keep telling him those farm hands are up to something, and he won't believe me!

I'm sure the communists are getting to them. I saw it on the news. The Reds are all over this island recruiting plantation workers to their cause.

Maybe that Dodong/Totong is a communist? We don't know him, or his family. He's not from around here. Why did Andy even hire him? He's too trusting sometimes, my husband. Puñeta.

Shit.

And it's not just something made up on the news.

Every time we go into town, I can sense it. An underlying—tension. I don't know what to call it. Something that's just—there. Palpable.

It feels like they're watching us. Waiting for us to make the wrong move so they can take our haciendas.

I went to the market with the cook, Manang Nita, the other day. A man was going from stall to stall speaking to the vendors. He tried to be inconspicuous, but I noticed him. And I heard him telling them to 'rise against the oppressors'. He called landowners—oppressors! He said it was our fault the rest of them were poor.

How is that our fault?

I can't speak for other hacendados, but we pay our workers well. Not only that, but we give them food for their families and provide them with huts to live in—on our land—during harvest season. What more do they want?

Someday—no matter how good we are to them—these people may still think the communists are right, then what do we do?

Andy isn't taking this as seriously as he should be. He isn't taking his work seriously.

It's as if the salary he gets from the family firm is nothing more than an allowance. It shows up in his bank account regardless of job performance.

Even so, he should at least show some pride in his work. Have some dignity. He must do—the—job! Be a leader. Run the plantation. Run the mill. Live up to the Yrastegui name and make a profit for the family.

Instead, he spends all day hanging out with his 'buddies'. If it's not breakfast with them here at the house, they meet for brunch at the club. Then, he comes back for a siesta. When he wakes from that nap, he goes for a walk to 'inspect the mill'.

After that, it's golf with the gang. Or pelota. Or tennis. Or any number of other useless activities.

How does he do it? The aimlessness and lack of ambition would kill me. But it doesn't seem to bother him. No, Alejandro Yrastegui is as happy as can be.

Puñeta.

* * *

'Mami!'

The voice of her daughter interrupted Alma's lamentations.

'Mami!' the little girl squealed again.

'What, Núria?!' the aggrieved woman screamed back.

She put her diary away before stepping out of her room.

It was at times like these that she missed Sombra and her desk of secret drawers.

Actually, Alma missed Sombra, full stop. She thought the hacienda too bright and airy. Too—*open*. There wasn't enough privacy with all the rooms seeming to flow into each other.

There were too many arches and portals, and not enough doors.

It didn't help that people kept dropping in uninvited— and unannounced.

Andy didn't mind, but she did. Which was why she appreciated bonsais. The dwarfed plants were all about discipline and control.

'Mami, Ena ban me dolly,' Núria, her three-year old, reported as soon as she stepped into the lanai.

The little girl took Alma's hand and led her across the room, pointing at the older sister on the couch ignoring her.

The five-year-old was seated next to a blonde life-size doll. They were having tea.

Ay, Alma groaned, *here were go again*. Her daughters were so close in age she presumed they'd take to each other and get along.

But she was wrong.

'Ximena,' she scolded the older one, 'Abuelo Federico gave that doll to both of you. How many times must I tell you to share? You cannot ban your sister from playing with it!'

'Mami, what is share?' Núria asked.

Ay, Alma sighed again. She wanted to pull her hair out. She wanted to pull *their* hair.

Why didn't their grandfather just get them each a ridiculous doll?
Where was the nanny?

'Luming!' she yelled across the house. 'Why aren't you watching the children?'

Alma marched into the kitchen wanting answers.

She didn't know how much longer she could do this 'rural idyll' in Sugarlandia.

Negros Island—for all its provincial charm, stately manors, and expansive haciendas—was no place for a cosmopolitan city girl.

She missed Sombra. She missed her family. She missed doors.

She missed there being—*more*—to life.

* * *

'So, your sister-in-law had a boy?' Andy asked jovially at dinner. 'That's great news, no?'

He was referring to Luísa, the wife of Alma's brother Freddie. After a miscarriage, the couple just welcomed a son.

'Please don't call her that,' Alma directed, annoyed. She was already in a foul mood from having to referee their daughters all afternoon.

'Don't call her what?' Andy managed through a mouthful of rice.

'My "sister-in-law".'

Alma tried to ignore everything irritating her at the dinner table. Which, at least, no longer included her daughters. The little girls were having their meal in the kitchen. She banished them for their earlier misbehaviour.

This couldn't go on. Alma had to convince Andy to move back to Manila soon. The girls needed to be in the right schools. It was the only way she could turn those scamps into proper ladies.

'But Luísa is your sister-in-law,' her husband stated, perplexed.

Alma rolled her eyes.

Sometimes the agility needed to manoeuvre his wife's emotional geometry flummoxed Andy. And he was still learning the language of her family's idiosyncrasies. It was not unlike traipsing through a minefield.

'That hussy forced him into marriage,' Alma declared. 'It might be legal on paper, but that's all there is to it.'

Alma swapped over her utensils after cutting her steak and poked a small piece of the meat with her fork.

'Ay, Alma, give them a break. Young love,' Andy said, slicing his meat with the wrong hand.

'I don't think you can call it love,' Alma said. 'Switch.'

She didn't want to correct him again.

'What?' Andy, confused. Again.

'You're cutting the meat the wrong way,' she couldn't help it. 'You have to switch over the utensils. Knife on the right, fork on the left. Cut. Then back again before putting the serving in your mouth. And no talking with your mouth full. Or elbows on the table. Please, you know this.'

Alma caught herself and hoped her tone sounded gentle. She couldn't understand how someone from such an aristocratic background did not mind his manners.

'Cariño, why do you get so worked up?' Andy put his hand over hers on the table. 'None of it is a big deal. Not who your brother married and why, or how I cut my meat.'

She said nothing.

Alma learned early on from her mother that if she had nothing nice to say, she mustn't speak at all.

Andy raised her hand to his lips and kissed it.

'Want some ice cream?' he asked her, smiling. 'I miss the girls. Let's go for a drive and take them to that new ice cream parlour in town.'

Alma had to admit—he was good to her, her amiable husband.

He was good *for* her.

She hated it. Hated that she had no actual reason to be angry at him—and yet, she was.

Alma's chest tightened. Her stomach clenched. She wanted to scream and didn't know why.

She wanted—*more*.

And she realized she wasn't going to get it unless she asked.

But Alma would never dare. Ask.

Her mother taught her that women must be content with what they have.

And they must carry their burdens silently.

In that was their dignity and strength.

Like her mother, Alma Castillo was nothing but strong.

* * *

'Do you truly need all that?' Andy asked his harried wife the next morning. 'We're only going for two weeks.'

'Not nearly long enough,' thought Alma.

They hadn't been to Manila in almost a year. Since Andy's grandmother, Doña Constancia, turned eighty-five. They were so busy then with Yrastegui events that Alma didn't have time for her own family.

This trip was going to be different. She would make sure of it.

'Best to be prepared for anything,' Alma replied to her husband as she ran between their bedroom and their daughters'.

She was packing like they'd never return to Negros.

Andy left her to it. He needed to give last minute instructions to the farm manager and speak to Dodong, the workers' supervisor.

It was the start of harvest season and not the best time to leave the plantation. But the christening of the first male grandchild was a big event for the Castillo de Montijo family. They certainly couldn't miss it.

Even if Alma disapproved of her brother's wife.

'Don't worry, *cabrón*,' Bertín told Andy later that afternoon. 'I'll come by every few days and make sure things are running smoothly.'

Andy trusted his old school friend and hoped for the best.

'And as I said, I can lend you some of my guards,' Bertín offered again. 'No charge. Just for while you're away.'

'Thanks,' Andy demurred, 'but I really don't want guns around the plantation.'

It was a conversation they were having more frequently. Other hacendados had already hired security guards to protect their properties from communist rebels. The guards were supplied covertly by a nearby military outpost.

Fact: It was a lucrative racket for underpaid soldiers. They secretly armed villagers and sent them to defend plantations. Taking a cut from the salaries of the previously unemployed.

The soldiers also received an off-the-books 'finders' fee' from fearful hacendados.

The whole thing turned Andy's stomach.

Negros Island may have been a world away from the capital city, but he was learning that corruption saw no borders—and fear could be a very profitable enterprise.

Was this what the future looked like?

'Buddy, I understand your hesitation,' Bertín, again, 'but it's a sure way to keep the commies off your fields—'

'Or invite them over for battle,' Andy countered. 'I appreciate it, *amigo*, I do. But for now, let me pretend that we still live in a civilized, peaceful world.'

Bertín burst out laughing.

'Coño, Alejandro—bless your heart, you *insensato*. Such a fool.'

Bertín slapped him on the back. 'I hope you're right, buddy.'

'So do I,' thought Andy.

So do I.

Chapter 10

La Famosilla y el Baile de Máscaras |
The Socialite and the Masquerade Ball |
Ang Sosyal at ang Sayawan ng Mga Nakamaskara

María de la Covadonga Castillo was beginning to feel a headache. A usual sign that she'd been at Sparkles long enough.

She was raised to disguise her fatigue, but there was only so much of the scene she could take.

'What time is it?' she leaned across the booth to ask her friend Patti. It was hard to read her small Cartier watch with the club lights pulsating. She only wore it because it was a graduation gift from her father.

Sparkles—with its state-of-the-art technology, foreign DJs, and exclusive disco remixes—was the hottest venue in town. Prime hunting ground for Manila's most eligible.

Which included the president's only son—notorious womanizer Felipe Rodríguez Jr. Also known as Pip.

The diminutive yet overly confident Pip fancied himself the king of disco. Hitting on everyone at Sparkles—except Manila's prize catch. Mainly because he didn't want to risk public humiliation.

Fact: Pip Rodríguez preferred women he could intimidate—and he suspected said catch wasn't among them. A small part of him feared that she was too good for a politician's son.

Even if that politician was installing himself as president-for-life.

The 'catch' was, of course, none other than the youngest Castillo de Montijo daughter—twenty-four-year-old Covadonga. Sitting in a booth, nursing an empty glass, surrounded by preening men she'd tired of.

'Chill!' her friend Patti shouted above the music. 'We've got at least two more hours 'til curfew!'

Anicleta 'Patti' Gálvez wore an easy-to-read, backlit, digital timepiece. A more practical gift from her powerful father. Anicleto. He was a general in President Amá's army.

The general always wanted his daughter to know when it was time to head home.

Until such time, Patti intended to flirt with Cova's cast offs.

'Catch up, Co-co girl!' Patti raised her fifth glass of whisky at her friend.

Cova shook her head.

The pair first met at the polo club a few years earlier.

Normally, Patti's father would not have been granted membership. But as a close ally of Amá Rodríguez—and the country under martial law—the club couldn't exactly turn the general away.

Like her father, Patti Gálvez was loud, brazen, and shameless. Everything Covadonga Castillo was not.

In their bell bottoms and platform shoes, the unlikely duo was known as Hi-Lo. An unflattering reference to Hi-Ro—an inexpensive chocolate cookie with a white cream filling. A local version of the American Oreo.

Naturally, the fair-skinned, light-eyed Cova was 'Hi-society'. Her darker sidekick Patti—with her wide nose and frizzy hair—was 'Lo-society'.

Hi-Lo.

But no one dared call them that to their faces.

As close as they were, Cova remained mindful of what she shared with her friend.

No one can be trusted, her mother warned, and Patti's bodyguards were a constant reminder that these were extraordinarily treacherous times.

For example, Cova didn't tell Patti about the night she made out with Susie Santos in the Sparkles restroom. They snorted some cocaine, and Susie got a little randy.

It was fun—for a bit—but Cova never did coke again.

Nor did she repeat the scene with Susie—who, on this evening, was busy trying to undress an American basketball pro on the dance floor.

'From the *tisoy* at the end of the bar,' the waiter startled Cova, handing her a flute of the club's signature cocktail. Rosé champagne with a dash of Grand Marnier. A swirl of crystal bubbles in pink and orange, with a single—imported—raspberry sitting at the bottom.

'He said to tell you . . . your beauty . . . sparkles . . . more than our drink!' the waiter scratched his head, struggling to be heard and stumbling over his English. 'Or something like that. I couldn't really understand.' He bowed, smiled shyly, and walked away.

Cova laughed. That was the cheesiest line yet. She rarely bought her own drinks at places like Sparkles—but the flattery still made her blush.

Glancing towards the bar, she made out the strong features of a light-haired, broad-shouldered man playing hide-and-seek with shards of light from the overhead mirror balls.

Inappropriately sexy shadows pulsed on his tight trousers.

His silky shirt was unbuttoned low, and the hair on his chest was shiny with sweat.

Cova felt a rush of blood between her legs. The mixed-race Spanish mestizo—aka tisoy—was just her type.

Apparently, he whetted the appetite of many in the disco, as evidenced by the number of heads—male and female—that turned to follow him as he strutted towards Cova.

'Hel-lo,' he said loudly upon his approach. 'I see . . . you are . . . dry.'

'Excuse me?' she pulled back, appalled.

'Dry? No drink? So . . . I send,' he stated, wondering why he'd offended her.

'Ah!' she giggled, noticing his thick accent for the first time.

'You don't really speak English, do you?' she asked.

'*¿Obvio?*' he laughed, shyly. 'I . . . learning.'

He has a kind smile—thought Cova.

'My name is Cristóbal,' he offered his hand. She shook it. It was soft.

'Cova.' She replied, charmed. He seemed to have no idea who she was. She liked that.

'Where are you from?' she asked, sensing he wasn't at all a Filipino 'half-breed' like herself.

'Comillas,' he answered, 'in Cantabria, North Spain.' He was used to people not knowing the small town.

'Ah,' she hadn't heard of it despite her studies in Europe. 'Must be pretty.'

'It is,' he confirmed. 'But you are . . . more pretty.'

Boy—thought Cova—*this will be fun.* She wasn't used to advances being so clumsily transparent.

'You're a long way from home then,' she smiled, coyly.

'Not any more,' he smiled back. 'I move here. To play—'

Of course—she thought—*a pelotari!*

Jai alai—a Basque racquetball game using wicker handbaskets— had become quite the gambling sport, and players were brought in from Spain to professionalize the matches. High speed, high stakes. Fortunes made and lost on the courts.

Cova heard about it from her younger brother, Freddie. He spent a lot of time at the fronton with his friends.

Some nights, Freddie came home with new cars and jewels for both their mother and his wife. He also talked a lot about 'investing' in something or other that was going to 'turn a quick profit', but Papá always told him it was 'too risky'.

Cova never understood much of what they said.

Mostly, Freddie spoke to their older sister, Maca. If Cova happened to be in the room, they ignored her, thinking she wasn't smart enough to 'get it'.

They were right, but Cova tried not to let that show.

She also didn't let them see that it hurt her. To be excluded.

Outside Sombra's walls, she wasn't treated like an intruder—everyone wanted to be around the enchanting Covadonga Castillo.

Cova learned early on how fascinated people were by her family. They swarmed her hoping for an invitation to Sombra or to a weekend at their rest house on the farm. Even just to be seen with her in public. Anything to be associated with the Castillo name. It held an odd kind of power that she took for granted.

Perhaps Patti was using her to climb the social ladder? To the rungs that couldn't be reached by newly acquired wealth or political pressure and brute force.

Cova looked over at Patti, throwing back whisky and laughing excessively with the men around her. She shook the thought from her head.

'Are you okay?' Mr Tight Trousers leaned over.

This guy—*Cristóbal, was it?*—was new to Manila, still unaware of the weight of her family.

'If they don't know who you are, or where you come from, you can be anything you want,' her mother had said. But this was the first time Cova understood it.

This Cristóbal was her blank slate.

Feeling refreshingly unshackled, Cova took another look at him.

She switched on her brightest smile and puffed out her chest. Wanting to get more than a peek at his bulging shadows.

In a heartbeat—two hours—time was up.

'Co-co, girl, *tara*—let's!' her friend Patti suddenly appeared and pulled at her elbow.

'Curfew,' Cova explained to Cristóbal, 'we must be home by midnight.'

'Or . . . jail?' he asked.

'Something like that,' she remarked.

'When can I see you again?' he leaned closer so she could feel his breath in her ear.

She also thought she felt the tip of his tongue. *¡Desvergonzado!*

Shameless—she liked that.

Cova noticed the shadow on his trousers grow larger.

Any other evening, she would've taken him to one of the private after-curfew parties at a friend's house. To *get to know* him better.

But not this evening.

Her first nephew was going to be baptized in the morning, and she had to look presentable in the House of God.

The next decision was an easy one. Cova took her lipstick from her purse and scribbled on a paper napkin. She then pressed it into Cristóbal's surprisingly soft hands.

'Come for merienda tomorrow afternoon,' she spoke in his ear. 'My nephew's bautizo. Be my guest at the reception.'

She kissed his cheek and was hurried out with Patti by her bodyguards.

When they were no longer in sight, Cristóbal unfolded the note in his hands.

He was perplexed.

There was only one thing on it—the Spanish word for shadow. *Sombra.*

* * *

That night, Cova snuck back into Sombra through the tunnels. Patti puked on her in the car, and she wanted to get changed before seeing her parents. They would not be impressed.

The Castillo children always greeted their parents when they got home, to let them know they were back in the manor safely.

That didn't necessarily mean they *stayed* in Sombra.

There were secret passages beneath the property that connected to old tunnels used by American soldiers during the War. With several exits by the river, just beyond Sombra's walls.

The underground corridors supposedly stretched like varicose veins across the city.

Cova only discovered them when she caught Freddie coming home one evening. He stepped out of a hidden portal by the chapel.

For Cova, it was like finding the key to a magic lock. A whole new world opened that made Sombra feel less like an isolated, inescapable fortress.

Since meeting Patti, Cova frequently used the tunnels to sneak in and out. Patti's father wouldn't give her a curfew exemption permit, but she was sleeping with one of her bodyguards and he knew how to evade the checkpoints. They moved around the city like glamourous outlaws—how could Cova pass up such adventure?

She did feel a little guilty because the secret portal was by the family chapel, but the thought of divine retribution didn't stop her.

Covadonga Castillo was all about breaking rules in the name of fun. Or so she told herself.

Often, as she sat in front of the mirror wiping her face before bed, Cova stared at her blood shot eyes and flushed red cheeks—wondering who she was underneath the make-up.

* * *

'You know that hides nothing, right?' Maca was waiting for her when she came out of their parents' room.

It caught Cova by surprise.

'Papá and Mami don't say anything,' Maca went on, 'but the smell of cigarettes and alcohol isn't covered up by your god-awful perfume or your change of clothing. You reek, Cova. Like a tramp.'

Cova felt punched in the gut. 'I only had a few glasses,' she explained, 'nothing outrageous.'

'I'm just telling you to be careful,' Maca said sternly. 'You're a Castillo de Montijo—your behaviour reflects on all of us. Don't forget that.'

Cova tried, again, to appeal to her older sister. 'But I've done nothing wrong—'

'Yet.' Maca cut her off and stomped away.

What is with her?—Cova wondered. Maca always seemed upset with everyone except Freddie.

'Cova!' Alma called across the courtyard to the floor above. She was up late watching a bootlegged film with Andy in the screening room.

'Oh my! I forgot you were arriving tonight!' An elated Cova ran down the stairs and hugged her eldest sister—who immediately pulled away.

'Uuff!'—Alma stepped back to take a breath—'that's some scent you have on.'

'So I've been told,' Cova muttered.

Alma was puzzled.

'Never mind,' Cova dismissed. 'Are you all here? Both little girls?'

'The girls and the husband, yes,' Alma beamed, then paused, taking a more considered look at her sister.

'Are you okay?' she asked, concerned. 'You seem a little—I don't know—unlike yourself.'

'I'm okay,' Cova lied, 'just a little tired.'

'Partying too hard?' Alma teased.

'Only on Saturdays,' Cova smiled. 'I have a job now, so I come straight home from work on weekdays.'

Alma was glad her youngest sister was doing something—*productive*.

'I'm just a secretary to one of Papá's friends, but at least I'm earning my own money,' Cova said proudly.

Which was more than Maca could say.

Macarena Castillo told people she didn't have a job because her many 'social causes' kept her busy, but Cova rarely saw her leave Sombra.

'Have you seen Lulu yet?' Alma lowered her voice to ask.

Lulu was what Freddie's sisters called his wife, Luísa. They let her think it was an affectionate nickname.

But it was short for 'Lukaret'—which is what they called her when she was out of earshot.

The name was a play on the local word for 'crazy person'.

'What did she do now?' Cova wondered. It was obvious her poor sister-in-law was miserable at Sombra, but Cova believed she brought it on herself. Always defensive and tense, Luísa didn't bother getting to know them—and it made the air around her less than amiable.

'For starters, she dyed her hair,' Alma whispered, conspiratorially. 'It looks like straw. Or, you know those coarse dry hairs that come out of corn? Like that. Dull, ugly yellow—so fake—it's terrible.'

'Poor girl,' Cova started, opting to be kind, 'maybe she's just trying to look good for tomorrow—'

'You mean she wants to upstage the baby,' Alma cut in. 'You know what she's like—always wanting attention for herself.'

'I think she feels insecure,' Cova offered. 'It can't be easy to suddenly be part of this family. And you know Freddie is no walk in the park.'

'True,' Alma acknowledged, 'but honestly Cova, that girl should be grateful. She gets to live here and carry our name—she's set for life.'

'¡Hermanas!'

A very drunk Freddie stumbled upon them very loudly from the back porch.

'How wonderful to see you here!' He gave them both a sweaty hug and tried to kiss each sister on the cheek.

'Where did you come from, Fred? You can't go see Mami and Papá like that,' Alma was mortified. '*Peor*, who saw you like that outside the house?'

'Ah yes, hermana, what could be *worse* than me "outside the house"—in any state? Haha!' Freddie guffawed, a terrible sound that resembled a congested carabao.

Alma was worried about her brother, the youngest of her siblings. In many ways, the twenty-two-year-old was still a child. An unruly boy on whose shoulders lay the family legacy.

Despite the attention lavished on him by their parents, Freddie seemed—*off-course*. Nowhere near becoming the man their father was.

Nowhere near being the man they needed him to be.

As Alma saw it, Freddie was undisciplined and recalcitrant. A school dropout who had no respect for hard work. Always after a quick-fix or a 'sure thing'. Always wanting to pull a fast one and game the system.

Then, when things blew up in his face—as they often did—he ran to Mami for help. Which only encouraged his recklessness and lack of thought. Freddie knew their mother would mollycoddle him regardless. Especially after—

No—Alma caught herself. She wouldn't let herself remember the *unmentionable one's* absence.

'Just get to bed, Freddie,' she told her brother. 'I'll let them know you're home and went straight up to Lulu—I mean Luísa—and the baby.'

She didn't want him upsetting their parents, which he would if they saw the state he was in—puffy faced, bleary-eyed—he was even drooling. His shirt wasn't buttoned right, and his trousers were stained. An embarrassment. Cova was used to him like that, but it was a shock to the visiting Alma.

She knew Freddie didn't hang out with other Spanish mestizos like himself—she understood how hard it was to be around people you sometimes felt inferior to. Even though they were notoriously lazy and spoiled. Little mama's boys who were never going to work a day in their lives.

Alma was convinced her baby brother would have been better off if he stuck with his high school buddies. A nice group of respectable tisoys from other countries—none of which had colonized the islands.

Lebanese mestizos, German mestizos, and one boy was even part-Swiss.

With their families relatively new to The Islands, those other 'half-castes' strove to make something of themselves. For starters—unlike Freddie—they all graduated from university.

Yes—Alma thought—*those boys would have been a good influence.*

But instead, Freddie spent his time at the jai alai fronton, with people the family didn't know. And he didn't even play the sport.

Ultimately, Alma was certain Freddie's misfortunes were Luísa's fault. If that trollop hadn't seduced him, Freddie would have finished school and had better prospects.

'Joder,' Freddie suddenly exclaimed. 'Fuck, look at the time.'

Alma and Cova turned to each other as their brother stumbled away.

He wasn't wearing a watch.

In his hurry to leave before his sisters started nagging, Freddie crashed into a centuries-old Ming vase that was in front of one of the courtyard pillars, just missing a glass cabinet filled with his mother's collection of ivory.

The Chinese antique burst into a flurry of porcelain pieces, but Freddie didn't even stop to dust himself off.

As his sisters neared the collision site, they noticed a plastic-wrapped packet among the ceramic fragments on the floor.

A tightly packed bundle of crisp hundred-dollar bills. Ten thousand dollars' worth.

It fell out of Freddie's pocket as he dashed away.

Chapter 11

El Regalo | **The Gift** | Ang Regalo

Some afternoons, Ricky Castillo strolled through the gardens at Good Graces. It got him out of his room—no doctor, no sharing circle, no marking in his *puto* journal what goddam day it was in the 'Lord's Good Year' of 2010.

No need to account to anyone for his 'thoughts and feelings'.

Or his lack of them.

He liked the sun on his face and feeling the grass beneath him.

He watched the clouds dance and listened for the song of the birds.

Oh, who was he kidding? He was no nature freak, but it was the only time they left him alone.

'Psst—psst,' a noise surprising him from behind a shrub.

He ignored it, thinking it must be the wind.

'Sir Ricky?' the same shrub was suddenly calling.

He looked around and approached it with apprehension.

It was an orderly. A young man he saw every day. He was crouching low, trying to blend in with the flowers.

'I have something for you,' the orderly whispered in the vernacular through the thick, blossoming bush. 'For your birthday. He says sorry that it's late.'

There was a shuffle among the twigs: 'I'll leave it here.'

Ricky stayed put until the orderly slinked away.

When he was alone again, he crept to the other side of the shrub. Among the roots—a small packet wrapped in plastic.

For a second, he thought his dreams had come true. He ripped open the pouch—but it wasn't a bundle of crank.

A mobile phone. Another of those cheap ones made in China.

A blinking light—and a message on the screen.

'Miss me? I'd nvr 4get u, FEDERICO d 3rd.'

Ricky deleted it. Not wanting a flashback to electric-green glasses and a coat of scales.

His hands trembling, he punched in Sombra's number—but the mobile was blocked from making calls.

It buzzed—and he nearly dropped it in the bush. An unknown caller was trying to reach him.

He accepted the call but said nothing into the phone.

'Happy birthday, Federico the Third.'

Ricky gasped.

'Click. Cluck. Click . . . you still owe me.'

Chapter 12

El Bautizo | **The Baptism** | Ang Binyag

Three years had passed since her miscarriage, but Luísa still wasn't 'over it'.

That's what Freddie said she should be doing—getting over it.

Other people told the young mother it would get easier, but it hadn't.

Part of her blamed Little Fátima. Her daughter was barely five and remembered nothing.

Luísa knew it wasn't rational, but if the precocious child hadn't disappeared into that wall those years ago, she might never have lost the baby.

She didn't know where to look for comfort.

Pot only did so much, and she didn't enjoy the hangover that always followed alcohol.

So, Luísa turned to the Church.

She didn't feel comfortable in the family chapel built in the garden by her mother-in-law—so she walked to the parish church down the street from Sombra.

She heard mass almost daily and confessed to a priest at least once a week. Activities neither her husband nor her young friends enjoyed.

Which meant that five years, one living child, and a miscarriage after she was married, twenty-two-year-old Luísa Acosta de Castillo still spent most of her time alone.

Or with a priest.

Who had become a close friend.

She was certain that's why God let her have another baby.

Finally, the long-awaited son. Federico Luís Castillo de Montijo III y Acosta. Baby Ricky.

Her husband Freddie should have been thrilled, but Luísa wasn't certain. He still came home late in the evenings and slept in a separate room.

The nationwide midnight curfew didn't seem to curtail his activities, and he knew his way in the dark quite well.

There were a few occasions when Freddie stumbled into Luísa's bed, drunk and half-conscious.

On those nights, he ravaged her. Like a man trying to relieve himself of rancour.

Luísa was certain that her husband used the secret corridors in the house to move around—but she didn't know how he entered and left the estate without being noticed.

Since her miscarriage, the young Mrs Castillo no longer ventured into the hidden hallway by her bedroom—it was a painful reminder of her mindlessness.

She did, however, keep in a drawer the photo of the handsome unknown boy that she found in the locked room. Occasionally bringing it out when she needed—release.

Just as she did that morning.

Yet another thing Luísa got used to doing on her own.

She checked her face in the mirror to make sure she didn't look as hollow as she felt. Her new jewellery laid out neatly on the dresser.

It was almost time for church, or in this case—the family chapel in Sombra's garden. For Baby Ricky's christening.

Freddie asked that she wear the jade set he brought her the week before. Necklace, bracelet, earrings—the works. A present from his new friend Harrison Chong.

Freddie was spending a lot of time with Harrison and a certain Edward Yang. Luísa had yet to meet them, but her husband had them stand as Baby Ricky's godfathers. Along with five other Chinese men he called his 'associates'.

Technically, most of them were Taiwanese—and only one was Catholic.

Freddie said making these men Ricky's godfathers would honour them and inextricably link them to the family. Which he hoped would lead to expanded business dealings.

As it was, Sombra's garage was like a showroom of Freddie's vehicles, and the house itself was speckled in jade and ivory trinkets. Plus, other Orientalia from his frequent trips to Hong Kong and Macau. He even found his mother a Cantonese supplier of monk fruit. The blasted gourd always smelled rotten to him, and yet she loved it.

Business was clearly going well, but Freddie Castillo wanted more.

His son would have eight sets of godparents because that was a lucky number for his seven Chinese associates—but the final godfather wasn't Chinese.

Mikey Reyes—godfather number eight—was introduced to Freddie by the son of Mang Eloy, the golf club storekeeper.

Mikey was the new young mayor of Manila. A nephew of President Rodríguez, with power over the city's ports.

Freddie planned his connections very well.

* * *

'Alma!'—Doña Fatimah summoned her eldest daughter to the grand salon—'Do you have the coins?' The guests were soon arriving, and she wanted everything in place.

'Yes, Mami,' Alma replied. 'Don't worry, everything's sorted.' She was rushing out to the garden to check on the tent canopies. Midpoint between the main house and the family chapel. The space designated for cocktails and canapés.

Sombra hadn't seen a reception this big since her engagement to Andy, and rain was forecast for the afternoon.

All three of Freddie's sisters were godmothers, and all three would be throwing coins. Nothing less for the first Castillo de Montijo grandson.

After every christening, it was tradition to toss coins at the guests for the children to collect. For prosperity and good luck. A celebration of new life.

The Castillos minted their own gold coins imprinted with the family crest and the name of the child being baptized.

Each coin was said to be worth a few hundred dollars.

Over the years, the Castillo coin toss became as much an event as their actual christenings.

'Have you seen Freddie?' Don Federico asked his eldest daughter as she dashed in from the garden. Iko always seemed to be chasing after his son.

'No, Papá,' Alma kissed him tenderly on the cheek. 'He must be here somewhere.'

Likely still passed out—she thought to herself—judging by his state the night before.

Neither she nor Cova had seen their brother since.

And they hadn't told anyone about the ten thousand US dollars that fell out of his pocket.

Alma tucked it away in her room, telling Cova she'd confront Freddie another time—his son's christening was not an appropriate occasion. Such a public event required the family exhibit a united front.

Frankly, Cova wasn't fussed. She never knew what Freddie was up to, and that's how it was best.

The only thing on Cova's mind was whether the pelotari from the night before would turn up.

'Attorney!' Maca gleamed as she raced to the new arrival—a dusky, clean-shaven, well-dressed man whom she led through the house towards the back yard.

His shirt was silk, his gabardine trousers seamless. His shoes were shiny and perfectly matched the burgundy-coloured leather belt cinched around his trim waist.

He was neither too tall nor too broad. With a thick head of jet-black hair, piercing dark eyes, and a wide toothy smile. She was thrilled to finally meet the famed personality.

The 'Attorney' took large confident steps and walked a little too close to Maca, though he seemed more impressed by the house than the woman guiding him through it.

They passed Cova in the courtyard, but Maca strode on saying nothing.

The man by Maca's side said nothing, too, but he noticed the pregnant silence between the sisters.

'Let me get you a drink in the garden, Attorney,' Maca was charming, afraid to lose his attention. 'Freddie will join us there shortly.'

The man she escorted was one of the baptism's most important guests—Attorney Armando 'Manny' Santos, the mayor's right-hand.

The politician-godfather was running late, so Attorney Manny would be his stand-in at the ceremony.

Fact: As customary, Manny was called 'Attorney' in recognition of his education. Like doctors, on the islands, such a show of distinction was also afforded to engineers and architects—their trades affixed to their names like a royal title.

Unknown to most, however, Attorney Santos only did half a year at law school. And he most definitely never sat for the bar exam.

Maca presumed the mayor was arriving with his presidential uncle—Freddie had told the family that the head of state would make an appearance.

Don Federico was not thrilled at the prospect, but Fatimah reminded him that their son should be able to invite whomever he wanted. It was, after all, his party.

What Freddie wanted were big shot guests to affirm his big shot status.

As always, Iko acquiesced to his wife.

* * *

Shortly after Manny's arrival, Freddie was found and roused. He dressed hurriedly, and the christening got underway on schedule. (The benefits of having a private chapel in the yard.)

At the marble baptismal font—which was to the side of the custom-made, hand-engraved wooden altar inlaid with mother-of-pearl—Luísa held the rosy-cheeked baby to her chest as if his breath were her own. Freddie beamed beside her like a captor.

The eight sets of godparents—Catholic and otherwise—stood solemnly around them like a dissonant choir of guardian angels.

Baby Ricky was silent throughout the ritual. He didn't even cry when holy water was poured over the thick tuft of hair on his head.

His parents took such seemingly innate propriety as a good omen. The priest knew better.

Afterward, the guests moved to the marquees in the garden for aperitifs. A remarkable procession of surly men in ill-fitting button-down shirts, gaunt women in see-through tops and skimpy skirts, and ill-advised Catholic schoolgirls who once hung out with Luísa.

Motherhood had a way of changing a girl's social life.

As Luísa went to put the baby down for a nap, Freddie got comfortable by the bar.

Alma circulated among the visitors hoping no one noticed her inebriated brother.

As hors d'oeuvres were served, a rock band played American covers and circus clowns performed tricks for the children.

Rain began to fall.

It was then that the mayor arrived. Without his uncle President Rodríguez.

Whom he swore would come by soon.

Attorney Manny stuck to the mayor like a male geisha catering to his lord.

Maca stuck to Manny like a guard dog with her master.

Several guests began to dance where they stood, and Freddie mingled with his son's godfathers—the assembly of questionable attorneys, entrepreneurs, an engineer, and a mayor.

Cigarette in one hand and a glass of whisky in the other, the *compadres* for life traded schemes shrouded in smoke.

On the sidelines, Federico and Fatimah observed it all like reluctant visitors at a zoo.

'Sometimes I miss the war,' Iko whispered to his unflappable wife.
'Why would you say that?' Timah was surprised.
'At least, back then we knew who the enemy was.'

* * *

'Make yourself useful and get me another drink, Luísa,' Freddie barked, puffing smoke at his wife seated next to him at the table.

It would've been his—well, it was difficult to keep track.

'Don't you think you've had enough?' she muttered, hoping that having company would keep him in check.

She was wrong.

Freddie got belligerent when he mixed his Johnnie with his Jameson and his Cuervo. She hadn't been around him in so long that she'd forgotten.

He laughed—again, like a choking carabao.

'¡Joder, coño!' he spewed at her. 'Who do you think you are to tell me what to do?'

His compadres said nothing. Luísa burst into tears.

She left the table and fled the marquee, dashing into the first doorway she could find. It was the storage room for pool towels and garden linens.

She realized she wasn't alone the moment she shut the door behind her. She felt for the light switch and flipped it on.

There, against a wall, was Covadonga—her skirt around her waist and Cristóbal's head between her legs.

'Oh my God!' Luísa screeched, 'I'm sorry—'

Cova noticed her sister-in-law's tear-stained face and pushed the pelotari away.

'Are you okay, Lu?' she asked. Breathless, but concerned.

'I . . . I . . . was just,' Luísa stammered as the strapping young man rose off his knees. His erection unmistakable in his tight tan trousers.

He wiped his mouth.

'Sorry you saw this,' Cova offered, only slightly embarrassed. Men didn't often do what Cristóbal just did.

'No . . . I . . .' Luísa was still at a loss for words.

'Did something happen, Lu?' Cova pulled her skirt back down. 'Cris—*porfa*—would you please get us some wine?' She smiled at him playfully.

'*Por supuesto,*' he replied, of course. His voice cracking under the weight of his lust.

'And fix your pants before you go,' Cova told him.

Luísa didn't know where to look as Cristóbal *adjusted* himself before leaving the room.

She also didn't know how much she could tell her sister-in-law. These Castillos stuck together like bananas.

But, ultimately, Luísa was too upset to hold back. Daring to tell Cova everything.

How awful Freddie was to her. How insecure and unimportant she felt. How unloved and unseen. And how much she hated being in the house.

Cova listened, unflinching. She didn't know what else to do. No one in Sombra ever spoke to her as openly as Luísa just did. She was both honoured—and horrified.

And she wasn't sure of the right response.

Cova Castillo was torn between wanting to make the crying woman feel better and defending her family.

She hoped she found a way to do both.

'He doesn't mean to hurt you,' she started, 'I'm sure of it. Freddie is just—you know—Freddie. He's a guy. He's young. That's what they're like, right?'

Luísa looked at her, unsure.

'I mean, he's just very sociable and likes to hang out with his buddies. They're also his business associates—so, really, it's a win-win for him. He gets to have fun—and make money.' *Good one*—thought Cova. It almost sounded true.

'Yes, but what about me?' Luísa's voice was soft.

Her pain and bare emotion made Cova slightly uncomfortable.

'He bought you that new car last week!' she remembered, triumphant.

'What's that supposed to tell me?' Luísa asked, distressed.

'That he loves you?' Cova didn't mean for that to be a question. 'I mean, he loves you.'

'He's never done what that guy was doing to you just now,' Luísa whispered.

'Oh—no,' Cova blushed, 'that wasn't love. I mean, we just met. We weren't, uhm—'

Cristóbal reappeared with their wine.

The conversation was closed.

* * *

'Attorney Manny, sir, telephone *po*.'

Maca was still by his side when the servant approached. She wondered jealously who would be calling her paramour on the Sombra line.

It didn't surprise her that someone needed him so desperately they tracked him down. That afternoon alone, Maca noticed how friendly he was with everyone. Even people he didn't know. It was as if he were the mayor and not Mikey Reyes.

'We're all politicians,' Manny shared as he swigged his sixth serving of Scotch. 'Officially, it is Mikey's post, but we're like family. We all campaigned for him, so we're all in power.' Manny's newly capped teeth gleamed like those of a magician. Devious and misleading.

Maca held on to it like a lifeline.

Manny excused himself and followed the servant to the phone in the house.

'Wherrrre'ssshhh Mann—Mann—nny?' Freddie slurred as he stumbled towards his sister.

'He went to take a call. Think you've had too much, Fred?' she asked, hoping no one was watching. 'Maybe you should go lie down awhile—'

'I'm fine!' her brother yelled, expelling a potent mix of fumes.

'Hush,' Maca lowered her voice and turned her head. 'Don't be a boob, Fred—it's your kid's baptism. Behave.'

'Or what, Maca?' he laughed. 'I can do what I want—I'm a man now. A man!'

She looked around again and tried to bring him aside. Glad their parents were in another corner of the marquee.

'Puñeta, Freddie—you're fucking twenty-two, hardly a "man",' Maca was irritated.

He laughed again. It made her angrier.

'I've got two kids now, you old maid—I think that makes me man enough.'

Before Maca could register the hurt from what he called her:

'So, you think that kid is mine?' he asked conspiratorially.

'What?' she was confused.

'Luísa's baby—do you think it's mine?'

'What the hell are you talking about, Freddie?'

'You know I only fuck her once in a blue ball,' he sputtered, 'maybe she screwed someone else and is passing that kid off as mine—'

'Shut up, Fred,' Maca was incensed. 'The boy looks exactly like you!'

'I don't know, hermana—'

Truthfully, she didn't know what to think either. Her brother's marriage was obviously not a happy one, but she insisted he stay with his wife. A separation was shameful—and would reflect terribly on the whole family. A dishonour that the rest of them didn't deserve.

Maca knew Freddie strayed—which was fine, so long as he didn't throw it in people's faces.

She even helped him hide his dalliances, sparing no thought for the wretched Luísa.

It was no secret they'd never accept her. The hussy who got herself pregnant for a piece of the pie. Loose-y Lulu was—*nothing*.

Unlike that wonderful Attorney Manny Santos. Such a strong character. Now there was a man!

Speak of the devil. Maca watched Manny rush back and head straight for the mayor— who was attached to some of the lesser clad female guests.

Manny whispered in the politician's ear and ushered him out of the marquee. Then, he made his way towards Maca—but leaned into her brother.

'Paré,' Manny whispered to Freddie. 'Sorry buddy, we have to go. I have to get the mayor out of here.'

'What? What happened?' Maca asked, overhearing him. They hadn't even tossed the coins yet.

'Someone tried to kill the president.'

Chapter 13

La Noticia | **The News** | *Ang Balita*

Special Bulletin: FINAL EDIT—APPROVED FOR USE
with **[INSERTS]**
News Alert || Manila, Philippines
27 September 1976 || Monday

[The Honourable] President **[and Father of our people, our dear Amá,]** Felipe Rodríguez remains in hospital two weeks after ~~a bullet grazed his arm~~ **[the attempt on his life]**.

Doctors at the National Hospital said the ~~president's~~ **[Supreme Commander's]** condition is **[now]** stable, **[but he still needs round-the-clock care.]**

[Our Esteemed Leader is recovering faster than expected because he was in excellent physical shape prior to being shot. Amá exercised regularly and maintained a protein-rich diet.]

[Pres. Rodríguez is also a devout Catholic and hears mass daily, even while in hospital.]

Felipe 'Pip' Rodriguez Jr, the **[righteous]** president's **[beloved]** only son, said the bullet missed his **[revered]** father's vital organs **[by the sheer grace of God]**.

[Sir] Pip is personally overseeing the investigation into the assassination attempt on ~~his father~~ **[the Supreme Commander]**.

He will also be supervising the military **[during the president's convalescence]**.

[The heroic] Pres. Rodríguez was shot along the Pasig River as he disembarked from the presidential speedboat at the mooring behind the presidential palace.

~~It was raining then, but~~ **[Amá's highly skilled]** security forces ~~claim to have~~ spotted the ~~alleged shooter~~ **[would-be assassin]** across the water.

The **[fast-acting]** presidential guards killed the ~~suspected~~ **[misguided]** attacker as he ~~reportedly~~ tried to flee after the shooting. **[A Kalashnikov rifle was found in his possession.]**

~~Witnesses said the man was only trying to fish for his supper when he was riddled with bullets.~~ **[There were no witnesses.]**

Police have identified the ~~alleged~~ shooter **[as 29-year-old tricycle driver Policarpio Macabenta]**. ~~They say he~~ **[The traitor]** lived in the ~~slum~~ neighbourhood of Happyland, on the riverbank opposite the palace.

Investigators are looking into reports that ~~he~~ **[Macabenta]** was secretly working for the **[so-called]** 'opposition' Democratic People's Party (DPP).

[A bank account in Macabenta's name received a deposit of twenty thousand pesos a few days before the shooting. The depositor was the unpatriotic, left-wing leader of the illegitimate DPP. The treasonous politician is now in police custody for questioning. A confession is imminent.]

In other news—another sugar mill burned to the ground last night as communist rebels continue their rampage across the central Visayan islands this harvest season.

[Since Amá was shot], insurgents have **[brutally]** attacked farms **[and incited plantation workers to riot]**.

Some sugar producers have ~~had to~~ cease**[d]** operations, ~~and~~ **[leaving]** many of the workers ~~are~~ at the point of starvation.

To help ~~paying~~ **[eligible]** landowners defend themselves from rebels, the military says it will provide weapons and ~~paid~~ **[duly licensed]** ~~paramilitary~~ **civilian guards**.

[The Honourable] Secretary of Trade and Agriculture, Eliseo Salazar, ~~says he~~ is working **[tirelessly]** to mediate and improve conditions for the sugar workers, but ~~he insists that~~ **[unprincipled and greedy]** landowners are refusing to cooperate.

Regardless, as the **[benevolent]** president's representative, Salazar ~~says he~~ is determined to reform the agricultural sector, expecting to make it less of a breeding ground for rebellion.

Meanwhile, in the southern islands of Mindanao, Muslim separatists pillaged their fifth Christian village in as many days.

The **[savage Islamic]** fighters destroyed homes, took possessions, and killed eighty people **[so far—including women and children]**.

Scores remain unaccounted, believed to have been taken **[by the brutal zealots]** as either hostages or slaves.

[In the last week, severed body parts were found along roads and on hillsides.]

Secretary Eliseo Salazar, also the National Security Adviser, is concerned that such violence signals the rebirth of the notorious Juramentados—a group of **[blood-thirsty]** Moro fighters known for their sweeping barbarism during World War II.

To aid ~~civilians~~ **[fellow Filipinos]** protect their families and their homes, the military will offer training and facilitate the acquisition of weapons in the southern islands.

~~The Presidential Palace has issued a statement that says:~~ Because of the **[precarious and dangerous]** state of the nation, the **[honourable and wise]** president is ~~going to~~ **[left no choice but to]** extend martial rule and expand the ~~already extra special super~~ emergency powers of the military and police **[indefinitely]**.

[The Gracious and Serene] First Lady Amelia Rodríguez has ordered the immediate arrest of all opposition politicians and declared a shoot-to-kill policy for any suspected rebels.

['It is terrible—just terrible—the horrid evil that is taking hold of our beautiful islands. These fiends, these bad people—they must be stopped. They will be stopped—with God as my Witness and my Warrior. I will do my duty—for I love you all.'

—**The Rt.Hon. Amelia Rodriguez, Supreme First Lady of The Philippines.**]

Until further notice, [**Her Serene Graciousness**] will also manage all judicial, legislative, and executive operations while simultaneously supervising the Central Bank.

Additional checkpoints will be set up nationwide, and extended curfew hours are now from 10 a.m. to 7 a.m.

[**Let us pray for our honourable leader and his courageous, God-fearing family.**]

God help us all.

Chapter 14

El Golpe | **The Shock** | Ang Pagkabigla

Doña Fatimah Castillo switched off the television and left the salon to get some air on the veranda.

Every day it was the same. A full month after the 'poor president' got 'shot', he was still in hospital 'fighting for his life'—and the country was 'falling to pieces' without him.

At least according to the urgent news bulletins that kept interrupting Doña Fatimah's favourite soap.

Every day, some new headline justifying the extension of martial rule.

Almost as if it were scripted—she mused.

It had been five years thus far.

Five years of trawling soldiers and military police with 'special powers'.

Five years of demonizing select 'enemies of the state'.

Five years of illegal abductions, disappearances, and imprisonments.

Hundreds of people gone—just like that—because they displeased Amá.

Maybe it was thousands of people. *Who knew for sure?*

That part was never in the bulletins.

Amá—Fatimah thought—*que ridículo.* Ridiculous.

After five years, Felipe Rodríguez—*the benevolent father*—controlled every platform, industry, and utility in The Islands.

And in his infinite wisdom, he decided what his forty-two million subjects needed to know. Many of whom were destitute and could barely read—though he denied that.

Five years of 'truth' according to a narcissistic sociopath.

Five years of eroding any notion of liberty and civil rights.

They were doomed.

Their lots were in the hands of a vainglorious maniac who hid behind theatre, ostentatious fashion, and pomade—the basic elements with which respectable despots cobbled together a façade.

Then, an assassination attempt. Rolled out, on cue.

Que barbaridad—thought Doña Fatimah—*Such madness. My grandson's christening forever marked as the day someone tried to 'destroy the nation' by shooting the president.*

She sighed. *What a farce.*

She was oh so tired of the melodrama.

Out on the veranda, the exhausted fifty-two-year-old poured herself some iced hibiscus-ginger tea sweetened with monk fruit. Another afternoon of mah-jong cancelled because of the monsoon.

On such a grey and agreeably morose day, it surprised her to find she missed the company. Or rather—the chatter.

You see, it was during those games with the wives of Don Federico's friends that Fatimah gathered crumbs of what was really happening in The Islands.

As they shuffled ivory tiles, the Doñas of Manila sipped sherry and anxiously smoked packets of imported cigarettes while exchanging rambling stories of increasing misery.

Oh, how their husbands struggled to keep them from ruin—paying all those bribes was going to leave them bankrupt.

And their children—their poor children—wallowing in loneliness and anonymity because they had to be sent abroad.

Without servants—No servants?—Can you imagine?

Such woes. . .

Another round of sherry.

That plunderer Amá was taking everything, you see. And at the rate he was going, Manila's Old Families of High Regard would be left with nothing.

Gone were the easy afternoons of trading salacious sagas of neighbourhood infidelity and libertinism.

Gone, too—over the last few weeks—was Doña Fatimah's high-minded daughter, Macarena.

Unlike the more intrepid Cova, Maca didn't seek employment after university. And she no longer associated with her lively school friends.

Instead, Macarena Castillo spent her time puttering about Sombra 'helping out', as she called it.

Since Baby Ricky's baptism or the 'assassination attempt' day, part of this 'helping out' seemed to entail spending time on the telephone with the mayor's right-hand fellow—a certain Attorney something-or-other. Fatimah could only just recall seeing him at the christening.

With her hair carefully brushed and her lips devoutly painted, Macarena eagerly prostrated herself by the telephone, convinced that Attorney so-and-so was an important man privy to important information. And as such, deserving of her admiration.

When the phone rang, Maca giggled and cooed—and she ooh-ed and ah-ed—in ways that turned Doña Fatimah's stomach.

One night at dinner, the suddenly optimistic Maca expressed to her parents how 'wonderful' it was that Amá took control of the plummeting peso. She dared tell them that his whimsical manipulation of the currency was *helping* the country.

For five years, Felipe Rodríguez used The Islands as a personal bank and treated its citizens like buffoons and criminals—yet, somehow, Attorney such-and-such had the 'socially aware' Macarena convinced this was beneficial for all.

Doña Fatimah wanted to slap her.

'Ka Timah, shall I still bring out some banana turón and mango rice cakes?'

Lydia's voice broke into her sombre musings.

It was three decades since the two women fought together during the War, but the head of Sombra's staff only showed such familiarity with its owner when they were alone.

'Yes please, Lydia,' Fatimah replied, 'thank you. Just a few pieces. For the children.'

The rain had stopped, and her granddaughters were playing on the swing set in the garden below—their laughter drifting up to her on the brittleness of the muggy afternoon.

Evidently, Alma's girls adjusted to life in Sombra very well. And Little Fáti was happy to have her cousins around to play with.

Albeit temporarily.

Alma and her girls remained in Manila for their safety. Andy was called back to sugar island right after Baby Ricky's christening or 'non-assassination' day.

He had to deal with what the grown-ups called 'The Challenges'.

The Yrastegui plantation was struggling, and the communists— and the creditors—were closing in.

Every night, Andy rang his wife from Negros with a litany of bad news. The commies were pressing him for money, as were the soldiers. One side called it 'revolution taxes', and the other— 'protection fees'.

'*Está hecha mierda*, Alma,' he said to his wife like an invocation at the end of every call. 'It's all gone to shit.'

Eventually, electricity to the Yrastegui hacienda was cut. Then, so was the water. Both utilities were owned by presidential relatives. When approached, they told Andy he needed to pay a 'facilitation charge'—and the matter would immediately be sorted.

Andy Yrastegui was astounded.

And disheartened.

He was powerless. His good name, his breeding, his background— meant nothing. And unexpectedly, he found himself under more stress than ever. Several hundred workers—and their families—depended on him. That's thousands of already impoverished people.

With things as they were, Andy wouldn't be able to pay their wages.

Nor could he hand out any more food.

Negros, the country's sugar bowl, was no longer the land of sweet opportunity.

It was the fuse on a powder keg waiting to be struck.

* * *

'*Hola*, amor.'

Don Federico arrived from work and joined his wife on the veranda, kissing her cheek as he put down his newspaper by the platter of caramelized bananas and coconut dusted rice cakes. He picked up a snack and took a hearty bite.

'Why do you bother?' Fatimah asked, indicating the daily. 'It's all nonsense. Always. Is there nothing the Mendozas can do to stop such garbage being printed in their paper? It's the same baloney on television.'

Baloney.

Federico paused to appreciate yet another American colloquialism his wife picked up from her favourite foreign shows. She peppered her speech with it. Sometimes sounding like an acerbic Army doctor from *M.A.S.H.* and other times like a guileless pioneer from the *Prairie*.

After more than thirty years together, Iko still found little things about Fatimah—*cute*.

He smiled. Faintly.

'Yes, Timah, a lot of—baloney.'

Federico stood next to his wife and looked out over the balustrade at the little girls playing in the garden below. The sound of crickets deafening in the pensive silence between them.

'Rafa Mendoza tells me'—he began—'that it's only a matter of time before they lose the paper. The government already takes a portion of their sales, and he can't hold them off much longer. Rodríguez is too powerful, and—as we know only too well—his henchman Salazar has no qualms about what they do to get what they want.'

Fatimah took a deep breath. Eliseo Salazar. Shafting people since World War II.

'We're on the verge of civil war,' she said flatly, not lifting her gaze from her grandchildren. 'This isn't good, Iko. These people will have us all turning against each other.'

She turned slowly to face her husband.

He sighed. 'You're right, cariño. Things are not good at all.'

This worried Timah. Her husband had never agreed with her on such matters.

But Federico Castillo no longer had the energy for optimism. He felt as old as the worn, stifling, granite skies above them—and he wasn't even sixty.

'Do you mean we're in trouble?' Fatimah asked.

Iko kept his eyes on their granddaughters as he gathered his thoughts for a reply.

The children played unaware of the looming darkness.

He watched the weight of the shadowless mango trees disappear beneath them. Sinking into the soaked, soggy ground.

He cleared his throat.

'There's enough set aside,' he told his wife, 'but our profit margin is not what it used to be. Our holdings are more heavily taxed and foreign investors have stopped coming into the country. Nothing is being built, and only government officials are spending. They're not the best people to do business with. We're having trouble renewing permits to stay operational—and we're being pressured to give up the farms.'

'But that's nothing new,' Fatimah jumped in. 'I know you don't like it, Iko, but just pay whoever needs to be paid—or—can we no longer afford to?'

Federico sighed. Again. Lately, he found himself doing it a lot.

'We're being squeezed everywhere, amor. I can't do much with our assets abroad right now because they are looking for any excuse to penalize us. More people are asking for kickbacks or favours—or both. And they're not subtle about it any more.'

His voice no longer had the lustre it used to.

'So, we're not in trouble yet—but we will be.' Timah summarized unceremoniously.

'We're doing all we can to prevent that.'

Her husband's reply failed to reassure her.

Once again, they stood side by side in silence. Enveloped by the nervous stillness that permeates a humid day after a rainstorm. When insects whirr incessantly, and leaves are heavy with the misspent promise of summer.

The saturated garden looked pallid—its colours whisked away by the trembling wind, its fruits lay sodden and rotting on the muddy ground.

Federico worked so very hard to give his family what he could. To build a home that would be their shelter. Somewhere they were safe.

Where none of his wife's demons could touch her.

He thought he planned for everything, but he hadn't planned for this. For greed and selfishness to rule men's souls so soon after a devastating war. For people to be so—*unkind*.

And unwise.

'Mami—Papá!' Alma rushed on to the veranda from the salon in a panic. 'I must get to Negros.'

'*¿Que sucede*, Almudena?' Federico was troubled by the look in her eyes.

'Bertín just called'—she managed to say—'Andy's missing.'

Fatimah gasped.

Don Federico wanted to wrap his daughter in his arms and protect her from the pain he saw colonize her face. It crushed his heart.

'I'll come with you, hija—we will sort this out.'

'No, Papá,' she looked to her mother for support. 'Stay here with Mami and the kids— please,' she begged. 'I won't put you in danger too.'

He was about to insist when Alma went on: 'Don't worry, Papá, Andy's father will fly out with me. He has many contacts on the island, and hopefully they can help us find Andy.'

'So, this is where the party is,' Freddie bellowed as he sauntered over. '*Oye*, Mami, I think I know why you never told us your real name—you're related to those crazy Moros on the news, aren't you?' he snorted. 'Joder, what a trip—those rampaging savages. You must be so ashamed of them—'

Fatimah's eyes went wide. Before she could speak, Don Federico whacked their son on the back of the head.

'Don't ever say anything so stupid to your mother again, do you understand me?'

It was the angriest they'd seen him. Even Doña Fatimah was stunned silent.

Freddie Castillo was just being 'Freddie', but this time, no one was amused.

'*¡Idiota!*' Don Federico smacked his son again.

'Ow!' Freddie rubbed the back of his head. 'Joder, Papá, you can't do that to me—I'm a grown man—'

'*¿Que coño dices?*' Iko was furious. '*¡Ojala!* If only you were a "grown man". We have been waiting for you to grow up since the day you were born, Federico José. You have been nothing but trouble— and now, you waltz in here like an *insensato* and disparage your mother? Apologize!'

Iko couldn't protect Alma from pain, nor could he shield any of his family from the world's unpleasantness.

He couldn't erase Fatimah's past, nor could he ease her heartache.

He failed to equip Maca with more confidence, just as he failed to imbue Cova with hope.

And try as he did, he couldn't make Freddie a better man.

But this much he could do—Don Federico could discipline his disappointment of a son for disrespecting his mother.

'I said—apologise!'

'Okay, okay—joder,' Freddie muttered.

The boy didn't get it at all.

'I'm sorry, Mami. I was only joking.'

Looking past him, his mother gave him a slight nod and said nothing.

His father was still livid.

'I just thought maybe that's why we haven't met any of Mami's family. You know—they're all nutjobs—'

'Freddie'—Alma jumped in—'just shut up and go—please.'

Tough crowd—Freddie thought as he walked away.

So much for treating them out to dinner with his latest ~~winnings~~ earnings.

* * *

Several difficult days later, Andy Yrastegui was found.

Or rather, returned.

He'd been abducted by that man Alma never trusted—that Dodong character—who was indeed working on the plantation as a communist spy. Alma was right after all.

Since Andy wouldn't pay the 'revolutionary tax', Dodong's cadre kidnapped him.

He was only released after his father paid—'the bill'. (It wasn't being called a ransom.)

Andy wasn't pleased, and Alma just wanted to go home. To Sombra. To her parents, and her daughters. To the guardians of her past, and the bearers of her future.

She was done with Negros.

So was Andy, and he convinced his father to let his young family move back to Manila.

The elder Yrastegui agreed, so long as they found someone to run the hacienda.

* * *

While her husband scoured Negros for potential plantation managers, Alma packed her diaries, her bonsais, and her family's belongings. She couldn't return to Sombra fast enough.

Every day, she rang her parents for updates on her daughters. It was the highlight of her otherwise tedious grind.

One morning, Almudena didn't have to place the call— Sombra rang her.

This was what she was told:

Don Federico and Doña Fatimah were getting ready for breakfast.

As always, Timah kissed Iko awake and went for her robe. When she returned from the bathroom, he was gone.

Just like that.

He was gone.

Mang Tining explained it was a heart attack. Manang Lydia wept in the background.

That was when Alma stopped listening.

Everything that followed was a blur. In slow motion.

She detached from the world around her and withdrew into her pain.

She and Andy flew back to Manila, leaving her father-in-law to deal with the hacienda.

At that point, it was the last thing Almudena Castillo de Montijo de Yrastegui cared about.

She no longer cared much about anything at all.

She was a rudderless ship in a storm.

Her father—her north star, her venerated source of stability—was gone. There wasn't space enough in that void for anything else.

Alma was upset with herself for not being with him when he passed.

She was angry at Andy for taking her away from Sombra when it counted.

She was furious at her father for dying.

Her father died.

He—died.

Leaving them all behind.

The ache—and the shock—was beyond anything they imagined.

Like many other well-loved children, the Castillo de Montijo siblings believed their parents immortal. They didn't know how to deal with such overwhelming loss.

It was something they were never taught.

From the moment Don Federico died, the house on Calle Sombra took on a different hue for each of them. The once grand manor of marvels became a shamble of shadows.

Sorrow moved in and ate away at the estate from all sides.

There was no escape.

No one could breathe when every room every hallway every corner every tunnel every arch every crevice every piece of furniture every curve every tile echoed with Iko's absence. It was so loud that it drowned out any hope for relief.

Doña Fatimah was so heartbroken she turned to stone. A tombstone. A marker of her departed beloved.

She was reduced to an embodiment of grief. The incarnation of her husband's absence.

Of where he once had been.

That was when—little by little, with every laboured heartbeat—Timah began to die.

Every moment, every second, pieces of her disintegrated.

As if they never existed at all.

That was when her children realized that no matter what the Bible said, there was no coming back from the dead.

But there were a million ways to die in a lifetime.

PART II

RUPTURE

Chapter 15

Las Últimas Noticias | **The Latest News** | Ang Nagbabagang Balita

10 November 2010 Broadcast || Wednesday || 1700 PST
Video Transcript || KBM-TNQR Network
Announcer:

Good afternoon, Islands.

In service of our Lord, I'm Larry Cabungay for the KBM-TNQR News Network.

Today's top story: President Facundo Marasigan's all-out campaign against illegal drugs is a resounding success. Since he assumed office in June, more than ten thousand drug pushers and users have been killed in police operations and other—uh—actions.

Meanwhile, Congress has voted unanimously to support the president's proposal to reinstate the death penalty for drug-related crimes.

Facundo 'Durog' Marasigan, Islands President:

Didn't I tell you bastards to be afraid? You should be! I am a man of my word, you *putang-inang* inbreds. I promised you the Pasig River would run red with the blood of criminals and other sick sons-of-bitches—and I have fulfilled that promise. So, you better watch out, you scrotumless assholes—my justice is mightier than Po'on Volcano. I am coming for you, or I am not a man! Remember, I am called 'Durog' for a reason—

Bam! (The president slams his fist on the podium).

Putang ina—dudurugin ko kayo—isa-isa! I will crush you—one by one, sons-of-bitches—until you fall in with my rules.

Crowd Cheers

Announcer:

We go live now to our reporter at the Manila Grandstand, where President Marasigan has just addressed the National Youth Symposium. Tess, over to you.

Reporter (shouting over cheering crowd):

It's mass hysteria! As you can see, people love him. Latest figures show the economy in a shambles: poverty is rising, the peso is depreciating, and human rights violations have become the norm, but Durog—as he is called by his supporters—has the highest approval rating of any president, even though more people have died since he took office six months ago than have perished over twelve years of martial law under the Rodríguezes.

Thousands are at this anti-drug rally, baying for the 'blood of evildoers'.

It's ironic that not only is his nickname Durog the local word meaning 'to crush', but it's also slang for someone 'smashed' on drugs. That irony, however, is lost on his followers. And don't make the mistake of reminding them because they are—let's say—*fiercely loyal.*

Announcer:

Uhm—yes, you got quite the response online after your last report on the president, Tess. The social media site shut down your account for inciting violence—

Reporter:

The case is still being investigated, Larry, but let me say this: I don't know why *my* account was shut when I was the one attacked and threatened with violence. Under this new administration, we journalists are treated like enemies of the state. Especially those of us who are female. Being on coverage lately has been—challenging. I have been accused of bias—and last week's presidential presser—

The transmission gets cut.

Announcer:

Seems we have—uh—lost our reporter's signal.

You will recall that Tessie Santo Domingo was mocked by President Durog after she—uhm—took a joke the wrong way on-air. She slapped the president when he—light-heartedly—kissed her during a live press conference.

Due to legal constraints, we are no longer allowed to play that video.

In other news: Pip Rodríguez, son of assassinated former president Felipe 'Amá Ipé' Rodríguez, has been named Interior Secretary—in charge of the police, public safety, and the effective delivery of basic services across the islands.

Secretary Rodríguez will also supervise a specially created anti-drug unit—which will receive the largest portion of the national budget.

Commercial Break

Chapter 16

Estado de Desgracia | **State of Disgrace** | Kahiya-hiyang Kalagayan

A playful knock on the door.

It swung open just as Cathy Miranda switched off the news. Patients were not allowed access to media—or communications devices—unless it was an emergency.

She wasn't happy about having to go against her own instructions.

'You wanted to see me, Doc?' he asked, boldly entering the counsellor's office.

'Yes, Ricky, please have a seat.' Cathy directed him to the chair in front of her desk.

'I knew you couldn't stay away from me for long.'

He plopped himself down and grinned like a child granted an extra snack.

This was their dance. He teased her, she looked past his false bravado. It was—*endearing.*

Though she'd never admit it.

'So, Doc, I hear there's been an election since I've been locked up—I didn't get to vote. Is it true the new guy is going all terminator on drugheads? What are they calling it now—*tokhang*? "Salvaging" like

127

back in the seventies? *Tinodas? Pinuksa? Kinatay? Kinitil?* What's the latest term?'

This was not the conversation she wanted to have with him.

'What does it matter?' she sighed. 'They're all just words for murder.'

'But he's only rubbing out the poor, right? Those from the slums? The wrong side of the river? At least, that's what I hear. So, I would've been okay,' he quipped.

'Really? They seem to be killing anyone who isn't in his circle. Or in the circles of his cohorts,' she paused. 'Which circle are you in, Ricky? You might piss someone off one day, and your kind doesn't fly any more under this administration.'

This wasn't how she normally spoke to him, but he had to realize these weren't normal times.

'Don't break my heart, Doc—money and class always fly. What the hell is happening out there?'

'Democracy, apparently,' she replied without irony. 'Majority rule. Mob mentality gone haywire. However you want to call it.'

Ricky Castillo scratched his freshly shaved chin, as if giving his next statement careful thought.

'Well, I think my uncle is back in government. Sort of. I mean, he wouldn't have an official post or anything like that, but he's been Mikey Reyes' bitch for decades. And Mikey goes where Pip Rodríguez goes. So, with Pip and his illegally inflated wallet back in town—that must be a circle that counts again, right?'

'I see,' Counsellor Cathy was unimpressed. She didn't bother trying to hide it.

It was indeed a circle that mattered again. Recycling was big on the islands.

Rinse. Spin. Repeat.

What was cast out had come back in.

Like the tide. Or a yo-yo.

Or dregs at the end of a typhoon.

* * *

Fact: After twenty years in exile, Pip Rodríguez returned to The Islands in 2008, like a despotic crown prince poised to claim his throne—the presidency.

Long story short, he fled Manila after his father was *actually* killed and his widowed mother was ousted as head of state a year later. (Yes, the first lady—and her army general lover—succeeded her murdered husband as joint dictators.)

The only thing Ricky Castillo remembered about those anxious days of political turmoil in the 1980s was that school was cancelled. As a young boy, he was yet uninformed of his father's machinations. (Freddie Jr was ignominiously involved with the greedy Rodríguezes.)

All the while, The Islands remained impoverished as unscrupulous clans took turns in power. Getting rich off the country's coffers.

It seemed that without a shared external threat, it was each to their own. A loose collection of tribal villages dissociated from its neighbours.

Like scattered lizard droppings on a cobalt floor.

In 2008, Pip arrived quietly from Latin America to do some 'cleaning'. He formed a twisted alliance with a little-known governor who ran his province like a feudal lord.

Facundo Marasigan.

It didn't take long for the dictator's son to turn the brutally self-righteous politician into an inescapable media behemoth. Marasigan was bold. He was brash. He was self-assured.

He was steeped in the kind of confidence that came from having money. So arrogant that he believed himself better than his peers because he raged against his privilege.

At least, he pretended to.

Voters loved it. He was one of them—a 'simple man'.

They didn't consider that it was easy to be a rogue when entitled. It made him fearless and gave him the audacity to do as he pleased.

Including mislead them into thinking him a simple man.

Marasigan wasn't fair-skinned, or handsome, or a colonist.

He liked to shock, and he liked to terrorize.

He cast himself as a home-grown scoundrel and lothario—and never second guessed his behaviour.

Pip understood the magnetism of such vanity.

Facundo Marasigan was a multi-faceted cad, and nothing was more attractive in a kaleidoscope nation of psychedelic politics and technicolour soaps.

By 2010, Durog was trending on social media.

Within the year, Durog Marasigan was president. His campaign, bankrolled by Pip and his family's secret stash of stolen loot.

In exchange, Durog would clear Pip's family of any crimes.

Pip saw himself president by the next elections.

* * *

'So, why am I in here, Doc?' Ricky asked. 'Did you just miss my company?'

She smiled faintly. The way she always did when Ricky tried to be annoying or haughty. It didn't suit him. Much as he tried. Anyone who spent five minutes with him saw it. The insecurity he tried to cover up. The—*softness*. And the anger he wore as a cloak.

Cathy Miranda took a deep breath and cleared her throat.

'Look, Rick, I'm just going to say this.'

He hated conversations that seemed serious. 'You want me. I knew it.'

It never got old.

'I'm sorry, Rick—but this is serious.'

'Yes, I will marry you,' he stated before she could go on. If he kept talking, there wouldn't be room for her to speak. My folks would love having a doctor in the family—Lord knows we could use your kind—an in-house psychiatrist—exactly what the Castillos de Montijo need.'

'Ricky.' She looked him in the eye, no smile this time.

He got it. This was serious. She meant it.

Silence.

Serious always meant *silence* to Ricky Castillo.

He stared back at the counsellor without a word.

'I don't want to make this about money, but the truth is—' it was. And it broke her heart to tell him. 'Your stay here hasn't been paid for six months.'

'What?' He wasn't sure he heard her correctly.

'A number of checks deposited into our account bounced. In the last two months, there were no deposits made at all.' She paused to let it sink in. 'We tried your parents, but neither of them returned our calls.'

'I don't understand.' Ricky shook his head.

'We let it slide because—you know—we knew your family was good for it. But the board says we can't host you much longer without pay. There are so many people on the wait list, some offering three times the fee just to get in. We're the top facility in the country, and with what's going on—thanks to Durog—everyone wants a stay at Good Graces.'

Ricky didn't believe his ears. This couldn't be happening. Unpaid bills? A Castillo de Montijo was never in debt. There must be some mistake. A misunderstanding. Most probably—his parents forgot to deposit the check. They forgot where he was. That seemed more plausible.

'Let me call my mom, Doc. Please. I'll sort this out. There must be an explanation.'

There must be—and he truly hoped it didn't involve Tukô.

'Of course,' his counsellor said graciously. 'You can call her from here. Figure out what's going on, and if there's no intention of continuing your treatment here, we must know soon. I'm so sorry, Ricky.'

He looked at her wordlessly. Lost. Numb.

'I'll be right outside.'

'No, Doc—please.' He held on to her arm as she rose from her chair. He didn't want to place the call alone.

The counsellor understood. She moved to the couch at the other end of her office, to give him at least a semblance of privacy.

The usually stunning view outside her window was misting over. It was almost Christmas and an early evening fog was rolling in. She could barely make out the volcano that sat in the centre of the crystal lake.

It's what the rehabilitation retreat was known for.

She always hoped the view gave her patients as much peace as it gave her—*nature's reminder that beneath the fog of addiction, there was clarity and beauty.*

It was on all their promotional material.

She heard Ricky mutter into the phone as he kept redialling a set of numbers.

Eventually, his call was answered.

'Hello?' Luísa said cheerily.

'Mom, joder. Are you fucking kidding? Why did it take you so long to pick up? This is, like, my tenth try. Where the fuck are you? Coño.'

He was manic, and he heard music coming through the receiver. It sounded like New Age jazz.

'Ricky, hijo, how are you?' His mother cooed into the phone. The wispy wail of some frail-sounding fairy trilled behind her. It was a Celtic soprano.

'Oh my God, are you stoned, Mom?' Ricky was aghast. It would explain the music.

'¿Como? Of course not, Federico. I'm at my temple,' she giggled, calmly. He didn't recognize her tone.

He also didn't have time for this.

'Mom, you haven't paid my bill.'

'What bill?' Luísa asked, bewildered.

'Rehab, Mom. My rehab bill.' He knew it, they forgot. 'I'm at Good Graces, remember?'

'Oh yes, of course, hijo. Your father handles all the bills. Do we have to pay there? They're always so nice—'

Jesus. And this was her sober. Or so she said.

'Mom, where is Pop? I tried him, too, but it kept going to a recording. Like his line's been cut.'

'Ah, Freddie,' she hummed. That was all.

'Mom?' He tried to get her attention back. 'Mom!'

'Hijo, stop yelling. I can hear you.' She was still humming.

Jesus. He tried again. 'Where is Pop?'

'You know your father—I have no idea. He never tells me anything.'

Great—thought Ricky—*typical.*

'You need to track him down, Mom. Please remind him to pay the bill.' He waited for a reply.

None came. All he heard were endless bars from that tinny Irish New Age song.

'Mom?'

'Hijo,' she replied as if in a trance.

'Are you okay?' He was genuinely concerned.

'Yes, of course,' she giggled into the phone again. 'Never better.'

Ricky was convinced his mother was on something. There was no way she could sound this anxiety-free without some sort of crutch—or heavy-duty anaesthetic.

'Listen, Mom, please tell Pop when you see him that he has to pay the bill. Do you understand?'

'Lalalalalaaalaaa,' Luísa sang, 'I have been praying for you, hijo mio. Everything will be okay, my son—you'll see.'

This was pointless. He could tell.

He covered the mouthpiece.

'Doc, can I make one other call, please? I don't think I'm getting through to my mother.'

The counsellor nodded.

'Okay, Mom, you take care,' he said sadly.

'*Ave María, gratia plena, Dominus tecum—*'

Ricky ended the call as his mother began to pray for him in Latin.

He tried the only other number he knew by heart.

The landline at Sombra.

He was sure his aunt Macarena would know where his father was. She always knew what was going on with him—and she was always home.

She pretty much ran Sombra since his grandmother's stroke a few years prior.

'Tita Maca? Oh, thank God—a grown-up!' He was so relieved to hear her voice.

'Ricky? Are you okay?' Maca was surprised to hear from her nephew. 'What's wrong? I thought you weren't allowed any calls?'

'Have you seen my pop? I called my mom, but she has no clue. Tita, the bills haven't been paid—and they're about to kick me out of rehab.'

'What?' Maca was horrified. What an embarrassment. It was bad enough there was a Castillo in rehab—but now—unpaid bills? Unspeakable! She couldn't allow this to happen.

'Please, Tita Maca—if you know where he is, please remind him— he needs to sort this out.'

Last Maca saw her brother Freddie, he mentioned a business trip. She helped him run their father's companies and presumed he meant another jaunt to Macau with his compadres.

But that was months before. She couldn't recall having seen him since.

'Actually,' Maca started, 'uh—'

Uh? What—uh? Ricky felt a familiar fear rise in his throat. He was going to throw up. This was not the response he expected from his aunt.

Maca was so busy doing things for her husband the last few months—what with the elections and all—that she realized she hadn't paid much attention to anything else.

She didn't know where Freddie was, and she hadn't even checked in on their mother.

'Let me ask the maids, hijo,' she told her nephew. 'He was away for work, and I haven't spoken to him since.'

'What do you mean?' Ricky was perplexed. 'Hasn't he been home at all?'

'Just a second,' Maca replied, ringing a bell to call for the help.

There was a muffled conversation Ricky couldn't make much of before Maca returned to the phone.

'Uh, seems he hasn't been home in a while,' his aunt sounded puzzled. 'Pepa said he hasn't even left any laundry. But don't worry, hijo—I'll pay what is owed to that place and send a car for you.'

'What?' he couldn't believe this. He wasn't ready to leave. Even he knew that.

'Sorry, Ricky, but we just don't have the funds right now to cover your continued stay there—it's the most expensive place in the country.'

Maca didn't have any funds because she gave everything she had to her husband. For him to spend on the elections. Not that he was running, mind you. But as the right hand of Mikey Reyes, the couple felt they should contribute to his senatorial campaign.

And they contributed—a lot. They needed Mikey in power. It's not like Maca's husband could've won a seat of his own.

When the Rodríguezes were exiled, anyone who was part of their pack became persona non grata—including Maca's husband, Manny, and his boss/best-friend-for-life, Mikey Reyes. No one wanted anything to do with them.

Lucky for Manny Santos, he was already married into the Castillo family by then. He moved into Sombra right after the wedding, and they lived in the manor—rent-free—ever since.

The couple occupied the western part of the house with their only son, Dito, while Ricky and his sisters were in the east.

Ricky knew that his aunt Cova and her husband Cristóbal moved to Spain in the mid-eighties, though he wasn't sure if they had offspring. They weren't great at keeping in touch.

Tita Alma's family, however, weren't strangers to him. They lived in the suburbs and visited Sombra on Sundays like clockwork.

Mass was said in the family chapel, then they all sat down to lunch with Aba.

Aba. How he missed his Aba. He felt her shutting down after her last stroke.

She was in her eighties but recovered fully. The doctors said there was nothing physically wrong with her. She just decided to disengage from the world.

Even more than she already had when first widowed.

Then, after Mang Tining died, followed by Manang Lydia, Fatimah grew impatient and uninterested in all but her grandchildren. She rarely spoke and drowned things out with the radio.

Every afternoon, Aba sat in her upstairs veranda, sipping iced tea and crocheting something or other. She scattered her projects throughout the house when she was done.

They were like cobwebs made of yarn. Marking places where love once thrived.

His older cousins said she was different when their grandfather was around—she even played the piano. But Abu Federico died shortly after Ricky was born.

How he wished he knew Aba Fatimah then, back when she was—*happy*.

'Ricky? Ricky? You still there?'

For a moment, he was elsewhere.

'Yes, Tita. I'm here.'

'Right. So, I'll track down your father, and send a car for you this weekend. There's no traffic on Sundays so it will be easier. Please tell your doctor—or whomever is responsible—to email me the bill. I will have it paid by tomorrow. I am sorry it has come to this.'

He knew his aunt Maca meant it. She was sorry—this was horrifically embarrassing.

Ricky Castillo was sorry, too. This was dreadful—he was going home.

Chapter 17

El Pantano | **The Swamp** | Ang Putikan

The scantily clad blonde woman was gyrating to Olivia Newton-John's latest hit when she was pushed into the pool by a naked Freddie Castillo.

He jumped in after her, then made a show of removing what there was of her underwear and tossing it at his friends. All without losing a grip on his glass of whisky.

Freddie's buddies stood by the water's edge—cheering him on—as he threw aside his drink, hooked the woman's legs around his waist, and began a rhythmic pumping while trying to hold her up against the wall of the pool.

The leggy blonde giggled like a schoolgirl. Her Lucite stilettos floating away. The pasties slipping off her nipples.

She coughed as she struggled to keep from swallowing more of the chlorinated water. An awkward duet with the yipping of Freddie's laughter.

They didn't look the least bit sexy, but little did during an orgy.

It wasn't the first in Sombra, and everyone knew Freddie got bolder when his wife was away. On some religious retreat or passed out in a pool chair from too much wine.

This particular evening, Luísa de Castillo managed to get to her room before passing out.

No fun—thought the blonde.

It was, however, understandable that Luísa left early—she did just have a baby. Another girl. Child number three for the fortunate Freddie Castillos.

Freddie knew that other people had their way with the mother of his children when she fell unconscious at these soirees, but he really didn't mind. It was 1981, he was a cool dude—and this was his chance to get freaky at home. If Luísa happened to get her freak on, too, then all the better. It made him feel less guilty.

Oh, who was he kidding? Freddie Castillo never felt guilty.

For him, the fun really started around midnight, after his sister Maca went to bed.

Unlike Cova and the boring pelotari she recently married, Maca and her husband, Manny, were always up for a good time. Relatively speaking.

Before disappearing, Maca always gave both her husband and her brother a peck on the cheek, saying goodnight with a wink and a jovial—'I'll let you boys have your fun now'.

But she had no idea how festivities progressed the second she left the pavilion.

The massive glass enclosure was built in Sombra's garden five years earlier. Freddie's first project after their father died.

It was by the pool. Detached from the main house, but not too far back in the yard that it was near the chapel.

There was a path to it paved with antique Chinese stones and lumber from old Spanish galleons.

It was a fantasy island unto itself. Surrounded by a cornucopia of flowers.

There were red firecracker plants and flame-coloured birds of paradise. Purple bougainvillea and bright yellow buds like small cobs of corn.

Pink and white showers rained down from a lattice of trees.

The pavilion itself was sound-proof and air-conditioned, specifically designed for entertaining. Tinted glass panels, plush velvet alcoves, shag carpets from England. Fully stocked bars, game tables, a service kitchen. Luxurious guest bathrooms, and even a 'sleep' area.

It boasted the latest hi-fi stereo system with the best built-in German speakers. There was also a hidden central mixer that controlled the intensity of each light fixture.

Setting the mood was of utmost importance.

Freddie called it 'the office'. It was, after all, where he conducted—*business.*

With Don Federico gone, twenty-seven-year-old Freddie Castillo took it upon himself to be head of the family.

The man of the house.

As such, he saw it his duty to replace the 'tacky' marquees previously used for Sombra's parties. The glass pavilion—the office—was much better suited to the kind of lavish events he was inclined to.

Ultimately, the exorbitant expense on the ostentatious structure was 'for the good of the family'.

With martial rule approaching its tenth year, the enterprising 'Don' Freddie Castillo and his brother-in-law/new-best-bud, Attorney Manny Santos, needed a comfortable—private—space to negotiate their many complex transactions.

You see, their businesses were not bound by the usual work hours.

Or, indeed, by the usual rules.

They had been giving a portion of their profits to Mang Eloy's son, who—for a price—used his 'family contact' to get them permits to move around Manila after curfew. (Fortuitously, Mang Eloy had gone from owning the golf club convenience store to working in government.)

But Freddie and Manny got tired of sharing.

Sombra offered a perfect venue to conduct their business. No one asked questions or monitored their activities.

And no one needed to be bribed to look away.

Their commercial interests were so diverse that they felt like tycoons, dealing in anything that could make them a killing. (Speaking metaphorically.)

No merchandise—or contract—was too large or too small.

They fixed jai alai matches, cockfights, card games, and horse races.

They bought and sold firearms as well as security personnel.

They made deals for Chinese traders eager to use their local connections.

And they began exporting Islanders to work in the Middle East.

The entire operation was really Freddie's, but Manny got a huge cut for being his 'lawyer'.

Well, for that and his personal ties to the ruling Rodríguezes. A bonus connection—aside from Mang Eloy—to the clan in the palace.

On the islands—at that point—you were nothing without it.

Not that Manny was himself a Rodríguez, mind you. But his close friendship with presidential nephew—Mayor Mikey—dated back to their boyhood at St John's Academy.

Mikey spent so much time in detention that he became friends with the janitor's son. From then on, they were keepers of each other's secrets.

Yes, the martial law years were lucrative for young Freddie Castillo. It was the perfect environment to harness his—*talents*.

'Beat that, buddies,' Freddie dared his friends when he finished with the spluttering blonde.

As he pushed her away and clambered out of the pool, the lights began to flicker—then, went off.

'Puta, coño—what's that?'

The lights flicked on again.

And then, off.

Freddie clumsily tucked himself into the first pair of shorts he could grab and stumbled into the pavilion in search of his brother-in-law.

Such flickering never happened at 'office' parties. They always paid extra so the power company would spare them the regular black outs.

They also had back-up generators, which kept the lawn drizzled with fairy lights twinkling like earth-bound constellations.

The tiny bulbs were all as blue as the crystal waters around Freddie's private island.

Maca told her brother she decorated Sombra in that colour to commemorate his financial success.

Truth was—Freddie cheated at poker to win the island, and Sombra was drenched in blue because Maca had read it's what Elvis did at Graceland.

You see, Elvis Presley was Manny's idol—and Maca would do anything to keep her husband happy.

There was such a glorious halo around the garden at these parties that fruits glistened on branches as jewels on a Russian empress' train.

And the glass pavilion shone like an heirloom diamond on her tiara.

In that kind of gemstone haze, Sombra's pool shimmered like a flawless Australian opal—until Freddie and his chosen blonde shattered the luminous water. And then, the flickering.

But the lights were back on when Freddie spotted Manny. He was so buzzed that he hadn't even noticed the power flux.

You see, at midnight—upon Maca's departure—the office staff laid out the 'buffet': large crystal bowls full of the best Colombian cocaine, porcelain dishes brimming with Quaaludes, and silver trays stacked high with doobies.

To balance the menu, there was a torrent of Beluga caviar and fresh oysters, and Cristal literally gushed from several fountains.

So, Manny was sprawled on one of the leather couches with blow up his nose and his trousers undone. A young girl in a very—*very*—short red dress trimmed in faux white fur stood over him, holding his brandy snifter.

Like Freddie, Manny Santos liked to drink.

And he liked his hand under the waitress' skirt while he was at it.

Across them, a group of men lounged in various states of undress, smoking hash as they watched some women perform sex acts on each other.

A throwback to the bacchanalian days of Rome. Only Nero and his fiddle were missing.

It was the advent of The Eighties, and this was the office Christmas party at the Castillos'.

Where the snow was as plentiful as Santa's 'helpers'—a playful name for 'polar' prostitutes. Whites, like the earlier blonde. Americans. Europeans. Australians. Anyone with pale skin in need of money. They were easy to find in 1980s Manila.

Freddie also palled around with Ahmed ibn Farquad, a young Kuwaiti-American billionaire who could bring anything—or anyone— into the country on his private jets. He proved quite useful in a bind.

Always on the office party guest list: actresses, models, and artists, plus all sorts of other 'interesting' people. The only rule was no fighting. Those who came with partners understood it was a free-for-all. Jealousy wasn't tolerated.

The last time there was a bust-up, one of the guests threw a jeroboam of champagne at Manny. He ducked, and the giant bottle smashed into the handmade family crest embedded on the porch wall.

The Spanish-tile mosaic crumbled to the floor in pieces.

It was still being reconstructed.

That put an end to Freddie's festivities *inside* the house.

Parties at Sombra. They changed quite a bit over the years.

* * *

Doña Fatimah was never seen at Freddie's socials. It was as if she no longer reigned over the estate. She still paid the bills but no longer bothered to feign an interest in people.

Fatimah focused on steering her late husband's companies. Hoping that soon one of their children could assume the reins.

At fifty-seven, the family matriarch was by no means old, but unless needed at Castillo Enterprises, she rarely went beyond Sombra's walls. A phantom choosing to be caged.

There were no more games of mah-jong or afternoons of empty chatter.

No navigating Manila society like its invincible monarch.

The widowed Fatimah only wore black and locked herself in her room before the sun set. Lost in a darkness all her own.

It was no different around the holidays.

Freddie's party was always on the Friday before Christmas, and Fatimah always stayed in her room until the following afternoon. Usually when the last guest tumbled out.

Timah preferred to roam the narrow passages of her mind. Desperate to hold on to fading images of a kinder existence.

Sometimes, she found solace in the unobtrusive company of Ka Lydia, her newly widowed housekeeper and oldest friend.

They would sit together in silence. Sipping sweet hibiscus iced tea and transfixed by the hypnotic movement of their crochet needles.

They sat in the wordlessness of wounded soldiers. Sombre and solemn. Stitching together frayed fragments of rapidly dissipating memories.

Other times, Timah sat alone on her veranda. Transported by the laughter of her grandchildren outside.

Alma and her daughters visited often from the suburbs. Everyone else still lived in Sombra.

Fatimah knew this was what Iko had wanted—the estate was built with room for all.

But sometimes—*sometimes*—she wished for peace.

For her children to be more ambitious and stand on their own.

Every night, she still prayed the rosary, but she found herself starting her days with a Quranic du'a—*would things have been different had she not turned from her roots?*

When she was most unsettled, she called for Freddie's boy, Ricky. The five-year-old was so much like her beloved Iko. The same light, wavy hair and winsome smile.

Like the grandfather he never knew, Little Ricky was gentle and kind.

Life will crush him—Fatimah thought—*if he's not fortified.*

She worried that-mother-of-his was 'too weak' to 'raise him right'.

Needless to say, Timah wasn't a fan of her daughter-in-law. She found Luísa frivolous and self-obsessed. A shallow girl who got pregnant to ensnare her son.

As Grandmother, it was her duty to step in and mould Little Ricky.

She prayed with him and read to him, in both Spanish and English.

She told him all about the adventure of creating Sombra, filling him with stories about his brave and wonderful Abuelo Federico.

Aba Fatimah was also concerned about her other grandson Dito—Maca's only child was always alone.

Or with his nanny.

The boy was three and still didn't speak a word.

Not that it even bothered his parents.

Maca was either 'too busy' with her brother or that so-and-so she married, and she made a career of 'supervising' Sombra.

Over the years, Freddie gave his sister a stipend—her 'earnings' from his projects. Maca 'invested' the full share of her inheritance from their father.

The stipend paid what few bills she had and left her enough to spend on her husband. Manny didn't seem to make much as a politician's right hand. At least, not that she—as his wife—was aware of.

Doña Fatimah was still waiting for that such-and-such to prove himself worthy of her daughter. She disliked how he strutted around Sombra as if he owned it. Monopolising the phone lines, hogging the screening room, and barking orders at staff as if they were slaves.

Not to mention how disinterested he was in his mute little boy. Rivetted instead by his bourbon and his beer—*and his blasted tournaments of filthy fighting chickens!*

Fatimah also noticed his fascination with Cova and her husband—*a sweet but aimless boy*. Manny tailed them like a butler when he was home.

Hounded by rumours of game fixing, jai alai had just been officially banned. So, while Cova worked, Cristóbal gained time to lounge by Sombra's pool with other expat players.

Bare-chested and oiled-up, Manny hovered around them with towels and drinks. Like a tsetse fly in Speedos.

Any wonder, then, that Doña Fatimah preferred the confines of her room? The sacred space she once shared with her beloved.

Oh, Iko. . .

The night of that 'office' Christmas party, Fatimah was roused from sleep by the sudden thump of the air conditioner restarting. The electrical surge hung in the air like poison.

She slept shallowly at best. But that night, it was as if something beneath her—above her, inside her—stirred, and she knew the demons of her past approached. Her long-suppressed torment—unshackled.

She shivered.

Pulling the blanket tight, Timah kept her eyes shut, believing that in the dark she saw Iko.

She waited eagerly for his return.

Longing to be devoured by the numbness of her pain.

* * *

'I'll go check on Mami,' Cova told her husband when the lights flicked back on. They were in bed watching a film during the power fluctuation.

After Freddie's last party, Covadonga Castillo de Pérez García knew better than to walk around the house in her nightgown—there was no telling whom she might encounter. That late at night, it was difficult to confine her brother's guests to the pavilion.

Unlike the other women in the family, Cova knew exactly how crazy things got at these soirees. Her evenings at Sparkles—though over—were not too distant a memory.

So, Cova threw on her dressing gown and slipped through a panel behind her bookcase. Opting to use the secret passage to her mother's room.

She hadn't been in the corridors since her nights with Patti.

Damn—she needed a flashlight. The old switch on the wall seemed grounded.

Cova thought to return to her room when she heard a rustling in the dark.

She was yanked into the void before she could get her bearings.

In an instant, hot heavy breath descended on her face as a beast began to devour her. It lapped at her lips and chewed on her tongue.

It clawed at her breasts.

Blood pooled in her mouth as a tide of torment besieged her.

It was a tsunami.

She was thrust against the concrete wall—rough on the lace of her dressing gown.

The beast was immense. Reeking of evil and sin and human sweat.

He was barefoot.

And hairless.

For a moment, she felt his chest on her face—then, his feet pushed hers apart.

He raised her dressing gown and shoved his fingers inside her.

She tried to scream, but he clamped his mouth on hers to keep her silent.

She tried to push him, but he was stronger. Despite being pickled in alcohol.

The beast turned her around and pressed his weight on her. Twisting her face and mashing it against the wall.

She was numb. Paralysed by a cocktail of dirt and tears and blood.

He grunted when he thrust into her. Like a deranged satyr at a bridal shower.

He bit her neck as he climaxed.

She felt nothing.

She had left her body.

Then, a light in her eyes.

A thud.

Her attacker slumped to the ground. Leaving his sticky fluid between her legs.

A light?

A flashlight.

Someone else was in the corridor.

A beam of gold shone down at the fetid lump on the floor.

She looked at her rapist—then up at the person who struck him.

'Julián!' Cova wept, collapsing into her brother.

Chapter 18

El Niño | **The Boy** | Ang Bata

He was the most beautiful boy Federico had seen.

Sharp firm nose, long dark lashes, deep-set almond eyes.

He had his mother's broad, open face and confident round jaw, and wore a similar expression of the dearest consternation.

His skin was silken cream, like the light from a soft morning sun.

He was born one glorious October dawn in 1945, and his cheeks bore the kiss of heaven.

The boy's hair was thick but fine and whispered the comfort of roasted chestnuts.

His ears protruded—just a little—like his uncle's.

Iko beamed. He couldn't believe this magnificent creature was part him and part Fatimah. That wonderful—*glorious*—woman had given him this—*miracle.*

He was so grateful to be alive. To have survived the war—the brutal Japs—and be alive.

To have left Spain—and crossed oceans—and be alive!

There was no greater gift.

This boy—*this boy!*—this—boy.

This boy—was *his*. The one good thing to come out of his miserable existence.

The baby cried.

And to Iko, the sound was the reveille of liberation.

He picked the boy up off the bed and cradled him.

His wife was hunched over a plastic pail on the floor, washing diapers by their solitary window.

'Are you certain, Timah?' he asked her again. 'You do not mind if we give him those names?'

A week had passed since they brought the boy home from the ramshackle medical centre where he was born. He came so soon after the war ended that Manila was still in ruins, and his young parents were too busy trying to survive to discuss appellations.

'My second name is the same as Ka Igmé's Christian one anyway, so it will be as if—'

'No need for explanations, Iko,' she smiled at her excited and anxious husband. 'Why would I mind?'

He'd been in such a state since her water broke. It filled her heart.

The night the baby came, Iko bravely guided them—in the dark, across the ravaged city—to get to the midwife. He showed no fear of potentially falling into unseen bomb craters or possibly encountering an unexploded mine under piles of debris.

But one look at the boy, Fatimah thought, and Iko turned into one of those paper boats her brother used to make when they were children—once they were put into the river to sail.

Soggy and shapeless.

Mush.

Her calm, level-headed husband—brought to his knees by a little baby.

She watched Iko rock the boy back to sleep as she hung the cloth diapers to dry.

They referred to him as 'el niño'—the boy—Fatimah was glad for something more permanent to call him.

'I thought you might, *perhaps*, want to name him—*possibly*—after someone in your family,' Iko was rambling, nervous about upsetting her. 'I mean, it's not like I have any relatives who would care—'

'Hush, my heart, don't speak like that. You have me,' she said, firmly. 'You have him. We are your family, and you are ours. That is all that matters. The three of us.'

Iko couldn't help but smile.

They had little food, no water, and barely a roof over their heads, but he had never known such—*joy*.

He had a son. His heart felt like it would explode.

From the shambles of that cursed war, he and Fatimah met and birthed this child.

'Oh—we must get him baptized,' Fatimah realized. She was still getting used to being Catholic.

'I will go see the priest tomorrow,' her husband agreed.

It was settled. They would name him after the only father figures Iko had known: Don Fernando, the captain of the ship that brought him from Spain to Manila, and Ka Igmé, their brave guerrilla leader.

Together their names meant 'fearless adventurer'—exactly what Iko wished for his first born.

A bold life of endless wonder.

Julián Fernando.

* * *

'What are you doing here?'

He shone the light on Cova and studied her closely. There was blood on her battered face and trickling out of her mouth. Bruises were beginning to welt on her skin.

She looked like she'd been thrashed in grit and grime. His beautiful baby sister . . .

'Who the hell is this?' he started kicking the body on the floor. It gurgled and sputtered.

'Who the hell are you?' he screamed at it. 'I am going to kill you—'

'Julián wait—Julián,' Cova tried to calm him down. 'Don't. Wait—shh.'

'Are you seriously trying to shush me? This monster—*raped* you. He—raped—you—'

A horrible sound, like that of a wounded bull, escaped Julián. The reality of what was done to his sister pummelled him like an iron ball.

It tore him apart.

He was—*too late. Always too late.*

'Shh, please, we mustn't upset Mami. She might hear,' Cova pleaded, not knowing where she found the strength to stay upright.

'What's wrong with Mami?' Julián asked as he carefully took hold of his sister.

'She's not been—herself—since . . . Papá—'

The body on the ground moved—groaned.

Julián kicked him again.

'Let's call the police, get this barbarian locked up.'

'It's not that simple, Juli.' The darkness seemed to be closing in, and Cova thought she might collapse had her brother not been holding her.

'Yes, it is, *hermanita.* I am your witness, I was here. I only wish I came upon you sooner. We will put this bastard away—'

'It's a different country, Julián,' she couldn't breathe.

'What do you mean?'

'He—he works for—the government,' she grabbed on to her brother's shirt. Trying to steady herself.

'What?'

'Things have—changed—since we last saw you,' she needed to lie down. 'We can't call the police—they won't help us.'

'What is someone like that even doing here? He must be a guest at that—whatever that was in the garden. I came through a tunnel by the chapel and waited for those people to leave—I fell asleep for a few hours—and they're still there.'

'Yes . . .' she felt weaker. 'Freddie's—*people.* They'll be there a while.'

She needed to be somewhere else.

'I'm glad I gave up waiting then. They were so high that I crossed the garden to the house without anyone noticing. But I should have come sooner, Cova,' his tone laden with grief. 'If I had, maybe this wouldn't have—'

Silently, Julián began to weep. Clutching his baby sister to his chest. His little—*Covado-do.*

After a heavy heartbeat, he pulled back to look at her—'How did he get in here? How did he know about these secret corridors?'

'I don't know.' In the fog of the moment, Cova wondered the same. 'Freddie must've told him, or maybe Maca.' She needed air.

'Maca?' Julián was confused. 'Why the hell would Macarena talk to a savage like this?'

He kicked the lump on the floor again.

Cova fell silent. She couldn't hold on much longer.

'—because.' She paused—

'That's her husband.'

* * *

The boy was good luck, Iko knew it from the moment the child was born. A few weeks early, but without any of the usual complications.

Since then, blessings rained on the young Castillo family.

For starters, he was finally able to find them a proper home. One with a roof that didn't leak and four concrete walls.

It had windows, too—*plural!*

And no narrow stairs that needed climbing.

Behind it, there was a small yard he could lay grass on and plant a flowering bush or two. It was perfect for his growing brood.

Julián—the boy—had turned one. And Fatimah was carrying their second baby.

Iko was thrilled.

Their new home even had electricity and running water. Thanks to a job that afforded him luxuries previously unavailable to them.

And he fell into it—*by sheer luck.* Which Fatimah called 'the grace of God'. She prayed her thanks with a rosary every evening.

Iko was employed by an American company doing post-war reconstruction. Rebuilding and fortifying all sorts of structures.

Hospitals, railroads, and dockyards. They also repaired Manila's bombed-out power grid.

Her nightly novenas answered, Fatimah got better at the Catholic thing quite quickly.

Iko was grateful for a prayerful wife. Such devotion would certainly make her a good mother.

With Timah in charge of their home, Federico busied himself learning all he could at work, dreaming of the day he'd set up his own firm. Something he could leave to their son. An enterprise that would benefit the country that had been so good to him.

He was a vagabond who found a home. His children would root him to The Islands.

He hoped they would also anchor his wife.

She, too, had been—*unsettled*—for so long.

Iko understood—as best he could—that Fatimah always felt quietly displaced.

Like many of her people did.

Treated like outsiders on their own land.

It made her—*tough*.

And angry.

And insecure.

Then—from what he understood—her own people cast her out as well.

He couldn't imagine the isolation she must've felt.

But she would never feel alone again. Not if he could help it.

Perhaps he should sell native products abroad? Like reeds, or coconuts. He discovered during the war how versatile they were. Too bad that healing fruit didn't grow on the islands.

Or maybe—*maybe*—he could work Manila's unused land? There was so much of it. Wide stretches of swamps, marshes, and grasslands—full of snakes and other unpleasant critters.

He could clear it and prepare the terrain for houses or schools—*and paved streets!* That would make it easier to traverse the expanding city.

Yes, that's what he would do.

Or maybe—*yes, possibly*—he'd find a way to do it all. The potential seemed limitless.

He, Federico Julián Castillo—from Montijo in Spain—could see it clearly: One day, he would build his family a *real* home. Just like the grand stone mansions he admired in Intramuros.

One that would stand firm for always.

That no war—or enemy—could decimate.

It would protect them and nurture them—and ground them.

He would surround it with every sweet-smelling, blossoming fruit and flower he could find. That way, all his beloved wife and children had to do was look out at their yard and see the face of God.

Yes!—Life would bring him more than he could hope for. He just *knew* it.

It was 1946—the war was over—and Iko Castillo was feeling good.

* * *

'We have to tell the family, Cova—we're not letting him get away with this,' Julián insisted as his sister came to. He was wiping blood off her face.

She'd collapsed in the hidden passage, and he carried her through the corridors to his old room. It looked exactly as he'd left it—which surprised him.

Cova lay on the bed stupefied. Numb, and in shock.

Her body felt as if it were someone else's, and her mind was frozen.

She felt time move around her, but she was standing still.

Like a photograph.

Or rather, the negative of a photograph waiting to be developed.

Cova felt like a strip of film soaking in chemicals just as the dark room door cracked open.

Ruined.

Marred.

Permanently captive in that half-state of grey.

An unidentifiable glob.

'They have a child, Juli,' she spoke softly.

'He should've thought of that before assaulting you.'

She was so confused.

Julián was home—cleaning her face—and she didn't know where to begin to unscramble her thoughts.

'Why were you there, Juli? In the corridor I mean. Why didn't you come through the front door?' she asked.

'I . . . I . . . It's better this way. Can't call too much attention to my being here,' he offered, rinsing the washcloth in a small tub of warm water on the bedside table. 'I would've come back sooner—when Papá'—the words caught in his throat—'but I couldn't. I truly—couldn't.'

He wrung out the cloth and gently wiped her brow.

'I think a part of me thought you died,' Cova whispered. 'Or that you just didn't love us any more.' She sounded like a child and she knew it. It broke his heart. She sounded like she hadn't aged a day since he left in '65.

She was thirteen.

'Oh, my little Dodo,' Julián wrapped her in a tight embrace, trying helplessly to console her. 'I am so, so, sorry,' his tears flowed again. 'Nothing could be further from the truth. Believe me, not a day has gone by that I haven't thought of you all. Especially you, my Dodo— *mi hermanita preciosa.*'

His beautiful, precious little sister.

Julián was always so fond of Cova. She was seven years younger than him, but in her, he saw the softest parts of himself.

The parts that needed to be—*fortified*—as their mother put it.

As the eldest, Julián took it upon himself to be Cova's guardian.

To look after her and side with her against the others. To let her know she was always, *always,* going to be okay.

But then, he was gone. Which was not his choice.

Had he stayed, maybe this horrible, dreadful—thing—would not have happened.

'Why did you leave, Julián? Papá and Mami never said. She's kept your room locked all this time. Hasn't let anyone in. Not to clean, or pack up, nothing. It's as if she's waiting for you to return.'

'That's not important right now, my Dodo. Let's get you cleaned—'

'I got married, you know?'

'I heard,' he smiled gently. 'Is he here? In the house? Do you want me to get him?'

'No!' Cova replied, more forcefully than she expected. 'Let him sleep. I don't even know what to say to him right now—oh God—'

She began to weep.

'I've got you, hermanita,' he whispered. 'I've got you.'

* * *

'Guess who I ran into?' Iko was exuberant when he got home from work that afternoon.

'They have a stall in the market—' he paused, waiting excitedly for her reaction.

Fatimah was bathing their baby girl while their son played with a few empty cartons on the floor.

She was exhausted.

'Tining and Lydia!' Iko exclaimed. They hadn't seen their comrades since the end of the war. While Iko and Timah headed to Manila, the others returned to their rural homes.

'They got married,' he continued. 'I knew it—didn't I tell you he liked her? I was right!'

'That's wonderful, amor,' Timah offered, hoping to placate him. The baby was fussing and getting bathwater all over her last clean dress.

Julián began to cry.

'How can I help, my love?' Federico asked, remembering his wife was doing everything alone.

'Please feed the boy, amor—his dinner's over there,' she gestured towards the corner they used for meals.

Iko picked up his wailing son and carried him to the table.

'They're selling vegetables from Tining's farm,' he continued telling his wife about the chance encounter. 'Well, it's his father's farm, but you know what I mean. They're selling vegetables but don't earn enough to sustain their families—I think they're feeding thirty people.'

Iko was visibly dismayed.

'So, I told them to come work with us,' he cut to the point.

'What?' Fatimah wasn't certain what her husband meant.

'I think it's time I leave Redstone and start my own projects. I have a few things lined up, and Tining can work with me—I trust him. And Lydia says she's good with children—she can help you with Julián and Almudena—'

Iko was so full of hope that Fatimah did not want to dampen his enthusiasm.

'I know what you're going to say'—he stopped her before she could speak—'how are we going to pay them? Well, if this land deal pans out, we'll get an advance. There will be enough to get us all started on the right foot. It will be so much work—I'll definitely need Tining's help.'

Iko beamed, as if he learned he was going to have another child.

How could she argue with that?

Fatimah knew the moment she laid eyes on him in the Japanese camp that this Spanish caballero was special.

She was right.

* * *

Feathered rays of silver light sliced through the heavy darkness in the room as the sun began to rise behind the shutters.

The chapel bell rang.

'*Misa de Gallo*,' Cova told her brother, the traditional advent service.

A mass was said every day—before dawn—for nine mornings leading up to Christmas.

'Mami has a priest come to the chapel so she doesn't have to go to the village church. She doesn't leave Sombra if she can help it.'

'Oh,' Julián said sadly. But he guessed as much from the tone of her last few letters.

Truthfully, he was both excited and afraid to see his mother. She wrote him less frequently over the years, and her notes got shorter. He could tell things were not going as he wished for her.

That's why he returned to Manila as soon as he could.

'Do you all still have breakfast together?' he asked his sister.

She sighed.

'No way.'

Silence.

Cova continued—'At this time of year, Mami might be in the dining room for her meals—in which case, some of us join her. But it can be very—uncomfortable. Mostly, she stays in her room. Everyone else eats where they want to, whenever they feel like it.'

'I see,' he replied, a textured bitterness settling on his palette.

He dipped the washcloth in the basin once more.

'Let's get you clean,' Julián said firmly. 'Then, we will speak to them about the bastard who breached this family.'

Chapter 19

La Violación | **The Violation** | Ang Paglapastangan

'She's lying,' Maca stated calmly, glad their mother had not come down for breakfast.

She was so tired of 'sweet' Covadonga's ploys for attention, and this one took the cake.

'No, she's not, Macarena,' Julián repeated, brusquely. 'I was there.'

Maca reached for a freshly baked croissant and slowly tore off a piece.

The Castillo de Montijo siblings—Maca, Julián, and Cova—were scattered around the long narra table in Sombra's dining room, just off the central courtyard.

The morning shone through wide panel windows and bathed the room in gold.

Above them, from where daylight struck, shards of light beamed rays of dazzling ice from Bohemian chandeliers.

The servants laid out a hearty spread then left the room. But only one of the masters had an appetite.

'And why should I believe you?' Maca laughed, purposefully buttering her pastry. 'I haven't seen you in, what, fifteen years? Why would I trust you over the man I love? The father of my child—'

She smiled. There was a glint in her eyes Julián hadn't noticed before.

158

It was frightening.

Cova told him speaking to the others was not a good idea, but Julián was still surprised by this response.

Instinctively, he balled his hand into a fist and felt for the ring he wore on his finger. Reassured by the warmth of the ivory against the cool metal braid.

'Seriously, Macarena?' He was aghast. 'I just told you your husband—the father of your child—raped—your sister—and that's all you have to say?'

Maca reached for the strawberry jam.

'Have you seen him this morning, your—husband?' Julián was incredulous.

Maca put the slathered piece of pastry in her mouth. It resembled an open wound.

She looked at her brother and pointed to her mouth. It was rude to speak with it so full.

She noticed a flash of movement across the entrance to the room— out in the courtyard.

Julián turned to see a little boy scurry behind a pillar. He looked at Cova, wondering if that was Maca's son.

'Ricky!' Maca called animatedly. 'Ven aqui, *crio*. Come meet your resurrected uncle, Juli,' she cackled.

The sinister sound grated on Julián's last nerve.

The child looked unsure.

'Ven,' Maca commanded, smiling ferociously.

Eventually, the five-year-old approached. Visibly terrified.

'This is Federico the Third,' she said proudly. 'Freddie's boy. I'm like a mother to him.'

Julián and the child eyed each other.

'Do you have any children, Juli?' Maca asked, unashamedly not caring for a reply. She noticed him play with a ring, but it didn't look like a wedding band.

'I do,' she proclaimed. 'Armando Federico—Junior. Named after his father, of course—and ours. Armandito, we call him. He's probably still asleep—he's only two—ay!—three, I mean—hahaha—I'm so bad with numbers.'

'Maca.' Julián called her attention back, evenly. 'We need to talk about this—'

'Por favor, Julián, please. There's nothing to talk about,' she tore off another piece of pastry. 'You've been gone a long time, there is so much you don't know.'

She reached, once more, for the butter.

'For starters, Cova is just desperate for attention. As always.'

Next, she reached for the jam.

'Her poor husband is no longer a star athlete and she's stuck doing menial secretarial work. Not the life of the party any more, eh, Cova? How things have changed'—Maca paused to ingest the last of her pastry—'My husband is a powerful man, Juli, and she's just trying to get noticed any way she can, *pobrecita*. No kids and a husband too busy with his amigos to pay her any mind, poor thing.'

A tear slowly made its way down Cova's swollen cheek.

'How can you be so cruel, Maca? I don't remember you like this,' Julián shook his head.

Cova pulled her torn dressing gown tighter around her battered body.

'I'm surprised you remembered us at all,' Maca smirked. She picked up a knife and cut into the omelette on her plate.

The kitchen door swung open, and Freddie stumbled in. Slightly unsteady on his feet.

His muddy, bare feet.

His hair was unkempt, and his half-opened shirt was unevenly buttoned.

He was wearing shorts, but they didn't seem to be in his size.

Freddie held on to the edge of the dining table and examined the breakfast assembly.

Slowly, he went from face to face, as if struggling to identify them.

'Hijo,' he recognized his son and called him over.

The boy stood still for a few uncomfortable seconds, then fled the room.

Freddie laughed—a baying, barking sound that irked Julián.

He took a few steps forward to grab a sausage from the middle of the table.

Only then did he realize who was there.

'Puta, Julián?' he exclaimed. 'Coño. Welcome back, hermano.'

Freddie staggered over to hug their eldest sibling, but Julián held himself away.

'Oy, Freddie, I think you should shower, no? I can smell—last night—on you,' Julián admonished.

The sound of a congested carabao again filled the large room.

'Coño, what a night, buddy,' Freddie laughed. 'Puta, you should've arrived sooner—you would've had a ball.'

He leaned down to whisper in his brother's ear. 'That's Olga you smell on me, and Tracy,' he winked.

Finally, he noticed Cova. Seated next to Juli, resembling a purple yam.

That's truthfully what Freddie called her.

'Joder, Cova, coño. You look like—*ube*! What the hell happened to you?'

'Maca's husband, that's what,' Julián replied, abruptly.

'Basta, Julián, enough! It's not funny any more,' Maca spat out as she put down her fork.

Freddie was perplexed. '*Espera, espera*, wait—clarify, please. *¿Qué está pasando?*'

Cova shrank further into herself.

'Our sister was assaulted—violated—by Maca's husband.' Julián explained.

Freddie began to laugh, then stopped when he realized he was the only one chuckling.

'Wait, you're not joking?' he looked around the table.

Maca had resumed her breakfast.

'Do I look like I'm joking?' Julián asserted.

'Puta,' Freddie shook his head. 'No.' It made him dizzy.

'No,' he repeated. 'No way, Juli. *Imposible.*'

He stopped to think, then remembered he didn't have to.

'I know Manny. Cabrón was so baked last night he passed out on the couch in the pavilion. After like an hour, he went up to bed—'

Freddie left out the parts of the evening when Manny fondled some Santa-clad waitresses, got a blowjob or two, and mooned their Chinese associates.

'We were all wigged out by the lights going *loco*,' Freddie continued. 'At least I was—did you notice it, Maca? Off, then on, then off again. I thought there was going to be another coup attempt or some sort of attack.' He guffawed, again. 'I asked Mang Tining to check the main breaker just now, but turns out, it was a city-wide power surge and I forgot to buy gas for the generators.'

Julián couldn't understand how the conversation went so off-track—*power surge? Gas?*

Maca continued to eat as Freddie prattled.

'Mang Tining called the electric company—they're upgrading the grid or something like that—no biggie.'

Julián had enough.

'This is a *big-gie*, Freddie—do you understand? Do you get what happened here? Do either of you get it? Look at her.'

He couldn't stand to see his youngest sister so hurt and so terrified, and he wondered why he seemed to be the only one in shock. He must speak to Alma.

'Oye, Cova,' Freddie said, pointedly, 'who did that to you?'

She looked from one brother to another.

And then, she looked at Maca.

Macarena had one eyebrow raised as she slowly chewed on the last of her omelette. Her back was erect and her eyes—unblinking—were on the mirror dominating the far wall. In it, Maca could see her battered sister's cowering reflection.

Cova lowered her gaze. She was oh so tired of this.

Of feeling like her home—her family—was a battleground.

'Cova, tell them,' Julián prodded. 'Let them hear it from you.'

Silence.

Freddie felt like he was waiting for one of his cockfights to begin. He wanted to place a bet.

Maca pecked first—he would've won.

'Juli, you may not know this since you abandoned us and all that,' a small—almost imperceptible—smile lifted the corner of Maca's lips, 'but your little Dodo grew up a floozy.'

'What?'

'She's a nympho, Julián, a slut. Everyone knows it. Her behaviour—in public—has not befit this family.' Maca finished with aplomb and put her utensils together on her plate.

'What the hell are you saying?' Julián slammed his fist on the table as he stood. 'How can you talk about your sister like that?'

Maca didn't flinch. She lifted her cup of coffee to her lips and took a sip. It was too hot.

'Tell them, Freddie,' she blew lightly on the scalding liquid. 'Tell them what Luísa told you, what she saw Cova doing before she was even married.'

This was all moving too quickly for Freddie. He was still a bit perplexed.

And then—remembering what Maca meant—he snickered.

'Ah, yeah—the Spanish *polla* was eating you out—right here in the house. In the linen room! Luísa said you were making all sorts of sounds—really enjoying it,' Freddie shook his head at Cova, chuckling.

'There was also that time you sucked off that surfer in Sparkles—some Australian I think, no? Whitey—bet he wasn't circumcised—right there on the dance floor—'

'That's not true—' Cova cried out.

'Please, Cova,' Maca dressed her down, stirring the liquid in her cup. 'Everyone knows the stories—all of Manila was talking about you. Papá would be so ashamed if he knew the truth.'

Maca beamed. Seeming to relish her sister's anguish.

'Do you know what they call her, Julián?' Maca offered, taking another sniff of her coffee. 'Your little—Dodo? They call her the "Castillo Coochie"—everyone got a jab. Isn't that right, Fred?'

Freddie giggled, nodding his head. 'Oye, from what I heard, you're pretty good, sis. Even the girls like you.'

Julián was gobsmacked—*What just happened? How did this get turned around?*

This was not a world he remembered. Or one he understood.

This was definitely not the family he missed being part of.

Who were these people?

And how were they raised by the same parents?

Maca put her coffee cup back in its saucer. She wasn't done.

'Bottom line'—she addressed Cova directly, coolly—'you're not even Manny's type.. Look at us, we're nothing alike. He can have anyone he wants—why would he want you? And if—let's just say—one day he woke up and found you attractive, we all know he wouldn't have to force himself on you. Please.'

She looked at their eldest sibling. He was seething where he stood.

'Have you seen him, Julián? My husband? He's super *guapo*. One of the handsomest men in the country. All the magazines say so.'

'Macarena—' he let her name slip out through gritted teeth.

'Julián,' she picked up her teaspoon to stir her coffee once more, 'I think we've all heard enough of this bullshit, no? Take it back with you to whatever hole you crawled out of. Go see Mami, as you planned, but don't you dare upset her with this nonsense. Thankfully, she stayed in her room this morning—do you remember where that is? Or will you need directions? Afterward, do us a favour and leave. Again. You don't belong here any more.'

She didn't even stop for breath.

'And Covadonga, whatever issues you have in your own marriage, don't take it out on others. It's not our fault you married a loser, *un huevón* with no job and no prospects. I've worked very hard to make my husband feel welcome here—in this home. In this family. You—of all people—will not ruin that. I will not have him treated like Lulu is. Understood?'

She paused a beat and put her spoon back on the saucer.

'We will never speak of this again.'

The temperature finally right, Macarena Castillo de Santos took a large sip of her coffee.

Cova fled the room in tears. Feeling assaulted—violated—all over again.

Left speechless, a shaken Julián followed her out.

Neither of them noticed the terrified little boy hiding quietly behind a planter by the open courtyard.

Overhead, thick heavy clouds swallowed the porcelain blue.

There was crack of thunder, and the boy began to cry.

A startled lizard fell off an arch and skittered down his arm.

Darkness descended, signalling an approaching storm.

PART III

JUNCTURE

Chapter 20

El Regreso al Hogar | **The Homecoming** | Ang Pag-uwi

Ricky Castillo didn't like the rain. But he never understood exactly why.

In the many hours spent with the therapist at Good Graces, the closest they got to an explanation was Sombra's courtyards.

There were too many.

And all of them were open-air.

To a young boy like Ricky, that meant rain always fell 'inside' the house, despite a roof and walls of stone.

It roared in torrents and bellowed iron sheets when there was a storm. Hurling thunder—and torment—throughout the halls.

In the tropics, where they lived, there was always some sort of storm.

Typhoons, low pressure areas, intertropical convergence zones—to name a few.

Young Ricky didn't understand why Aba Fatimah wouldn't fix the gaping holes. She laughed and pinched his cheeks each time he asked her.

So, every day he came home from school bracing himself, convinced that thunder would eventually smack him down.

Or that too much rain would drown his family.

His nanny told him it often flooded in parts of the marshy city.

Even as a grown-up—in the dense, rebel-held jungles of the southern islands—he was more afraid of rain than the armed fighters he was there to photograph.

Fact: When he was ten, Ricky Castillo tried to build a boat. Using fallen branches in Sombra's yard after a storm.

Aba read to them about some old guy with animals surviving a flood, but cousin Dito wouldn't help him with his ark.

The younger boy just sat under the macopa tree—holding his nanny's hand—watching Ricky. Much of the bright pink fruit was on the ground, looking like teeny-tiny unwashed babies' bottoms.

Dito picked one off the lawn and took a bite.

Hours later—as his nanny helped him wee into a bush—Little Dito broke his silence. Echoing the people in Aba's book.

'God will save us, primo'—Dito muttered through another mouthful of macopa—'just be good and pray.'

Then, he crossed himself as his nanny tucked him back into his shorts.

But how good did young Ricky have to be? His mother always prayed and still God never sent Pop home in time for dinner.

Before the sun set that afternoon, it was ready—Ricky prayed and pushed his boat into the pool.

It came apart.

Cousin Dito said he must not have prayed correctly. Then, he licked another blushing fruit like a baby's bottom.

Aba Fatimah told them rain was good for Sombra's garden. It kept the fruits plump and juicy, and the flowers bright and happy—just as Abu Federico always planned.

The rain—Aba said—was Abu's 'miracle from heaven', which left a fresh coat of rainbow colours after every storm.

Sombra was beautiful—Aba said—because it rained.

Ricky wished he knew why he didn't take his Aba at her word.

* * *

It was raining that November day he returned to Sombra from Good Graces.

Tita Maca sent a new chauffeur in Aba's old Benz to pick him up. It was just respectable enough to not give off the wrong impression.

But Ricky was shocked by the impression he got behind Sombra's walls.

The once-imposing metal gates looked battle-scarred, and the driveway was potholed and uneven.

The broadleaved trees stood forlorn, and the flowers were soddened and wilted.

The lawn—usually manicured—was overrun by a legion of weeds. And rotting fruit lay on the ground like exploded bombs.

Ricky felt as if he were back in the southern islands' bullet-sprayed villages. Gripped by the inescapable dread of being under siege.

There, generations lived frightened and traumatized, as people with guns—rebels, soldiers, and warlords—waged endless combat around them.

He remembered it so clearly—the *fear*. It was—fossilized.

It was a time before the drugs took over.

* * *

He was a junior photographer then for the Mendozas' newspaper. A job they gave him—seven years earlier—as a favour to his Aba.

Lifestyle Section. Sometimes, Features. It was easy, but uninspiring.

So, he volunteered to go to the restive south—to the most troubled parts of Muslim Mindanao. People were poor, guns were abundant, and lawlessness prevailed. Under the cloak of a separatist, religious struggle.

He wanted to see where Aba Fatimah was from. She never spoke of it—not even a hint of the name of her tribe—but he needed to trace his roots.

To find her family, and maybe—to understand.

Aba Fatimah didn't want him to go—so, he lied and told her he'd be elsewhere.

Ricky learned early on that lying came easy to the men in his family.

The Castillo women were strong and could be brutal in their certainties, so the men—like his father—learned to skulk and speak in whispers.

Inevitable then that he and Dito would also be most comfortable in shadow.

But Ricky's editors weren't swayed, fearing he'd be kidnapped. A Castillo de Montijo would fetch quite a ransom.

Undeterred, he used a false identity and went on his own. Lying, after all, came easy.

It was a life ago.

Before he was colonized by meth.

* * *

A freed man—and no wiser about his Aba's past—Ricky sat in her Benz, uncomfortable beside the unfamiliar chauffeur. His mouth ajar as he stared out the rain-smeared window.

The estate was blanketed in mud. Resembling the marshland that it once was.

As if the earth was reclaiming what it owned.

Sombra looked—*unkempt*. A word that Ricky had never used to describe it.

It looked neglected. Far worse than the last time he was home.

Had it been almost a year since they stuck him in Good Graces? A year since his maritime meeting with The Lizard.

As the Benz wound slowly up the rutted drive, Ricky gaped at his grandmother's grim 'garden of miracles' and his grandfather's drenched 'coat of dreams'.

An eternity later, the manor appeared—a spectre of the home that it had been.

The car stopped at the front door and a young girl he didn't recognize came to greet him.

He couldn't feel like any more of a stranger.

Then—as he dreaded—there it was. The moment he stepped through the portico.

The unwelcome but familiar burst of roaring thunder. Coursing tumultuously through the darkened hallways.

He was home.

'Aba?' he asked the girl, as she shook rain from the umbrella that she used to shield him.

'In her room, señorito,' the girl replied, shyly.

She tried to take his duffle bag, but he insisted on carrying it himself. He was certain it weighed more than her. She looked as thin and frail as a young banana plant.

When the girl noiselessly scurried away, Ricky skirted around the courtyard towards the main stairwell. Feeling assaulted by the pounding of the rain against the stone floor.

He was careful to avoid the puddles of murky water. And the battalion of tiny reptiles scuttling past.

It wasn't evening yet, but Sombra was already leaden in shadow. Heavy clouds sat overhead, casting a gloom that gnawed at the house and settled in.

The walls dripped with sadness, and the paintings—long lifeless and imposing—seemed haunted.

Ricky feared what he would find in Aba's room. His grandmother hadn't been the same since Manang Lydia died. She was more reclusive and reticent—and she had stopped sweetening her tea.

The last time he saw her, Aba joked that she was tired of being the last one waiting in the 'departure lounge', wondering why her 'flight' still hadn't boarded.

She was in her eighties, but Ricky knew she was healthier than she let on.

Or so he hoped.

He stopped and took a breath—the rain—did neither.

He was finding it difficult to see.

Only a handful of Sombra's many lights were on, throwing uneven textures on dulled corners and archways.

The bulbs were not the usual shade of elegant yellow but dissimilar watts of weary white. Radiating ghastly gashes as stark as the light in a hospital basement.

Glaring.

Blatant.

Intrusive.

As if the harshness was meant to shock patients into healing.

That's where they used to put mental patients—in hospital basements. In windowless rooms alongside the morgue.

Ricky's mother was admitted there once, though no one was supposed to know that.

Not even her own children.

They were told she was on vacation.

But cousin Dito informed him otherwise. He'd overheard his mom Maca talking to Ricky's dad.

Ricky went to see his mother in the hospital, but the doctors wouldn't let him through.

He never forgot how blunt—and ugly—those basement lights were.

It made him understand why Aba Fatimah insisted on golden halos in Sombra.

Another unholy crack of thunder.

Alone in the long, dark hallway, a familiar anxiety rose within him. He was defenceless.

Instinctively, he braced for an attack.

Other than the rhapsody of the downpour, there was only silence. Overwhelming and bristling.

Like that of an anxious country on the eve of war.

'Aba?' he reached her door and gently knocked.

Another unfamiliar face came to greet him.

'She's on the veranda, señorito,' the unknown woman opened the door to let him by. 'I'm Emmy, po, sir—her nurse.'

He smiled politely and made his way to his grandmother.

She was in a wheelchair, staring out into the garden. A wistful look on her face.

He bent to kiss her.

Slowly, Doña Fatimah lifted her head to her visitor. His cheeks were fuller than the last time she saw him, less ashen. His eyes were focused and not blood-shot. He had no scabs or scratches. His hair was neatly trimmed, and his chin was clean-shaven.

Iko...

Ricky.

Tears began to flow down her cheeks.

'Aba, please don't cry,' Ricky gently wiped her face. He didn't know if they were tears of sorrow or of joy. Joy hadn't been seen in Sombra for years.

She squeezed his hand. The one that took hold of hers. It let him know she was all right.

Aba wasn't told he was in rehab. They said he was away 'on a job'—shooting magazine covers in Japan. Or Korea. It didn't matter which.

They kept forgetting that stupidity wasn't a consequence of age.

Fatimah knew exactly where her poor little Ricky was. She'd seen it brewing, over time, in his eyes.

The self-hatred—and anger—at his inutility.

His inability to grapple with his parents.

How it ate away at him—the rottenness of the world.

He was—too *soft*—Fatimah thought. She'd failed.

Her beloved grandchild needed restoration and—*reinforcement*.

'How are you, mi niño?' she asked, not sounding as frail as he expected.

'I am well, Aba—now that I am home.'

He lied.

And they both knew it.

* * *

Ricky had dinner with Aba in her room that Sunday afternoon. No one else was home, and he was glad to have her company.

The maids said his aunt Maca left for lunch and had yet to return. His uncle Manny was out somewhere 'working'. So much for Sunday family meals at Sombra.

Both Ricky's sisters were abroad, and his mother was—elsewhere.

His father's whereabouts—of course—unknown.

Apparently, Dito was back from his postgraduate studies. But stayed sheltered in his room as always.

It was only when Aba turned in for the night that Ricky left her.

His own room was exactly as he'd had it. Other than fresh sheets on the bed and a general cleaning.

He threw his duffle bag aside and ransacked his drawers, searching for his old cameras. Anything he could use to make money. He wouldn't be reliant on his father.

The police still had his precious—pricey—Canon. Unlikely to return it with the investigation still open.

Puta—shit—maybe Dito's dad could recover it. Surely Tito Manny had the right connections under this hashtag president. They're both super tight with those Rodríguezes.

When Dito didn't pick up his call on the intercom, Ricky walked across the house and knocked on his cousin's door.

He turned the knob—it was locked.

'Primo, it's me.'

There was a muffled shuffling behind the door and then a thud.

'Wait, paré, just a sec,' came Dito's mumbled reply.

A few interminable moments later, the door creaked open.

'Really, dude? I've been away for ages—and this is the welcome I get?' Ricky joked seeing his cousin's expressionless face.

Dito was still shorter than him but stockier. Burly almost, if not for his thin calves and short arms.

He had thick dark hair like his father, Manny, and skin like burned sugar. His nose was wider than Ricky's—and his teeth were small.

He was still dressed from church.

'Hey man, how's it going?' Dito did not move from the doorway.

'Can I come in or what, paré?' Ricky teased.

'Uh,' Dito seemed—nervous.

They stared at each other in silence.

Then, reluctantly, Dito let his cousin through.

'What's up?' Dito asked, trying to casually glance around his own room.

Ricky looked around, too. Less casually.

The ceiling lights were off.

The TV was on but muted, and a radio on the bookshelf played soft pop music.

Above the bed, there was a crucifix. And an abundance of religious statues and lit candles were crammed in an alcove beside the bathroom.

Before it—on the floor—a small pillow.

The laptop on Dito's desk was frozen on a screensaver of a desert sand dune.

There was a sharp ping noise in the background. And then a few more. In staccato.

Like when messages come through on an electronic chat.

'Am I disturbing, primo?' Ricky teased. 'Were you—praying?'

'No, not at all,' Dito switched off the silent TV. And then, the radio. He pushed down his laptop screen.

'You look well,' he added, unable to think of anything appropriate to say.

Still awkward after all this time—Ricky smiled at his odd little cousin.

'I need your help, Dits—can I still call you just Dits?' He got right to it.

'Of course, dude—and I'll help if I can.'

'Great,' Ricky replied. 'Actually, I was hoping your pop could help—'

He saw Dito visibly shirk. A small automatic movement his younger cousin seemed to make whenever his father was mentioned.

'Uh, I don't know, man—I haven't talked to him in a while. You know how—busy—he is,' Dito offered.

'Yeah, but—well—two things, really. One, nobody seems to know where my dad is, so I'm hoping your dad can find out. And two, cops took my camera when they busted that party I was at. You know the one—at Chucho's? From where I was dragged directly to Good Graces?'

Dito nodded. Of course, he knew. All of Manila was still talking about it—nearly a year later. Which was incredibly unusual in a city where outrageous things happened with every heartbeat. Like waves crashing on the coastline. Or blinking.

In Manila, scandals broke like rain.

But the incident at Chucho's was—'epic'. It had all the usual characters—and elements—rolled up in one, so there were still a million ways to rehash the stories.

Russian hookers, A-list film stars, C-list wannabes. Brazilian models, self-proclaimed artists, blustering news readers. All carousing with hotshot entrepreneurs, smugglers, drug lords and scions of political dynasties. Often, the latter were one and the same—third and fourth generation 'public servants' who got rich turning government into a family business.

Chucho's party was raided by narcs. Blasting sirens, geared up agents—the works. They barrelled in alleging an 'anonymous tip'—but everyone knew the only tips that cops responded to were monetary.

The narcs claimed they intended to bust a drug lab, which wouldn't have been extraordinary in Manila. #Truth. Some of the poshest mansions in the most tightly guarded neighbourhoods were leased to outsiders and used as meth labs. It's how the trade remained undetected and grew so large. The rich and powerful were involved.

Deliveries were made in heavily tinted, often bulletproof, luxury cars. Also by city ambulances and other government vehicles.

There were fishing boats and yachts that moved 'products' across the islands, and private submarines—like Tukô's—collected foreign supplies dropped at sea.

It was sheer luck that Chucho's house wasn't an active meth lab, but police inadvertently stumbled into a drug feast.

Ricky was there taking pictures. That was all.

Another 'job' for his private client/tormentor—Tukô. His abductor demanded shots of certain guests in compromising positions. One never knew—he said—when such photos would come in handy.

Ricky Castillo was a perfect patsy. Everyone knew him, so his presence—and his camera—didn't raise eyebrows.

Not that it mattered. People got too plastered to care that they were being photographed.

The first thing the narcs took was Ricky's brand new DSLR—evidence, apparently—in what was likely to be some turf war between crime lords/politicians.

Before he knew it, Ricky was back in rehab. Whisked away by his Tita Alma.

An arrest would've disgraced the family.

His parents, yet again, were missing in action. His father, presumably, away on business. His mother, undoubtedly, just—'busy'.

Likely engrossed in Korean telenovelas.

Those shows were all the rage in Manila, but his mother, Luísa, would never admit to being hooked. She said it didn't make her seem very intellectual.

After all the years, she was still trying to impress his father's sisters.

As it was, Ricky felt his mom spent too much time in front of her sixty-five-inch 3D-capable LED Samsung Smart TV.

When not glued to imported dramas, she was tuned to fundamentalist religious programmes. Or binge-watching pirated screeners about New Age theory. The 'Law of Attraction' and all that malarkey.

She was still waiting for her prayers to be answered.

'I need the camera back,' Ricky pleaded with his cousin. 'I can't afford a new one, and I need to work—so I can keep clean. Please, primo.'

It was that stupid ark all over again—Dito thought—why didn't his cousin ask his high-society friends for help?

This was the secret Ricky guarded most of all: he didn't really have any friends.

Chapter 21

Los Payasos y/o los Piadosos | **The Clowns and/ or the Pious** | Ang Mga Payaso at/o ang Mga Maka-Diyos

'Body of Christ—'

Manny Santos looked positively virtuous laying the thin, white wafer on the elderly woman's tongue. His smile was turned down, his eyes—purposeful and serious.

When he held his breath, his engorged belly only half-peeked out over the top of his custom-tailored trousers.

He was also wearing an expensive *barong tagalog* shirt, which— as it was appropriately untucked—gracefully covered up any protuberant imperfections.

'Amen,' the elderly woman replied to him before stepping away and letting the next communicant forward.

'Body of Christ,' Manny repeated. With a sincerity oozing out of him that was almost believable. Lord knew he had enough practice.

He was so convincing it almost covered up the stench reeking off him.

Tennessee bourbon. Just a few shots—at breakfast—for motivation.

It was hot in the ornate basilica that morning—what with the flood lights and throngs of people—but his undershirt successfully absorbed his sweat. Leaving no traces on the sheer pineapple fabric of his barong.

Manny Santos was confident he looked—*exemplary*.

Positively respectable—as an Attorney should be.

He felt perspiration trickle down from his armpits.

'Amen,' purred the well-endowed young woman in front of him. She left a bright red lipstick stain on his hand as he pulled it back from her mouth.

There was a twitch in his crotch that he ignored. (The barong covered up any protuberance.)

His focus—at the time—was on distributing the holy communion wafers in his chalice.

Yes, Manny still put the wafer in people's mouths. Directly on their tongues, to be exact.

'Body of Christ—'

It was no longer the way communion was distributed—what with public hygiene standards and all—but sixty-year-old Armando 'Manny' Santos was a man of tradition.

And this was the biggest—most important—show on the islands.

All the notable politicians attended this Sunday mass at this church.

As did movie stars, super athletes, and other social 'influencers'.

The service marked the start of Advent, forty days until the celebrated birth of Christ.

It was televised, so—technically—free publicity.

Oh, how the Islanders loved the Christmas season. They loved TV almost as much.

Naturally, this high mass—with its grand ecclesiastical trimmings and gaudy star power—was the most watched event of the year.

To be featured—nationwide—assisting in such a sacred exercise, was invaluable for Manny's image.

And that of Mikey Reyes, of course. Whom—*naturally*—Manny was standing next to.

Mikey was also holding a golden chalice, distributing holy wafers like political favours. The former Manila mayor had become a congressman, but he planned to run for senator in the next elections. And it was never too early to start 'pre-campaigning'.

Not that Mikey would have trouble winning a national post.

Since #Durog became president six months earlier, the old Rodríguez gang was back in the country—or out of hiding—and getting the opportunity to 'serve the people' again. #GoodTimesforOldCronies #CorruptionRocks #YayforPipandMikey

#AndMannyToo

#Durog's approval rating was the highest of any president, though he behaved like a blinkered mob lord overseeing his turf.

#ThePeopleLovedAStrongman #GoFigure

It didn't seem to count against him that his idea of fighting crime was extermination. No trials or due process. Unarmed suspects were simply executed in 'shoot-outs' with police.

Rubbed out by cops dressed as—cops.

To be fair, there was some initial public shock, but Islanders quickly grew accustomed to seeing bullet-riddled bodies.

Cadavers littered roadsides and blocked gutters. Either wrapped in packing tape like presents—or covered by newspapers like rotting fish or pig carcasses from a rundown market.

Like lizard droppings in an unkempt house.

Often, there were cardboard signs tacked on the dead: 'Crime does not pay', 'Don't sell drugs like me', or other such elementary variations.

A gruesome homage—#throwback—to the puritanical era of scarlet letters.

More theatrical than anything in the martial law years.

Six months in and only the leaders of the Catholic Church still raised any questions about the deluge of corpses. There was that niggly sixth commandment after all. #ThouShaltNotKill

But—#Fact—Islanders, in general, were comfortable with contradictions. They enjoyed cheese in their ice cream and salted fish with chocolate porridge.

So, not even holy condemnation diminished #Durog's appeal. He was a national rock star whose every performance was applauded.

He usurped the bishops' pedestal, and anyone associated with him was virtually anointed by the gods.

Durog himself, however, did not bother with godly nonsense. And—#Fact—he only ate boiled vegetables and stewed plantains.

* * *

Doña Macarena Castillo de Santos was rarely seen in public, but for an occasion this important, she sat up front. Feeling the envy of every woman in the basilica.

Her husband Manny was so elegant in his barong, and he still had a full head of his own hair.

She admitted there was a little more of him than there used to be, but he was still handsomer than all the men in Manila. Regardless of what the magazines were saying.

Doña Maca flicked her wrist with a flourish, expertly cooling herself with a folding Spanish hand fan. Confident she was finally the Castillo de Montijo that mattered.

She hobnobbed with the most powerful and ran Sombra like it was hers, certain that her mother must be grateful. After all, it was she—the discounted middle child—who stepped up.

As far as Maca was concerned, her elder siblings shirked their responsibilities and abandoned the family. Julián—thank goodness—was gone. And suburban Alma was submerged in bonsais, marital bliss, and Andy's shadow.

What a waste—Maca sneered.

Surely, she would inherit Sombra—*who else could Mami leave it to?* At fifty-six, Freddie was still too irresponsible if unsupervised.

There was their youngest sister to consider, but Maca never spared her a thought.

Nor allowed her name to be mentioned.

Cova may as well have not existed.

As she fanned herself in the basilica's front pew, Doña Maca smiled at the other ladies in the congregation. Judging those whose baubles were larger than hers—*No accounting for taste or breeding.*

She only knew them from the papers and off TV—a new, moneyed class that grew like amoebas. Rapidly and craftily.

Across the aisle, she spotted the best of them—the infamous Eliseo Salazar.

He survived the stain of being a Rodríguez crony and recreated himself as an enterprising private citizen. A mogul with a horde of successful companies. Call centres, courier services, pharmaceuticals. All respectable and above board.

Salazar had even been appointed ambassador to China by a previous president—and he wasn't dispirited when #Durog recalled him from the post.

Instead, he announced he'd run for governor of his hometown.

He was campaigning for the post unopposed.

Maca couldn't help but admire him. Unlike Durog, he even bothered to come to mass.

At the back of the basilica—with the hoi-polloi and the servants—her fresh-out-of-rehab nephew, Ricky, watched proceedings closely.

He stood behind one of the imitation Baroque columns. An old Pentax camera around his neck.

There were dark rings under his eyes and a scruffy shadow on his chin. The close-cropped hair on his head was unwashed, and his face had a pallor.

He looked tired and dishevelled, like he'd been drinking.

But Ricky had only had coffee and a pack of Marlboros. He was up all night, chasing cops and corpses. Hoping to sell the photos to international news agencies.

In the chancel, a hand-picked choir of orphans began singing another hymn. To accompany a long queue still waiting to receive communion.

Who knew there were so many people in Manila without sin?— Ricky smirked.

He brought the Pentax viewfinder to his eye, zooming in on select faces in the crowd.

It had been a while. He wasn't sure who was who—or *with whom*—any more.

Attending Sunday service was still the quickest way to get back into Manila's social scene. It's where the latest plastic surgeries were unveiled, and family additions were introduced. New couples were announced, and broken families were disguised.

Occasionally, a pre-marital baby bump or two might even be spotted.

It was—*pantomime*, Ricky scoffed.

What people wore spoke to their status. So, many dressed as if in costume.

Ricky always thought it the best telenovela in town. His mother's extravagant Korean dramas couldn't compare.

He trained his camera on the tag-team serving communion—his uncle Manny and his uncle's lord-and-master, Mikey Reyes. The vapid politician was a godfather at his christening. But that 'sacred' connection never served Ricky.

He barely knew his godfathers—which was why he relied on an actual relative to help him. Especially one who always boasted that red tape was no impediment and insisted that legalities were a mere suggestion.

A week had passed since his uncle Manny swore to track down his father. But despite behaving like his proximity to power gave him run of the nation—he did have a chauffeur-driven car with government plates—it seemed the unelected, unofficial 'official' couldn't deliver.

No one had seen Freddie in quite a while.

Even Aba Fatimah was asking after her son.

Tita Maca just repeated he was away on business.

As the choir's poignant rendition of 'Anima Christi' ended, Ricky lit another cigarette and snuck a smoke.

The communion line finally thinned. And Manny headed back to centre stage—the altar—to return the chalice.

He barely acknowledged his son, who was standing next to the priest as his assistant.

Dito stumbled as he stepped forward to take the golden goblet from his father. Then, he scampered aside to wipe it clean.

He hated Sunday mass at this basilica and couldn't wait for a parish of his own.

* * *

'Tito Manny!' Ricky rushed to grab hold of his uncle before he drowned in the exiting crowd. His first chance to possibly catch him.

Unsurprisingly, he also caught a whiff of bourbon.

'Hijo,' Manny exclaimed at his most avuncular, 'so good to see you here.' He was certain there were cameras rolling.

Maca stepped forward to be closer to her husband, proud that he was getting shuffled away by 'The People'.

'Tito, any news of my pop?' Ricky asked as an over-dressed herd jostled them out of the church.

Manny shook his head solemnly. *The cameras.*

'Not yet, hijo, but keep the faith.' He dramatically clapped a hand on his nephew's shoulder.

'What can I do to help the search, Tito?' Ricky pressed, ignoring the smell of alcohol.

'Ricky, *luego ya*,' Maca muttered under her breath. This was not the time to be harassing her husband about unofficial—unimportant—non-political matters. Especially with Ricky looking so grimy. *¡Que horror!*

'We can talk about this at home,' she dismissed.

'But he's never home, Tita—' Ricky began to say.

'Because he has so much work, hijo,' Maca offered immediately. She beamed. *The cameras.*

'*Venga*, smile at The People,' she told her nephew. 'We need to get Congressman Mikey to the Senate—it'll be good for the family.'

Then, as if she just remembered, 'I'm sure your pop is fine—you know how he is. He's likely with Harrison Chong, or one of his Saudi friends—gallivanting around the world on their private jets or yachts, *ya sabes*.' She chuckled. *Smile.*

Ricky felt a hand try to sweep him aside. With all the people around them, he almost couldn't be sure whose it was. Almost.

'Tito! Tito Manny!' he tried again.

But Manny and Maca Santos were opportunely engulfed by the crowd.

'Jesus,' he mumbled to himself.

'Ricky? Ricky Castillo? Is that you?'—a voice out of the multitude.

He didn't turn his head.

Joder.

He clutched his old Pentax to his chest. He'd done so well to stay low-key.

'I can't believe it'—the voice was closer—'you're out!'

Shit.

Laura Herrera. The biggest loudmouth in town. Editor-in-chief of *Island Elite*—the self-proclaimed 'top' society rag in the country.

She was also the leader of the Rah-Rah Girls. A pack—named after her, of course—of young, party-hopping gossips.

She gave him a quick hug and the perfunctory air kiss on each cheek.

'How long have you been back?' she asked. 'Despite the—uh—outfit, you look great. They must've treated you well at Good Graces.'

He was uncomfortable. It was obvious.

She didn't notice.

'Come on, dish. Who else was there with you?' A playful gleam in her eyes. 'Just between us, I swear!' She giggled.

'Quite a few of you went missing after Chucho's party, and we all know the cops didn't make many arrests, so—?'

He grimaced.

'Wow, *ha*,' Laura kept going, 'I see you're back to being the silent, broody type—don't take this the wrong way but *parang* I liked you better when you were on something—we had such fun then, *no*, Ricky-Dicky? Remember?'

She casually leaned in and grabbed his crotch. In the massive crush of people, no one noticed. Live cameras and mobile broadcasts notwithstanding.

'Laura—' he smiled awkwardly and pushed her hand away. 'House of God.'

He gestured upwards solemnly.

She laughed.

''*Sus*, Tricky-Dicky, when did that ever stop you?'

He spotted his cousin in the crowd. *Thank God.* 'I have to go,' he said, abruptly.

She turned to see what caught his eye.

'Ah, Batman and Robin are back together, eh?' she chuckled, flirtatiously. 'Are your adventures going to be different now? I mean, with you—*freshly laundered*—and him in his new—*costume*—and all—'

'Dito! Dito!' Ricky tried to get his cousin's attention.

It was always difficult to manoeuvre through crowds at his height, but Dito Santos would spot Laura Herrera anywhere. She was always the loudest and most garishly dressed.

This time, it was her fascinator that called his attention. Bright purple with a burst of peacock feathers. Only she wore head gear to church in Manila.

Advent colours, he noted. At least, she always bothered to match the occasion.

'Hello, Father Dito,' Laura greeted cheerily, tailing Ricky to his cousin. 'I'm supposed to call you that na, *di ba*?' she teased the would-be priest.

He squirmed. Too late to get away.

Dito offered her an uncomfortable smile. Not unlike his cousin's.

'Uh, not yet. My ordination isn't for another few weeks.'

'That's near na, ha! So, that's pretty much a done deal, right? No sex forever?' she winked.

The two Castillo cousins had uneasy smiles plastered on their faces. They were struggling to stay polite.

'I'm just teasing, boys—lighten up. Ay, well, I better go—I see my Rah-Rah Girls over there—we have a merienda to get to at the Esquivels',' she explained unnecessarily. 'See you boys again at Misa de Gallo—and Ricky—next time, try to dress *naman* to impress.'

Laura pinched his balls before walking away. 'Say hi to your sisters when they get back.'

Ricky and Dito stayed put until her plume disappeared into the circus of churchgoers.

The cousins turned to each other dumbstruck. A moment.

Maybe two.

'You look like hell,' Dito spoke first. 'Your sisters coming back for Christmas?'

'God knows,' Ricky couldn't stop himself. 'Shit, sorry, didn't mean to take the Lord's name in vain, or whatever.' He rubbed his palm across his face. 'Puta, dude—hard to get used to this.'

'What? Me ordained a priest?'

'Yeah, coño,' Ricky answered. 'Ah, joder, I did it again. Sorry for swearing.'

'Stop, dude,' Dito reassured him coolly. 'You don't have to keep apologizing for shit.' He smiled. 'Priests are people, too, you know.'

It was going to take getting used to—his odd little cousin—a priest! Growing up together, Ricky supposed he should have seen it coming, but he didn't.

He wondered how much more he didn't know about his family.

His expat sisters, for example, rarely called. All he knew was that Fátima—the older one—divorced an uber wealthy British banker. She lived off alimony somewhere in the south of France.

Pilar—his mother's 'dearest Pili'—was twenty-nine. Five years his junior, she switched boyfriends—and locations—faster than trendy diets.

Occasionally, she sent him a postcard, but he didn't know how she afforded all that travel.

Like Fáti, Pili was unemployed. And over the years, the allowance from their father had decreased.

Since Freddie's recent disappearance, they got *nada*.

'Can I get a ride back home with you, primo?' Ricky asked, lighting another cigarette. The crowd was down to a trickle.

Dito nodded and led them wordlessly to his old Toyota.

They walked in companionably awkward silence.

'Uh, did you catch my dad?' Dito eventually—hesitantly—muttered.

'Yeah, dude'—Ricky inhaled—'no news'—exhaled. 'And your mom insists this is just my dad *being* my dad.'

'What do you think?' Dito asked as he manually unlocked the car doors.

Ricky stubbed out his cigarette and wiped a palm across his face. It was the warmest December he could remember.

'He's gone AWOL before, but not for this long. And never without leaving us some money. I mean, he's left nothing. My mom doesn't know how she's going to keep up donations to her charities—dude, she's asked me for money—and it's not like I have anything left to sell.'

Dito nodded sympathetically. He didn't know what else to do.

Purposefully, he got behind the wheel and rolled down his window. Waiting to turn on the ignition until Ricky was in the passenger seat.

* * *

When they got to Sombra, Dito told Ricky he'd offer a special prayer for his father. He had a distinct Sunday ritual of supplications and ablutions.

As soon as he got to his room, Dito switched on the TV. It didn't matter what was showing, he kept it silent.

Then, he put the radio on to his favourite pop station. An Irish boy band was crooning their latest hit. He enjoyed the sound of young boys in harmony.

He carefully shed his shoes and brought out a tissue box.

After unbuckling his belt and removing his trousers, Dito took a seat at his desk and powered up his laptop. Logging into his VPN to hide his electronic movements.

He brought himself out of his underpants and went in search of his usual Sunday fare. An entire website dedicated to photo-shopped images of Johnny-Tobee de la Cuesta-Wagner. A cherubic local actor who drove the girls crazy.

Jon-Tee had slim shoulders, a bright grin, and innocent eyes. A button nose, long fingers, a clear complexion.

He looked like one of those androgynous Korean popstars. With shiny black hair and a soft, dimpled chin that Dito wanted rubbed against his crotch.

He also dreamed of licking Jon-Tee's waxed-clean torso. It looked as smooth as a blushing baby's bottom.

Dito stroked himself until release. The guilt always came after he climaxed.

As a man of God, he mustn't feel such pleasure.

He took a tissue from the box and wiped himself clean.

Then, he got down on his knees and made his way to a secret drawer behind his altar. As always, he needed to be disciplined.

He unlocked the drawer and brought out a velvet case. Inside—a well-used, knotted cattail whip made of leather.

A gift from the priest at the ultra-conservative all-boys private school he attended. His special mentor taught him how to use it to cleanse his sins. The more it hurt, the more he was absolved.

But sometimes during flagellation, he climaxed again.

A cycle he was not particularly proud of.

When he finished, he'd go and visit Aba. To pray with her, play cards, or just sit in quiet contemplation.

On clear nights, they'd spot a firefly or two from her veranda. And sometimes, stars streaked a silver trail across the sky.

His mother rarely entered Aba's room. His father never dared to cross her threshold.

For Dito, it was the only place in Sombra where the silence was less painful.

Chapter 22

La Mesa Redonda y el Invitado de Honor |
The Round Table and the Guest of Honour |
Ang Mesang Bilog at ang Panauhing Pandangal

There was nothing Doña Almudena Castillo de Yrastegui hated more than social gatherings. Be they small get-togethers—where it was more difficult to disguise one's disinterest in superficial tête-à-tête—or the large, pretentious assemblies—where people threw around their meaningless titles and overdressed to be seen and validated by strangers.

She found all such events tedious and dull.

But her husband thrived on them.

In fact, he was an absolute star.

Everyone loved the affable Don Alejandro 'Andy' Yrastegui.

He was funny, charming, and—as Alma kept finding out from other people—ready to help anyone he came across who needed *helping*.

Which cemented a unique—but unintended—servile loyalty.

Your driver's son has dreams of becoming a pilot? Andy arranged to get him into flight school.

Orphanage in need of funding? Done.

What about building homes for impoverished families? Well, Andy did that, too. He was even known to get his own hands dirty. Heavy lifting, hammering, painting. No matter how remote or underdeveloped the area, Andy was there with his fellow BoBs.

Yes, BoBs—Band of Brothers. A group of businessmen who not just golfed together but assuaged their privilege by giving their hobby a humanitarian purpose. Beyond putting, they 'held meetings' on the green to discuss how to improve the world.

In Manila, it was a status symbol to be a BoB. Though it was in the group's creed that members work discreetly.

That didn't mean there weren't BoBs who relished being 'inadvertently' photographed helping the less fortunate. It was no secret that the 'accidental' presence of the press could be arranged.

So, this was the scene: The BoBs—gathered at a large 'unintentionally publicized' event. It was the first Friday of December, time for the annual Band of Brothers Gala.

Andy was president of the group for the third time. Which meant all eyes were not just on him, but on his elegant, elusive wife.

Alma hated it.

As the lead BoBee—wife of a BoB—she was expected to play hostess to more than three hundred formally dressed, preening status seekers. Also known as—guests.

All of whom came to the gala to be noticed.

The guest of honour was none other than the hashtag president—Facundo '#Durog' Marasigan.

It made Alma's skin crawl.

This was the man who took everything ugly about The Islands and made it—*acceptable*. He put it onscreen, online, and on the record. The greed, the viciousness, the swearing. The pettiness, the dishonesty, the bigotry.

The new president made the private—public. He did away with shame and propriety. The things that made a society—*civilized*.

#Durog did away with manners.

Yet despite that, even the hashtag president wanted to be accepted by the long-standing, well-mannered class.

So, in their presence, #Durog Marasigan appeared the most decorous S.O.B.*

As Alma and Andy learned first-hand.

'Good evening, President BoB.'

#Durog immediately offered Andy his hand at the receiving line in Manila Dynasty Hotel's grand ballroom. Ignoring the frantic rush of his coterie of bodyguards.

'What an honour to be your *Special Other Brother at this gala.'

Before Andy could reply, Durog turned to the woman trying to stand in her husband's shadow.

'Madam BoBee Yrastegui, long have I wanted to make your acquaintance.'

They were eye to eye. He was much shorter than Alma expected.

She didn't dare look down at his scruffy shoes or notice the uneven creases on his trousers.

He smiled.

Alma saw that his teeth—though all there—were varying shades of faded orange. From a light honey-amber to a darker burned carrot/caramel colour. A pale spectrum of betel nut juice that some poor dentist must have tried to bleach. She hadn't noticed it on TV.

So, the 'anti-drug' president had a betel nut habit? Alma filed that away for later discussion with her husband.

Durog's hand was outstretched a little longer than appropriate before she took it.

She said nothing. Showing none of her discomfort at the proximity of such boorishness.

Oblivious, Durog turned back to her husband.

'President Andy—may I call you Andy?—I understand Cardinal Toledo is slated to say tonight's invocation?'

Durog Marasigan was a direct man, an uncommon trait in polite company in The Philippines.

He was also not the Manila archbishop's greatest friend.

'Yes, Mr President,' Andy replied evenly. Aware that the leader of the country's Catholics was also the president's most rabid critic.

'It's tradition for the chief Catholic clergy to say the opening prayer at BoB Galas.'

'Yes, I understand.' Durog dismissed, displeased. 'But tonight— will be different, yes?'

He smiled at Andy. A horrid flash of speckled orange.

Andy said nothing.

'President Andy, I am here—what does Toledo have to say that is more important? Is he more important than me?'

Andy wasn't sure if the Philippine president was serious or merely showing off his much touted 'humour'—as offensive as it seemed.

#Durog was known for off-colour, off-hand remarks. He called them 'jokes'.

He joked about torture, he joked about murder, he joked about rape. He joked about genocide and had most people in stitches.

Again, he won the presidency with the largest landslide in Islands' history.

And he did it without the help of that insufferable Eliseo Salazar, the prehistoric busybody who fancied himself a kingmaker.

Because he wouldn't work with Salazar—or Tukô, as the fearful called him—#Durog owed Pip Rodríguez a few hundred billion pesos.

He was repaying the former dictator's son with government contracts and side deals. Durog learned a thing or two about creative accounting when he was a mayor.

Running a small town meant easy access to kickbacks, and debts were repaid however possible without showing your hand.

In small towns, everyone knew each other, and everything was personal.

Durog ran the country in similar fashion.

So, as lord of a larger fiefdom, that fricking turd Toledo would not be saying no *putang inang* invocation in his presence.

'But Mr President, surely you would rather relax and enjoy the evening instead of having to go on stage and—'

A squawk burst from the bleached betel nut mouth.

'Oh, my dear man, I find being on stage most enjoyable.' Durog slapped Andy's shoulder, sniggering like an unoiled door.

Andy did not know what to say.

'Have Toledo sit at my table. Tell him I am relieving him of his duty so that *he* can relax and enjoy the evening. Okay?'

Andy looked at his wife.

'Don't worry, President Andy. Toledo and I go way back—we have a *personal* connection.'

And with that Durog dove into the sea of awaiting sycophants. Also known as—guests.

'Did you see his mouth?' Alma whispered as the president tromped away.

'What about his mouth?' Andy was trying to work out what to tell the cardinal. There was no way Durog was not getting what he wanted.

'He chews betel nut.'

'You think? It would explain why he acts the way he does. Maybe he's high all the time and just concealing it.'

'That doesn't excuse his behaviour. *Por Dios*, Andy, why did you allow him to come tonight?'

'Amor, I am only the president of the BoBs—he is president of the country. How could I not have him as guest of honour?'

'Dishonour, more likely.' She shook her head.

The servers began to show the gaudy, gossiping guests to their assigned seats. Each one fluttered like a common maya bird thinking itself a peafowl.

She didn't want to be there, but it was her duty. She was Andy's wife. She was the lead BoBee.

Oh, how Alma hated social gatherings.

* * *

'So, tell me, Madam Alma, why is your brother not as good looking as you? Do you have different mothers?'

Alma nearly choked on her sea bass. #Durog Marasigan howled with laughter.

She quickly scanned the ballroom—grateful the other guests were focused on their meals.

'Freddie is the father of Ricky Castillo, no? The photographer?' the regrettable guest of honour continued. 'Kid's not bad, but he should stick to features. He lacks the eye for news. Why haven't I seen his byline lately?'

Alma gulped. Not about to tell the anti-drug president that her nephew was just in rehab.

But Durog didn't wait for an answer. He moved on to another topic he deemed enjoyable.

'Your daughter—the one on TV—she is abroad, no?'

Alma glanced at her husband seated beside her. He took a sip of his water.

'I see her sometimes—with all those white people on her channel. Good for her, no?'

The Yrastegui parents thought it best not to reply.

Across them at the table, Cardinal Toledo squirmed.

'You must be very proud of her—your daughter—the international reporter. *Mabuhay*—Island pride!'

Durog raised his glass in mock appreciation of her work.

'What was her name? Some fancy Spanish one, no? Who can even pronounce it with that letter X—Chee-my-nah? Hee—or is it *High-my-na*? High-mee-nah? Hymen?' Durog laughed, showcasing his orange speckles.

An uncomfortable silence settled on the presidential table.

'You know, Andy, as her father, you must be worried. There she is—gallivanting across those dangerous, distant lands—'

Andy put down his near empty glass of water.

'At the rate your daughter—Hymen—is going, she will end up with some unknown foreigner's dick inside her. And you wouldn't want that, would you, Andy? Some strange white guy's sperm in your grandchild?'

Immediately, Durog clucked his disapproval. 'You wouldn't know his family, his background. Better tell your daughter to come home. If not, that's how you lose them.'

Andy didn't know what to say. And he didn't want to look at his wife, certain he would see murder in her eyes.

Never had they been subjected to such impolite—*obscene*—conversation. Especially in public. At the esteemed round table of honourable BoB Gala guests, no less.

Andy tried to steer the talk in a different direction. But Durog wasn't having it.

'When your daughter returns, you must send her to my palace—I am sure she would enjoy an exclusive evening with the president—how many people can say that?' he smirked. 'Well, a few maybe—but not many.'

He winked at Alma.

She was horrified.

'I am only joking, of course. You should see the looks on your faces,' he laughed again. 'Ay, this fucking country. That is the problem—too many of you have forgotten how to laugh.'

'But it is not funny that you have allowed thousands of people to be killed,' Cardinal J. Arturo Toledo could no longer take it. 'In the name of a fabricated "drug war". Preposterous.'

The silence shifted. Durog stopped laughing.

'Do not judge me for doing the Lord's work—His vengeance is mine, did He not sayeth?'

'That is not the correct quote—' the cardinal began to explain.

'Arturo, those—animals—need to be cleared off our streets. Their drug use has turned them into savages. They are not human beings, but a danger to themselves and the rest of us.'

Alma thought Durog would spit on the floor. She'd seen him do it countless times on TV after saying that exact phrase.

But Durog Marasigan didn't spit. This was—after all—the annual BoB Gala.

'Pareng Art,' the president suddenly addressed the cardinal as if speaking to an old friend. 'We are the same, you and I, we both act in the best interests of the public.' He paused. 'At least, you *claim* to be acting in the public interest.'

Toledo turned red. He had told the public not to vote for a madman.

And Toledo knew the president better than most.

* * *

'Art, I need your help,' the mayor entered the sacristy from the back. Surprising the priest laying out his vestments for afternoon service.

'What can I do for you, Facundo?' Arturo Toledo asked his old friend. They met as boys in the small provincial school run by French missionaries.

Mayor Facundo Marasigan spat betel nut out the window and promptly prepared another leafy bundle to chew.

'It's Celia, my daughter,' began the mayor's confession. 'Jerry raped her, paré—I caught him.' A low growl of pain escaped Facundo. 'She's only thirteen—he was so smashed—so *'tang-inang* smashed! He hit me then ran off without his pants.'

Jerry—as Toledo knew—was the mayor's illegitimate son with his political rival's sister. A town secret that no one dared acknowledge.

'Go to the police, Facundo. Let them handle this.'

'Are you crazy? No one can know—it will ruin her. It will ruin me!' The mayor was overwrought.

'So, how can I help you?' Toledo asked.

'Tell me what else I can do to—fix this—to get justice for my daughter. You and I both know the police are useless.'

'Vengeance is mine sayeth the Lord,' the priest reminded him. 'You must find it in you to forgive your son, Facundo—to "overcome evil with good"—Romans Chapter 12—'

'Putang ina, are you joking? Your *lecheng* God let this happen! Do not talk to me like a priest, paré—I came to you as my friend.'

Toledo knew not to get in the way of Facundo's temper. He said a silent prayer.

The mayor spat his chewed up betel nut into the chalice.

There was a knock on the sacristy's main door. It was the volunteer who helped the priest clean the chapel.

'Father, there's a call from the mayor's wife—' she stopped, surprised to find the mayor with the priest.

She said no more.

The two men rushed to the mayor's house. His daughter had hung herself from a ceiling fan.

The next day, Jerry's body was found floating in the river. Riddled with bullets from the mayor's—untraceable—gun.

* * *

'I made no false claims about myself,' President Durog Marasigan was still regaling the table. 'The people knew whom they were electing, and I'm sure I don't need to remind you that I won by a landslide.'

He smiled at his old friend Arturo Toledo, Cardinal Archbishop of Manila.

'The people want me, Arturito—not you and your silent God.' #Durog wiped his mouth with his neatly folded napkin. 'I am a man of action. As I said—I take the Lord's vengeance as my own. There is absolutely nothing wrong with that.'

Alma was about to speak when Andy grabbed her hand underneath the table. He shook his head, pleading with her to let it be.

She didn't want to cause her husband discomfort, but she also couldn't stay silent.

'Are there not more important national concerns? The alleviation of poverty, perhaps, or ending armed conflict?' Alma asked the hashtag president. Unable—refusing—to say his title.

She smiled. Hoping to mask any rancour.

'You know,' he put down his napkin and addressed her like a child, 'all these—important matters—are connected. The little clashes across our islands—the warlords, the Moro rebels, the armed groups linked to foreign terrorists, even the outdated communists—they are all funded by crime. Robberies. Kidnappings for ransom. Piracy. Extortion. Smuggling—goods, cars, guns. Drugs. Even human trafficking. And crime is rampant because of poverty. Everything is about money or the lack of it. Who doesn't want to be rich? Ask resourceful turncoats like Eliseo Salazar. Look how far he's come from the War and that convenience store in a golf club. There are no political movements, only personal interests—an old adage. But here's something you may not have realized, Madam Alma—crime fuels insurgencies, insurgencies keep our islands lawless and our people poor. Poverty means more crime. Round and round. For money. See? And if you keep people poor, you keep them powerless. That's why they need a leader like me.'

Alma knew this was not an argument she was going to win. And her poor husband looked like he was about to pass out.

So, she said nothing.

Durog winked at her again, his betel nut mouth smiling ferally.

'Quite a feisty woman you have there, President Andy. You are a lot like your sister Doña Macarena—I have met her many times through Attorney Manny.'

Alma was not about to get into a conversation about her family tree. And she didn't appreciate Marasigan making it appear to the other guests like they were—*connected*.

The lights flickered and dimmed, signalling the start of the programme.

Cardinal Toledo tried to stand to head for the stage, but #Durog's bodyguards held him down in his seat.

The president gleefully stomped forward, gripping every hand he was offered along the way.

At the podium, he waved like a rock star and raised his face to the spotlight.

He grabbed the mic, adjusting it to his height.

'Good evening, BoBs—and honourable guests.'

He grinned, playing the crowd like an experienced ringmaster at the circus.

'I am supposed to lead the prayer,' a smirk, 'but come on, you know that's futile, no? Deep down, you know there is no God. You have been lazy, fooled by a long-standing—imported—colonial—illusion. We are Islanders, '*tangina*—grasp your roots, claim your power! Why let a false, white-washed Being tell you how to live? In this world, we each do what we can. A few of us get rich, and then—we all die. Sometimes, people like the BoBs are helpful—so thank you, BoBs. And thank you, President Andy. The rest of you can kiss my ass—which I am pleased to point out—you all have. So, enjoy your free dinner and your commercialized consumer Christmas. I will see you in the New Year as we welcome the Year of the Rabbit with a fiesta in Chinatown.'

#Durog then uttered something in Mandarin. Which few people in the room understood.

Not that it mattered. It wasn't said for the benefit of the BoBs, but for a select overseas audience that would get wind of the president's statement when the 'unintended' coverage of the Gala went viral.

In that moment, #Durog furtively granted Chinese traders open access to Islands' seas. They paid him greatly for such an undisclosed privilege.

He smiled. Just a few more rounds of bleach and his teeth would be white.

Chapter 23

La Caza y los Que Rebuscan en las Basuras |
The Hunt and the Scavengers |
Ang Pangangaso at ang Mga Namamasura

'Another day, another bomb.'

His cousin Ximena ended the call just as Ricky heard the explosion. She hung up too quickly to hear him wish her well.

He shut his mobile and walked back into the flashy all-night convenience store.

At that late hour on a Saturday, it was full of young people who worked in twenty-four-hour international call centres—all cardigans and scarves over casual, trendy outfits. Incongruous with the tropical heat but increasingly a common sight in modern Manila. Their air-conditioned offices occupied most of the city's new real estate.

They barely looked old enough to drive.

So damn fresh and cheerful—thought Ricky.

He was only thirty-four but couldn't remember ever feeling that—carefree.

The agents spoke to each other in the vernacular, glad for the chance to put their put-on foreign accents on hold for the length of a large bubble tea and a cigarette.

Ricky knew their job afforded them a lifestyle that might otherwise have been out of reach, but just like his, it had its pitfalls. He met more than one call centre manager or two at Good Graces.

As he walked through the gaggle of agents to the back of the store, no one gave Ricky a second glance. He looked like any other bar-hopping, privileged tisoy trying to be 'street'—all pale-skinned, mixed-race entitlement in faded designer jeans and a wrinkled T-shirt.

Ricky wasn't trying to look *anything*—he just hoped to blend into the crowd.

He took a packet of gum from a shelf and tucked it into his pocket. These big mini-mart chains would never miss it.

Chewing gum helped calm his nerves since he gave up smoking.

And lately, Ricky found himself wanting to smoke—a lot.

He was so anxious—and desperate—he even called *her*. He'd been home three weeks from Good Graces and still no word from his father. It was nearly Christmas.

When Ricky opened the door to the convenience store's closet—yes, the closet—a tattooed bouncer lifted a velvet curtain along the back wall. Dito was waiting at the bar on the other side. A rare occasion when Ricky was able to drag him away from his prayers.

El Armario de Cervantes—Cervantes' Closet—was one of those small, speakeasy-style bars that could only be found if you knew where to look.

Such places might entail walking into the storeroom of a twenty-four-hour minimart, going past the greasy garbage bins of a Korean fried chicken eatery—or trudging through a men's toilet at an all-night petrol station.

The truth was Dito only agreed to go to keep an eye on Ricky.

Or so he told himself.

'So, did X-men have news for you?' Dito mumbled as Ricky took a seat. They called their cousin 'X-men' because like those superheroes, she always behaved as if she were saving the world.

Ricky downed the shot of whisky on the counter and nodded.

'No shit, paré,' Dito was so incredulous he surprised himself by swearing.

Ricky asked the great Ximena 'X-men' Yrastegui for help—and she came through. They couldn't believe it.

The 'always busy' cousin X-men was the only other person Ricky could think of with potentially useful contacts. Thus far, Tito Manny and his 'official sources' had turned up nothing on his father.

X-men—Ximena—was Tita Alma and Tito Andy's eldest child. A TV reporter working somewhere in Iraq.

Or Afghanistan.

Or some other bumhole war zone. Which her mother never failed to remind them.

Ricky wondered why his cousin left when there were conflicts enough on the islands.

But then again, it meant one less Yrastegui around.

Something about those cousins always riled him—their air of superiority simply because they didn't live in Sombra.

Not in what they called 'Aba Fatimah's house'. Or off inheritance from Abu Federico.

And we're—what? Moochers? Sombra is our house, too, you know? A soundtrack that looped in the back of Ricky's mind for as long as he could remember. He and Dito had lived in the manor since birth. It was the only home they knew.

Abu Federico built Sombra for the family, and each member of that family had a right to be there. #Fact.

Ricky was also irked by his Yrastegui cousins' irritatingly impeccable manners. So hoity-toity, as if they were European royalty.

They sat up straight and never put their elbows on the dining table.

They chewed quietly and didn't speak with food in their mouths.

They held doors open for others—pulled out chairs—and knew which utensils to use and when.

The maddening mantra of his childhood—*fork on right, knife on left, unless you're slicing*. He heard Tita Alma repeat it enough times at family meals.

Not that she was even correcting her own children. She likely did that in the privacy of their own home. Of which she also, repeatedly, reminded them—the Yrasteguis had their own estate.

Tita Alma took Castillo family events as an opportunity to correct the children of her siblings. At the rate she did so, she clearly felt they needed improvement.

Her siblings never stood in her way. Such was the order of things in the family.

'Breeding has nothing to do with one's bank account,' Tita Alma always said. Or was it—'money can't buy breeding'?

Whatever.

The Yrastegui-Castillos were all about saying 'please' and 'thank you'. And not questioning their elders unless invited to.

Ricky clearly failed on all accounts.

He hated—and was grateful—that it was his Tita Alma that put him in Good Graces.

So, yes, the Yrasteguis bugged him—but he had hoped Ximena didn't think herself above helping family.

As it said on the crest in Sombra: *La familia primero*. Family first.

'She knows people in Taipei with ties to Harrison Chong,' he told Dito. 'They're tracking down his movements as we speak.'

For the first time all month, Ricky was almost optimistic. The elusive ~~Chinese~~ Taiwanese tycoon was one of his godfathers, but he couldn't remember the last time he saw him. If at all.

Harrison and Freddie were old friends and associates—they might just be travelling together through some exotic corner.

Ximena said she also tapped underground contacts in the Middle East. Private—*sketchy*—sheikhs who no one wanted to admit Freddie knew.

After all, Freddie was friends with incredibly wealthy people who didn't like being featured in society magazines like *Tatler, Hello,* or *Island Elite*. Their schedules weren't on the publicized party circuit.

It didn't, however, mean they weren't partying.

* * *

'Praise Him—alleluia! Let us sing, sing, sing—and rejoice!'

The jubilant lyrics scrolled silently along the bottom of a large TV behind the bar, as a casually dressed gospel choir swayed in frenetic—inaudible—godly glee.

'Why the fuck is that on in here?' an inebriated hipster screeched at anyone who could hear him. And in such a small space, they all could.

Ricky and Dito wondered the same.

'Bingo! Bingo, paré,' Ricky struggled to get the bar manager's attention off his phone.

Eventually, the skinny millennial turned to him.

'Yes, sir—what can I do for you?'

'Look, paré,' Ricky tried to sound cool, though it bristled that he was addressed as an older person. 'I'm not trying to shit on your high, but don't you think it's kinda weird to have that religious crap on in a bar, dude?'

He pointed at the TV.

'It's ironic—dude.' The perky millennial smiled, ironically.

Ricky stared him down.

'Actually, po, sir,' the millennial again, 'my staff demanded it. Without it, they wouldn't come to work on Saturdays because that's when this Brother Sunshine insists they attend his service.'

Fucking Brother Sunshine—they both thought, turning back to the muted TV.

A plump man with curly hair and a long bleached beard sat on a high-back wicker throne like a newly crowned beauty queen. The chair was outlined in fairy lights and made to look like the sun.

His Royal Sunspot—Ricky gathered.

The 'solar' star wore round glasses like John Lennon circa 'Imagine' and looked like a jaundiced combination of several emojis.

At the end of the choral performance, His Presumed Holiness arose like a grand vizier in a billowing tunic.

Around his chest—a garland of big, bright tropical flowers. Hibiscus, frangipani, and yellow bells.

Yup, Brother Sunshine.

Apparently, BS was the most popular evangelist in the country.

Not only did tens of thousands of Islanders attend services in his purpose-built Sunshine Stadium, but millions more across the globe watched his sermons on a dedicated satellite channel.

The twenty-four-hour Sunshine International Network. (Abbreviation at viewers' discretion.)

From what Ricky could tell, the self-aggrandised preacher was riveting the crowd with promises of miracles and redemption from hell. (The subtitles didn't keep up with his pronouncements.)

'Primo, paré—look,' Ricky directed Dito to the monitor.

Behind this Brother Sunshit was a massive wall of LCD screens. Each one flashing a flurry of images. It was like a Hollywood game show.

Then, the screens froze to form one giant visual.

Against a black backdrop—emblazoned in yellow—the name of his rapturous congregation.

The Church of Omnificent Neuro-theosophy. (C.O.N.)

Registered and trademarked.

Dito gagged on his beer. His enlarged eyes—glued to the screen.

Ricky was doubled up in laughter.

A moment later, their mirth turned.

'Uh, primo'—Dito elbowed his cousin Ricky in shock—'look.'

Ricky downed another shot of whisky before returning to the screen.

There, next to Brother Sunshine, was his mother, Luísa. Her hands in the air, her eyes shut tight, and her flowing hair a tousled— *seaweed green?*

Ricky was flabbergasted. This must be her latest—'church'.

Dito tried not to laugh at his cousin's parental misfortune, but he was still chuckling into his beer when Brother Sunshine introduced his next guest.

Helplessly, the cousins watched as Congressman Mikey Reyes appeared on stage. Behind him, flushed red and grinning widely, was Manny Santos—waving imperially at the crowd.

Suddenly, Dito no longer found the Sunshine show so entertaining.

'Bingo, paré,' Ricky sidled up to the bar manager again. He was looking to score a hit.

It was a split-second decision. Impulse. *A weakness.* He needed something stronger than whisky after this Sunny shitstorm.

'I can't even—' the bar manager retorted, trying to keep his voice low. 'If any of that junk is found here, they'd fuckin' shut me down. Or shake me down. Or both!' He shook his head. 'Dude, *naman*—'

Bingo, the bar manager, looked around to make sure they hadn't attracted unwanted attention. 'Sir, please don't approach anyone else here with that question, po, or I will be forced to throw you out.'

And with that, Bingo slinked back into the shadows.

By its very nature, Armario was dark and discreet. A sanctuary for select clientele.

But in #Durog's Manila, little was sacred but Durog.

And Durog disliked anything he couldn't control.

Before the hashtag president was elected, speakeasies were in fashion for the sake of it. But #Durog's brutal policies unintentionally cultivated the trend. The number of hidden bars grew exponentially out of necessity.

Not that alcohol was prohibited, but people like Ricky needed a 'safe space' to mingle. Or fly solo. Somewhere less visible that they could go without raising eyebrows. Or risk being recorded to go viral on social media.

Armario was private, served tapas, and had the best whisky and gin menus in town.

It was set up by three twenty-something Kastilas fleeing unemployment in Spain. Converse migration, if you would. Decades after desperate Islanders sought work in Europe.

A whole century after the colonisers left, there was a new generation of Spaniards seeking opportunities like Ricky's grandfather had.

They arrived to find islands still gripped by a colonial mentality.

Not that Ricky was complaining. Such racial bias worked well for the pale-skinned likes of him.

Whereas they stood out in some of Manila's grimier areas, in Armario, the Castillo cousins felt at ease.

Ricky stiffened. They were being watched.

And this time, he knew his paranoia wasn't drug induced.

Seated in a small booth nursing a gin and tonic, the ogler— a tiny candle flicking tongues of light across his face—looked vaguely familiar.

'Can I help you, dude?' Ricky approached his watcher without warning.

The spectator wore a button-down, long-sleeved, checked shirt and magenta trousers. They were visible in the dark.

Typical Kastila—Ricky thought. So preciously—European.

Only a Spaniard would wear such a colour. Or a member of ABBA.

But other than his clothes and his bearing, the ogler didn't look too continental.

'Eh, sorry, I didn't mean to stare. You just look a little—familiar,' the watcher smiled, warmly.

Ricky snorted. 'Then we thought the same thing.'

'I just arrived—from Spain,' the ogler shared.

No shit—Ricky thought, but he was outwardly polite. 'To work?'

'No, to visit family,' a shadow crossed the Spaniard's face. 'Well, maybe. I try—'

'Maybe?' Ricky repeated.

'Long story,' the guy laughed.

'Isn't it always?' Ricky smirked as he took a seat and motioned the server to bring them another round. 'Let me buy you a drink and you can tell us. That's my cousin at the bar, and we need a distraction.' He waved Dito over to join him at the watcher's table.

'My name is Diego—*bueno*, Diego Federico. Eh, you can call me Hugo.'

Expectedly, the ogler pronounced his name the Spanish way.

'Well, *Oo-goh*—there seems to be a lot of that going around,' Ricky retorted, as his cousin slid into the booth. 'I'm Federico Luís—Ricky. And this is Armando Federico—Dito.'

The Spaniard was stupefied. *Was Federico that common a name in Manila?*

'Our grandfather was Federico,' Ricky explained. 'We were named after him.'

'Me, too.' Hugo exclaimed.

They stared at him, unbelieving.

'Eh—' for half a moment, Spanish Oo-goh seemed unsure. Then, he decided to proceed: 'My mother is the daughter of Federico Castillo de Montijo, but she warned me about saying that in Manila.'

The two other boys were gobsmacked.

'Who—who's your mother?' Dito muttered.

'Cova. Covadonga Castillo? My father is Cristóbal Pe—'

'The pelotari,' Ricky interjected in disbelief. He found old posters of his uncle Cristóbal in Sombra.

'That was a long time ago. He, well, he does other things now.'

'Like what?' Ricky wondered what a former star athlete of a none-too-common sport did in retirement.

'This and that,' Hugo seemed uncomfortable. 'Whatever he can.'

'Such as?' Ricky was still curious. Only momentarily distracted as their drinks arrived.

'Eh, he was a bus driver once—also a cook in a small café near our house.'

'You live in Salamanca, right?' Ricky asked, downing his newly arrived whisky. Aba Fatimah had once mentioned it, but she didn't seem to know much else about Tita Cova's family.

Hugo nodded as he swirled the slice of lime in his glass. 'My mother is the marketing director for Las Olivas de Oro,' he paused, expecting them to know what that was.

They didn't.

'It's the top exporter of Spanish olive oil,' he said, proudly. 'Its headquarters are in Salamanca.'

Ricky and Dito nodded silently, not sure what to say.

'So, you are the sons of—?' Hugo prompted.

'Freddie,' Ricky told him. 'And this loser nursing a beer is Tita Maca's *unico hijo*, the golden boy who will save us all by becoming a priest.' He pinched Dito's cheek as he teased.

Hugo ordered them another round.

It was going to be a long night of getting to know newfound cousins.

* * *

'Man, of course you looked familiar—we're related,' Ricky proclaimed. 'But poor you, you look more like Dito than me.'

Dito said nothing. He was used to keeping his mouth shut when he wasn't amused. Or however else he might be feeling.

He knew Ricky was joking, but he deplored being seen as the less attractive cousin. He was aware of what was said behind his back. Joining a religious order didn't make him naïve.

Or stupid.

Truthfully, Dito wasn't too thrilled about having another male cousin. Bad enough that Tita Alma's son was fitter and taller than him and Ricky—now there was this guy.

Hugo said he was in Manila to see Aba Fatimah. She was getting old, and he wanted to meet her. He felt it important to understand his roots.

Ricky grinned. He knew exactly what cousin *Oo-goh* meant.

But for some reason—Hugo told them—his mother Cova tried to talk him out of it.

So, he lied to her and pretended he was in Ibiza.

'That's where my sister Pili was a few months ago,' Ricky muttered. 'Probably slept with half the island. No clue where she is now though.' He took a swig of his newly served glass of whisky.

Dito shook his head, signalling Hugo not to ask any questions.

'Tell us more about your family. Do you have siblings?' Dito redirected the conversation.

'Yes, two sisters,' Hugo replied. 'They're adopted.'

Oh!—Ricky thought, the alcohol churning in his head. 'Are they hot?'

'Dude,' Dito kicked him under the table.

'What? If they're adopted, it's not incest, right?'

Hugo wasn't sure he understood. 'Does everything come down to sex here?'

'Of course,' Ricky said a little too loudly, too quickly. It made the almost-ordained Dito shift uncomfortably in his seat.

'Doesn't it always come down to sex—anywhere in the world?' Ricky went on. 'It's taboo in so many cultures. And for us Catholics— in how many ways is it off limits? Eh, Dito?'

Dito gulped, hoping Ricky only addressed him because of his impending ordination.

'Primos, what's forbidden is seductive,' Ricky paused for dramatic effect. 'Right, Dits?'

No response, so he went on.

'And once seduced, you're owned. It becomes all you can think about. You are a man possessed.'

A darkness glazed over Ricky's eyes.

'Eh, are we still talking about sex?' Hugo asked, lightly.

'Sex, drugs, death—power—it's all the same,' Ricky sneered.

'You left out rock and roll,' Dito muttered, drolly.

'Don't be trite, coño.'

'Wow, Rick, big word, paré—trite.'

Ricky tapped Dito's cheek a little harder than was playful.

Dito was used to it.

Hugo was not.

'So why haven't you come to Sombra?' Ricky turned his attention to the new guy.

'I did—yesterday,' Hugo said, 'but they didn't let me in.'

'What? That's crazy,' Ricky looked to Dito for agreement. 'We'll take you to Aba, no, Dits?'

'Uh, yeah, sure,' Dito replied, a little terrified at the prospect.

There must be a reason they hadn't heard about Hugo, or why he wasn't let into Sombra. Dito wasn't sure he wanted to know what it might be.

Chapter 24

La Reunión y la Oscuridad | **The Reunion and the Darkness** | Ang Muling Pagsasama-Sama at ang Kadiliman

'*Hay Moros en la costa,*' Doña Alma de Yrastegui lowered her voice to let her husband know that someone was approaching. The coast was no longer clear, and their conversation might be overheard.

'Seriously, Mom?' Núria admonished as she took her seat next to her father at the dining table. 'I can't believe you still say that when we know what it means. Defeats the purpose, no?'

She stirred the cup of coffee she made for herself, revelling in the tinny clinking sound of the teaspoon against her grandmother's china.

'Plus, it's 2010. That's just kinda rude'—*clink, clink, clink*, as if for emphasis—'and racist.'

Her father, Don Andy, grimaced, but that didn't stop her.

'I never understood how you all use that phrase considering who your mother is. How is Aba okay with that?'

Núria Yrastegui Castillo de Montijo stopped clinking her silver spoon against the porcelain cup and took a small sip of her coffee, fully aware she rankled her mother.

211

Doña Alma shut her eyes to keep from rolling them. As if on cue, Don Andy reached out to squeeze her hand.

Bathed in the soft glow of the morning sun streaming in, the three Yrasteguis looked like an ersatz holy trio in Sombra's massive dining room. Sitting wretchedly at one end of the long narra table, surrounded by empty chairs.

Like agnostic apostles too early to the Last Supper.

It was a common Spanish expression—there are Moors—i.e., Moros/Muslims—along the coast. Taken from a historical warning for Christian residents to prepare against an attack.

The Castillo de Montijo grandchildren heard it often through the years, each time they chanced upon their parents discussing 'grown-up' matters.

Such as when the Yrastegui sugar plantation was overrun by 'Challenges' in the 1970s and Don Andy was kidnapped by communist rebels.

Núria was only three or four, but she recalled a lot of Moros on the costa then.

Decades since and she was still unclear as to what went down during said 'Challenges'.

You see, in the Castillo family, there were many *delicate* issues that the 'adults' didn't want 'los críos'—the kids—to know. So, they whispered to each other in Spanish, not realising the *críos* eventually picked up smatterings of their 'secret' language.

Growing up, Núria felt that understanding the family history was like putting together a puzzle without knowing that many of its pieces were missing.

As she said earlier, it was 2010, the Castillo críos were in their thirties and forties. It was no longer cute—nor accurate—to see them as children.

And Núria had run out of patience for puzzles.

* * *

Like most men in his family, it could be said that the Reverend Dito Santos y Castillo de Montijo was used to stumbling around in the dark.

But this time, he was surprised by how it upset him.

'How long have you known about this?' he asked his cousin Ricky, who was leading them through Sombra's tunnels to their grandmother's room.

'A while, dude,' Ricky replied, distracted. He scanned the path ahead with the torch on his mobile phone. 'How did you not know?' he inquired, unperturbed.

Dito stopped in his tracks and adjusted the borrowed shirt he had on. He was uncomfortable enough wearing someone else's clothes, he didn't also need to feel out of place in his own home.

His teeth were clenched tighter than they normally were.

*Our Father—fiat voluntas tua—*A breath. *Thy will be done—*on earth as it is in heaven.

Exhale.

'How exactly was I going to know about this if you never told me?'

Ricky snorted, not realising how distressed his cousin was.

'It's no big deal, primo. My dad showed me—I think he was drunk—said I should know where this was—*just in case.* Whatever that meant.'

Ricky flashed his light to the left, then to his right. He wasn't going to admit being lost.

He hadn't used the tunnels in years, and after the night they had, he was still a bit shaken.

He turned to Dito briefly. They both looked ridiculous in the borrowed—*pastel-coloured!—*button-down shirts they were wearing.

Further behind, new cousin Hugo was snug in his lilac gingham.

*At least they're clean—*Ricky reminded himself, as he spun back around and led them forward.

Taking another deep breath, Dito readjusted his ill-fitting, honey melon shirt and trailed him.

* * *

A thin, young girl in a maid's uniform entered the dining room, interrupting the haloed family's silence.

She looked about fifteen and was carrying another platter of eggs from the kitchen.

Scrambled, this time.

Without making a sound, she set it down next to the collection of fried eggs, between the mound of garlic fried rice and the heap of sweet, cured pork.

It had been a while since Núria had a full-on Filipino breakfast, and she worried the food would get cold before she had a chance to dig in. Her mother, Doña Alma, was a stickler for everyone being seated before starting a meal.

Her father—the imperturbable Don Andy—was enjoying his second cup of hot chocolate.

Núria was on her second café con leche.

It was almost ten-thirty. They'd been at the table for over an hour.

Núria sighed, this was so like Tita Maca.

She was convinced that her mother's younger sister kept them waiting on purpose. It was the kind of subtle power play her aunt enjoyed.

Núria pointed this out to her mother on a previous occasion, but Doña Alma refused to believe that her sixty-year-old sister would be so petty.

'Don't be silly, hija,' Núria recalled her mother saying then.

Well, who's silly now? Núria rolled her eyes and sighed.

She and her parents left their suburban home before seven in the morning to beat holiday traffic and get to Sombra in time for this 'urgent' family breakfast.

With Christmas only weeks away, it could take more than two hours to travel ten kilometres—even on a Sunday.

That said, they arrived with minutes to spare.

The woman they came to meet, however, was late. Even though she lived in a comfortable suite—*upstairs!*

* * *

'Talk about a literal rite of passage,' Ricky recalled, snickering as they went. 'I'll never forget it—I just turned fourteen—Pop took me to White Stallions with some of his buddies.'

Ricky paused and shone his mobile light at Dito: 'Remember that place?'

No reply.

'First time I saw naked women,' Ricky declared. 'In the flesh, dudes! And I got to fu—'

'I don't care,' Dito cut him. 'Please stop talking about your dick already.' He trained his torch light on Ricky's face. 'Why didn't you tell me about these tunnels if you've known about them for—what—decades?'

'*Calma*, dude,' Ricky laughed at his cousin's discomfort. 'It was between me and my pop—"top secret", you know?'

He turned and started down the path again—'I presumed your dad would show it to you at some point. Like on your White Stallions night.'

'Is that a joke?' Dito was incredulous. 'You know my dad—when has he ever shared anything with me? Or taken me anywhere? He's always drunk, and treats me like I'm his biggest secret—the one thing he's ashamed of—'

Dito's voice cracked. Again, Ricky stopped to look at him.

Oh, dear God—his father couldn't find out how they spent the evening. His mother, Maca, would be even less thrilled.

Dito's chest tightened, and his heart sank to his stomach. He dropped his arm and the light from his mobile swung to the floor.

'Eh, primos, I think that's still the Tanduay talking, no?' Hugo suggested as he came up behind them.

It was potent, that local rum. He had it for the first time that night before. At Armario, the speakeasy. Well before—*everything else*—occurred.

Hugo Pérez-García Castillo de Montijo appreciated the smooth amber liquid, but not as much as Ricky and Dito seemed to. They drank it—literally—like water.

It was their chaser between shots of other spirits and beer, as if they were competing in an alcoholic Russian roulette.

Hugo began to think his newfound relatives might have a drinking problem. Which could explain why his mother never had anything stronger than iced tea.

When the bar closed, he suggested they sleep it off at his hotel, but that's when things went—askew.

¡Por Dios!—how he hoped his mother would not find out.

'How much further?' he asked, feeling a sourness climb his throat.

'Not far,' Ricky swore, checking another tunnel with the mobile torchlight.

All these hours later, sneaking in to see their grandmother no longer seemed like a good idea.

* * *

Bai Fatimah Suhaira binti Hadji Datu Khaled Talal Mohammed al-Hakim Al Abdullazuljani sat on her veranda staring blankly at her kingdom, lost in the familiar strains of an old ballad.

At eighty-seven, she lived much longer than she expected.

Much longer than she wanted.

She spent the last three decades a widow.

Soundlessly, the morning dimmed around her. A shadow began to steal across the yard.

It was raining the day she met her beloved.

He was emaciated, unconscious and bleeding.

¿De donde es?—she asked him where he was from. Never imagining how their fates would entwine.

Alhamdullilah, thank goodness she knew where the camp commander hid his monk fruit. He imported it especially from China.

She hadn't seen one since she left her childhood home.

'Like an egg, anak,' her mother showed her how to crack open the sacred fruit. 'Then throw it all into the pot of boiling water.'

It was the only way to extract the sweetness.

Mother—

Nearby, a nurse sat reading a gossip rag, her job reduced to making sure Doña Fatimah's old cassette player was on loop.

The señora's current favourite was a compilation from her granddaughter, Núria. Songs from a time before the War.

It was music Bai Fatimah was raised with, melodies she learned from her father.

He liked to sing, that much Doña Fatimah remembered. But she could no longer conjure up the timbre of his voice.

It was once the most comforting sound in the world.

Father—

He taught her how to play the piano. They had a grand one at the centre of their home. It was specially crafted for the esteemed datu—another present, like the fruit, from Chinese traders.

Oh, how her father liked the gentle melodies of Bach, Chopin, and Mozart. *Like raindrops on the ivory*—he used to say.

Fatimah preferred more vigorous pieces—like their traditional gong music—stirring, emotive, robust. Russian gypsy songs and Spanish flamenco. Rhapsodies that struck the keys like storms.

As a compromise, her father taught her the poppy song—a misleading, gut-wrenching tune purportedly about a flower. Its notes progressed like an approaching tempest on a scalding metal roof. In expert hands, a deluge of skilfully measured emotion.

Ka Timah played it often during the war. A favourite she shared with both her beloved and the Japanese commander.

She stopped playing piano when Iko died.

But on days like this, the tentative rhythm of the rain brought her back to her youth. When she was known as the blessed daughter of Datu Khaled.

To a time when the world was friendlier, and all her life stretched out before her.

On days like this, with the tap-tip-tippy-tapping of rain, she wondered where she'd be if she never met the gentle Spaniard.

Or, indeed, if she had stayed in her village in the southern islands.

What if she had married that boy Hatif and lived among her people?

Timah wondered how her old friend Lydia would have felt knowing she was really a princess.

As it was, after they moved into Sombra, Ka Lydia was never comfortable addressing her by name. Timah was a rich man's wife, and

Lydia and her husband Tining—the chiefs of their household staff. Servants who were part of the family.

It was not an uncommon arrangement in The Islands.

Fact: Fatimah missed her old companion.

After both their husbands died, the two battle-scarred women clung to each other's presence as reminders of what was. Once or twice, they even let themselves speak of regrets.

Fatimah had many but leaving her father's village wasn't among them.

However, her children—and Lydia's—were another matter.

She didn't worry too much about Alma. Her eldest daughter was always strong and evidently happy.

On the other hand, Maca laughed too much and too loudly. But the mirth never seemed to reach her eyes.

Cova—How she wished she knew more about her youngest daughter.

Covadonga used to call in secret and write her through Lydia, but she heard nothing since Lydia's death a few years back.

Fatimah never understood why Cova left Sombra. Surely her husband Cristóbal could have found work in Manila. Freddie—*so enterprising*—would have helped him.

And then, there was Julián. Her biggest regret of all.

Doña Fatimah shut her eyes. Allowing herself to be transported by nascent rain.

* * *

'Do you think my mom knows about this?' Dito wondered anxiously as he swept the dank corridor with his phone's torch.

Ricky truly couldn't believe his cousin lived in Sombra all his life and didn't know about the hidden passages. It's how they got into the house that morning undetected.

They were dropped off at Sombra's main gate, but Ricky led them around back near the river. To one of the estate's secret entrances. After the night they had, they couldn't have anyone in the house see them.

'I presume so, no?' Ricky replied, trying again to regain his bearings. 'Unless—only the men in the family needed secret portals— *you know*—to let their playthings in and out.'

'Was Abuelo Federico that type of man?' Hugo, bringing up the rear, was astounded.

'What? No!' Ricky spat out. 'No way,' he repeated more calmly. 'My dad and Dito's dad—for sure, but not Abu Federico.'

'At least not the way everyone talks about him,' Dito mumbled. 'People tend to romanticise the past—'

'Tio Julián doesn't seem the type either,' Hugo mused.

'Who?' Dito aimed his torchlight at the new guy's face.

There was a sudden clap of thunder.

Deep within Sombra's walls, it reverberated like a peculiar, muffled *snap*.

'Puta!' Ricky jumped.

Another strangled crack—snap, snap—and the fevered scurrying of lizard feet.

Terrified, Ricky shut his eyes.

'Wait—' then abruptly flashed them open. 'Julián?' he repeated the name. 'I think I remember.'

* * *

Unperturbed by the rain, Núria stared at the grated cheese on top of the fluffy *ensaimada*—it stopped melting. The toasted sweetbread had been on the table so long it grew cold.

Fricking Tita Maca.

She likely knew why Núria's parents wanted to see her and was putting off what was sure to be an awkward conversation.

Núria wouldn't miss it for the world. Her sister Ximena called the night before from Gaza—it was not going to be a pleasant meal.

Not that their increasingly infrequent visits to Sombra were pleasant any more.

It hadn't been for years.

* * *

In the dark labyrinth, Ricky flashed his torch from one cousin to the other as rain intensified its muted dance on Sombra's roof.

The growing hum-thrum-drumming awakened his memories.

'There was a guy here—years ago. I hadn't seen him before—or since, I think. Wait, another time—I was up a tree? . . . Saw a man with Aba in the garden. Damn, I can't really remember. But that one time—your mom was super pissed,' he told Dito.

Then, he turned to Hugo.

'And—your mom, too. I think it was her. Everyone was upset. It was around Christmas, like now. I'm sure of it. It didn't used to rain in December, but it rained then. I remember crying—my dad got me the entire Playmobil pirate set—and an Instamatic camera with a built-in flash—just so I wouldn't tell anyone what I saw. Yeah, Juli. I think they called him—Juli.'

'I never heard of a Tito Julián—or a puto Juli. Shit! Why am I always the last to know?' Dito clenched his fists hoping to stop his tears.

Hugo didn't realize he was opening a can of worms.

Such was the danger of not being raised around family—you didn't learn the rules. What to say, what not to say. What to ignore, what to believe, how to pretend.

The events of the previous evening fast-tracked a fraternal bond among the cousins, but it wouldn't make up for the missing years.

Frankly, Hugo didn't know much about the family history either, but he was certain his mother had an older brother named Julián.

And Tio Julián lived in Boston.

How was it that his cousins had no idea?

* * *

'I am so sorry I kept you waiting,' Doña Macarena de Santos entered the dining room as if she were an ancient Egyptian queen welcoming the emperor of Rome.

She took the seat at the head of the table.

Bulbous South Sea pearls dangled from her ears like miniature chandeliers, and multiple strands of the expensive gem were festooned around her neck.

She wore a diamond-encrusted watch and a Chinese silk top that Núria swore she saw at the bargain market. A shoppers' paradise—a feast of fakes and imitations—that her aunt would never admit to visiting.

Núria didn't put it past her mother's sister to pass off knockoffs as branded items. Funnily enough, her aunt Maca was the only one at the table who even cared about labels.

'Núria,' her father said quietly, indicating she should get up and greet her aunt with a kiss. *As if she wouldn't*—Núria and her siblings were raised properly. She would never give this woman the satisfaction of having something to criticize Alma for by being remiss in her manners.

'Morning, Tita Maca.'

'Hija,' Maca gave her niece the most cloying of smiles and waved her back to her seat. 'Shall we? Manny will be late, and the boys are likely still asleep. You know how it is—Sundays.'

No one said a word.

Núria reached for the food and made fast work of the pork *tocino*.

'I'll get right to it,' Alma began. 'Ximena called from Gaza last night—did you catch her on TV? She was reporting live all evening because of those awful rocket strikes. So terrible the things she has to witness.'

Maca smiled politely and shook her head.

'Sorry, I was busy supporting Manny in his pre-campaign for the congressman. They were at the Sunshine Stadium and I had to make sure it looked ok on TV. I tell you, what a crowd—that Brother Sunshine is so popular, and he chose to endorse Mikey—*pero oye*,' she lowered her voice dramatically, as if to reveal a state secret.

'Guess who was there? On stage!' She didn't wait for a reply— 'Lulu, *la loca*.'

'What do you mean?' Andy inquired after consuming his fifth hot-chocolate-dipped churro. 'Luísa was campaigning?' He ignored the derogatory nickname Maca used and hoped the sisters-in-law might be on the same page for once.

'Por Dios, of course not,' Maca laughed at the suggestion. 'Lulu was there, as in she was part of his congregation. What do they call themselves? Sunbeams? Sunrays?'

'What?' Alma didn't think there was anything that could still shock her about Freddie's wife, but she was wrong. She did try with the woman but found her wanting. She had no conversation, no intellectual pursuits, and she only seemed to care about something if it directly affected her.

At some point, it seemed that no longer included her own children.

Which was why Alma always stepped in—from Fáti and her divorce to Pili and her exploits.

Then, of course, there was Ricky and his tragic drug problem.

Those poor kids—Alma thought. *Ay, Freddie*—

Freddie!—Of course! That's why she called this meeting.

* * *

Doña Fatimah didn't see the wall in her bedroom slip open. Or the mad tumble of haphazard boys falling through.

The lads shushed their grandmother's nurse and snuck over to the veranda as quietly as they could. The booming rain was redolent of resonant gongs.

'Aba?' a familiar voice called above her nostalgia. 'There's someone here to see you.'

Fatimah couldn't believe her eyes. Freddie's and Maca's boys were standing before her with another young man who looked so much like Julián.

Well, Julián—if he were a little more—Islander.

She lifted her arms as if they were made of lead. The dusky young man came forward to grasp them.

'Julián?' she whispered.

'No, Aba,' Hugo replied gently, using the term of endearment for the first time. '*Soy* Hugo. Cova's son.'

* * *

'Why didn't you tell me about Freddie?' Alma demanded.

'What about Freddie?' Maca retorted.

'Where is he?'

'Oye, he's a grown-up—*yo qué sé*—I'm not his *yaya*.'

'I'm not saying you're his nanny, Maca, but you live in the same house—you must know what's going on with each other, no?'

Maca pointed to her mouth to show her older sister that she was not about to be rude and speak while chewing food.

'You live in the same house'— *Que puñetera*—Little shit.

She hated how Alma always found a snide way to point out they were still living in Sombra, off Mami.

Alma took her sister's silence as an opportunity to fill it.

'Ximena's been talking to Ricky—he's very worried. He says Freddie's been missing for months. Months, Macarena—and you haven't noticed? Or—you know where he is and you're just not saying?' Alma posited.

That would be par for the course. Those two were always thick as thieves. Over the years, Alma heard a million rumours of what her brother was allegedly involved in, but Andy—always optimistic and generous—brushed the stories aside and assuaged her anxieties.

Alma chose to believe her husband and turned a blind eye. Ten-thousand dollars once falling out of Freddie's pocket notwithstanding. She opted to trust her brother then when he said it was from an investor.

It was easier that way.

'Just tell us,' Alma repeated, coolly, 'what is he hiding from?'

'Like I said—yo qué se—how should I know?' Maca put a pause in her indignation. 'Wait, why do you think he's in hiding?'

'What else could it be? I presume he's got himself in some sort of trouble—again.'

Maca hadn't considered that. She needed to think and looked away from the sanctimonious Yrastegui gaze—three of them staring at her expectantly like pontifical buffoons.

'Business wasn't going too well,' she muttered, 'but he didn't give me details.'

'Ximena said no one she contacted has heard from him—which, apparently, is unusual,' Alma explained. 'Why did you not tell me any of this, Maca? Did you not think it important? Or did you not think it important that I know?'

'Once and for all, Alma, not everything in this family is about you.'
Maca was exasperated. If their brother was missing, why was she being
made to feel as if she had done something wrong?

Andy put his hand over his wife's, knowing it would calm her.

He hated seeing the sisters like this. As they got older, they seemed
to disagree more frequently. Especially over family matters.

As always, Freddie engendered trouble. As if the rest of them didn't
already have other concerns.

'What does Luísa say about this?' Andy asked.

'Who cares?' Maca replied. 'Lulu doesn't even know what's
happening with her hair, what would she know about her husband?'

The young girl in the maid's uniform rushed back into the
dining room.

'Señora, Señora! Ang mga señorito—' she was catching her breath.

'*Ano yun,* Pepa?' Maca didn't have time for this. *Good God*—she
cursed—they don't make the help like they used to. This waif from
Tining and Lydia's hometown was practically useless, and she kept
swallowing her words, making her near impossible to understand.

Maybe she's just stupid—Maca considered. *Uneducated—and
dumb. Typical.*

'It's so hard to find good help these days,' she told Alma, conspiratorially.

Pepa repeated what she saw on the kitchen TV—'Ang mga
señorito—*na-aresto!*'

'What?' Alma nearly choked on her water.

Núria immediately checked her mobile for news alerts.

There it was, in less than 180 characters. Trending. *Fan-
fricking-tastic.*

Núria handed over her smartphone—'There are photos, Mom.'

This was a curveball even she didn't expect.

High-definition mugshots of her cousin—the señoritos—going
viral, which included their clearly printed—complete—names.

Federico Luís Acosta Castillo de Montijo III.

Armando Federico Castillo de Montijo Santos.

And—*Diego Federico Pérez-García Castillo de Montijo?*

Wait—Núria thought—*who's that?*

Chapter 25

Las Brasas | **The Embers** | Mga Baga

Micro News Feed

Philippines Trending Topics: Sunday, 5 Dec. 2010
#CASTILLOdeMONTIJO
#CastillosCastigated
#StickyRicky
#OopsIDidItAgain
#DurogDominion
#FatherDitoBa

Manila Tonight News @MNL2NYT • 12mins
BREAKING: **#CastillodeMontijo** Scions arrested for drinking alcohol outdoors & nudity. Defied public drinks ban, brawled with police. #CastillosCastigated #DurogDominion
Full story, images: btly./ph1

Replies: 260K | Likes: 480K | Reposts: 1.5M

KiligNaKolehiyala @KnK69 • 11mins

Replying to @MNLY2NYT

OMG they're so handsome! More pix pls! #CastillodeMontijo #StickyRicky #studs

Replies: 560 | Likes: 3,308 | Reposts: 2,150

Devout Follower of the Lord @SantoSantito • 11mins

Replying to @MNLY2NYT

Isn't one a priest? Shameful! #CastillodeMontijo #FatherDitoBa #CastillosCastigated

Replies: 10 | Likes: 40 | Reposts: 0

Writing My Life Away @JournoWannaBe • 10mins

Replying to @MNLY2NYT

How is this news?! Who cares abt d rich boys? People are getting killed by state actors & this is ur headline?! #CastillodeMontijo #DurogDominion #DeadDemocracy

Replies: 0 | Likes: 3 | Reposts: 0

Money Money MamSir @3MShady • 10mins

Replying to @MNLY2NYT @KnK69

Any1 hv pix of #StickyRicky nekkid? Did he bare all? Share *naman dyan*! #CastillodeMontijo #HubbaHubba #TrickyDicky #fullfrontal

Replies: 790 | Likes: 5,378 | Reposts: 2,016

Motorin' Mother @Lurker562 • 9mins

Replying to @MNLY2NYT @SantoSantito @KnK69

So much for rehab! Poor guys. Let's pray for them. Who's the other boy? #CastillodeMontijo #NewGuy #relapse #OopsIDidItAgain

Replies: 19 | Likes: 28 | Reposts: 15

Flip Island Fraternist @ManilaBoi71 • 8mins

Replying to @MNLY2NYT @Lurker562 @SantoSantito @KnK69

I hope dey rot in jail! Dey $houldn't be exemPt frm d rule$ ju$t cuz dey rich.
#CastillodeMontijo #CastillosCastigated #DurogDominion

Replies: 753 | Likes: 1,208 | Reposts: 1,516

Fans of Facundo @Durog4Evr • 8mins

Replying to @MNLY2NYT @ManilaBoi71 @Lurker562 @SantoSantito @KnK69

Bet they were high. Why weren't they shot? Kill them all! Druggies!!
#CastillodeMontijo #DurogDominion #PapaCanUsaveMe #unfairtreatment

Replies: 69 | Likes: 58 | Reposts: 109

Hope de la Cruz @FilipinasForJustice • 7mins

Replying   to   @MNLY2NYT   @ManilaBoi71   @Durog4Evr
@SantoSantito

I'm praying for u. Dat language is not necessary. No trial, no justice. God bless.
#CastillodeMontijo   #CastillosCastigated   #DurogDominion
#humanrights

Replies: 3 | Likes: 1 | Reposts: 6

Brown Man Standing @BMSgwaping • 7mins

Replying to @MNLY2NYT @JournoWannaBe @ManilaBoi71
@Durog4Evr

Who are these peeps anyway? Why are we subjugated to Tisoys—
bcuz dey whiter than us? #CastillodeMontijo #CastillosCastigated
#colonialmentality

Replies: 9 | Likes: 89 | Reposts: 10

Up In Arms for Country @DurogDynamos1010 • 6mins

Replying   to   @MNLY2NYT   @ManilaBoi71   @Durog4Evr
@SantoSantito @BMSgwaping

Dat family is corrupt! Dirty money! Mafia! Only way to get rich here. $ystem must change! Thank God for #DurogDominion!
#CastillodeMontijo #CastillosCastigated

Replies: 3,705 | Likes: 21,508 | Reposts: 51,760

Nimfo Naypi @MadamDutdutan • 4mins

Replying to @MNLY2NYT @KnK69 @3MShady @Lurker562 @SantoSantito @BMSgwaping @FilipinasForJustice @DurogDynamos1010

Send me PM. I have close-up of Ricky's 'tisoy manhood. *Indays—*it's B*G! <3 (1)
#CastillodeMontijo #CastilloCock #StickyRicky #OopsIDidItAgain

Replies: 907 | Likes: 10,568 | Reposts: 7,516

Chapter 26

El Desenredo | **The Unravelling** | Ang Pagtatastas

'Unbelievable,' Doña Alma handed the phone back to her daughter. 'Can't you keep this house in order, Macarena? I have tried not to say anything, but you haven't even decorated for Christmas, and it's almost the 25th—'

'Don't come here and judge me,' Maca aimed to soften her statement with a false grin. 'This doesn't concern you—they're not your children.'

'Precisely,' Alma asserted without raising her voice. 'My son is at Wharton getting his MBA. And yours—the priest—is getting arrested.'

Maca seethed. She didn't need this in her own home.

She picked up her smartphone and scoured her alerts. 'Let's just be grateful it isn't drug related.'

Unnoticed, the morning light vanished from the windows. Expunged by a sudden heavy downpour.

As the family sat there wordlessly scanning their mobiles, the young maid switched on the lights.

The chandeliers—a few bulbs out—threw a pale, tired glow over the room.

'Seems they were drunk,' Maca surmised from her newsfeed. 'I'm sure it was Ricky's idea. Walking the streets with alcohol has been banned in certain areas—he probably didn't know, being away in rehab all this time. Ay, my poor Dito. Nothing to get hysterical about. Locking them up for the night should teach them a lesson.'

Andy rose, wanting to be helpful. 'I'll go get them from the station.'

He bent and kissed his wife's forehead, squeezing her shoulder before leaving the table.

Núria didn't know whether to accompany her father or stay for the bout of the century.

'Manny can't be tainted with this,' Maca clucked. 'And that boy is not coming here.'

Núria stayed and poured herself a cup of cocoa.

'What boy? Cova's son? He has every right to be here,' Alma reminded her sister.

It surprised Núria to know that her mother had news of her enigmatic aunt in Spain.

'After everything that woman did?' Maca shook her head.

There was a flash of lightning—and the skies rumbled.

'That was over thirty years ago, Maca. And as I recall, you drove her out,' Alma stated.

Maca laughed. 'Ay, Almudena, that woman *left*. She made that ridiculous accusation, then ran away. Like you all have. You. All. Leave. I'm the one left here—taking care of Mami— dealing with reality.'

The maid returned with a tray full of dishes. She made to set a few more places at the table.

'Pepa, *ano yan*?' Maca told the young girl to leave it be—no one else was expected at this galling reunion.

'*Sabi po ni*, Señora—'

The maid's meek reply—barely audible over the rain—shocked them. Their mother was coming down for her meal. Doña Fatimah hadn't done that in years.

And apparently, she had company.

Maca should've realized the day would go to hell. It always did when the magnificent Almudena was involved.

Fact: Sombra was *Maca's* domain. *She* was in charge.

But matters seemed to be cascading out of control. Freddie was missing, the boys were in jail—and her mother was suddenly coming down to the table for brunch.

She didn't like it.

Núria hid her smile in a cup of cocoa.

* * *

Out on the veranda, surrounded by her grandsons, Doña Fatimah was speechless. Her tears speaking for all the years gone by.

As the rain beat like gongs a cadenced *kulintang*, she let Hugo paint her scenes of life in Spain. Each stroke slashed a deeper wound into her soul.

'Where is she?' From the bedroom, her daughter's voice pierced through their tender tableau.

More voices—then, a flurry of advancing footsteps.

In the commotion, the three boys rose to stand behind their Aba.

'Mami?' Alma was first to come upon them. Followed by Maca, gawping angrily.

'Hi Aba,' Núria pushed past her irate aunt to kiss her grandmother. Then, she grinned playfully at the rank and file of cousins. They looked like startled sentries assembled around their queen. 'Good morning, boys.'

'Núria.' Her mother, Alma—*the killjoy*.

'What are you doing here?' Maca's rage finally found its words, but she didn't dare direct it at her mother.

'G'morning, Mom,' Dito replied sheepishly, praying no one knew about their evening misadventure.

What a circus—Nuria thought of her relatives. Acrobats trying not to tip the balance.

* * *

Downstairs, Pepa ran out the front door to respond to the buzzer. Someone was at the gate and there was no longer a security guard to let them through. There hadn't been a guard on duty in quite a while.

Señora Maca had cut back on Sombra's staff.

Not that Pepa was complaining about the extra work. She was glad to still have a job and a place to live.

She felt her pocket for her good luck charm—a golden medallion she got from her elders. She gave it a rub before opening her tattered umbrella.

It was a long way to the gate—on foot—in the rain.

'Freddie Castillo?'—two men confronted her as she cracked open the pedestrian door.

A third man held a massive golf umbrella over their heads.

Behind them, two dark-coloured, heavily tinted SUVs were waiting. Their engines running, and their wipers at top speed.

'He's not here, po,' Pepa replied respectfully in the vernacular.

'When will he be back?' the stouter man growled.

She scratched her head. 'I don't know, sir.' Was she expected to be her master's keeper?

'You tell him the Suarez brothers sent us. He will know who we are.'

Pepa nodded, nervously.

'And tell him we're not as stupid as he thought.' The balder one ripped up some papers in her face.

It terrified her. Exactly as he intended.

Just then, returning from his jaunt to the police station, Andy's car pulled up to the gate from Calle Sombra. He stepped out and approached the men towering over the shivering Pepa.

'Can I help you?' he asked, opening his own umbrella.

They glared at him through dark glasses—then, backed down.

'We're here for Freddie,' the men stated, almost in unison.

'I see, but he's not here right now,' Andy replied, calmly moving closer to Pepa.

The men looked back at their heavily tinted vehicles.

'Can we give him a message?' Andy's voice was steady.

The bald one spat on the ground as the other one answered. 'Tell him we know the papers were faked. We want our money back or we're going to be forced to take what's ours.'

'I'm sorry, papers?' Andy wondered what they meant.

'The house,' the bald one said, after spitting. 'He sold it to us for three hundred million pesos.'

'Which house?' Andy looked from one visitor to the other.

They laughed. Then, pointed at Sombra.

* * *

Three generations of Castillos were gathered in potent silence on the matriarch's veranda.

On the cassette player, another Spanish classic began to throb with the rain.

Doña Fatimah steeled her gaze on her daughters. Neither dared speak nor look directly at her.

Alma was trying not to stare at Cova's son.

Maca tried not to slap her own son in the face.

Núria was dying to pepper them all with questions.

The boys tried their best not to look like chumps.

The nurse broke their stalemate with a message—Andy had returned and would wait for the señoras downstairs.

* * *

'Firstly, the boys were not at the precinct,' Andy started once his wife and her sister were seated.

The adults were back in the dining room, where the food on the table had cooled.

'The police said it was some sort of misunderstanding. The boys were released before I got there—'

'We know,' Maca snapped, impatient. 'The children are upstairs with Mami.'

'Oh?' Andy glanced at his wife. She nodded a weary affirmation.

'Bueno, así que no hay Moros en la costa'—he rejoined, wiping his brow—'on to a more pressing matter.'

Assured that there were no eavesdroppers, Andy recounted his exchange with the men at the gate. All the while, laying bits of paper on the table. Muddy remnants of the visitors' ripped up documents.

'How could you hide this from me, Macarena?' Alma was alarmed.

'Why do you always presume the worst of us?' Maca countered.

Alma glanced at Andy in mute exasperation. He said nothing as he wiped his glasses on a table napkin.

'I'm not hiding anything,' Maca was adamant. 'And poor Freddie has done so much for this family—'

'So why do those men think they own the house?'

'I have no idea!' Maca hated it when Alma's indignation was well-founded.

'Okay, okay,' Andy calmly put his glasses back on. 'I'm sure there's a perfectly logical explanation for all this.'

He said it without quite believing it.

'Maybe Mami gave him the deed to the house to use as collateral for a loan—or something,' Maca knew that wasn't likely to be true.

'So, he goes and sells it to those goons?' Alma wondered how she got saddled with such siblings.

'I'm sure those men are just trying to fleece him,' Maca insisted.

'Then how do you explain this?' Alma spotted something in the bits of paper. A name—a signature—that was legible through the dirt.

Maca shook her head the moment she saw it, unable to believe what her sister was insinuating.

'That must be a forgery,' Maca stated with bold assurance. There was no way her clever—*handsome*—husband would be so stupid.

'It seems Manny was a witness to this deal?' Andy read.

'That's a lie,' Maca wanted them to stop the persecution.

'Where is your husband this morning, Macarena?' Alma struck a nerve she knew her sister tried to shield.

'I told you he had a late night campaigning with those Sunbeams. He needs his rest.' She didn't mention he was *resting* someplace else.

'These are extortionist ploys, Almudena, you should know that. People always want what they can't have. They can fake it all they want, but without the *real* papers, they have no actual claim.'

'Are you kidding?' Alma countered. 'This is the Philippines—I know people who have had their houses sold from under them with less.'

'Okay, okay,' Andy again tried to calm the sisters. 'Maybe Manny's contacts can help us locate Freddie. We must get to the bottom of this— and find the original deed to Sombra—before those men return—'

'Manny has tried, you know?' Maca needed to make it clear. 'But there's nothing on Freddie. His phone is off—he can't be tracked— and no one has seen him. He wouldn't just vanish without telling me unless he had no recourse—'

'Where is Luísa?' Andy wondered, since no one else did. 'And where would Fred hide that much money without a bank account?'

'What do you mean?' Maca wasn't pleased that she had to ask.

'No bank will touch him or his business,' Andy stated, then he saw the look of horror on Alma's face. He softened his tone—'That's only what I hear.'

'*Cuentos*. Rumours. All lies,' Maca concluded. 'People are just jealous.'

But Andy knew it was more than gossip. He had tried—as long as he could—to protect his wife from her brother's duplicity.

From the kitchen, Pepa peeked at the diners. Uncertain if she should serve them any more food.

'How did he expect to get away with this?' Alma was stupefied. 'He fakes the sale, takes the cash—and disappears?'

They sat at the table in shared but silent dread.

The breakfast spread before them, cold and covered in congealed oil.

Outside, the rain—a clap of thunder—kept steady vigil.

And a gecko began to wail out of turn.

* * *

'Mom! Mom!' Núria thundered into their ossified quiet with more disquieting news.

'Aba—Aba,' she repeated like a toddler just learning to speak. 'Hurry, hurry!'

By the time they got to Doña Fatimah's room, she was gone.

Just like that.

Exactly like Don Federico.

PART IV

EXPOSURE

Chapter 27

El Silencio y la Actuación | **The Silence and the Performance** | Ang Katahimikan at ang Pagganap

Julián Castillo always jumped when the phone rang in the middle of the night. Certain it would be news he didn't want to hear.

More than forty years had passed since he left Manila, but he still felt as if he occupied someone else's life and his own would one day call to reclaim him.

Forty years, and he still felt like a fraud.

In the early hours—that fifth of December in 2010—his sister Cova woke him with a call from Spain. She was his only real link to 'family'. The word had taken on a bitter taste.

He and Cova stayed in touch after the—*violation.*

Despite their age difference—seven years—they were the only ones among the siblings who understood each other. Both having been driven away from home.

Maca and Freddie were no longer the playful children he remembered. And Alma—well, Alma always stood alone.

So, it was Cova who bothered to ring Julián.

She had just sat down to breakfast when she heard from Hugo. Turned out her son wasn't in Ibiza like he first told her.

It was a very brief transcontinental conversation.

Their mother was gone. There was not much else to say.

Julián was determined to make the funeral. He still regretted being absent for his father's.

But back then, he had no choice. Had he left—without a green card—he could not have returned to the States.

Fact: Julián Castillo de Montijo overstayed his visitor's visa. Like many other desperate—*undocumented*—migrants.

It was the only way to protect his family. He couldn't taint them with his secrets.

Working in restaurant kitchens and office backrooms, Julián paid for night school—part-time—and got his degree.

Eventually, he found someone to marry. Thanks to her, he was granted residency. The precious US green card.

Which meant that five years after his father's death—fifteen years since he first left The Islands—Julián could finally slip back to Manila and see his widowed mother.

It was 1981. How Sombra had changed.

How his siblings had—evolved.

That was when he stumbled on to that animal raping Cova in the tunnels.

Family.

The word turned his stomach.

As quietly as he could after his sister's call, Julián put on his robe and made his way—in the dark—from the bedroom to the kitchen. Focused on brewing himself a pot of ginger tea.

By the silver sheen of the winter night outside his window, he filled the kettle with water from the tap.

In those early hours, a snowstorm swirled around the brownstone.

Mechanically, Julián took an empty mug from the cabinet and reached into a drawer for his processed monk fruit sweetener—*damn*—empty, too.

He left the pack on the counter, then sat at the table with his mug.

Waiting for water to boil.

* * *

It was so hot that afternoon that steam rose from the asphalt. His sneakers stuck to the pavement as they played hoops.

He remembered sweat trickling down his bottle of ice-cold soda, and he invited his friends for a swim right after school.

Tino was already home from his classes when they got to Sombra. Clearing leaves from the pool, barefoot and in shorts.

It's what Tino did most afternoons. When he wasn't helping the gardeners weed the lawn or the drivers clean the cars.

They were like brothers—Julián and Tino—since they were children. Extended family, living in Sombra, with all their siblings. Safe in a carefree kingdom all their own.

Except the Castillos had the big rooms in the castle, and Tino and his little sister, Nena, shared a smaller room—near the kitchen— for staff.

Tino and Nena were the only children of Mang Tining and Manang Lydia—Julián's parents' oldest friends. They ran the estate.

It made no difference to Julián that they were employees. They were—*family*.

That molten afternoon of liquified pavements, Juli and Tino played football in Sombra's garden with Julián's classmates—the sons of other wealthy clans.

Tino was always shy around those boys, but he got into the game and forgot that he was only barefoot because his lone pair of slippers was broken.

The boys played a heated match. Chasing each other, kicking and laughing.

By afternoon's end, they were all barefoot, shirtless and in shorts.

At one point, Julián fell over on the poolside pebbles.

Tino was atop him, playfully pinning him down.

In the tussle, Julián felt a blade against his back. He froze—then realized it wasn't a blade at all.

Tino moved.

Julián squirmed beneath him.

He felt the sweat from Tino's chest slide down his back.

In Juli's shorts, his own dagger throbbed erect.

They were fifteen.

Juli blamed the hot Manila weather.

They jumped into the pool—Tino, too—and showed off their form in strokes.

* * *

The kettle sang, startling Julián back to his Boston brownstone.

It was cold. His joints hurt. The snow still swirled.

He dug his feet into his sheepskin slippers and pulled his robe tighter around his body.

In the silver darkness, he rose slowly from the kitchen table.

He reached for a teabag and poured hot water into his mug.

* * *

It was fifty years since Tino first kissed him.

Or did he kiss Tino? Julián really wasn't sure.

They were sixteen. It didn't matter who did what—just that it happened.

They kissed, and things changed evermore.

* * *

In Boston, a sallow light came on in the kitchen.

'Are you okay?'

Julián nodded, raising his steaming mug.

'Just made tea. Couldn't sleep. Go back to bed.'

A look of concern.

'Don't worry,' Julián assured, 'I'll be there shortly.'

He breathed in his tea.

The smell of ginger brought him home.

* * *

Juli and Tino were always close, that was no secret. But they both knew that not all 'best friends' did what they did when alone.

They wrestled—and they grappled—and they—*played*.

They were—*best friends.*

They had no other term for what they were.

* * *

After high school, Julián was sent to America for an Ivy League education. It was the sixties—they were wealthy—the world was waiting.

He posted letters and photos back to Tino. Wanting to share his new adventures with the only person—besides blood relatives—whom he trusted.

They were, after all, the best of friends.

Juli wrote Tino that no one knew about the Castillos in America. They'd never heard of Sombra, nor obliged him to *be* a certain way.

Among strangers in a new country, Julián didn't feel like he was being gauged. He was himself, and not an idealised—or resented—Castillo de Montijo princeling.

Before then, Juli only felt like that with Tino.

But Tino began to see him as the master-in-waiting.

'Master' Julián only returned to Manila in the summer. Tino was always too busy with chores to—*play*.

Tino told Juli to go swim with his old schoolmates. Or write letters to his new blonde friend, Sarah.

Tino was certain that Julián had better things to do than hang out with the dark-skinned boy who cleaned his pool.

He was certain Julián would find a new best friend.

One day—two summers later—Juli was at the polo club with Don Federico. Having lunch with other rich men and their sons.

Tino was home, as of course was expected. Waiting for Juli with a bottle of rum.

He reread the letters full of promises about their special friendship. That Tommy meant nothing to Juli, and he never kissed a girl. Only Tino—Juli wrote—touched his soul.

Gulping the rum, Tino replayed their kisses. Wishing they didn't have to keep it secret.

He was so tired of feeling bad because of Juli.

He was tired of feeling like his life was—*less.*

He was angry and depressed. And alone.

That afternoon, Tino trashed the tool shed in the yard that he just tidied.

He yanked out flowers and peed in the pool.

He also stumbled on the gardener's prized *paltik.*

The home-made gun was wrapped in rags and stashed by a sack of fertiliser. No one would have found it—had they not known where to look.

When Julián returned to Sombra that afternoon, he went straight to his room—and seated on the floor, by the bed, Tino was crying.

The lights were off. He smelled of earth.

He finished the rum.

'Enjoy your lunch?' Tino drawled as Julián switched on a lamp.

'Are you drunk?' Juli's tone was even, not unlike his father's.

'Does it matter?' Tino struggled to stand.

Julián reached over to help him up.

''Tangina, really?' Tino tried not to raise his voice as he pushed Juli away.

'What's wrong?'

'What's wrong, you ask?'

'You're worrying me, Tino.'

'About time.'

'Buddy—'

'Don't *buddy* me, you asshole.'

Julián was shocked. He'd never seen Tino so—upset.

Still clutching the rum, Tino began to pace the room like an injured dog.

'What's the matter, Tino? You're scaring me—'

'How do you do it? You go on with your days—like nothing—'

'Not so loud, Tino.'

'Ah, not—so—loud. That's the fucking problem. We are never—loud—Julián.' Tino stopped pacing and scowled. 'We kiss we fuck—we fight—in the shadows. Like that stupid couple in the 'tang-inang musical you like so much—singing foolishly about hiding from the lecheng moon! I can't any more. We're sick.'

'Tino, oye, please,' Julián lowered his voice. He didn't know who was home and didn't want to attract attention.

'We're not—sick, Tino. We just—can't behave a certain way in public.'

'Why?'

'Because it's—unacceptable.'

'Puta, paré—unacceptable. So, what do we do? *Ganito nalang?* Forever be in hiding?'

'I suppose so. I mean, I don't know.'

'You leave—you go off and leave me—and I have to stay here—suffocating—dying—without you.'

Julián was silent for a breath.

'You want to come with me?' He would say anything to make his friend feel better.

'How? How will I go with you, Juli? I am not a rich man's son—there is no escape for me.'

Julián never saw it that way.

'You can run, Juli, to your classes in D.C., or New York, or wherever you are—while I stay here like your 'tang-inang mistress, waiting for you to take a break from your real life and pay me some attention.'

'I send you letters—'

'Consolation prizes! I don't care about your friends Tommy and Michael and Peggy. Do they know about me?'

Julián was confounded.

'Do they know about me?' Tino's voice cracked.

'Yes.'

'What have you told them?' Tino taunted.

Julián stared at him.

'Have you told them that I suck you off?'

'Tino.'

'Have you told them you suck me off?'

'Tino, don't talk like that, please.'

'Why? Make you uncomfortable? Too uncouth for the great Julián Fernando Castillo de Montijo? *Bakla ka*, Julián. A faggot—like me. This is your fault—'

'Hush, Tino, hush. We were just boys—*playing*. Life doesn't have to change because of a few—trysts.'

Tino's heart exploded into weighty shrapnel. Julián heard the pieces clatter to the floor.

He shook his head.

'Let me speak to my father,' Julián offered. 'I'll ask him to let you come to the States with me—we can both study there—I'm sure he will think it's a great idea—'

'What are you talking about? Do you really think the son of your maid will be sent to study with you in your Ivy League school?'

Julián felt the hot sting of iron in his chest. He'd never thought of Tino that way. That 'maid' was Manang Lydia, his mother's closest— and only—real friend.

'Trust no one, Juli,' his mother Fatimah always told him. 'The only people you can rely on are in this house.'

'I am not your brother, Julián,' Tino spat on the floor. 'I am not your cousin. Apparently, I am nothing to you—except a boy you once *played* with. A boy no one can truly know about.'

'That's not what I meant, Tino.' Julián hated having caused such pain. 'I will speak to Papá, you don't have to feel this way. You are not the "maid's son" to me, you know your parents mean so much to mine—'

'Only because they fought the war together. It doesn't make them equals, Julián. Your father pays them a monthly wage— that is all.'

Tino raised the empty bottle of rum to his mouth, then threw it on the carpet.

It landed with barely a sound.

Julián was not prepared for such a conversation.

Dusk began to whisper through the bedroom's wooden shutters. Stirring shadows that crept in with the fading sun.

Julián shone like a golden, sun-kissed dream—Tino shut his eyes, desperate to stop the pain.

He pulled out the paltik and put it against his brow.

'Tino!'

In the radiant haze, Juli rushed to wrestle away the gun.

They grappled. And they tussled.

A shot went off.

'No, no, no—'

Julián folded himself over his bleeding lover, cradling his head and kissing him where he could.

Moments later, his mother—Doña Fatimah—came upon them. She walked through a panel that swung open along his wall.

She was chasing a bang that echoed through the hidden corridor by her room.

Doña Fatimah feared the Moros had finally found him. That the rival tribe had come for her eldest child.

She feared it from the moment he was born—retribution—for the life that she had cost them. That boy, Tarek, whose defilement chased her from her home.

To her relief, there were no Moros in her son's room, but what Fatimah saw instead filled her with both dread—and wonder.

She didn't know what to make of the two boys on the floor.

'Julián?' her voice trembled.

She read the heartbreak in his eyes without a word.

'I tried to stop him, Mami,' her beautiful boy explained.

She nodded, not needing—nor wanting—to know the rest.

'I tried, Mami—but he—'

'Hush, hijo. Don't say anything. Just—hush.'

Fatimah's head spun. Her chest tightened.

She saw black.

She was glad her other children weren't home.

She felt for her father's ring—the well-worn braid of ivory, gold and silver—still a comfort on her finger after all the years.

She said a prayer to God—or Whomever might be listening. And pondered what to tell young Tino's parents.

Oh Lord, his parents!—Tining and Lydia survived the war, but losing a child would be an impossible battle to bear.

Once she calmed herself, Fatimah rang the kitchen on the intercom. Trusting that only another mother would not judge.

'Lydia, please come to Julián's room. I need . . . we need—to talk.'

On the floor, Julián wept inconsolably. Cradling Tino's body to his chest.

After a few interminable minutes, the bedroom door creaked open.

Lydia struggled to breathe at the sight of her son in a pool of blood. Transfixed by an indescribable pain.

'Tino!'

She took his lifeless body from Julián, hoping the power of her will would bring him back.

'Sorry, po, Manang Lydia, I'm so sorry,' Julián repeated. Convinced he was to blame for Tino's death.

Lydia said nothing through her tears.

Together—a lifetime later—Fatimah and Lydia cleaned the room in silence. Then they decided what best to tell their husbands. Not expecting the men to understand what—*transpired*—between their sons.

'Are you sure about this, Ka Timah?' Lydia was anxious. But she was also too ashamed of the truth.

Timah nodded. This was for the good of all.

Their crafted tale was that vengeful Moros came for Juli. Tino protected him and got shot in the chest.

Fact: This was not too far-fetched a story.

In The Islands, vicious rivalries between families could run for generations. Over anything from disrespect and honour to land and cattle.

'An eye for an eye, a tooth for a tooth' was the way of justice. Leaving many a clan blind and toothless.

So, Bai Fatimah told Iko they had to calm the blood feud, and it was best if Julián just—disappeared.

No police. No records. No investigation.

Again, not at all uncommon on the islands.

Desperate to protect his family, Don Federico smuggled their son on to a ship bound for Hong Kong. Money bought silence, and potential witnesses looked away.

The journey wasn't easy for Julián. The smell of hemp—and the sea—still made him sick.

From Hong Kong, Juli flew to California. To start afresh with a share of his father's fortune and an ache that turned his battered heart to stone.

They told him to lie low and avoid all Islanders, or anyone who might know where he was from.

They wished him well—his parents—and begged him not to return.

It was for his benefit—and the survival of the family.

It was the best that Doña Fatimah could do for her son. In Manila, he would be judged, and the family disgraced.

It was the best that Fatimah could do for her husband. Iko worked so hard to build their name—their reputation—and this would stain it.

In the years that followed, Doña Fatimah de Castillo did wonder if somewhere in her heart she must have known. Her beloved son Julián was—*different*. If she didn't see that, then what kind of mother was she?

But if she *knew*—and let it be, then she raised him—*incorrectly*.

Either way it was looked at, she had failed.

* * *

Tino was buried quietly in Lydia's home province. Far away from the city, with no link to the Castillos and Sombra.

Julián's siblings were only told that he had left, and that—from then on—they must never speak of him. They were teens but saw how the matter upset their parents, so they swore to not distress them again.

Tino's sister, Nena, was only ten. For her, it was simple: Her brother was a hero, and he was gone.

Juli's room was locked and shuttered to the light. That final day forever cloaked in gravid silence.

It was a secret the two mothers never spoke of. Just another of the many silences that bound them.

Don Federico felt both guilty and grateful. His son lived, while Tining and Lydia lost their boy.

He assured the couple that they'd be employed for life.

He sent their daughter to school—as he had done with Tino—and paid for everything else they needed.

His home would be their home until they died.

* * *

Morning broke in heavy concrete across Boston. An ashen light gaped through the naked brownstone window.

Julián was still seated at his kitchen table. Holding an undrunk mug of tea, grown stale and cold.

This was how he risked reliving it when he relived it. Which wasn't often in all the years gone by.

He recounted events in staid stops and starts. In sober images of calcified trauma—in black and white.

In stone and steel.

In hefty blocks of numbness.

With ginger tea—and his mother's ring around his finger.

She gave it to him before they sent him to Hong Kong.

To shield him—she had said—from all evil.

A well-worn braid of silver, ivory, and gold.

Julián Castillo was sixty-five years old that December morning Cova called. His hair was grey, his eyes were weary, his back was sore.

His life—as his mother feared—had not been simple. He got divorced—they stayed friends—he had no children.

Juli worked hard and locked away as much pain as he could.

He worked with numbers—an accountant—so as not to deal with people.

He hated attention—and carried his shame like a responsibility.

The braided ring did indeed protect him—from forgetting that he hurt the only people that he loved.

Oh, how his mother enjoyed Manang Lydia's iced hibiscus ginger tea. Especially sweetened with dried monk fruit stewed in the pot.

In the tropical summers, the jug of ruby liquid sweat profusely.

At his Boston window, the sun began to gasp for air.

Cova called—once again, it was time for a performance.

Their mother died.

It was time to go home.

Chapter 28

La Cabalgata de Navidad | **The Christmas Pageant** | Ang Pamaskong Prusisyon

The only thing Covadonga Castillo de Pérez-García recognised about Manila were the colourful fairy lights. Streaked throughout the city like sanding sugar on a garish cake.

They were draped on trees and outlined entire buildings. Glistening at night like electric rain or neon perspiration in tyrannical humidity.

Dios, it was hot—much hotter than Cova remembered.

There used to be a gentle breeze in December. Enough for sweaters, light cardigans, and knee-high socks. She was not prepared for the blistering evening.

Or the bedlam of garments that greeted them upon exiting the airport.

Through a wire fence, swarms of people in flipflops, discordant shorts and T-shirts waved and shouted at the new arrivals. *And madre mia, how they all pressed in.*

Cova was not prepared for the utter anarchy that accosted her when she stepped back into the life she'd left behind.

* * *

As they drove from the airport in the hotel's airconditioned Benz, she stared out silently at a slow parade of seasonally dressed shop windows.

Giant Santas. Candy canes. Snowmen. Reindeer. Gingerbread houses. Bells.

Jesus and three flamboyantly bejewelled Wise Men.

Sidewalks weren't spared the holiday treatment. Neither were the—usually ignored—traffic islands.

Bridges, roundabouts, and overpasses were also flecked in exuberant—*excessive*—displays of cheer.

It's just how Islanders did Christmas. Celebrating from September to January, it was the longest yuletide in the world.

'So much has changed,' her husband Cristóbal gushed. Wide-eyed and enthralled in the backseat beside her. There was so much more 'city' than he remembered.

The sweeping green spaces were gone. Overrun—like mould—by chaotic stacks of wood, metal, cinderblocks, and spears of glass. Obscured by massive billboards featuring foreign celebrities and local—*politicians?*—selling everything from condoms to hair plugs and skin bleaching products.

He gawked through the heavily tinted luxury car windows. Every inch so crammed that it blocked out the evening sky.

It took them nearly three hours to travel the seven kilometres from the international airport to the understated Tsang-Du Colony Hotel. Tucked within the new business district carved from an army base.

Cova hoped the boutique chain would be a quiet place to stay. She didn't want anyone knowing they were in the country.

Other than family, of course.

Alma offered them room in her house, but the suburbs were just too far in holiday traffic. And staying at Sombra was clearly not an option.

An elegantly dressed security guard let them in to the well-appointed lobby. But not before putting them through a full-body scanner, examining their bags, and reminding them to leave all weapons at the door.

Yes, indeed, it was a very different city—Cristóbal concluded.

Cova frowned. Nothing had changed in over thirty years.

* * *

It would not have been the first time that Macarena Castillo de Santos failed to hang Sombra's holiday lights. She barely bothered after Freddie lost his private island in '85.

Which was also around the time her husband Manny lost interest in being home.

The tiny turquoise lights went from being celebratory to mocking. Blinking reminders of their unacknowledged failures.

But this Christmas 2010 was going to be different. Maca and Alma agreed to decorate Sombra like when their father was alive—and the Castillos de Montijo would be merrier than they had been in years.

Aside from lights, there would be ornaments and lanterns and tinsel. Life-size figures of seasonal favourites and banks of artificial snow.

No one would know that the family was bereaved.

No one—but family—could know that Doña Fatimah was gone.

The sisters needed time to get family affairs in order. To sort finances, find lost documents and missing deeds. The essentials to protect what they owned. They worried about creditors and loan sharks, Freddie's enemies—and fraudulent 'friends'.

Like the men who came to visit earlier that week.

Maca was so afraid of losing Sombra that she let Alma make the decisions.

Not because Alma was smarter, but because—after all—she was the older sibling. And if things went wrong, it would be *her* fault.

'Señora,' the idiot maid was again troubling her for something.

'What now, Pepa?'

There weren't enough string lights. She needed money to get more from the store.

* * *

Dito Santos' hands trembled as he lit another candle in the chapel. He couldn't burn enough to pray for his Aba's soul.

He wished her peace.

He wished himself the same.

He was convinced they were the reason she was gone.

How it haunted him, the look on Aba's face when she breathed her last. Her eyes went wide, as if dismayed and horrified.

As if—in that split second before death—she saw the depths of their deceptions.

Dito felt responsible for her final expression.

So, there he was—in Sombra's dim, family chapel—alone.

Sort of.

Aba Fatimah was with him, lying before the altar—in a box.

He and Ricky snuck it in through the tunnels after dark. His mother insisted they not be seen bringing a coffin into Sombra.

Normally, his uncle Freddie would handle such a task, but no one had yet been able to reach him.

* * *

As they lugged the wooden coffin through the tunnels, Dito told Ricky he was certain they killed their Aba. They shocked her with that Hugo's presence. It made her sad, it made her emotional—it made her angry.

And it enraged his mother, Maca, beyond belief.

It was their fault—Dito repeated to Ricky—they triggered Aba's stroke.

Then, he paused, and altered what he said—'No, wait. This all on you, jackass.'

Had he not been carrying a coffin, Dito would've punched his cousin.

'If you didn't drag us to Armario that night, we wouldn't have met—*Oo-goh*—'

Ricky stopped walking, the puto coffin was heavy.

'Without Hugo, the night wouldn't have been such a disaster. We wouldn't have drunk too much, and you—maybe—would not have whipped out your puny dick at the cops!'

'Dito—'

'No, paré, I am so tired of your shit. We wound up in jail, man! Now look at us. We're smuggling a frickin' coffin into our own house. Putang ina!'

Ricky swore he heard Dito choke back a cry.

'Dits, Dits, look at me, primo.'

In the dank tunnel—the lights of which were reconnected for this very smuggling operation—the two cousins faced each other from opposite ends of a simple wooden coffin.

It weighed a lot more than expected.

'I'm sorry you got dragged into my, my—shit. Hey, at least I'm not on meth any more, right? I mean, I have a drink now and then, but I am trying to cut down, paré. I know how fucked up I was—'

'You're not the only one fucked up in this family, Ricky. Don't act like you have a monopoly on misery.'

Ricky was stunned—and chastised—by his younger cousin's—*candour*.

He wished he could be as honest in return.

But Ricky couldn't tell his cousin—the almost-priest—that cops followed them that night hoping to grab him.

He couldn't tell Dito that those officers moonlighted for one of Tukô's many rivals—an actor-turned-politician who owned casinos.

The cops knew Ricky was a druggie and tried to blackmail him—he'd be dead if he didn't do as they asked.

In exchange for his life—and his cousins' freedom—Ricky agreed to help them bait The Lizard.

Click, cluck.

'Great,' Dito sighed, startled. 'Last thing we needed—a puto gecko in the tunnel. That stupid clacking will echo around us like the theme from some horror film—'

Cluck, click.

Ricky froze. He couldn't help but think that Dito was right.

This was all his fault.

* * *

That evening in the chapel, Dito was on his knees praying a second rosary. Ignoring the din of his mother barking orders at the help outside.

He felt guilty for seeking solace in images of the actor Jon-Tee. Guilty that his grief whipped him to a frenzy.

If not for Ricky, there would be no need for absolute contrition.

If not for Ricky, on her last breath, Aba Fatimah might not have looked at him aghast.

* * *

As always, Luísa Acosta de Castillo wasn't sure what was going on. Her son bundled her into a borrowed car without explanation.

They hadn't seen each other in days.

'Is this Dito's, hijo, why are you in such a hurry?'

She stroked his arm, trying to get him to slow down.

'How did you find me?'

She was at Brother Sunshine's compound.

Not like she was difficult to find.

Luísa posted everything on social media. From the moment she woke up until returning to bed. She checked-in at every location, and geo-tagged every thought and activity. As if that were the only way to validate her existence.

Ricky wished he never taught her how to use social media.

'We need to get you home, Mom.'

She didn't understand. If her son meant Sombra, they both knew she was never welcome.

'There's a—family emergency.'

Luísa Acosta couldn't help her smile. Thrilled that—*at last*—she counted as family.

* * *

Julián Castillo de Montijo had just showered and changed when his sister arrived at the hotel. He gave her an hour to settle in before ringing her room.

She picked up immediately, jumpy from the second she landed.

'Cova? Are you ready?'

Cova and Juli were both at The Tsang-Du—the new hotel was owned by people they didn't know. And it was close to one of Sombra's hidden gateways.

'I can't do it, Juli, I just can't,' Cova implored. 'I can't go back into those tunnels.'

She lowered her voice as her husband Cristóbal came out of the bathroom. He presumed her tears were over her mother's death.

Cova went silent, Julián understood. They agreed that she should place a call to Alma.

Their sister would know what to do.

* * *

When Núria Yrastegui arrived at The Tsang-Du's basement carpark—which was selected as the meeting point because it was less exposed to prying eyes—there were two more people waiting for her than she expected. With their chauffeurs given the Christmas weekend off, her mother sent her to collect the visiting 'grown-up' siblings.

She immediately recognised Tita Cova. Her aunt looked like a younger version of her mother, Alma. With lighter hair, which was similarly—neatly—pulled into a ponytail.

The grey-haired man beside her aunt must be her uncle Julián, but Núria wasn't sure which of the two white men with them was Tito Cristóbal.

She looked again. And surmised it must be the tanned one. Broad-shouldered, smartly dressed, with twinkling eyes.

'You must be Núria,' her newfound uncle Juli offered his hand.

She took it, slightly awkward at such a business-like invitation.

'Oh my, you look just like your mother,' Cova smiled.

'I was about to say the same of you, Tita Cova.' Núria gave her aunt a careful hug. The woman looked so fragile and—*afflicted*.

'You might not remember Tito Cris?' Cova turned towards her husband.

The bronzed former athlete gave Núria a kiss on each cheek and a warm squeeze.

'And this is Greg,' said Tito Julián. 'My—partner.'

O-M-G—Núria tried not to look surprised. Another piece of the jagged family puzzle.

She shook Greg's hand and grinned wider than she had in days.

She couldn't wait to bring them back to Tita Maca.

* * *

Almudena Castillo de Yrastegui was on autopilot. She felt as if she had 'Grief' on speed-dial.

First, she lost her father, which—though years prior—felt like yesterday.

Next, Andy's parents passed away. One quickly followed by the other.

After that, her oldest friend died.

And then, her mother.

Truth be told, Almudena no longer knew what she was feeling. The past week was an out-of-body experience. Nothing in her life— or her upbringing—prepared her for having to hire an embalmer—in secret—and paying him a 'premium' so he would tell no one that they snuck him into Sombra to 'handle' the family matriarch. (Imagine the scandal if that got out.)

Maybe this was why people chewed betel nut!—Alma hadn't recognised herself in days.

She sat in Sombra's back porch nursing a glass of iced tea.

It was almost dinner time, but Maca was still in the garden ordering around what was left of Sombra's staff. They were hanging the last of the Christmas lanterns.

'That's it, Pepa, right there. No, a little to the left—the left, Pepa! Good God, don't you know your left from your right?'

Maca threw up her hands and returned to Alma in the porch. 'This is why these people never get ahead in life. And they move so slowly—¡Por Dios!—so lazy. At this rate, we'll never get dinner served on time.'

Alma said nothing. She knew not to engage in her sister's—drama.

'Oye, Maca,' she tried again, 'we can't have them stay in a hotel.' Her younger sister was stubborn, but so was she.

Especially when she knew that she was right. Which—as established—was always.

'This is their house, too, Macarena,' Alma said, evenly, as her sister poured herself a glass of iced tea. 'And frankly, at this point, I think the more of us here, the better.'

Maca considered what Alma said—they'd been at it all day—and then, agreed.

Puñeta—if this was the only way to keep them from being thrown off the estate, then fine. *The more the merrier.*

Anyway, just as their parents planned, Sombra was big enough for all of them. So large that they wouldn't even have to see each other if they didn't want to.

And Maca didn't want to see anyone besides her husband.

Just then, the gardener switched on power to the extension cords in the lawn.

Colourful star-shaped Capiz shell lanterns began to shine, a music box played carols, and tiny Christmas lights twinkled along like constellations.

For a moment, Sombra looked like it did when they were—*happy*.

When their father made paella and roasted lamb on weekends, and their mother led them in prayer and played the piano.

For a moment, Alma and Maca felt like—sisters.

As he walked in, Andy saw the same pain sweep across the women's faces. Exposed— briefly—in the reflected glimmer of dazzling lights.

He just picked up their three other children at the airport. All the Yrastegui-Castillo offspring—except Núria—lived abroad.

'Andy!' Alma breathed, grateful when she saw him.

He walked over, nodded to Maca, and kissed his wife.

'Are the kids all right?' she asked him. 'Even Ximena?'

'Yes, amor, don't worry. They're all upstairs freshening up. They'll be out soon.'

'And Hugo?'

Andy dropped him off at his hotel on the way to the airport.

'Still packing. He'll take a hotel car to the village church and walk over.'

They didn't want strangers driving into Sombra. Anyone could be lurking in the shadows, waiting to attack.

Throughout this exchange, Maca kept her eyes on the colourfully bedecked garden.

So, before they even discussed everyone moving into Sombra, Alma already had Hugo packing?—Did her opinion count for nothing?—*Puñeta.*

'Where is Dito, Maca?' Alma hadn't seen him in hours.

'Ay, you know my son,' she flashed her sister a disingenuous smile, 'he is likely praying somewhere.'

'And Manny?' Andy inquired.

'What about him?' Maca snapped, not knowing where her husband was. Probably out campaigning with Mikey. Yes, that was it.

'Cálmate, Maca.'

She always hated it when Alma told her to calm down.

'Por favor, please, we have to be civilised,' the great Almudena began her sermon. 'I hope you reminded him to behave. He mustn't say anything to anyone in that Durog Marasigan's circle about Mami—we don't know who is connected to whom. When the others get here, we will figure out what to do. Together.'

La Familia Primero: Unida y Protegida.

Family First. United and Protected.

It was the Castillo de Montijo motto. After all the years, it was barely visible on the reconstructed mosaic of the family crest on the porch wall.

(After all the years, Manny still denied it was his fault it was shattered.)

* * *

As instructed, Pepa was rechecking the décor on the gate when Ricky pulled up in Dito's car with Luísa. She had time as the beef stew she made for dinner needed longer on the stove. Señora Maca did tell her to mind how she juggled her chores.

'Good evening, señorito,' she whispered, shyly.

As she let them by, she handed Ricky a package that was dropped off for him earlier.

He put it aside, wanting to rush his mother up the driveway to the house. He hoped to get her changed before anyone saw her 'Sunshine' outfit.

Her tie-dyed skirt, her green-streaked hair, her orange lipstick.

'Here you go, Mom,' he pulled right up to the front door then helped her out. 'You'll feel better after a hot shower. I'll just park and come check on you, okay?'

He waited until she entered the house before getting back behind the wheel.

In the privacy of Dito's car, Ricky unwrapped the package Pepa gave him.

A mobile phone—*fuck his luck*—there was no escape.

A light blinked green. Then, a silent ring.

'You are costing me a small fortune in mobile phones, Federico the Third.' Click. Cluck.

'Sorry . . . they keep being taken from me.'

'Yes, yes—the police, then rehab, and now, the police again, no?' The Gecko chortled.

'Yes, sir.'

'Cluck, you have had a string of bad luck, my boy—click—you know I can help turn it around.'

'Yes, sir.' Ricky didn't know what else to say.

'Hijo?' Luísa came back out to look for her son. She was scared to walk through the house alone.

'Ah, your mother is home.' Click. Click. The Lizard heard her.

'Eh, ah, yes. But my father—isn't.' Ricky whispered, miming to his mother that he was on a call.

She wandered off.

'I see. Click. But you are trying to reach your father for me, yes?'

'Yes, sir. Of course. It's almost Christmas, I'm sure he'll be home soon.'

'He'd better be.'

The line went dead.

Ricky tried to catch his breath. At least, he no longer wet himself when Tukô called.

He pulled out a cigarette and lit it.

He thought Tukô only wanted him to take photos at that wretched party—but, apparently, blackmail material wasn't all he was after.

The Lizard tried to use Ricky to bait his father, but Freddie disappeared before he was trapped.

Ricky didn't know how the two men were acquainted, but it was no secret that upsetting Tukô was bad for business.

¡Joder, Pop!

Repeatedly, Ricky began to hit the steering wheel, raining cigarette ash all over Dito's car.

He didn't know how to shake a fucking lizard.

He didn't know how to lose the puto cops. So many different factions out to get him.

At Chucho's party, the narcs let him go when he swore to lead them to Tukô. But the recent night in jail reminded him that his empty promises would one day cost him. His thighs still hurt from the beating that he got. From another set of crooked cops within the precinct.

They said they acted on orders from #Durog and it was—*personal.*

Ricky didn't know what the hell that meant.

* * *

When Hugo Pérez-García got to Sombra that evening, he was deceived by the Christmas paraphernalia around the estate.

Trains of tinsel, strings of fairy lights, and dancing fountains.

He thought that he'd arrived at a jolly reunion.

Poor chap, he knew nothing about his family.

It was the first time he would see his mother, Cova, since he lied to her and left Spain for Manila—but she was too busy to even notice he'd arrived.

She was in the parlour off the main courtyard with her siblings.

Hugo heard voices and stopped before the portal.

* * *

'Let me get this straight,' Julián paced the Ottoman carpet in the centre of the room, twirling their mother's ring around his finger. 'Freddie *sold* the estate—and none of you knew?'

'Not exactly,' Alma shook her head, still in disbelief. She was perched on the edge of their mother's favourite armchair. With her back straight, her hands on her lap, and her legs crossed at the ankles. 'Those men *claim* he did, but he couldn't have done so without Mami's permission—'

'There's no way Mami let him sell Sombra.' Cova asserted from the couch. Of that, she was certain. When last they spoke, their mother told her she put all their names on the estate's title—so, they shared ownership.

Yes, she spoke to her mother. It wasn't often, but Cova called covertly, telling the maids she was an old friend of the family.

Fortunately, Maca rarely answered the landline phone.

'And how would you know?' Maca glared from across the parlour. She was seated alone at the antique card table.

'Maca.' Alma's look silenced any further questions.

'Bottom line,' she went on, 'Andy looked into Freddie's affairs—he's broke. He has no bank accounts, no records, and no documentation. Even his companies were shells, and his businesses—*bogus*. Unless Mami secreted money somewhere, it looks like Freddie ran Papá's legacy into the ground. And we can't find the title to the estate.'

Maca was silent, feeling responsible for her brother. But damned if she'd admit that aloud. She picked up the playing cards on the table and shuffled them.

'So, we could be dispossessed, there's no money, and Freddie—for whatever reason—owes a ton to unsavoury characters?'

'Yes, Julián,' Alma confirmed as he stopped pacing.

'Now these characters are going after anything they can,' he continued to spin his ring. Julián may have been away for decades, but he knew that an-eye-for-an-eye was still the law of the islands.

'Exactly.' Alma looked over at Andy by the window, needing the comfort of his warm and steady gaze. Her lovely husband nodded in her direction, letting her know that he was at her side.

Andy Yrastegui knew his place in Sombra and kept his mouth shut. This was a *family* matter—the Castillo siblings had to hash things out amongst themselves.

'All right. So, what do you suggest we do, Alma?' Julián asked, not wanting to usurp her position as the long-time elder. He lost his place when he left the country.

'Well, we must keep looking for the papers, and for Freddie. He might be hiding with the help of some of his—*associates*. Maca, Manny has to pull strings, find a way to smoke him out.'

Cova flinched at the mention of that name.

Maca pretended not to notice.

In the corner by the Christmas tree—near the bar—Cristóbal sat with Greg. Nursing their drinks in silence.

'Tomorrow,' Alma suggested, 'we should all go to mass in the village church. Present a united front. Our siblings are here from abroad, it's a happy occasion.'

By this time, Julián realized there were no vengeful Moros after him. His siblings, on the other hand, still knew nothing.

His heart broke all over again at the memory of what their mother did to protect him. Of the story that she told to make him leave.

'Wait,' Julián suddenly remembered, 'Mami had a brother—' a man with large ears whom he once met. The man wore a brimless cap and a colourful tadjung—which, as a child, Julián had called a skirt.

'Should we find him?' Julián looked at each of his siblings. 'If he's even still alive.'

* * *

Stuck in gridlocked traffic, Núria felt like a driver-for-hire. Wishing instead that she were at Sombra for the Grown-Up siblings' reunion.

But with the chauffeurs off, she was sent on all sorts of errands.

Can you imagine what traffic's like in a place with no respect for rules?

As best she could, Núria criss-crossed the crowded city—buying drinks, getting dessert, and finally to The Tsang-Du. To collect her aunt's and uncles' suitcases.

It seemed there would be a family sleep-over at Sombra for Christmas—*Oh joy.*

She turned up the radio—her favourite carol had just come on.

* * *

At the other end of the river, in the Palace, the president was singing into a mic—a surly version of a song about a father and son.

Only a handful of people were in his audience—including Pip Rodríguez, Mikey Reyes, and Manny Santos.

Yes, Manny Santos—Maca's husband—was at the Palace. He finally breached the inner circle of power.

He swirled expensive whisky in a vintage crystal glass, while reclining in a luxurious leather chaise. Pretending to care about corporate takeovers, drug wars, and stem cell therapy.

There was a nurse injecting vials into their arms. Pip convinced them it would keep them young and virile.

#Durog needed all the help he could get.

The president had not been well for months, but he told no one, certain his enemies would take advantage of perceived frailty. Many waited in the sidelines to take control, and he would be damned if he were outlived by that troll Tukô.

Durog coughed. A red-orange glob bubbled to the side of his mouth.

The room went silent as he spat it out.

'Don't look at me like that,' he glowered at the assembled.

'Are you sick?' Pip asked, feigning concern.

'No.' Durog snapped.

'Is that the truth?' Pip again.

'The truth!' Durog laughed. 'Puta, Pip, you and I both know that the only "truth" that matters is what you can get people to believe.'

Pip smirked and gulped down the last of his Scotch.

'Sir,' one of the president's assistants approached his easy chair and whispered in his ear.

A wide grin crossed Durog's face—'Show him in.'

A thin, bespectacled man in his mid-forties entered the hall. Crisp shirt, bespoke trousers, expensive leather shoes. Stanford degree borne firmly in his bearing.

'Little Boylet,' Durog smiled, snapping his fingers to the rock song on the karaoke.

'It's Boy-Tiny, Mr Marasigan,' the Ronquillo scion corrected. His family had run the power company since its inception. And everyone knew Boy-Tiny was his nickname from birth.

'It's Mr President, Tiny Boylet,' Durog smiled, with barely hidden contempt. 'I wanted you to know I am dissatisfied. Too many power disruptions in Mindanao—'

'Our supply lines keep getting attacked and our plans for a plant in Latîan—'

Durog wasn't pleased that he was interrupted. 'Fix it.' The 'or else' was left unsaid.

Boy-Tiny was promptly shown the door.

'Sir, Mister Cotiengsu is here,' another presidential assistant announced.

Durog waved his hand, indicating that the music be stopped as the Chinese-Filipino businessman was led through.

'Buboy—' Durog exclaimed, leaning back into his chair. 'What a pleasure.'

Pip, Mikey, and Manny exchanged glances over the unexpected guest.

'What can I do for you?' Durog beamed at the casually dressed entrepreneur. The man seemed nervous and kept his gaze down.

'I, uh, we—uhm, need your assistance, po, Mister President.' Buboy Cotiengsu was anxiously rubbing his palms together. He peeked at the others in the room.

'It's all right, you can say whatever you need to in front of them. I have no secrets,' Durog grinned as if it were true.

'Uh,' Buboy cleared his throat, 'you were right, sir—we need your help. We keep receiving threats and so many of us have had children kidnapped for ransom. We need—assistance.'

'You need my protection.' Durog corrected.

Buboy nodded. Fully aware that the threats to their wealthy Chinese-Filipino community were likely also coming from the president's people. Forcing them to acquire the services of his private militia-for-hire. It's what the former mayor was known for. Just one of the many side hustles from his small town that he kept going.

'Good,' Durog nodded, as he prepared another bundle of betel nut. 'And chicks? For your casinos?'

Another of the president's sidelines: supplying women for sex work where 'appropriate'.

The way #Durog saw it, if there were 'hookers', there'd be less rape.

If there were hookers, his daughter—and his son—would still be alive.

'Uh, yes, Mister President, of course. I will speak to our council and arrange payment,' Buboy Cotiengsu knew how to protect his interests.

Durog smiled, waving him to a chair. A glass of whisky was swiftly put before him.

The president spat out betel nut and snapped his fingers. His bodyguard switched the music back on.

An old Filipino ballad began to play.

#Durog wiped his mouth and raised the mic—to warble about the pain of losing an errant child.

* * *

None of the Grown-Ups felt like dinner after the family meeting. But Pepa brought Luísa a tray of stew. Freddie's wife was alone, watching TV in her suite.

Cristóbal went to swim a few laps before bed.

While the children were in the chapel keeping vigil with their Aba.

Maca was the first to leave the parlour and turn in.

Andy and Alma stayed, politely inquiring after Greg—who apparently was a law professor at Harvard. They hid their surprise that, at such a time, Julián brought back a—*friend*.

'It's late,' Cova rose slowly, with a slight nod at the others. She expected her husband to be done with his swim and back in their room.

It was quite a trek from the parlour to the north wing guest suite she had asked for—which was far away from their old quarters.

On the landing—it was dim—she saw a figure. Her chest thumped a thunderous bolt of dread.

The figure moved—it was Hugo—she caught her breath.

In the shadows—in this house—he looked like his father.

'Mamá? Are you okay?'

She never thought she'd have to see that beast again. But here she was, back in this cursed city with that brutal rapist.

'Hijo, I'm just tired. Let's talk tomorrow, hm?'

She passed her son on the staircase without a glance. Too afraid of the weakness—and the shame—that he resurrected.

In the guest suite, as her husband showered, Cova sat at the dresser.

This was her least favourite part of the day.

She looked in the mirror as she wiped off her make-up, the vivid mask that made her someone else.

It was easier to be someone else.

Somewhere on the ceiling above her—or in some unseen, damp corner of the room—a goddam lizard clucked its evening dirge.

Over and over, like a puto pounding bassline. Cluck click cluck—reminding her why she left.

How she missed Salamanca's comforting silence.

Click. Cluck. Click.

Puñeta—it was going to drive her mad.

Chapter 29

Los Rumores | **The Buzz** | Ang Alingawngaw

ChatsApp

GROUP CHAT: THE 'RAh-RAh' GIRLS

Admin: Laura Herrera/Members: 28

---

10 December 2010

'OMG, girls, know who's back?! Covadonga Castillo! In the FLESH!'

'Wow! She really exists?'

'LOL, you make her sound like some intangible icon'

'She is! Only heard about her from the parentals. She's like the original 'it' girl—before whitening soaps and all that'

'Where'd you see her? Did she look as fabulous as I imagine?'

'If she was that *sosyal*, why'd she disappear? I mean, look at the Islander mom of Enrique Iglesias—she's all over the magazines in Spain'

'I bet she's here because that guy arrested with Tricky and Dito is her son! OMG! He's guapo ha, but not as white as I expected. I mean, isn't his dad some super-hot jock from Spain?'

269

'My mom said she dated him back in the 70s. Before he met Cova. For sure he was after her money'

'Yeah right, because your mom is prettier than Cova Castillo #not'

'How do you even know what Cova looks like? She was like—before our time!'

'Google is my friend, no? I did a deep dive'

'Well, I saw her at the Tsang-Du with some men'

'What were U doing there naman, Chiqui?'

'Same thing as Cova by the sound of it—some men! Right, Chiq?'

'Gaga! Not funny. But yes—LOL'

'R u still doing that, girl?'

'Why shouldn't she? It pays, no? Bumps up her allowance from Daddy'

'$$$ometimes. Other times it's about fun ☺'

'She looked good, for her age. Cova. A little tired though, thin, but not bad. Maybe she had work done'

'Or it's the Moro in her—u know they're part Moro right? And u know what they say about Asian skin—LOL'

'Wait, speaking of Google—check out Ricky's latest pics. He's gone dark, man! What happened to his glossies? Tragic. Such gloom and doom. Why'd he go all—newsy?'

'He needs a good shag—aren't you doing him any more, Rah-Rah!'

'Gaga—he dumped Laura remember?'

'Hoy naman, I wouldn't say he "dumped" me!'

'Our Lady Rah-Rah is now after the Yrastegui cousin—Tita Alma's son'

'4get it, Ra—no matter how much skin bleaching soap you use. He only likes *chinitas*'

'Yikes, his mom would love that—a chinky-eyed Yrastegui, the horror!'

'I hear he likes them anyway he can get them!'

'What about his sisters? You never hear about who they're f*cking'

'OMG, is that all that matters to you?'

'Who someone sleeps with says a lot about a person'

'WAIT! Speaking of shags—my tita is the girlfriend of Attorney Manny—she just told my mom that Ricky's dad has been kidnapped! The family got a ransom demand by text!'

'What??? Why?'

'By whom?!'

'Moros, *daw*—for money—I guess'

'My other chat groups are blowing up—yeah, daw—some Moros sent a text—asking for a billion pesos to free him!'

'I'm confused—aren't they related?'

'I hear the Castillos no longer have that kind of money'

'Are you kidding?'

'Oh shit'

Chapter 30

El Moro | **The Moor** | Ang Moro

Rashid Sulayman was never good at fasting. He didn't understand why he had to go 'without'—*on purpose*—when there was such abundance around him.

He swung at the mosquitoes swarming by his head, and with his other hand, he grabbed the fattest banana on the tree. Not caring that it was hardly ripe.

Alhamdulillah—Thank God the fruits hung low.

Rashid knew that abstaining was a necessary show of good faith. Literally. So, when in company, he fasted. He didn't want to risk appearing like a bad Muslim.

From the holy month of Ramadan to Muharram, including this blessed day of Ashura. One occasion for abstention seemed to bleed into the next. The opposite of indulgent Christian Islanders over Christmas.

For Muslims like him, the holiest of times meant no food, no drink, no women.

At least not in daylight.

Rashid wasn't sure how that translated when there was a storm and most of the day was dark.

He looked up as the visible slivers of stone-coloured sky began to grumble through the trees.

The breezeless jungle shuddered around him.

Mindanao, the largest of the southern islands, wasn't previously in the path of typhoons, but apparently, this 'climate change' thing *changed* that.

Rashid did not enjoy living 'off-the-earth' on the most temperate of days, but it was worse when rain converted the forest into a bog.

He wiped his brow with the back of his hand.

Truth be told, Rashid Sulayman thought it would be terribly difficult to stay away from alcohol and the profusion of women, but when one's life depended on it, he found himself surprisingly motivated.

So motivated that he married Rawah Al-Tumawiri Muklagitan just before Ramadan.

Since then, the tribe took any delays in his shipments more—*graciously*.

He was even promised an additional wife—when he was 'ready'.

Which meant when he delivered on his promise to bring in more money.

He peeled the unripe banana and took a bite.

Rashid could once turn anything into a fortune. But in his advanced years, he found 'work' rather challenging.

Then again—another bite—he could never really be called a hard worker.

He didn't have the discipline for manual labour, nor the patience for being out on the boats.

He was unlike many of his tribe.

But—then again—they didn't really expect him to fit in.

Regardless, it could never be said that Rashid Sulayman didn't try.

In fact, he tried his darndest to not stand out.

'There you are,' one of the younger men stumbled upon him among the fruit trees. 'Don't forget to reinforce your windows so the storm doesn't blast into your hut again.'

Rashid quickly hid the banana he was eating.

'Ah, yes, Abu Wadi, of course. I am actually gathering wood for a barricade.' Surreptitiously, he swallowed the morsel of fruit in his mouth.

'Do you need help?'

'No, thank you,' Rashid raised his bolo knife to convince Abu Wadi of his confidence. 'I am fine.'

The younger man knew that Rashid wasn't being truthful, but he had more important things to worry about.

He readjusted his belt of bullets and trod on.

The tribe was always ready to help Rashid—with anything. As if he were truly family.

Or—*an imbecile.*

Inadequate. Unable to survive on his own.

He hated it.

It might not have appeared so, but Rashid Sulayman was a survivor. Just like the rest of them.

His battles may have differed from theirs, but he too spent his whole life on a frontline. Facing numerous enemies out for his blood.

A rumble of thunder coursed through the dense vegetation.

In the quivering silence that followed, he heard a soft rustle in the brush.

Rawah—his young wife—was returning from doing laundry in the lake. A chore his first wife had never done.

'Rashid—' she gasped. 'You frightened me.'

'I'm sorry, *dayang,*' he lowered the bolo, liking how the term for 'beloved' felt in his mouth. 'I was trying to gather us some wood.'

She said nothing, still trying to manoeuvre being married.

'For the windows,' he explained. 'And the cooking. And—things.'

She noticed his eyes rake over her body and resisted the urge to pull her tadjung tighter around her. The thin cloth marked every curve and protrusion.

A mosquito landed on her uncovered arm.

Another roar of thunder.

The jungle quaked, and the sky grew darker still.

Rawah slapped dead the insect on her arm. It itched.

'I best get back to camp and put this away before the storm,' she indicated the tub that contained their newly washed clothing.

Rashid nodded. Not knowing what else to say to his new bride.

He watched her fix her headscarf and walk deeper into the trees.

Their camp was tucked away from roads and dirt paths. Far from any civilians.

It was by a small assortment of nearly imperceptible stone ruins. A few damaged pillars and grave markers overrun by tangled vegetation.

The locals believed it the remains of an ancient sultanate's palace. There was nothing like it in all the islands.

But there were never any tourists, and no one looked for the living that far from shore.

It was the perfect encampment. A warlord's fiefdom ensconced in rebel-held land.

Neighbouring villagers—and government soldiers—acknowledged the unseen perimetre. No one dared cross unless they were in the militia or had business with them.

These particular fighters were an enterprising bunch.

A few kilometres east of their camp, there was a mountain range they mined for gold. From afar, it resembled a giant anthill. Numerous blast holes pockmarked the denuded soil.

The warriors cut down and sold the trees, sharing the profits with the town mayor. He made sure they weren't troubled for environmental licenses, permits, or taxes.

To the south—where Rawah had just come from—was the great lake once abundant in fish. But the water was spotted in algae and no longer as deep as it once was.

No fish had been caught there in months.

To the west were the lush Latîan Wetlands. Hundreds of thousands of fertile acres rich in untapped oil and methane gas. A perfect site to generate power for the island's poor.

At least that's what the stories said.

Even on the news.

But no one knew for sure. There was never a ceasefire long enough between warring factions for experts to wade in and confirm any hidden resources.

Thousands of people lived off the wetlands. On rice and maize farms, and sandbars that disappeared and reappeared with the tide.

It was at the centre of the southern island of Mindanao. The mystical heartbeat of the marginalised Moro nation.

Another rustling from a clump of trees.

A group of men carrying assault rifles burst forward.

'*Assalamu alaykum,*' Rashid greeted, getting out of their way. 'Where are you headed in such a hurry?' He feared they might be under attack. They certainly weren't rushing for a shipment. There wasn't one scheduled to arrive that night.

'*Wa'alaykum salaam,*' Faisal stopped, a bit out of breath. 'To the rowboats in the mangrove forest. We must check on the trawlers along the coast. The men weren't expecting a storm when they headed out yesterday.'

Rashid nodded. Of course. It was one of their more lucrative ventures.

The trawlers siphoned oil from tankers travelling the open sea between Mindanao and Indonesia. Those waters were rarely patrolled, and the oil sold for a mint on the black market. Enough to make the whole endeavour worthwhile, considering they split the profits with a few ship captains, the local coast guard, and the roundup of necessary government officials.

If they failed to dock and unload the boats before the storm, all that income could be lost.

'Rashid, your contact knows we're grounded tonight, yes?'

Rashid nodded. He wasn't about to tell them his contact hadn't taken his calls in days.

After the men disappeared into the brush, Rashid scanned the woods to regain his bearings. He still got lost returning to camp.

The absent rain hung heavy, and he struggled to breathe.

He couldn't make out the markers he'd left on the trees. *Goddamit.*

Somewhere in this blasted jungle, Rashid knew there was a clearing.

A small patch of grass dotted with bamboo huts on stilts.

It looked like any other assemblage of rural dwellings. Especially from above. Those darned military flying drones would never spot anything out of the ordinary.

But these thatched roof 'dwellings' housed some of the island's most prolific gunmakers. And other such unlicensed entrepreneurs.

Including bomb experts and—shall we say—*chemical engineers.* Trained in the science of making crystal meth.

Most of the products went abroad, but they also had a devoted domestic following. Sold by the gram in tiny sachets, even the poorest Islander could afford a hit.

Any ingredients not locally available were smuggled in from China, Thailand, or Myanmar. All they needed was a rustic lab for blending, and—*viola*.

This *special* village—with its extraordinary homes—was shielded by the rebel flag. The armed impresarios hid behind the Moro cause.

Their homespun enterprises supported the rebellion, and the rebellion kept their industries afloat.

A win-win situation.

That's how Rashid presented it to the warriors a decade earlier, when he and his associates first broached them with the scheme.

Things were going well—until he got too greedy.

Rashid's other—*legal*—business interests were waning, so he took a little—here and there—to make up the difference.

On retrospect, it wasn't a good idea.

He moved into the jungle camp when his creditors and other—less reasonable/former—partners came after him. With a hold on his passport, it was an easy place to disappear.

And the intrepid fighters would protect him for as long as it was profitable.

So, Rashid had to remain—*cost-effective*.

With the rains, the gold mining wasn't going too well. Their best miners were minors, and the last storm buried many of the children in landslides.

The gun-manufacturing was compromised, too. Government troops were taking a larger share of the profits, insisting they deserved it because they were the reason business was booming. You see, police needed cheap, untraceable guns for the president's 'anti-crime' campaign. They didn't want the murders of suspected 'undesirables' linked to them.

So, Rashid was counting on his evasive Taiwanese contacts to keep the warriors gainfully employed.

His phone vibrated in his trousers.

He pulled it out.

'About time, paré. Where's the shipment? They're getting antsy.'

Rashid looked around to make sure no one would witness his anxiety.

'What do you mean—diverted?' He swatted at another swarm of insects with his bolo.

'I have people waiting. The fishing boats went out every night this week—but nothing. They said there were no packages in the water for them to collect. Not one. There's a storm coming, and now the oil is in danger—paré, we need this.'

He scratched his chin. It itched more frequently since he grew a beard.

'Come on, man. The governor is breathing down my neck, we haven't paid him in weeks—'

Scratch, scratch, scratch.

'What congressman? Chongki, I know more people than that goon. Trust me, that bastard will double-cross—you can't be serious—Salazar? I've told you that slippery dinosaur can't be trusted.'

Rain began to fall. In increasingly insistent drops.

'Shit. I have to go, man—storm's here—I'm still not back at camp. I'm starving. Yes, yes, I will pay you for that soon. I swear I have money coming in—yes, I am sure. No, paré, I am not lying to you. Jesus.'

Call ended.

He lied several times.

'Frickin' Chinks,' Rashid muttered under his breath. These Chinese people were all the same—always suspecting they were being scammed when they themselves took shortcuts.

The arrogance—as if their money could facilitate everything.

He warned Tukô about dealing with them, but he wasn't heeded. And that's how he got caught in the middle –'*Tangina!*

There was a succession of crackles and crunches. And like the rain, the noises got louder.

A deluge of fighters was rushing back to camp. Their weapons rattling across their chests. Their flipflops clattering in the mud.

It was the same rumpus when they ran to or from battle.

His heart stopped. He would never get used to it.

To him, the slap-slap-rattle-rattle signalled impending doom.

In his panic, Rashid slipped on wet soil and landed on his backside. Splat on the banana that he hid earlier.

His rear end was splotched in fruit and soaked in mud.

As if he soiled himself.

Oh, how he hated this climate change thing.

By the time Rashid got to his hut, his wife was preparing dinner. Some rice and what vegetables survived the last typhoon.

He tucked himself into a dark corner of their one-room home and removed his soggy cotton trousers. Slightly embarrassed at the state of them.

He peered at Rawah bent over a make-shift stove, her soft face caressed by shadows from the low flame. There was no twitching between his legs.

Dammit.

She was not—*unattractive*—his young wife. Though she was nowhere near his usual type.

Short, small-breasted, with few curves, Rawah had pleasing brown skin. Her eyes were almond-shaped, and her long black hair was pulled up in a bun. The way the other women must be wearing it—he surmised—under their hijabs.

Yes, even in the jungle, all their women wore headscarves.

They were nothing if not devout.

Especially Rawah.

She was the granddaughter of Hadji Datu Wazilah Al Tumawiri, revered founder of the country's Islamic separatist movement: The Native Army for Moro Emancipation, or N.A.M.E.

Her mother was his only daughter.

Her two uncles—known as Abu Wajid and Abu Omar—broke away from N.A.M.E. when their father began peace talks with the government in the 1980s. They believed Datu Wazilah, as he was widely known, was making too many compromises in his old age. So, they set up their own Society of Armed Moros for Emancipation.

Or S.A.M.E.

As if that wasn't confusing enough, Rawah's father—Abu Jafik Muklagitan—was still not satisfied. He wanted something more radical and extreme than his brothers-in-law.

He wanted a fundamentalist Islamic state. Traditional and deeply conservative. Just like Saudi Arabia. Where men ruled unquestioned, and women were never seen unless shrouded in black.

So, Abu Jafik created his own faction of fighters prepared to do anything to make that happen.

Calling themselves F.I.S.T.—Fighters for Islamic Statehood and Territory—they terrorised civilians, extorted money where they could, and dealt in narcotics.

He was Rashid's main associate. The chief of *chemical* engineers.

Abu Jafik was as hot-blooded as they came—exactly as Rashid expected of all Moros.

Unfortunately, Abu Jafik's daughter was nowhere near as—*passionate*.

'There's a nearly dry tadjung on the line.' Rawah pointed at the tubular fabric hanging on a string between two shuttered windows. One of the boys must've secured it for her in Rashid's absence.

'Thank you,' he muttered, grabbing the still-damp cloth. He found it difficult to move wearing the restrictive wrap-around, but he had little other choice.

His phone buzzed again. He put it away without looking at it. No one had the number but his Chinese partners, and he had enough bad news from Chongki for one day.

As they sat down to dinner, rain fell in booming metal sheets while bullfrogs and geckos croaked a thunderous concerto.

Rashid felt entombed. Imprisoned by the boisterous night and the sinister light of a lone gas lamp.

An unexpected rapping at their door.

'Rashid,' Omar yelled from the portal, 'my father is calling for you.'

Rashid changed into trousers and struggled to follow his wife's cousin across the drenched camp to the leader's hut.

Omar's father—Abu Omar—was sitting cross-legged on the bamboo floor.

He was a short, stocky man a few years younger than Rashid.

But he always carried a Kalashnikov—wore several belts of bullets—and so demanded respect.

He sported a red bandana around his head and a scraggly beard sprouted from his chin.

Over his right eye, he wore a black patch that he thought made him look frightening.

'*Talbos ng kamote?*' Abu Omar offered, inviting Rashid into the hut. His gold Seiko timepiece glistened in the amber gaslight.

'Thank you.'

Rashid took the rustic tea made from sweet potato leaves just to have something warm and stop his body from trembling. He was soaking wet. It's not as if the rebels made a habit of carrying umbrellas in the rain. And he gave up using banana leaves for shelter after the first time he tried it. Not only was it ineffective but he realized it made him look—*silly.*

Which was the last image he wanted to project in such—*esteemed*—company.

'How is married life, Rashid? My niece treating you well?' Abu Omar laughed, vulgarly.

'Yes, Abu Omar, very well.' He felt just a little odd speaking to the middle-aged man about his twenty-two-year-old niece in such a manner.

Rashid was only fifty-six, but his new wife was young enough to be his grandchild.

Not that he was complaining.

'Listen,' Abu Omar set down his tea, 'the proof-of-life video and updated ransom demand was just sent to the Castillo family, as you instructed. Took a while for the clip to upload over the shitty signal here, but the footage is certainly more dramatic than our initial text message. It should frighten them. You are certain they will pay?'

Rashid smiled. 'Of course. Trust me, the family has more money than they realize. You know how it is, parents always tuck things away for a rainy day and don't necessarily tell their children where the stash is. This will loosen the purse strings, for sure.'

For the first time in days, Rashid felt—*relief.* The ransom would solve all his—their—problems.

'Well then, we should have thought of this kidnapping sooner!' Abu Omar laughed again. 'They will try to haggle—these families always do. How long should we negotiate before giving a deadline for decapitation?'

Rashid nearly spat out the tepid tea.

'Is that necessary, Abu Omar?'

'Rashid, you know better than to ask. I am neither my father nor my gutless brother.'

It would not be the first beheading in the camp.

Not all ransoms got paid, and Abu Omar's fighters—whom he could always later denounce as 'rogues' under 'illicit' orders from Abu Jafik—had their own brand of justice.

They were feared for it.

An eye for an eye.

'Another thing,' Abu Omar scratched his crotch, 'in a few hours, when the storm is at its height, we will go to the wetlands. My informant tells me a rival clan has breached our territory. Of course, we shouldn't wage war during these holy days—but Allah, most exalted and sublime, has given us this perfect opportunity. We mustn't waste it. So, I need all the men I can muster.'

'Of course, Abu Omar.'

Again, Rashid had no idea what he was doing, but there was no way he wasn't going to be useful to these people.

He could handle a rival clan. *Take a gun, point, and shoot*—how hard could that be?

He drank his tea, then returned to his hut.

* * *

After an unsuccessful attempt at coupling with his young bride, Rashid was roused by Omar's men.

'I'm coming,' he told them. Wishing he meant that sexually. *Dammit.*

Under cover of storm and darkness, a combined group of warriors got into canoes and slithered through the marsh to the rival's huts.

Once past the gnarl of mangroves, the men in the lead canoe began lobbing Molotov cocktails. Rapidly engulfing the front row of grass huts in flames.

In the chaos, Abu Omar and his men raided the small village. An assault of fire and fury.

Rashid was shooting his handgun indiscriminately—all the while, searching for a place to hide.

Crouching by a stack of wood, he noticed an unburnt hut to the side of combat.

He dashed into the dark shack and surprised a man inside gathering—*documents?*

Instinctively, Rashid shot him in the back. The man fell flat on the bamboo floor. His papers scattered about him like confetti.

When Abu Omar found him, Rashid was still staring at the gun in his hand. The body—unmoving—at his feet.

He'd never killed anyone before.

'Good job, Rashid. You are getting better at this every time.'

Rashid didn't know if he was shaking from the gunshot or the cold.

He was going to be sick.

'A few more excursions and you will be a pro,' Abu Omar grabbed Rashid's arm and lowered it. He stood there—paralysed—as the warriors ransacked the home.

What looked like building plans were set alight and a photograph fell to the floor.

Rashid wasn't sure why he bothered to pick it up.

His face went white.

It was dark—surely, he couldn't trust his eyes.

'What is it?' Abu Omar snatched the photo and turned it to the flame.

'My parents,' Rashid found himself saying.

'What are you talking about?' Abu Omar didn't know if this was yet again another of this man's tricks. He looked closer at the sepia image in his hand. 'This is Datu Khaled's clan—that's the daughter they disowned—Fatimah. I recognise her from a photo my father had. She is older here, but it is her.'

Rashid looked from the photo to Abu Omar. 'Fatimah is my mother's name—'

The raid leader said nothing. For a beat. Or two. They stood there like statues in the bristling firelight.

Then—

'Bai Fatimah binti Datu Khaled is—your mother?' Abu Omar glared at him.

'I don't know what her full name is—she never told us.'

'Ah, this again—your ridiculous claim to knowing nothing about your mother—though you insisted that she was one of us,' the warrior was incredulous. 'But it makes sense now—you are all *disgraceful*.'

Rashid stared at him confused. Abu Omar kicked the dead body on the floor.

'This is Ismail, son of Datu Adil—her brother. You just killed your cousin.' Abu Omar laughed. 'They've been our enemies for years, since the day your mother killed my uncle.'

Rashid was certain none of this was true. His mother would never have done such a thing.

'Ismail was going to desecrate our land by building a power plant— without paying for our permission,' Abu Omar barely blinked. 'We get so little news out here that I did not know you were related. Seems your family has a way of making trouble.'

Rashid remained silent. Not often at a loss for words.

He saw something click in Abu Omar's one exposed eye.

No—

There again was the warrior's vulgar laugh.

'I am Tarek Muazzil,' Abu Omar stated his birth names. 'Son of Datu Hatif Wazilah Abdulrahim Al Tumawiri. My father named me after his brother, Tarek, who was killed by your mother.'

He relished the retelling of his family tragedy.

'Bai Fatimah was supposed to wed my father as recompense, instead she fled. Like the shameful coward that she is.'

Tarek Muazzil—otherwise known as Abu Omar—pointed his gun at Rashid.

'What about you, Rashid Sulayman, or should I say—Freddie Castillo?'

Rashid—Freddie—shook his head. Terrified at the anger burning in Abu Omar's eye.

'I converted, remember?' he pled with the rebel. '*La ilaha illa Allah*—'

He declared the creed of faith three times when he first joined the camp. As required for converts. Believing it a magic spell of sorts that would transform him from a frog or a pumpkin into—*anything else.*

'La ilaha illa Allah,' Rashid repeated. 'Clean slate, no? I am Muslim now. A Moro, like you. I bring in money—I married your niece—I'm family, coño!'

Abu Omar smirked. 'And you are still the son of Bai Fatimah, daughter of Datu Khaled.'

The one-eyed commander slowly wiped his bolo on his rain-soaked shirt.

'My father told me not to bother with vengeance, but look, Allah—in His infinite wisdom—has put you in my path,' Abu Omar grinned. 'How can I turn away such a present?'

'Abu Omar, please, there must be another way—'

'Are you a coward like her, Rashid?' the warrior traced the blade with his finger. 'My dear Freddie, are you not prepared to die?'

Chapter 31

El Descubrimiento | **The Discovery** | Ang Pagkatuklas

The room had not been opened since October 1976, from the day that Don Federico Castillo died.

Only he and his wife knew of its existence, and a widowed Doña Fatimah could not bear to be in there.

It was hidden behind a panel along their bedroom wall. An enclosed, windowless chamber that held everything dear to the family patriarch.

A few photos, some books, and his most private papers.

There was a ceiling fan, a small sofa next to a drinks cabinet, a specially crafted narra desk with a multitude of drawers, and his favourite reading chair.

It was *his* space. His—*refugio*—as he called it. His refuge.

When his eldest son turned sixteen in 1961, Don Federico showed him where it was. *Just in case* anything happened to him. He counted on Julián to step up and tend to the family.

Don Federico told his first born that all he'd need to know would be in this room.

He kept meticulous records. Details of where his money was, whom he owed, and who owed him. Notes on anything that crossed his mind and his concerns for the future. Pages and pages of plans to grow the family business so that his children never wanted for anything.

Don Federico would make sure they didn't struggle like he did.

* * *

Julián Castillo did not like lying to his father, especially when they were in his refugio. It felt like committing a sin inside a church confessional.

He was twenty the last time he was there. The night after Tino died.

'Are you certain you didn't see their faces, hijo?' Don Federico was at the drinks cabinet pouring them some sherry. The fortified wine from his native Spain always soothed him.

'I didn't, Papá. I—I didn't see—anything.' Julián was seated by the desk with his head bowed. His mother told him that the truth would only cause his father further pain.

Julián hadn't been able to look either of his parents in the eyes.

Don Federico sighed as he set down two glasses of sherry on the desk. Sombra was built to be impenetrable to outsiders. *How did those Moros get in?* He still couldn't believe the story.

He walked to the bookshelves across the room and pulled out a large encyclopedia.

He brought it with him to the desk and lay it down, taking a seat across Julián.

'Mira,' Federico began, wiping his hand over the book's front cover, 'your mother—as you know—is from the south. Before the war, she'—he took a breath—'well, she was accused of something she did not do, and she's feared reprisal ever since.'

Julián admired his father's conviction, considering it was unlikely he was present when this alleged wrongdoing occurred.

Don Federico retrieved a small key from a secret panel on his desk and turned it in a hidden lock on the book.

It was a false almanac. Where the pages should've been, there was a safe box.

He carefully removed its contents. Putting some photos and postal envelopes on the table.

'These are from your mother's family.'

Julián was surprised by his father's concealment.

He understood that his mother cut all ties to her family when she left Mindanao in the 1930s, but suddenly—before him—was a stack of handwritten letters his father said he received from a man named Adil. His mother's brother.

'Go on,' Federico indicated his son pick one up.

The top envelope was addressed to 'Celestino Magpantay, care of Castillo de Montijo Enterprises'—*Mang Tining*.

It was dated earlier that year—31 March 1965.

'Assalamu Alaikum, dearest brother Don Iko,' began the letter's cursive script.

Blessings be upon your house and family.

I would like to thank you for the assistance you sent for our mother's hospitalisation. While appreciated, your generosity was unnecessary. I am doing well as a university professor and my children are gainfully employed. We would not want to owe you a debt. Mother's doctors are uncertain how much longer she has, but she says we should not feel sorrow for she has lived heartache enough for three generations. I did not know what to say in response.

How is my stubborn sister? I trust you and she are well. I pray that one day she will forgive me for failing her. It will forever be my burden. Are the children well? Do send a new photo. Mother is eager to see how they have grown.

By the time you receive this, it will be Eid al-Adha, the holy festival of sacrifice. My son Ibrahim and I went to Mecca last year and completed the Hajj. It is my dream to send my younger boy, Ismail, with his mother when he is of age. Alhamdulillah for decent wages.

Julián looked up to see his father's eyes were shut, his chin resting on clasped hands.

Don Federico seemed deep in thought—or in prayer.

Julián returned to the letter, not wanting to disturb.

I have enclosed the latest photograph of my boys—should you ever be in a position to show my sister. The photo of you with your first born is tacked on our mirror. I want my sons to know the reaches of our family, and how far an education can lead them.

With my respect and friendship, Don Iko.
Eid Mubarak.

Julián turned the page. That was the end of it.

It was signed 'Adil'.

His father took a sip of sherry. The glass Julián was served remained untouched on the table.

'I met Adil during the war,' Iko recounted, setting his glass back down. 'In the jungle, before your mother and I were even married. I ran into him again just before you were born. In Quiapo. He was looking for work to pay for passage home to Mindanao.'

Julián lifted his eyes off the floor and chanced another glance in his father's direction. The older man seemed to be gazing far beyond the confines of the secret room.

'Your mother wanted nothing to do with him both times.'

Julián remained silent.

A few breaths later, his father turned to face him.

'When I saw Adil in the Quiapo market, I gave him all the money I had,' Federico disclosed. 'It wasn't much, but what little was in my pocket was more than he'd seen in months. He was nothing but bones, ashen, pale as a ghost . . .'

Julián looked down at the black-and-white photo that came with the letter he just read.

He'd seen the man before. This—*Adil.* He was wearing the same clothing—a dark shirt, a traditional tadjung wrapped around his waist, and that visorless cap on his head.

In the photo, the man looked almost regal standing between his two sons.

He also seemed slightly better fed.

But there remained a haunted air about him. An undeniable anguish in his sunken eyes.

'You met him when you were a little boy, maybe three or four?' Don Federico told Juli. 'We kept in touch when he returned to Mindanao, and he came by with a present a few years later—we were still living in that small apartment in Pasay, do you remember?'

There was a slight smile on his father's face, then, he sighed. 'Ay, what am I talking about—you were too young.'

At that moment, Julián wished he did remember. It seemed a much simpler time for his parents.

'Bueno,' Iko continued, 'the first time Adil wrote, it was to say he got home safely. Fortunately, the landlord gave *me* the letter because if he'd given it to your mother, that would've been the end of it.'

Federico looked his son in the eyes, as if trying to transmit a lifetime of secrets.

He reached for his sherry and took another sip.

'Adil wrote again when their father died. I didn't know how to tell your mother.' He set the glass back down. 'Every time I brought up her family, she shut down. So, for months, I said nothing. Eventually, of course, I told her everything and she agreed to write them. We sent along a photo—one of those portraits that we sat for after your first birthday—' Iko paused. 'As far as your mother was concerned, that was the end of it. She didn't want anything linking her back to them—in case the aggrieved rival family got wind of it.'

Until that moment, Julián didn't know that his mother's story about a vengeful clan was true.

His father took one more sip of sherry, emptying the glass.

'I couldn't cut them out like that—they're the only other family she had'—he took a breath—'so, I kept in touch with Adil.'

Iko got up and poured himself more sherry.

'Every now and then, I would send him money. To help care for their mother. He always sent it back, but with some news. I told him to reach me through my office, addressing the letters to Tining. That way, it wouldn't trouble your mother. She didn't need to know. We didn't write frequently, just enough that we weren't complete strangers.'

He returned to the table and put his glass down next to his son's.

'Apparently, after your mother left Mindanao, Adil tried to repay the debt the other family insisted they were owed. He offered to marry that datu's daughter, but they wouldn't have it. Marrying a boy from your mother's tribe was considered beneath them, but had your mother wed their son, she would've been *advancing*.'

Don Federico gave Julián a sad smile. 'I had hoped this troublesome matter would resolve itself. Instead'—he sighed heavily—'here we are.'

Federico shut his eyes again and shook his head. In the golden light of the stained-glass desk lamp, his son thought he aged beyond his forty-six years.

'Julián, hijo,' Iko's voice was almost a whisper. 'I am telling you this so you understand a little about your mother, where she comes from and why she is so afraid.'

Julián always thought his Mami the strongest person in the world.

'I will write Adil,' his father continued. 'We will sort out what is going on.'

'No, Papá—' Julián's sudden move nearly toppled the glasses of sherry on the table. 'It's all right, I will go away as Mami said. It's for the best. I mean, what do we really understand about these feuds? No? *Mejor*—let it be.'

There was a poignancy to Julián's realization that his parents believed they were each protecting the other. It was not his place to tell them otherwise.

Seeing his son's resoluteness, Federico gave him documents to take to Hong Kong. It would give him access to a bank there and a share of the family's wealth.

Iko told his eldest child to use the money to complete his education. Then, to find work in the States—or set up a business.

Julián would have to fend for himself.

But if he needed anything, he was to reach his father through a lawyer in Hong Kong.

Once he left The Islands though, Julián didn't want to ask for help. He felt he'd burdened his parents enough.

He most certainly would never use his father as a bank account.

Over the years, there were many complications for a man—like him.

He felt shame, he felt anger, he felt self-hatred.

Over the years, his letters home through the Hong Kong lawyer grew infrequent.

Until he heard through the grapevine that his father had died.

* * *

'Jules?' Greg Parker stepped back into their guest bedroom from the bath. 'Are you all right?'

Julián was staring out an open window into Sombra's garden. Mindlessly swirling a glass of dark amber sherry.

He almost forgot he had company.

'Sorry, I know this isn't how you would've wanted to spend the holidays.'

'Nothing to apologise for,' Greg approached and gently rubbed the grieving man's shoulders. 'It's been a long few days. I know how difficult this must be—what's that smell?'

Julián smiled sadly. 'Dama de noche, an evening jasmine. It grows along this outside wall and only blooms in the dark.'

He cracked the window wider and took a deep breath.

'Reminds me of my mother—' he shut his eyes. 'My father used to call her his little "poppy"—his *amapola*'—he took another deep breath—'but my mother, she always smelled of jasmine—'

Greg nodded. The scent was—*comforting*.

He would've liked to have met the legendary Doña Fatimah—he heard endless tales from Jules and Cova. It pained him that he couldn't ease his husband's sorrow.

'Why don't you try and sleep?'

'I can't,' Julián sipped his sherry and faced his partner. 'I have to figure out if my parents stashed away money. If not, I don't know how we can pay Freddie's ransom.'

'Couldn't you borrow from someone?' Greg wondered why they didn't just ask for help. From Andy, for example.

'No.' Julián was adamant. 'We must resolve this ourselves. Money is not a matter to trifle with. We wouldn't want to burden anyone or owe them such a huge amount.'

He turned back to the window and breathed in the crisp December night—his finger tapping his mother's ring against the glass of sherry.

Moments later, he set the glass down on a table. 'I think I'll go back to my father's office and keep looking through his papers.'

'Shall I help?' Greg ventured. Julián seemed a different person since they set foot in Manila.

'No, no. It's all right,' Juli kissed his husband's cheek. 'Thank you.'

* * *

In the hallway, the Swiss grandfather clock on the landing struck 2 a.m.

Julián heard a thump down the corridor to his right. It was dark.

'Joder, shit.'

One of his nephews.

'Ricky?'

Thud-thud. Thump.

'Are you all right?' He helped his brother's son off the floor.

'Thanks, Tito. I tripped on the puto rug—'

'Are you just getting home?' Julián worried his nephew was inebriated.

'Yes. Was in Pasay. Working,' Ricky checked that his camera wasn't damaged. 'Under this president, dead bodies appear like stars—after dark. The photos sell big time, especially abroad. I can make money to put towards the ransom.'

Julián had been away so long that he didn't think he could ever be as blasé about murder.

But on the islands, it was par for the course. Like the Christmas season beginning in September—and rain.

Or abductions as viable means to make a living.

Somewhere on the ceiling, a gecko clucked.

'Why are you up, Tito?' Ricky ignored it. 'Still jetlagged?'

'Possibly,' Julián sighed. 'I'm going to look through your grandfather's papers again to see if I can—I don't know—find anything useful.'

'Let me help?' Ricky offered.

Why not?—Julián considered. It felt like a torch-passing of sorts.

* * *

Like his uncle before him, Ricky had no idea the refugio existed in his Aba's room.

But he saved his questions for later.

'Could you start on those boxes?' His uncle pointed at a stack behind a chaise longue. 'I'm told those were brought over from his main office after he died—and no one's looked through them.'

The boxes were full of documents and records from Don Federico's workplace at Castillo de Montijo Enterprises, including a file of medical papers and unopened letters from Mindanao.

'Who is Celestino Magpantay?' Ricky called out, surprised at the speed with which his uncle approached.

Julián skimmed through the file, putting aside hospital bills in the Magpantay name—which were likely paid by his father. It was the pile of unopened letters that might be useful.

Silently, he read each one.

Ricky scanned the pages after his uncle put them down.

There was news about some Ismail fellow returning from Saudi Arabia more devoted to Islam than ever. Apparently, he was there on an engineering scholarship and learned the ultra-conservative ways of the Wahhabis. Or so the letter-writer feared. He—the letter writer—also worried about this Ismail's growing interest in guns.

Another letter was brimming with pride over 'Ibrahim's' teaching certificate. Then, it went on to speak of the writer's 'uncertain health' and wondered why there hadn't been a response from Manila in months.

The unanswered months turned to years.

The letters were all postmarked after Don Federico died. None later than 1981.

There was a photo included in one of the envelopes.

'Tito Julián,' Ricky ventured, taking a closer look. 'I think I've seen this man—'

Julián's silence encouraged him to go on.

'He was here, in Sombra. Abuelo Federico had already died, but Aba spoke to this guy in the yard. I remember 'cuz he was wearing what I thought was a skirt,' Ricky smiled, shyly. 'I was up in the macopa tree and saw her give him an envelope. It had money in it, but he wouldn't take it. Back then, I had no idea her family was Muslim.'

It played back in his mind like an old film clip. Faded, and in stops and starts.

'Only time I saw Aba cry.' Ricky remembered feeling helpless as he watched his indestructible grandmother shed tears. 'After he left, she stood in a corner before entering the house—by the wall covered in dama de noche. She didn't know I could see her. When I asked her about it later, she told me to stop being silly.'

Julián nodded sadly. His Mami was the strongest person in the world.

'For years, I thought I'd seen things wrong,' Ricky stared at the photo of an elderly man in traditional Moro dress. He was flanked by two other men looking just as serious.

* * *

'This one is Ustadz Ibrahim Abdullazuljani,' pronounced Alma's eldest daughter—the reporter—as she handed the photo back to her uncle. 'Head of the Moro Union of Moderates. An academic. Ran for a seat in Congress. Lost. Well-respected, but too clean. You know how it is. Without using intimidation and cash, there's no prevailing in island politics. Especially now.'

Ximena Yrastegui, walking encyclopedia and unbridled commentator. Apparently, jetlagged, and also an insomniac.

Still tossing and turning when the church bells rang for the pre-dawn advent mass, Ximena decided to wander into Aba's room and sit alone in her absence.

Instead, she found Julián and Ricky going through heaps of papers. The men had been foraging all night.

Julián pieced together that the academic was Adil's eldest son, Ibrahim. The other one—an engineer possibly radicalised in Saudi—must be the younger Ismail.

'Why do we have photos of prominent Moros?' Ximena asked. 'Does this have anything to do with Tito Freddie's disappearance?'

Before Julián could speak, Núria burst into the room.

'Quick, everyone downstairs! Tita Maca has news—' she stopped midsentence at seeing Ricky.

She wasn't going to be the one to tell him that they received a video clip of his father—blindfolded and on his knees—surrounded by armed men.

Chapter 32

Los Forasteros | **The Outsiders** | Ang Mga Tagalabas

'Sorry, Luísa, you froze. Could you repeat that?'

Luísa Acosta de Castillo—Freddie's (legitimate) wife—switched her laptop camera off and then on again. A trick she learned from Pili, her youngest daughter, who occasionally—*infrequently*—called over the internet from Europe. (Or wherever Pili found herself at the time.)

'Is this better, Reverend Shirley?' Luísa asked the person on the other end of the video call. The connection in Manila was so slow and unreliable—she hated wasting time sorting it out.

'Yes, I can see you now,' the robust blonde woman on the screen nodded her pixelated head.

Luísa said a quiet prayer of thanks—Reverend Shirley charged a hundred dollars for half an hour, regardless of connection quality. Plus a premium, because it was the holidays.

The worst Christmas of Luísa's life.

Not counting the year she lost her baby, the one she miscarried before having Ricky.

But then again, that miscarriage took her down a 'blessed journey of faith'—as Brother Sunshine termed it. She'd been exploring all sorts of paths to enlightenment ever since.

Luísa supposed that, at the very least, she should be grateful for the inducement to spirituality.

It led her to Reverend Shirley in Montana, USA. An astrologer and energy healer making waves on the worldwide web.

For her regular client, Reverend Shirley delayed dinner with her family. (30 minutes = $100.00, not counting the holiday premium).

Thank goodness for the digital age.

Luísa didn't know how to handle her desolation otherwise.

'So, your husband isn't back yet?' Shirley repeated what she thought Luísa had said.

'No, and we've heard nothing since the proof-of-life video days ago.'

Luísa began to hyperventilate, remembering a blindfolded Freddie on his knees surrounded by armed men wearing balaclavas. She clutched her chest.

'Julián—that's my husband's brother—I didn't even know he had one until now—he's gay—lives in the States—Boston—is that far from Montana? He's still so handsome—I saw old photos—I found his room by accident, you see—well, I didn't know it was his—anyway—that's not what I wanted to talk about. I called because Julián is back—and he says the family has no money for ransom—I don't know how that's possible— and what does that mean for my husband—what if they kill him?'

'Don't worry, Luísa,' Reverend Shirley in Montana had never quite dealt with a situation like this one. 'Your husband is—fine.'

'Are you sure? Is that what the angels say? Is it in his star chart?' Luísa was hopeful.

'Yes, yes,' Shirley's eyes were shut as if listening to something far away—or bored. 'That's what the spirits are telling me. Your husband is—fine.'

Luísa sighed, relieved.

'However, your children,' Shirley pulled a card out of her tarot deck, 'they're—away?'

'Yes. Well, my daughters are,' Luísa nodded. 'They escaped Manila. They escaped this house. They have their own lives. They didn't even come back for their grandmother's—' Luísa stopped, fearing she might say too much. Alma was clear about what should be kept private.

Reverend Shirley nodded. 'I see. And you are alone.'

'I have my son.' Luísa said abruptly. She was beginning to feel sorry for herself.

She didn't like the feeling.

Reverend Shirley noted her client's distress and pulled out another card.

'What is it?' Luísa tilted her head, trying to peer into her laptop screen as if she could see to the other side.

'Your family is grieving,' Shirley pronounced.

'Yes,' Luísa knew there was no point hiding anything from this amazing clairvoyant. 'My mother-in-law died two weeks ago, we can't tell anyone—and we've been worried about my husband. It's—a terrible time.'

'So much grief. So much death. Too many secrets.' Shirley enumerated. 'No wonder you've been unable to see the light of the Universe this Christmas. With such darkness around you, you cannot feel the love.'

Luísa nodded—*Exactly*. 'Which is why I need you to clear the energy, please, Reverend Shirley—I am tired of being in the dark.'

* * *

It was always light out by the time Attorney Manny Santos got back to Sombra from the Palace.

Since the Christmas season began, the president's gatherings with his 'advisers' ran longer and later. Entailing loads more—*flesh-pressing* and *chin-wagging*.

Yes, Attorney Manny Santos snagged himself a coveted spot as a 'close-in' ~~crony~~ of President Hashtag. (No one called them the 'mafia' in public without being jailed.)

One by one, the Close-Ins were lined up and assigned to positions of great importance. The Central Bank, the power company, the national water system, the sugar industry, the rice authority, tourism, gaming, etcetera.

Where there was money to be made, a #Close-In was put in charge.

Having reaped all he could from the Castillos, Attorney Manny recast his lot with the kingpin of the new social order. (Oh, how he loved democracy!)

He and Durog first met through Mikey and his cousin Pip Rodríguez, but it was a claim to similarly miserable childhoods—and a mutual love of Elvis—that cemented their affinity.

'Manny! Thank God you're finally home,' Doña Maca whimpered, reaching for him as he stumbled into their bedroom.

He evaded her grasp.

He was exhausted.

There was enough drama around #Durog—didn't the woman realize how much effort went into constantly agreeing with a narcissistic madman?

He kicked off his shoes. 'What now?'

'Didn't you see my text? I sent you their message—'

'What text, Macarena? I don't have time for this.'

'Freddie—' Maca's voice cracked. 'The investigators say there's still no news. It's been almost a week, Manny—my poor brother—they'll kill him if we don't pay ransom.'

Maca checked her mobile phone again. Manny took a deep breath—his wife relished this 'distraught woman' routine.

He'd been around politicians long enough to know a play when he saw one—and this 'kidnapping' was textbook. He almost wished he'd thought of it first.

He sighed.

'Maca, I was with the president all night—the president! I have friends in the highest places—I told you I would handle this Freddie matter.'

It took all Manny's strength to keep from smirking—*Freddie, that bothersome bastard.*

'Speaking of the president,' he puffed his chest out and slowly unbuttoned his shirt. 'Guess what he gave us for Christmas?'

Maca was not so easily distracted—her mind still on her brother.

'You are looking at the new COO of LIsPoCorp*.' Manny threw his shirt aside.

She looked at her husband as if a light switched suddenly on. 'What?'

'Mikey is CEO, of course—I'm his deputy. The power company needs new leadership. The grid was heavily damaged by the storm in Mindanao and—'

'But the Ronquillo family has run the electric company for generations'—Maca was baffled—'why would they give up control now?'

'Because they have no choice!' Manny didn't like being questioned. Maca flinched.

He took a breath.

'The government—*has no choice*—but to take over LIsPoCorp because Boy-Tiny Ronquillo is incompetent, nothing like his father. Under Tiny, the company had no contingency plan and failed to provide a basic service to the people of Mindanao—our fellow countrymen— in their hour of need.'

Manny repeated similar explanations so often he actually believed it—wonderful how easily history could be revised.

'I see,' was all Maca replied.

'The position comes with the penthouse of Paradise Towers—you know the one—was called Manhattan Skies while being built? We get the top three floors, two helipads, full staff. All our bills will be paid. I thought you'd be pleased.'

'I—am.' Truly, she was. Manny didn't know how anxious she'd been about being broke. She hadn't told him about the Castillos' impending impoverishment.

Alma was clear—they couldn't risk Manny informing opportunists like Durog.

Truth was, Maca kept silent because the loss of wealth—and so status—embarrassed her.

But this presidential posting erased any reason to be ashamed.

All the nights she had to share her husband with his *political* work finally bore fruit.

She was going to be Doña Macarena, Mrs Attorney Manny Santos—of *Las Islas Power Corporation (LIsPoCorp).

They would be rich—and important—on their own.

The Honourable Santoses—it was going to be wonderful.

'I'm going for a swim,' her husband announced.

Macarena watched as he—unthinking—removed his trousers and pulled his underpants out of his butt crack. At sixty, her husband was still such a glorious man.

She approached him and tried to lay her hand on his sturdy, smooth chest.

Manny turned away and headed for the bathroom to change. He saw the longing in Maca's eyes. Once or twice in the last month, she even tried to *touch* him. It was terrible.

In front of the full-length mirror, Manny appraised himself as he rubbed coconut oil on his hairless body—*Not bad for a senior citizen.*

He adjusted his crotch in the tight white Speedos and stepped back into the room.

'Have the maid bring me breakfast in the gazebo.'

It was nearly noon. Maca simply nodded as he walked out the door.

* * *

Locked in her room, with her eyes shut, Luísa Castillo silently tallied her woes as Reverend Shirley prayed over her via the internet.

1) Her husband was gone—had been for years, if she was honest with herself.

2) Her daughters—Pili and Fáti—had also abandoned her. Both left the country as soon as they were old enough, and—

3) her son was in and out of rehab. Lost in a darkness all his own.

Luísa never knew how to reach them, let alone make them love her.

So, she worked on loving herself. It's what all the books said she should do.

Or what her friends said the books said she should do. (Luísa hadn't actually read anything herself.)

She was in her fifties and still trying everything on trend—feng shui, energy crystals, Jesus, Buddha, reiki—Reverend Shirley, the internet healer. She didn't know where else to turn.

Life was supposed to improve when she married Freddie Castillo de Montijo, but it hadn't.

She didn't feel important, or popular—or loved.

What else was there to living?

'Our time is almost up, Luísa,' Reverend Shirley pronounced from Montana. 'Unless you want to donate another fifty dollars—for extra time?'

'Yes. Yes, of course.' Luísa reached for her last functioning credit card—a supplementary Amex her eldest, Fáti, gave her for emergencies.

* * *

Hugo put his credit card away, remembering—almost too late—how adamant Ricky was that no one be able to identify him.

'Sir, how much did you want?' the man behind the cage bars smiled at him warmly, Santa hat perched jauntily on his head.

Hugo's stomach churned—he wasn't sure what to do.

'Sir?'

He wiped his brow. He'd never done anything so—*nefarious.*

'Sir?'

How'd he let himself be talked into this?

Why was he so desperate to feel like part of the family?

Que imbécil—this could land him in jail.

Him. *Not Ricky.* Him!

As if he hadn't upset his mother enough—*Joder.*

'Paré, hurry up,' a gruff voice behind him urged.

Hugo checked his mobile. It wasn't even noon.

'If you don't want any more chips, sir, please let me serve the next customer.'

How was there a line in the casino so early in the day? At Christmastime, too.

Hugo moved aside to let the agitated chain-smoker forward. The man shoved a heap of chips to be cashed.

Hugo counted the remaining tokens in his hand. Value: two thousand pesos.

His few weeks in Manila taught him that was barely enough for dinner at a proper restaurant.

'Mr Castillo de Montijo?'

Hugo turned to find a smartly dressed man had sidled up to him. He wore a wireless earpiece and there was a bulge under his shirt to the side of his torso.

'Would you come with me, sir?'

Mierda. Ricky asked him to do one thing and he messed it up.

* * *

Pepa was always impressed by the number of mobile phones the attorney sir had. There were at least five on the table in the gazebo.

She didn't know where to move them as she set the place for his meal. He must be a very important man indeed to need all those devices.

One of them rang.

Pepa nearly dropped a plate. Oh, how she wished Señora Maca hadn't fired Beverly. The more experienced maid was better at serving Sir Attorney.

Manny rose from the pool to check the call. It was from a number he didn't recognise.

Ordinarily, he would've ignored it, but with his new important post—he figured he should answer. The call came straight through to him and not his assistant—so it must be an equally important person at the other end.

Click.

'You are not an easy man to track down, Armando.' Click, cluck.

'Tangina—Tukô. Damnit.

'Secretary Salazar,' Manny tried to sound pleased to hear from the elderly politician. 'Merry Christmas—'

'Let's not pretend you're glad I'm calling. You've been eluding me for some time now, Armando—you and Freddie. And don't feed me this bullshit that he's been kidnapped. We both know those "rebels" have been working with him for years.'

Manny didn't know what to say—*Good Lord*—the old lizard really did know everything.

Pepa quietly scurried out of the gazebo to get the sir his food.

'What can I do for you, Mister Secretary?' Manny pulled his wet trunks out of his buttocks. He hated addressing Tukô by a title he no longer held.

Indeed, the old man hadn't been a government minister in years. At least not under the last two presidents. But on the islands, people clung to designations as if they were gold.

'You owe me, Armando.' Click. Cluck. 'Blaming Freddie for everything doesn't get you off the hook. I'm no fool, my boy—and yet, you keep making that naïve presumption.'

Manny knew better than to speak. He shut his eyes, feeling the onset of a migraine.

'As you suggested, I had a—talk—with Freddie's son a while ago now,' Tukô continued. 'But the boy hasn't given me anything truly useful. A few compromising photos of select personalities, but no lead on that new Chinese triad or his father. I want my money, Armando—maybe I should've *talked* with your offspring instead—'

Manny held back a laugh—Tukô would gain nothing from harassing Dito. That spineless loser had no secrets and never got in trouble unless dragged into it by Ricky.

His son's only weakness was a blind faith in his cousin—and God.

'Do not for one second think I meant little Dito.' Click, cluck.

Manny held his breath.

'What is it now, Armando? Ten? Fifteen? Must be at least thirteen, no? Click. Do you even know how many children you have littered around? I must say, your latest bastard is cute. Yes, I have seen him. Cluck. That tramp of yours is also screwing my worthless son. She tried to pass the baby off as his—but the DNA test proved otherwise. God is good. I have enough spawns in my family to tend to.'

Shit—Manny didn't know about this new one. He really should have been more careful about birth control.

No—he corrected himself—those stupid women should've been more careful. Clearly, they got pregnant on purpose. Who could blame them? He was so attractive—with his thick head of hair and his deep bronze skin. The epitome of a beautiful, virile islander. An easy mark.

Manny offered to pay for abortions—albeit illegal on the islands—
but the girls refused to have them. So—*tough shit*—it was their choice.
He wasn't paying for anything after that.

'Armando, since neither you nor Freddie have repaid me what you
stole—and don't bother saying you didn't do it, I'm not as stupid as
your women—you are going to give me access to the power grid. I hear
you and Ipé's idiot nephew, Mikey, will be managing it.'

Again, Manny did not know what to say. But confident of his place
in Durog's inner circle, he dared to be cocky. The president and Tukô
had been at odds for years—supposedly over a business deal gone sour.
Maybe he could play the two men off each other.

'Let me consider it, Mister Secretary,' Manny proposed.

Click, click. Tukô was no longer the most feared man in
the country.

'What's in it for me?' the duplicitous 'lawyer' inquired.

The clicking stopped. A chilling laugh pierced through the phone.

'What's—in—it—for—me?' Tukô repeated. Click, cluck. 'Your
life, Armando—that's what's in it for you—I might be persuaded to
let you live.'

More laughter. Cluck. Click. The line went dead.

At that moment, Pepa was returning to the gazebo with a tray of
scrambled eggs and garlic fried rice.

'Inday! 'Day!' Manny snapped his fingers at the young girl, calling
her by the term commonly used for indistinguishable servants—girl.
Shortened to and pronounced—'die'.

''Day, bring me my whisky—and a bucket of ice.'

Pepa froze, unsure what to do with the tray of food she was so
carefully balancing.

She was halfway across the garden, by the pool. Does she return
to the kitchen? Does she put down the tray on a sun lounger? Or does
she go towards the table in the gazebo? Beverly would have known
what to do.

'Now!' Manny yelled at her.

'Yes, sir—Attorney,' Pepa nodded, half-running back to the
kitchen with the tray.

Attorney Sir Manny always made her nervous.

* * *

'That is not Ricky Castillo.'

Hugo stood unmoving between two burly escorts, unable to clearly see the man speaking.

The only light in the dark room came from a wall of security monitors showing every inch of the casino in black and white.

'That—is not—Ricky—Castillo—' the man repeated through gritted teeth, a cigarette dangling vulgarly from his lips.

He blew out acrid smoke and threw an ashtray across the room. It hit the padded wall with a dull thud.

He stepped towards Hugo, squinting.

Up close, the angry man's face was pale and waxy. His nose—wide.

His eyes were slits behind thin, round-rimmed glasses.

'Who are you?' the man glowered in English with a heavy Chinese accent.

Hugo had never been so terrified in his life. Not even when he went rock climbing without ropes in Andorra.

Maybe it was just as well he wasn't raised in Manila—he wouldn't have survived all this—*adventure.*

'I said—who are you? Answer me!' The man slapped him on both cheeks.

Hugo began to shake.

It was Ricky who made plans to cheat at Baccarat. Ricky who was friends with the dealer from their 'party' days.

It was Ricky who arranged entry to a high-roller game that was fixed for him to win.

Ricky who was desperate for money to free his father.

But it was also Ricky who was paranoid about being shadowed by cops.

Ricky who didn't want to be spotted on security cameras.

So, Ricky asked Hugo to go in his place.

New cousin Hugo. Manila virgin.

'No one knows who you are, primo,' Ricky implored.

And that—Hugo thought—was precisely the problem. No one knew who he was.

At the ripe old age of twenty-eight, Hugo Pérez-García found he barely knew himself.

That night at the casino, Hugo got carried away by the opportunity to be someone else.

Evening rolled into day, and he turned his cousin's pre-arranged win into losses.

He should've stopped when he was told to—instead, he moved on to another high-stakes table. The dealer wasn't as accommodating.

Uff—he reeled from a punch in the stomach. One of the burly escorts was cracking his knuckles in preparation for another blow.

'I know everything that happens in this casino,' huffed the cigarette-puffing Chinese man. 'No croupier can cheat without me agreeing to look away. That table was prepared for Ricky Castillo. So, I will ask one more time—Who the fuck are you?'

When Hugo failed to reply, the escort struck him again.

He doubled over.

Behind him, two narcs stepped out of the shadows. They wore vests emblazoned with the name of the agency.

'We've wasted enough time, Fu Ming,' said the shorter agent. His pot belly pouring over his straining trousers. 'Do we plant the drugs on him or not?'

Slowly, Hugo realized he had blundered into a sting operation—Ricky was being set up for arrest.

What did his cousin do that they wanted him so badly? Thus far, his experience with Island police had not been reassuring.

'Can you cover the forty million that Freddie owes?' the agent asked.

Hugo shook his head. Wondering if this maybe wasn't about Ricky—but his father?

''Tangina,' the narc cursed.

The men began to speak to each other in a flurry of Tagalog, occasionally peppering their conversation with English words. Those were the only ones Hugo understood.

As well as a few that sounded like Spanish.

Droga—drugs. *Millones*—millions. Operation. *Presidente*. Freddie.

'Now—one last time—tell us who you are and where the fuck is Ricky Castillo?' the lead agent threw back the wallet that they took off him earlier.

Hugo began to cry.

'*Pucha naman*—you limp-wristed waste of space!' The narc spat at Hugo's feet then punched him in the gut.

'Get him out of here,' the Chinese puffer ordered his burly guards. 'And you,' he addressed Hugo again, 'give that fool Ricky a message from the Dragons: If he doesn't stop fucking with us, he will be liable for his father's mistake. Freddie owes a lot of people—and we all want our money back. If we don't get it, one of us will make sure he pays, one way or another.'

The angry Chinese man exhaled a cloud of smoke.

Then, he clapped his hands together in Hugo's face—'Game over.'

* * *

To Pepa, it was like going through an obstacle course—a round of *patintero*. How she hated playing that game as a child in a rural backwater. She didn't like being chased within its narrow lines and risk being tagged out because she was clumsy on her feet.

She felt for the lucky medal in her pocket.

To get Attorney Manny Sir's drink from the bar, Pepa had to walk across the main courtyard from the kitchen towards the east lanai. Running the danger of encountering any of the señoras and señoritos of the house.

Gripping her talisman, she stopped abruptly under the archway before stepping into the terrace.

The two foreign girls she'd admired for days were splayed on the sofas. Glued to their big shiny mobiles.

They were the daughters of Señora Maca's sister, Señora Cova— the beautiful, thin one from Spain.

These girls were also very pretty—with their tall noses, long golden hair, and bright, sparkling eyes.

Under whirling ceiling fans, they chattered in Spanish, just like the glamorous women in those Mexican telenovelas that Pepa watched.

She didn't understand a word, of course, but she gazed at the Spanish visitors awe-struck—imagining their conversation was dubbed in Tagalog. Just like the telenovelas.

She stood unmoving by the archway, hoping they hadn't seen her.

* * *

'Did you get a good picture of the house? With all the Christmas décor? I still can't believe Mamá kept this from us.'

'Right? I mean, we had a right to grow up here, too—like the cousins. We could have each had a suite!'

'Yea! She totally deprived us—#unfair.'

'Haha! And yes, I did get a photo of the entrance—it has over five hundred likes already—#heritage.'

'Nice, #TropicalChristmas. *Que suerte*, how lucky they are. Meanwhile, we've been stuck taking summer jobs and doing chores in boring Salamanca—'

'Tell me about it. Our cousins live like royalty—and they have maids!'

'Shh, here comes one now.'

The two blonde girls smiled politely at Pepa. Her head bowed, she didn't dare look them in the eye.

Do something, Pepa, Sir Attorney is waiting—she rubbed her talisman and took a few tentative steps. Then, she hurried across the lanai—like a small, soundless lizard—to the bar.

She felt the visitors' gaze—and their silence—and wished they'd look away as she searched for Sir Manny's bottle of Scotch. She wasn't sure she was reading the labels correctly.

Blue and gold—Pepa told herself. Sir Attorney drank the rusty liquid in the blue and gold bottle.

* * *

The blue-striped 10 ball missed the side pocket by a hair—Cristóbal couldn't believe he was losing to Greg.

They'd been playing pool in the game room for the last hour, trying to keep themselves occupied without being disrespectful of their spouses' grief.

The walls were plastered with photos of the Castillos looking happy. Weddings, christenings, Christmas mornings, vacations abroad. They shimmered in the daylight streaming in from the windows.

Greg noticed there were no photos of Julián. Or Cova.

He lined up his cue stick.

'But it is odd, wouldn't you say?' Greg pressed Cristóbal as he prepared to strike the ball. 'I mean, she's been lying in that chapel for, what—almost three weeks? That's longer than Lincoln at the capitol when he died.'

Cristóbal smiled, unperturbed. Greg missed his shot.

'Shouldn't she have been buried within twenty-four hours? It's a Muslim custom—'

'Yes, but she's not Muslim any more,' Cristóbal explained. 'She converted before marrying Don Federico.'

Cristóbal missed the pocket, again.

Greg moved around the table.

'Okay—but surely even as a Catholic—you find this a little odd?' He stopped studying the balls and looked Cristóbal in the eye. 'We're cooped up in here as if something's about to attack. They don't let us help with this matter of the abduction—*an abduction*—for Christ's sake. They don't let us into their—grief—or anxiety—or whatever else—and honestly, I'm uncomfortable that you and I are playing pool—for the love of God—while this strange spectacle goes on around us.'

Cristóbal laughed. Not unkindly. 'Haven't you realized by now that the Castillos live by their own rules?' He offered the observation without any rancour.

'I think I finally understand why Jules had to leave—this place can drive anyone mad,' Greg could barely contain his frustration. 'It's like walking a tightrope—a ludicrous balancing act between how you feel and how you're supposed to behave.'

'So very un-American, no?' Cristóbal jested. Greg didn't crack a smile.

'Why did you and Cova leave? I can't imagine it's a decision you regret.'

'Ay, Greg, there are many things I regret—and that is among them.' Cristóbal finally got a ball in. 'I often imagine what my life—our lives—would have been like had we stayed in Manila. Maybe my wife would not have had to work so hard—'

Coño. Missed, again.

'Maybe she would be closer to her siblings and not feel left out. Like this morning, she's still asleep because she took a sedative, but the rest of them are probably already huddled together plotting something.'

Cris smiled and stepped back to let Greg get closer to the table.

'That's why I insisted our girls come to meet the other children. To bond.'

'Why in God's good earth do you people keep calling them that?' Greg put down his cue stick. 'The "children". They're adults, for Pete's sake.' He was flummoxed.

Cristóbal clapped him in the back—'They'll always be the children to us, to family.'

* * *

Don Andy Yrastegui had represented the Castillo de Montijo family on many occasions. Officially, and unofficially.

Not only was he the spouse of Don Federico's eldest daughter, Andy was also part of one of the oldest Spanish—Basque—industrial clans in the Philippines.

So, when Don Andy asked the chief of military intelligence to meet him at the Manila Grand Hotel after they got the first ransom demand, General Catacutan went without question.

In a private penthouse suite, Andy told the general about Freddie's abduction, asking for his help—and his discretion.

To not inconvenience the Castillos, General Catacutan agreed to keep investigators off the estate—and instead, set up a base of operations at the hotel. On Don Andy's bill, of course. He leased The Grand's entire top floor for that purpose.

Every morning for a week, Andy rushed over for updates. Hopeful that investigators had triangulated the kidnappers' location or gleaned any pertinent information from dissecting the ransom footage. He'd seen it done many times on those foreign FBI shows.

But this wasn't scripted television.

Or the FBI.

* * *

Pepa was giddy with triumph as she returned to the gazebo with the ice bucket and the golden bottle of whisky. She always felt foolish around new people—especially if they were pale-skinned and from abroad. But she found what she was sent for and escaped the Spanish girls in the terrace without tripping on her feet. Thank goodness for the lucky medal.

She was still flushed with joy when she bent over the table preparing the sir's drink. She didn't notice him come up from the pool behind her.

Suddenly, she felt cold water seep through her uniform, and something like a policeman's club was pressed to her back. She was trapped against the table.

Manny laughed at the young maid's helplessness. She was immobile, her arms rigid at her side. He liked that.

'Do you feel how happy I am to see you, *inday*?' he growled in her ear. 'And not only because you brought me my Scotch—'

Attorney Manny Sir always made Pepa nervous.

He spun her around and invaded her mouth. She gagged on his tongue and couldn't have screamed if she tried.

He shoved his hands under her uniform—she struggled to push him away.

He was such a powerful man, Sir Manny Attorney.

'What the—?!'

The voice was one Manny did not recognise.

'Who the hell are you?' the attorney demanded with righteous indignation.

The interloper looked like a faggot—yes, *a faggot*—why did people get so upset when he used that word?

Well, this boy looked like a. . .what were they calling themselves? Mono-sexual? No, wait—*metro-sexual*—what does that even mean? Yet another stupid name for the same thing— limp-wristed pretty boys who dandied about looking delicate and prissy. In bright pastel colours and pressed button-down shirts. They looked—*European.*

This fop was darker than others Manny had encountered, but—like the rest of them—this dandy appeared to smell of gardenias and lime.

'I'm Hugo, Cova's son.'

Manny swatted the young girl away—his eyes locked on the intruder—his erection distinct through his swimsuit.

Pepa ran back to the house as fast as she could.

Oo-goh—interesting name. Manny looked the boy up and down. Cova—

He hadn't seen Cova since she arrived in Manila. He reckoned that was likely due to his wife's careful choreography.

Cova.

No wonder this self-righteous boy looked familiar. Thick hair, steely gaze, strong presence. He reminded Manny of—of—*himself*—when he was younger.

Almost as handsome, thought Manny of the European dandy.

Definitely handsomer than Dito.

'So,' Manny approached the boy like a snake about to sting his prey, 'your father is—?'

'Cristóbal. Pérez-García.' Hugo replied, upset at the insinuation. 'Who else?'

Manny nodded, then shook his head, laughing. 'Of course. Of course he is.'

Like a preening cockerel, Manny ran his hands through his wet hair. Still thick and black despite the years.

'First time in Manila?' he slowly circled the boy—the young man—better said.

'Yes,' Hugo was curt. This *gilipollas* was a little too close for comfort. He'd had enough of questionable characters for one lifetime. 'And you are?'

'Attorney Manny Santos,' he puffed out his chest and patted his stomach as if it were a tight six-pack. 'Soon to be running the power company. I am married to your Tita Macarena.'

Hugo thought it a strange way to introduce oneself, but then again—as he'd discovered—there were many 'strange' things about Manila. About his family.

About Sombra.

'So, Oo-goh, have a seat. Tell me about yourself,' Manny invited with a broad grin.

'I am going to the chapel—to sit with Aba.' Actually, he was searching for Ricky.

With that, the eldest of Manny's bastards left him behind.

* * *

Reverend Shirley wasn't in the habit of telling on her clients, but this one was special. She paid double for 'news' and always added a massive tip.

So, for Madam, the Revered Shirley was flexible about her rules. What harm, after all?

For Madam, she stayed up past midnight, Montana time.

'Good day, Madam,' Reverend Shirley answered the video call from Manila. Her Island clients were keeping her busy.

'Hello, Shirley.'

The middle-aged American astrologer was face-to-face with an overly made-up woman wearing curlers in her hair. Her lips were yet unpainted, but her ears were already dripping in diamonds. 'You have news for me?'

'I believe so,' Shirley replied. 'I spoke with one of the women you asked me to keep tabs on, and I think you'll find this quite interesting, Madam Marasigan.'

* * *

'Yes, President Marasigan, he's right here.'

Andy was pacing the hotel room when the call came in. Four investigators were huddled around a laptop, the others watched television or yammered away on their mobiles.

A map of Mindanao was on a large white board on the wall—a big red circle marking the area they believed Freddie was in.

'Sir Andy?' a young soldier handed him the phone.

#Durog was—*sympathetic*. Telling Andy that he put the entire military on alert—ordered to assist in the search and rescue.

'You know, Andy, maybe you should just pay the ransom—'

'What? I thought we weren't supposed to negotiate with these people?'

'Yes, yes,' the president tried to muffle a cough, 'but you know, sometimes it makes more sense to—shall we say—(*another muffled cough*)—bend the rules. I'm sure you agree, anything for family, no?'

* * *

'*Mahal*, let me powder your face na, it's almost time for your segments.'

Durog was in the Palace studio, waiting to record his holiday messages for the public.

He spat into crumpled tissue paper and put a finger to his lips to shush the First Lady. She was fussing over him with Andy Yrastegui still on the other end of the line.

The First Lady was in truth #Durog's mistress, the woman everyone called Madam. His wife—the mother of his legitimate children—was never seen in public and stayed in his hometown several hundred islands away.

'Hang on, Andy, there's something I must attend to,' Durog muted the mic. 'Relax, mahal. I'll be ready, love. You know I don't need make-up—my people appreciate reality.'

The president looked in the mirror, liking the unfiltered reflection that stared back at him.

'This is perfect.'

He coughed again. Madam wiped the corners of his mouth with her hankie.

'Your cheeks are grey in patches, mahal,' she was concerned. 'We must even out your skin tone, so your health isn't questioned again.'

His health. Indeed. The one thing he couldn't control.

Sixty-one-year-old Facundo 'Durog' Marasigan went into politics because it was the only way to be in control, but since becoming president, things seemed to be slipping from his grasp.

That mongrel Freddie Castillo, for example.

Durog should've realized the entitled *Kastilang hilaw*—half-baked Spaniard—would screw him over. It wasn't his first transaction with the infamous King of Shortcuts.

Undeclared fact: When Durog was mayor, Freddie Castillo persuaded him there was a fortune to be made from transiting contraband through the town's port. They even smuggled out an entire forest of trees despite a national logging ban.

If he didn't work with Freddie, someone else would have.

Their partnership flourished until Freddie siphoned more of their profits into his pocket.

'Sir,' Durog's cousin—and private investigator—marched in unannounced. 'I have confirmation—' he nodded at the First Lady, who was pressing powder into the president's face. 'Madam's intel was right—the Castillos are bankrupt, and I can't trace a title for the estate.'

Durog swatted away Madam's hand and checked that the phone he held was still on mute.

'Tangina—what to do. Should he take Sombra? It was on prime land. Without papers, there was no proof of ownership. He could create some patriotic excuse for its sequestration. Was that disrespectful? The old lady did just die.

His other phone rang—an assistant showed him the caller ID: Manny Santos. Durog shook his head. He already had something on the Castillos.

He coughed once more, then released the mute button on the phone in his hand.

'Andy, I have to go. Pass on my condolences to the family. Such a shock when someone you love dies so suddenly—especially for the rich. You people end up scrambling to get affairs in order—like chickens during a typhoon.'

The president laughed until he gagged and coughed up more blood.

He wiped his mouth on the back of his hand.

'Would be a shame to lose that beautiful estate, Andy—so inconvenient.'

Andy froze.

#Durog hung up.

* * *

'Please turn down the television,' Cova beseeched her nieces. She just woke up and felt besieged by the frantic images flashing on the screen—the presenters shouting like circus barkers.

Frankly, it was like the morning shows in Spain. Mindless chatter and rumours dissected as facts.

'Sorry Tita, I'm keeping an eye on the weather. The rains haven't stopped over Mindanao and if the damage gets worse, I may have to get out there,' Ximena explained.

'Ay, hija, can't you take a break this once? It's Christmas Eve,' Alma was both horrified and proud—everyone could see it.

'Mom, you know there is no—'

'No break from the news,' Núria chimed in. 'We know.' It was a familiar refrain from her older sister.

Ximena cast her a sideways glare.

'Girls.' Was all Alma needed to say.

She made room for Cova on the sofa and nodded her head towards the jug of iced hibiscus ginger tea on the table. Pepa didn't make it as well as Manang Lydia had, but it was a regular—*reassuring*—feature of afternoons at Sombra.

'Was it always this hot at Christmas?' Cova whimpered, vigorously flicking a hand fan.

Before anyone could reply, something on the television caught Ximena's attention. She immediately turned up the volume.

It wasn't an update on the weather.

Chapter 33

Las Noticias de Última Hora | **Breaking News** | Ang Nagbabagang Balita

News Copy / BREAKING/ 24 December 2010
Presenter Read:

This just in—a slew of casualties in **Mindanao**—as the ceasefire between government forces and rebel groups collapses.

Members of the Special Forces were on a secret recon mission last week when they stumbled into an active *rido*—which is a blood feud between warring clans in the south.

Military chief, **General Estefanio Angkan**, said soldiers may have been deliberately misled by their informant. They entered a contested area and unknowingly engaged with Muslim clansmen who were battling each other.

The soldiers believed they were under attack.

Fighters from the separatist **Society of Armed Moros for Emancipation (S.A.M.E.)**, and the extremist breakaway faction **Fighters for Islamic Statehood and Territory (F.I.S.T.)** also thought they were being attacked—and retaliated.

A text message from S.A.M.E. said government forces trespassed on their land—and they were defending themselves.

Roll CLIP: General E. Angkan, Military Commander:

'It was a horrible mis-encounter. It should never have happened. But, you know, it's been raining hard, and accidents in the field—in an unmarked jungle or marshland—while under the fog of conflict—are not unusual. We are deeply sorry for the loss of life.' / **END CLIP**.

Presenter Read:

At least thirty soldiers were killed—and more than fifty fighters and civilians.

Entire villages in the Latîan Wetlands were destroyed.

According to leaked reports—among the dead are S.A.M.E. founder Tarek Muazzil Al Tumawiri, better known as **Abu Omar**—and **Ismail Adil Khaled Abdullazuljani,** an alleged criminal warlord known as 'The Engineer', suspected of kidnapping people for ransom.

Several of Abdullazuljani's hostages are also believed to have been killed—including billionaire industrialist **Freddie Castillo de Montijo**.

Officials have yet to confirm the fatalities as bodies have been difficult to identify.

* * *

Back to Segment on 'How to Make Holiday Hooches'

(While we pursue a reaction from the Castillo family.)

Chapter 34

Detrás de Las Noticias de Última Hora | **Behind the Breaking News** | Sa Likod ng Nagbabagang Balita

The microphones were still off, yet the slap across the plump man's face reverberated around the studio.

'*Putang ina!*' Durog shouted. '*Mis*-encounter? Really? You stupid eunuch!'

The military liaison took the assault like a statue, but his cheeks turned the colour of raw pork.

'Sorry sir, we didn't know what else to call it—it was unintended. An accidental shot fired. We didn't know those people were there—'

Durog glared at him, still recouping his energy after the smack. 'You didn't know what else to call it? The national armed forces—Did. Not. Know. Those People. Were. There?'

'The informant led our men to a clearing—we were scouting a suspected terrorist lair. There was heavy rain—the Moros were already shooting at each other. Or it was a trap for us—'

Durog slapped him again.

'So easy to lay everything on the Moros, no? And what—calling it a "mis-encounter" would disguise that it was a—*mis-take*? Is that supposed to make it more palatable to the public? You killed people we were talking peace with—and civilians—then, you tried to hide it?! You stupid, stupid man!'

'Sir, orders from General Angkan—'

'Ah! And now you throw the general under the bus? What kind of soldier are you? Have you no respect for the chain of command? Tell the general I want a full debrief as soon as he's back from vacation. Now get out of my sight.'

Durog coughed. Madam waited for the army major to leave the studio before rushing forward. She was careful not to give the impression that the president was—unwell.

'You mustn't get worked up like this, mahal, it's not good for you.' She wiped his mouth, worried that his face was purple.

'Did you hear that? Mis-encounter! Idiots! Are we that incompetent? Does no one act *intentionally* any more? That's the national defence force. How do you blunder into battle? Or worse—bungle into a trap? If the Moros were indeed trying to ambush our troops, why was it so easy? They walked right into the fracas. Someone's going to pay for this. Where is Pip Rodríguez? He is my security adviser—why isn't he here yet?'

Durog scanned the studio for his assistant. The room was dotted with members of the presidential production crew waiting to record the official year-end video.

Durog's man in question was cowering in a corner behind the cameras.

'You—get me AJ!'

This was not the way Facundo Marasigan envisioned his first Christmas at the palace.

Not that he believed in Christ or anything so silly as God, but he did hope to get a break during the holiday and watch a marathon of Elvis films. He'd asked Madam to download his favourites for screening in the palace's newly updated movie room.

'Sir, AJ.' His assistant handed him a mobile, the encrypted one he used for sensitive conversations.

Durog kissed Madam's cheek and moved to a less populated corner of the studio, grumbling into the receiver without preamble. 'Is it true?'

'Sir.' The voice on the other end crackled, seeming further away than just the southern reaches of the small country. 'Many dead. Shooting . . . *buzz* . . . Abu Omar . . . fire . . . Freddie . . .'

Durog appreciated that AJ always spoke as if in Morse code, but this time, he needed more.

'Do you have the bodies?'

'Yes . . . *crackle* . . . no . . . cordoned. Bodies . . . pieces. Burned.' AJ didn't offer any certainty.

Durog tried again. 'So, you're not sure who's dead?'

Only an irritating buzz got back to him on the phone. *Shit*. They really must sort out comms across the islands.

'AJ?' *Buzz*. 'The informant, who was it?' *Buzz, crackle*.

'One. . . Tukô's man. *Crackle*. We took care of him . . . few thousand pesos. *Crackle, buzz*. Got him to tag that electrical engineer . . . *buzz-buzz* . . . Ismail . . . causing my family too many problems.'

'Whatever makes it easier for us down there, AJ. We don't need any more splinter groups.'

'Yes, sir.'

'Now, find me Freddie Castillo. Dead or alive. And I may just forgive you for not telling me he was there to begin with.'

'Sir, I—'

'You must realize by now, AJ, that I have all the power, regardless of how much Freddie is paying you.'

AJ was silent—intentionally. Again, the only sound coming through the phone was the crackling of the connection.

Durog cleared his throat. 'I will say that Freddie is dead—that will upset Tukô. And AJ, if we're not getting our investment back, it would be best if Castillo—disappeared. Understood?'

From Durog's tone, AJ took that the conversation was over. But—

'Ah, Ramil, I almost forgot. I need you to sabotage another power station. Make it look like storm damage—or better yet, an insurgent attack. Anything. Just take down the electricity. We need to announce a takeover.'

'As you wish.'

It had been a while since Ramil was called anything but AJ—or Abu Jafik.

* * *

Across the studio, there was a mild ruckus. Interior Secretary and Security Adviser Pip Rodríguez finally arrived.

Madam pointed out where Durog was standing.

'What the hell happened?' Pip stormed over just as the president ended his call.

'It's under control.'

'Is it?' Pip strained to keep his voice down. 'How the hell did Castillo end up in Mindanao? Abducted? And now—dead? How did we not know this?'

Durog appeared calmer than earlier. 'That's what I was going to ask you, but I'm certain Tukô is behind this. Freddie screwed him, no?'

'Freddie screwed us, too!' A vein throbbed on Pip's neck. 'What's AJ been doing? Can we still trust him?'

'Yes, of course.' Durog grinned coolly, motioning for Pip to take a breath. 'I've known him since grade school—he's my cousin, really. Well, distant relative. On my mother's side. I've helped them a lot over the years—he wouldn't dare double cross me.'

'He didn't tell us about Freddie—'

'Maybe he didn't know. I will have people check into Tukô. Meanwhile, Ronquillo's engineer has been removed, and AJ's men will deal with the power grid, as we intended. We'll have Mikey in position by New Year's Eve.'

Exactly the lackey they needed to pave the way for Chinese contractors. The cut he was getting would make Durog rich beyond his dreams. Richer than his father who was a governor, and richer than Pip Rodríguez.

He'd even be wealthier than the Old Rich Castillos de Montijo.

If his calculations were correct, the Chinese deals would make him more powerful than that damned, death-defying Tukô Salazar.

And if his illness killed him first, his family would still be comfortable for generations.

'Remember what I told you, Facundo,' Pip detested not being in charge. 'You have to keep the people scared—'

Durog was amused by the impertinent reminder.

'I know, Pip. If people are scared, they are powerless—I am not new to this. That's why I wage my war against crime and drugs, remember? And it's perfect cover for eliminating our enemies.' He winked conspiratorially.

Out of the corner of his eye, Durog saw Madam call his attention. His private nurse—in civilian clothing—had arrived with his injection.

'Not now!' He yelled across the studio.

Purposefully, Durog strode to his faux office set-up in front of the cameras, indicating Pip get out of shot.

'Bring them in,' #Durog was ready to record his year-end broadcast.

In single file, a queue of local officials entered. Each wearing a shirt printed with Durog's face.

The floor director signalled the start of recording.

A portly man in his forties was instructed to step forward. Without warning, he was slapped by the head of state. His dentures rattled in his mouth.

'Mayor Lamutak, tell the people how sorry you are about what you did.'

The mayor shook silently in place, unable to respond. #Durog hated such impotence.

'Cut!'

Durog Marasigan did not like being interrupted. Especially when he was on a roll.

'Sorry, Mister President—an urgent call for you,' the floor director explained.

Durog's assistant approached with another encrypted device.

'I hope this is not a bad time,' the line was crisp, and the caller was cordial.

Durog snapped his fingers for the mics to be shut off.

'Premier Xiao, what a delight.' One did not keep the Chinese prime minister waiting.

'My son-in-law tells me you've reached an agreement?'

'Yes, Premier Xiao, I will make the announcement soon.'

'And the former ambassador—Salazar—will not be an issue?'

'Don't worry. Eloy—I mean, Secretary Salazar—no longer wields power here. I decide who gets government contracts, and your son-in-law will get the power grid upgrade.'

'And the matter of Harrison Chong?'

'Yes, the ah—drug lord. We tracked down his local partner. He's been killed in a—special operation—in Mindanao. This should disable their network.'

'Good. We wouldn't want a rogue Chinese national involved in such transnational problems. Especially when it's in conflict with our—interests.'

'Of course. We are in your debt. You have helped me—us—much more than the West ever has. China is our most powerful neighbour. We are fortunate to be treated as family.'

'The transfer has been made, Mister President. Happy holidays.'

Durog was already counting his proverbial chickens, smart enough to not put his eggs in just one basket. And no one paid as much as China.

It was simply a matter of—*business*. Anyone with the chance would have done the same.

Durog looked over at Pip Rodríguez—pacing in a corner by the door—ignorant of the president's upcoming betrayal.

Suddenly, the floor lights in the studio began to tremble. The spotlights on the ceiling shook. The ground seemed to rise and roll, and the walls around them groaned.

After a moment or two of confusion—

'Earthquake!'

Chapter 35

Los Ensombrecidos | **Those in Shadow** | Ang Mga Nasa Lilim

Outside the hospital's emergency room, Ricky Castillo searched his pockets for a lighter. He was desperate for a smoke.

It was a long month and he'd seen enough dead bodies up close to last a lifetime.

Not that the Christmas Eve earthquake—*thank God*—led to any casualties other than frayed nerves and shaken structural foundations.

The country escaped the impending Big One yet again.

But between sitting vigil with his grandmother (still lying in wake at Sombra) and chasing corpses from #Durog's criminal 'clean-up' crusade, Ricky Castillo had been busy.

Intentionally too busy to grieve for his father.

Out of habit, he felt for his lens cap, making sure it was back on his camera.

The Intramuros Public Hospital was his last stop for the night.

He'd followed paramedics with the bullet-riddled body of a suspected drug user—a petty thief, shot in the Old City's slums by the usual gun-toting, tandem-motorbike-riding, 'anonymous' vigilantes.

It was the fifth such murder that night.

The photos—dramatic and gory—were sure to bag him another headline.

Finding the lighter, Ricky lit the last stick from his battered pack of Marlboros and took in the ashen evening.

The city was darker than usual. The crescent moon was waning, a haze concealed the stars, and much of Manila—like Mindanao Island in the south—had been without power for days.

A maintenance issue or another.

The grid tripped up by a storm, or something to do with earthquake aftershocks.

There was possibly even a communist attack on a power plant.

A variety of options—according to the news.

The hospital was one of the few places in Intramuros with a back-up generator—a deficiency the newer, richer districts didn't suffer.

Around the emergency room entrance, a single string of fairy lights twinkled.

A faded paper lantern in the shape of a star blinked in accompaniment.

Ricky was leaning on a grimy wall underneath a 'No Smoking' sign.

He puffed on his cigarette and watched its smoke dissolve into the night.

'Rick, paré—Merry Christmas.'

He was approached by a dishevelled man juggling several bags across his chest—another freelance photographer who worked overnight.

Ricky smiled perfunctorily in wordless acknowledgement. It took years for such colleagues to speak to him—a Castillo de Montijo—as one of their own.

'Hey, sorry about your dad, paré. Shit, and your grandma *pala*. 'Tangina, super shit Christmas, huh?'

Super shit Christmas, indeed.

After news broke of his father's death in a military op gone wrong, rumours spread that Doña Fatimah succumbed to shock and a broken heart.

The family remained silent on the matter.

Regardless, Freddie's death exempted the Castillos from any public displays of seasonal joy—there was no longer a need to play happy family at the Christmas mass in the basilica.

Which was just as well since they'd all been treading on eggshells.

With everyone in the house—except for his sisters—Sombra was a powder keg set to go off. The unspoken tension so brittle that the sound of crickets could shatter the façade.

Ricky found more solace in the tumult of the city's streets than at home.

That Christmas in 2010, the family did away with the customary midnight feast of honeyed ham, stuffed turkey, and roasted pig. There was also no coterie of yuletide sweets, and obviously, no gifts exchanged.

Mourning was in full swing.

Even the country's president offered his condolences.

'Have you got another cig, paré?' his colleague eyed him, hopeful.

Ricky shook his head, indicating the crushed packet on the floor.

The man rummaged through his bags for his own pack.

Then, he held out a hand to bum a light from Ricky's stick.

'Has the military turned over your dad's corpse?' He lit his cigarette.

Ricky grimaced. Hating that many Islanders had no qualms about asking the most personal—and inappropriate—of questions.

To be fair, no harm was intended.

Almost imperceptibly, Ricky shook his head.

'Keep at them until they do, paré,' his colleague returned his cig. 'Bet they don't want to hand him over because you'll see that they shot him themselves. Typical. Friendly fire, collateral damage, whatnot. I heard they actually dropped a bomb and wiped out more civilians than they're saying.'

Ricky wished the man—whose name he couldn't remember—would stop talking.

'Any plans for tomorrow, paré? New Year's Eve. I hope naman the lights will be back by then.'

Again, Ricky shook his head. As indicated earlier, nothing about the season gave him cause for celebration.

'You—Rick Castillo de Montijo—have no plans? Don't you always say there's no excuse not to party? I would've thought you'd need the pick-me-up—'

Just then—a burst of colours spattered against the charcoal sky.

It was followed by a series of loud explosions.

'See? The Island Spirit,' his colleague chuckled. 'Even if they can't afford it, Islanders will spend on fireworks to welcome the new year.'

'Right. And tomorrow, as usual, we'll be back here to see how many of them have blown off their fingers in the process,' Ricky shook his head. 'People never learn.'

'Or maybe'—his colleague cocked an eyebrow and smiled—'they always just hope for better.'

The conversation was interrupted by a blaring siren. An ambulance with tinted windows was heading towards them.

Its lights were flashing, its side panels—emblazoned with the seal of a province fifty kilometres south of Manila.

When the vehicle came to a stop, Ricky noticed it wasn't carrying a patient.

He knew what that meant—it was his lucky night.

He excused himself from his chatty colleague and approached the orderly stepping out of the van's front cabin.

'Paré,' Ricky whispered, 'Santa sent me for Rudolph.'

The orderly nodded, understanding the code used for their drug clientele.

'Let me just do this drop.'

The orderly opened the vehicle's back door as two men dressed as doctors came out of the E.R. They took an ice chest from the van.

Easily several kilos—Ricky calculated. Not at all stunned that the ambulance was transporting narcotics.

Such vehicles could zip through anywhere unimpeded, and the governor of this particular province was a big supplier of crystal meth.

Drop done, the orderly approached Ricky. 'How many?'

Ricky held up a finger. He didn't have enough money on him for more than a gram.

The orderly ruffled through his trousers and brought out a small packet of meth.

They made the exchange through closed fists.

'Uh, paré,' Ricky inched closer. 'Are you passing The Village?' He hoped to hitch a ride back to the exclusive, gated community that Sombra was in—he was tired and didn't want to risk getting robbed or kidnapped by hailing a taxi.

The neighbourhood known as The Village had grown around the Castillo estate over the years—a well-guarded assembly of tree-lined avenues and lesser mansions belonging to wealthy families. It was as much a landmark of Manila as The Slums, which had sprouted—higgledy-piggledy—in all the other available spaces.

The orderly motioned towards the ambulance's side door.

With barely a glance at his colleague, Ricky threw away his cigarette and hopped aboard.

* * *

Father Dito Santos relished putting on his priest's habit, and by candlelight, there was something almost—*romantic*—about it. An additional ethereal glow to the sacred white cloak that shielded him from the world and its sins.

Thank you, power outage.

Dito was confident that the holy garment elevated him from people's judgement. It didn't matter what he wore underneath. Designer or bargain clothing. Leather shoes or flipflops.

It didn't matter how smart he was—or how charming.

It didn't matter that he wasn't tall or attractive.

Dito Santos was officially a priest. Ordained most blessedly on Christmas Day. In time to say the public memorial mass for his Aba Fatimah and his uncle Freddie.

It was planned for the sixth of January to coincide with the Feast of the Epiphany, which marked the official end of the Christmas season.

No longer just assisting, Dito would concelebrate the mass at the village church with the eminent Archbishop of Manila. They would be standing at the altar side by side.

No one could look down on him any more.

Father Dito appraised his reflection in the mirror, solemn and saintly in the glimmering candlelight.

Unlike Sombra, the old rectory at Saint Jeremiah wasn't hooked up to a generator—item one on Dito's new list of things to do.

His church should be prepared for any eventuality. Regardless of its neighbourhood's financial state.

There was a soft rap on the door.

'Enter,' Dito called out in a practiced tone. Savouring being the man in charge.

'Father, the line for confession is getting long.' The church volunteer smiled at him widely. Shiny, soft cheeks with a touch of macopa fruit blush.

Dito had specifically chosen the clean-cut teen from the congregation to assist him. The church was always busiest in December as people rushed to get pardoned for their sins.

Who didn't want to start the new year with a clean slate?

'I'll be right there, Samuel. Thank you.'

Father Dito patted down his habit and grinned. He was finally a significant man.

* * *

In Sombra's private chapel, the remaining children of Don Federico and Doña Fatimah Castillo held vigil. One more day until they finally buried their mother. But they would have to wait to inter Freddie until the military handed over his remains.

Doñas Almudena, Covadonga, and Macarena were sitting a foot apart, in silence, before their mother's coffin. Each praying a rosary of her own.

On the altar behind Doña Fatimah, they had put a framed photo of Freddie, in place of what they hoped was the temporary absence of his remains.

In the image, their younger brother was immortalised in his twenties. Standing on the beach of the island he once owned.

His beige trousers were folded above his ankles, his button up shirt—untucked and billowy in the yellowed breeze.

He was barefoot at the water's edge and smiling cheekily.

The photo was taken by his then six-year-old son, Ricky. Freddie had just given the boy his first camera.

In the pew across the aisle from his sisters, Julián was on his knees. Weeping quietly into his clasped hands.

The in-laws—Greg and Cristóbal—sat together to the side.

The family chapel was flushed with gaslight. Maca hadn't maintained the estate's generators. That was always on Freddie's half of the list of responsibilities.

She chanced a sideways peek at her sisters, certain they were judging her.

Well, when her husband Manny took over the power company in January, Sombra would never be in the dark again—and that would be thanks to her.

A few rows back, Núria sat with Hugo and his sisters, amazed at the Grown-Ups inability to offer each other comfort.

So stoic and isolated in their grief. Motionless and mute. Like statues. Or bonsais.

Núria's heart broke for the stunted, orphaned children that they were.

* * *

In the ambulance, Ricky Castillo struggled to stay awake. Despite the siren's loud wail.

He hadn't slept in days.

Actually, he couldn't recall the last time he'd slept at all.

He felt his pocket for the sachet of crystal meth—*Could anyone blame him?*

With everything going on, it was a wonder he was even upright.

He looked out the window as the ambulance whizzed through the blacked-out city—*So much for tragedy being a great leveller.*

The wealthy districts—where people afforded generators—shone like rare diamonds in a stack of coal.

'Going home?' the ambulance driver peered at Ricky in the rear-view mirror.

He shifted uncomfortably in his seat, hoping to remain anonymous. 'Uh, I'll just hop out along the way. Where are you headed?'

'Senate president's house,' the orderly turned to face him. 'End of year party.'

Of course.

The said politician lived on Calle Oro, three streets from Sombra. He could walk home from there.

When they arrived at The Village gate, the armed security guards noted the provincial government seal on the tinted ambulance and waved them through without question.

Ricky asked to be let off before they turned into Calle Oro.

'Sir Rick,' the orderly rolled down a window and held something out to him.

Ricky was surprised they knew his name.

'Saves us the stop at Sombra.'

As the ambulance rolled away, Ricky tentatively opened the zip-lock bag he was handed.

Inside, another cheap Chinese mobile.

It rang.

'Why do you keep misplacing your phones, my boy? Makes it so difficult to reach you—I might think you are avoiding me.'

Ricky was stupefied.

'I am sorry to hear about your father, click, he was like a son to me.' Tukô Salazar almost sounded genuine.

Ricky could no longer distinguish the tone.

'Our cat-and-mouse is getting tiresome, no? Come work with me, Castillo the Third. We can—*assist*—each other. You can start in one of my call centres, then I will move you to E-Mart. You could make a fortune.'

Ricky heard rumours that Tukô was grooming a new generation of 'associates'. With his social connections and unhealthy proclivities, he certainly saw how he might fit the bill.

Tukô's international 'call centres' occupied entire floors in some of Manila's finest buildings. The posh offices—in the centre of the new business district—handled underground global sales of highly addictive prescription drugs.

He was also behind E-Mart—an online site that connected buyers and sellers of high-powered weapons, narcotics, and even people. A dark web eBay for the unscrupulous.

Tukô always evolved with the times. It was the secret of his longevity.

'Click, look how far I've come from my first convenience store. I'm really just a salesman providing a service—I make it easy for people to get what they want.'

For a moment, Ricky considered the offer. Wondering if he had the stomach for the job. It would mean infinitely more money for less work, and he wouldn't have to keep chasing corpses.

'You can call me Mang Eloy, my boy—your father did.'

What would Aba think about all this?—But then again, she was no longer around to disappoint.

'You know what they say about a parent's debts, no?' Tukô clucked into the phone. 'Do you need time to think, Castillo the Third? I'll wait. You have until after the memorial. Click-click. You do know there is only one answer? Cluck, click. Happy New Year, Don Federico.'

The line went dead.

Coño—it suddenly dawned on Ricky that with his father gone, he was the patriarch's last living namesake. The honourable heir.

Federico Castillo de Montijo III—*El Señor Don.*

Thing was, Ricky failed to understand that outside of Sombra—without an inheritance—that no longer mattered.

As he pondered his fate, Señor Castillo found himself walking down a dim Village street pocked with unlit, dilapidated mansions. Abandoned homes—in the richest neighbourhood of modern Manila—rotting away unkempt.

How could people neglect their family homestead?

Federico III didn't want Sombra to end up like that.

* * *

Ximena Yrastegui returned to the family chapel and flicked on a light switch.

She and Pepa had been helping Don Andy with one of the generator sets. Her father had learned a lot from his days at the sugar plantation.

Ricky arrived as a spotlight came on above the main altar. It shot a beam over Doña Fatimah's casket.

In the frame behind her, a shadow fell across the photo of his father. Ricky had taken it the day an undertow almost swept him away.

He tried to shake the memory, locking his attention on Ximena reorganising gas lamps.

'Look at her, still stage managing everything.'

Ricky turned to Cayetana Yrastegui standing behind him. Ximena and Núria's always-impeccably-turned-out sister. Alma and Andy's third and youngest daughter. As close to a black sheep as the Yrasteguis had among them.

Cayetana—or Tana—lived in L.A. Or New York. Or London. Wherever the jobs were.

'Remember that stupid play she made us perform over and over as kids?' Tana grumbled in Ricky's ear. 'The really boring one she "wrote and directed" when she was, like—ten or something? Remember? About that dude who was shot?'

'You mean *Bobby Kennedy, the Musical*?' Ricky offered.

'That's the one!' Tana clapped him on the back. 'I mean—WTF, right?' She rolled her eyes. 'An American politician who was, like—dead—before we were born. He wasn't even president, right? Wasn't he killed before he could win? Fuckin' Ximena. Such a loser.'

Ricky wasn't about to chime in and remind Tana that may have been where she got her start in acting. He knew better than to get between the literal 'drama queen' and the TV reporter. *Goddamn Yrasteguis.* Overachievers, the lot of them.

Truth be told, he did wonder why as a child—growing up in Manila—Ximena was obsessed with the Kennedys. Was she intrigued by assassinations or unfulfilled potential?

Ricky scanned the chapel for his mother, unsurprised by her absence.

Shit—Who would care for his widowed mother? Surely his aunts would let them stay in Sombra?

That's if his aunts were inheriting the estate. Or would it go solely to his uncle Julián? He was, after all, the rightful eldest.

But Tito Julián lived in Boston—did he even want Sombra?

Who would pay for the upkeep of the estate?

Ricky realized he had no idea. The family never had such conversations.

He looked again at the photo of his father on the altar—his aunts and uncles silent in the pews before him.

What if the unfulfilled was all there was?

What if that, in truth, was the legacy?

* * *

When Father Dito arrived from Saint Jeremiah the next morning, he found Ricky passed out on a couch in the patio. Barefoot, shirtless, with his trousers undone.

Tin foil, some sort of pipe, and traces of white powder on the table.

Fuck—Dito muttered under his breath. He kicked his cousin's dangling leg and tried to rouse him.

'Rick. Ricky,' Dito shook him, frantic. 'Puta, paré—get up!'

Ricky groaned.

'Are you kidding me?' Dito shook him again. 'I can't believe you did this again—and you left your shit out. Clean this up before anyone sees you.'

Ricky flicked a bloodshot eye open. Then, another.

'Ho, ho, ho, his holiness is here,' Ricky growled. 'To what do we owe the honour?'

'Keep it down, dude—what the hell were you thinking?'

Ricky tried to sit up on the couch—he fell back and put his hand inside his jeans.

He stared blankly at Dito, saying nothing.

Frankly, there was nothing he could say.

Then, his eyes fell on the wall mosaic behind his white-robed cousin.

He raised a heavy arm and tried to point—'Joder, look at that, paré.'

Dito turned, unsure what Ricky meant.

'The coat of arms, Father—the puto family coat of arms.'

Dito looked back at his disrobed cousin. 'What about it?'

'Haven't you ever wondered why it's all cracked? You can see where the pieces were reapplied, the glue is dis-coloured. It looks so fuckin' ugly and cheap. Like it's made in China—'

'It's old, man,' Dito said, calmly. He remembered what Ricky was like when coming down from a high. It was not pleasant.

'So, what if it's old? Abuelo Federico must have put that there with pride, man—¡*Orgullo!* You know about pride, no? And now look at it. Smashed up—filthy—cobwebbed.'

Dito would not be baited. 'Have one of the maids clean it then, they probably just overlook it. You know what they're like—'

'Maids? Puta, dude, we're, like, down to two—in this whole house. Can you imagine? Your mom fired most of them, even the really good cook your father liked—remember her? He was probably fucking her—'

Dito had no patience for reminiscing, and he learned years ago to stop paying his father any mind.

'Come on, Rick, take a shower. Get dressed. We're burying Aba today, remember? I'm saying mass in the chapel.'

* * *

Somehow, Federico Castillo III managed to make it to his room. It was as dishevelled as he was.

He stopped in shock when his eyes fell on the bed. A blonde woman lay prone and naked—*Shit*, had he called Lenya? He had no money to pay her!

A flash of memory—some time the night before, he walked to the senator's party on Calle Oro—Hugo's sisters went along for the 'local' experience.

The blonde stretched languidly and turned to her side—another woman curled up behind her.

WTF?

Ricky staggered forward to get a better look—¡*Joder!*—The blonde wasn't his favourite Russian call girl—it was Merche, one of Hugo's sisters from Spain.

The other woman was an infamous 'Rah-Rah Girl', from the pack of that nosy writer Laura Herrera.

He couldn't remember the Rah-Rah Girl's name, but her father was some mayor, and people knew she moonlit as a high-society escort.

Why the hell were they in his bed?

He stepped on a used condom on the floor.

More rubbers were scattered around his rumpled sheets.

Coño—another flash of memory struck him. He shut his eyes, remembering their writhing bodies.

* * *

As the morning sun cut through the shutters of the guest room, Doña Covadonga de Pérez-García sat at the mirror. Confronting the hairline cracks in her weary reflection.

It still surprised her to see evidence of time's passage.

She always felt like she hadn't aged a day over thirty, although her body ached in places she could no longer ignore.

How it crushed her that what lay past was more than what was ahead—her tomorrows dwindling faster than she would like.

The life she'd led was not what she'd expected.

She dabbed on powder, hoping to hide each regret that left a mark upon her face.

* * *

Across the house, there was a quick knock on a heavy closed door. It opened before Luísa could answer.

'Lulu,' Maca entered her sister-in-law's bedroom uninvited, 'brand new day—and tomorrow, brand new year. You must be eager to get your life back on track after all this—unpleasantness.'

Luísa sat up in bed, perplexed. She barely had time to grasp that she'd been widowed.

Freddie hadn't spoken to her in years, but there was a part of her that still—*loved*—her husband. She didn't know what else to call the emotion.

Luísa watched Maca flip open the window shutters. 'I can't blame you needing to get away and see your daughters—such a pity neither of them could come to be with the family.'

Selfish little brats—Maca concluded wordlessly.

'Don't worry,' Maca continued without looking at her sister-in-law. 'I will pack up Freddie's things while you're away, so you won't have to do it yourself. And we'll put aside what you leave behind in the meantime.'

In the meantime?—Luísa wondered where Maca thought she was going.

'Ay, your daughter called *pala* earlier, did I not mention?' Maca went on as she scanned the room. 'You were asleep—maybe too much Valium? Anyway, we had a chat—and she's sending you a ticket. Isn't that wonderful? You'll be in Europe by next week! And don't worry about the memorial. We've handled everything.'

What is she talking about?

'But—Ricky?'—was all Luísa could think to say.

'Ricky is a grown man; he can look out for himself.'

And with that, Doña Macarena left Luísa's room.

* * *

Ricky pushed away Merche's hand as she reached for him—it wasn't easy to ignore her naked breasts.

'You have to get out before anyone sees you,' he told his cousin, bending down to pick up her clothes off the floor. 'Where's your sister?'

'Buenas, primo,' Merche smiled at him, seductively. 'She left the party with some movie producer. He said he would make her a star.'

'Seriously?' Ricky threw the discarded clothes on to the bed. In no way was he amused. 'Mierda, I shouldn't have brought you to that party.'

The mayor's daughter moaned. Another pair of breasts for Ricky to evade.

'You have to leave,' he implored the awakening Rah-Rah Girl. 'No wait. Actually, we'll be in the chapel shortly—hang here a while, then please, sneak off the estate.'

* * *

Later that morning, on the last day of the year, the Castillo de Montijo family quietly buried their matriarch by Sombra's chapel. Joined by what remained of the household staff.

With the sun sighing prayers into the powder blue sky, they lay Aba Fatimah next to her husband. Embraced by flowers and sheltered by a robust molave tree.

Birds chirped and wind chimes tinkled softly in the breeze.

The garden was every bit Aba's magical carpet, Abuelo Federico's 'miraculous' coat of dreams.

Father Dito led them in a sombre goodbye. He would do the same before a larger crowd the following week. #Pride

A public memorial service was planned in the swanky village church, a special mass on the Feast of the Epiphany.

The holy day marked the end of the Yuletide season, when the Three Wise Men brought their gifts to the infant Jesus.

* * *

'Psst, niño bonito, golden boy—'

Ricky turned to see two cops wave him over. He was walking to the village store for a packet of cigs.

'You said you'd get us on Tukô's payroll, did you forget?' one of the cops casually asked him.

'No, not at all. I just need time,' Ricky couldn't keep track of what he said to whom. He'd been telling people whatever they wanted to hear so they'd leave him alone.

Maybe he shouldn't have left Sombra through the front gate.

'Naku, niño bonito, you better hurry. The way you keep lurking in The Slums, you might get killed in a dark alley, by mistake. Be careful.' The cops chuckled as they ambled away.

He turned a corner and was soon approached by another pair of men. Faded jeans, creased designer shirts, branded shades.

'Well, hello Ricky, how was the funeral?'—He couldn't tell whose goons they were.

'So, has the government turned over your father's body?'—As if that fell under polite conversation.

Ricky looked from one man to the other, too tired to be scared or to care.

'Anyway, just a reminder—we'll come for you after the sixth. Tukô says you're to start in the call centre—unless you know where your father stashed the money?'

This again?—Ricky shook his head, defeated.

Goon Number One removed his sunglasses and looked Ricky in the eye.

'We don't believe that for a second. You're his son—who else would he trust?'

Ricky tried to hide the quiver in his voice—'I know nothing'—fearing he was about to cry. 'Why does no one believe me?'

The man who'd spoken put his shades back on, then patted Ricky rather forcefully on the cheeks.

He tapped his wristwatch and walked away without another word. His companion trailing right behind.

It was not the first time Ricky wished he still had his car. It would've spared him the walk—and the unexpected company.

But he sold his Hyundai a while back when he was desperate, smoking through the proceeds in a week.

Across the street, a heavily tinted SUV kept pace. Shadowing him from the moment he left Sombra.

Chapter 36

La Epifanía y la Despedida | **The Epiphany and the Farewell** | Ang Epipanya at ang Paalam

Like the Three Wise Men on a quest for Jesus, Ximena, Núria, and Cayetana Yrastegui were searching for a saviour. Anyone who might redeem them from their mother.

Doña Alma had been doling out instructions like presents all morning.

Unsurprisingly, the eldest of Doña Fatimah's daughters assembled her own children early at the village church. To oversee preparations for their Aba's memorial. If they must say a public goodbye, they would do so in style.

Said 'style'—of course—being 'with quiet dignity'.

Fatimah would've disliked such attention, but because of the family's standing, there was an expectation to be allowed to partake in their grief.

Which was why the private Castillos acquiesced to a public commemoration.

A panoply of personalities was anticipated, a cross section of The Islands' moneyed classes. From industry titans and property moguls down to cultural icons, rival politicians, and the agnostic hashtag president himself. The privileged natives and the venerated half-castes.

'The candles, Tana, hija, make sure they're lit—*oye*, each one, eh? Then, please check that Dito has the frankincense for the final blessing—don't forget the seating arrangements—'

'Núria, the flowers—that can't be all of them—really? Well, hija, please make it so that the calla lilies at least aren't obscured by the ferns. They have to be distributed just so—that batch—over there—it's not visible—see?'

'I don't understand what you mean, Ximena, just fix it. You're the one who knows about lights and sound systems—as long as the string quartet is not louder than the priest. And remind them, no singing—'

Javi Yrastegui, the girls' thirty-year-old baby brother, was distributing missalettes at the main entrance. He volunteered. It kept him far from his mother barking orders at the other end of the church.

From where he stood, there was a long, pristine white carpet rolled down the central aisle leading up to the marble altar. It was flanked by a cortege—five feet tall—of potted ferns.

White lilies were scattered among the leaves like angels' feathers, and elegies were offered by tall, thin candles in silver holders.

It was elegant—and understated. A catwalk fit for a solemn procession.

* * *

There was nothing understated about the present Manny Santos gave his wife back at Sombra—a banquet of diamonds and sapphires set in white gold.

He had just returned from an all-nighter with Pip and Mikey.

At least, that's what he told his wife.

Doña Maca waited for him before going to church for the memorial. It wouldn't do for her to show up unaccompanied.

'What are you miserable about this time?' Manny growled. 'I'm here, aren't I? And I brought you a gift.'

He pushed the necklace at her, insisting she try it on. He'd ~~stolen~~ taken it from the woman he spent the night with. Knowing he would need to appease his wife.

She smiled politely. 'Thank you, my love—' and made to kiss him.

He walked away.

'I have to change,' he said, entering the bathroom.

Maca sat at her dresser and appraised her reflection, the bejewelled necklace was undeniably stunning. She appeared every inch an intimidating matron. Exactly as a powerful man's wife should look.

The day suddenly dimmed outside her window. The sky turned a dull shade of grey.

'Oye, when are we moving to that penthouse your office is giving us? Honestly, I don't know how we are expected to fit all our things in an apartment—surely, we can get them to pay for us to stay in this house?' Maca called out to be heard through the shut bathroom door.

No reply.

She spoke louder as thunder rumbled above them—'The president is coming to the service, no? So nice of him,' she paused, 'especially as he isn't the church-going type—shows how much he thinks of us. Maybe I can talk to him about our living arrangements—'

Still nothing from behind the closed—and locked—bathroom door.

'Isn't it wonderful that Dito is concelebrating the mass?' her last attempt at getting a rise from her husband.

They never talked about it, but all things considered, Maca was proud of their son. Their one conjugal accomplishment.

Undoubtedly, his nanny had much to do with how he was raised, but that was just the way with privileged children. And Dito Santos was truly fortunate to have had a nanny.

As he was finally ordained, they were blessed for life. What a gift it was to be mother to a priest.

'Wear your finest barong—' Maca called out again. They must look their best even in mourning. 'Remember, all those people will be watching—'

It was going to be a pageant no matter what they called it, and she was not about to be upstaged by her sisters.

Her son—*the priest!*—was concelebrating the mass.

* * *

Alma had finally ticked off everything on her list, if only the rain would tarry.

As people began to trickle in, she had Andy gather their children to one side of the church. Then, she gave them a talk to rival a sports coach at a championship.

'This is it kids, after this we can return to our house and resume our lives. We say our goodbyes,' her voice caught, and she paused for breath, 'then we move forward as best we can.' Another pause. 'Such is life, no?'

Alma looked to her husband for strength and stood a little taller. 'Now remember, everyone is watching, so best behaviour. We don't want to call attention to ourselves.'

'Mom,' Tana, of course, interjected, 'the mass is for our family, how can we pretend to not be seen?'

Andy shook his head at his impetuous daughter, not the time or place to taunt their mother.

Alma was about to retort when a rush of whispers swept through the growing congregation. The other Castillos were arriving.

There was a titter of recognition when Cova entered the church—many of her contemporaries were in attendance.

She was still as beautiful as they'd recalled—*so delicate and stylish*—and time had been kind to her striking—*how guapo*—agile husband.

Oh, look her daughters are so pretty—so blonde and European!

The titter dropped to a murmur when Julián was spotted, the current crop of social butterflies didn't know he existed. They were too young to have memories of the 1960s, the years before the eldest Castillo de Montijo left Manila.

'Uh, hon, mind hanging back with the kids?' Julián whispered to his American partner. Greg was surprised at his husband's hesitation.

'It would be best,' Julián explained. 'I'll sit up front with my sisters.'

'Won't their spouses be with them?' Greg wondered.

'Yes, but, uhm, less questions this way.' Julián concluded.

'Are you embarrassed to be seen with me?'

'No, of course not,' Julián wasn't sure how to make him understand. 'It's just . . . this is Manila—best not to give them anything to talk about.'

Julián patted Greg's arm in consolation, grateful for Maca's entrance across the threshold.

There were gasps as his jewel-encrusted sister glided down the nave, with Manny at her side shaking hands with the crowd.

She was the wife of LIsPoCorp's new COO, the fortunate woman beside the man in charge of the power grid.

Doña Maca was confident they were the couple to admire. Her Old-World stature gave his New-World influence a priceless sheen.

All she needed to cap her reign was full ownership of Sombra.

She had plans that her siblings could not top.

* * *

Through a side door—without fanfare—Freddie's widow Luísa was ushered in by her skittish son. They both looked like they hadn't slept in weeks.

Ricky didn't want them to be fodder for the horde. And he was convinced they were being followed by sinister forces.

In a daze, Luísa slowly scanned the church before taking her seat—'Hijo, your sisters?'

'They're not here, Mom, remember?' he was impatient, but tried to console her. 'You'll see them soon—you're flying to Fáti in France tomorrow.'

Truth: Ricky was angry that his sisters hadn't come home, though they always said they felt like strangers among family.

He began to wonder how much that had to do with their mother's position in the clan—Pili and Fáti were daughters of the unpopular daughter-in-law.

Whereas he was the only son of the progenitor's namesake.

'Tomorrow? Already?' Luísa recalled she wasn't happy about this plan, one that Maca had imposed on her. 'What about you, hijo?'

'I'll be okay, Mom, don't worry,' he tried to smile as he followed her into the pew. She got on the kneeler, brought out a rosary, and shut her eyes.

He was glad she'd be out of the country. Somewhere safe, in case one of his father's 'frenemies' came for them.

There were certain facts that Ricky didn't trouble his mother with:

1) He was stuck—he had no passport to exit the country. Tukô, or someone more powerful, had got it revoked.

2) He was at a loss. He didn't know what to do once the memorial was over. After everyone left, how would he manage the estate alone?

3) He had to lie low and find a way to rid himself of the Lizard,

a) and #Durog's minions,

b) and the thugs of his father's other 'associates'.

Coño—he was a Castillo de Montijo, *dammit.* How did they forget that he was untouchable?

'Rick?'

He jumped when Ximena touched his arm.

'Hey, you ok?' she noticed his anxiety.

'Of course—'

'Are you lying?' she muttered under her breath as she slid in next to him.

'Of course,' he chuckled, conspiratorially.

She smiled at him sadly. Wishing there was something she could do.

Ximena had seen a lot of pain in her line of work, but she couldn't imagine what it was like to lose a parent.

'We'll get to the bottom of this,' she offered, unsure how.

'We can try,' Ricky scoffed, 'but we both know there are no straight answers in these islands—'

Ximena sighed—'Guess you're right.'

'—just multiple layers of bullshit. I mean, who knows what's really going on,' Ricky stopped to look around. 'We're all sitting ducks, unaware we're being screwed—'

He took a breath, then leaned in closer to his cousin. 'Do you know Tukô?'

'You mean former secretary Eliseo Salazar?' Ximena whispered back, sarcastic. 'Legendary sleaze ball? Rodríguez crony? Master criminal?'

Then, she too looked around, and leaned in. 'Why? Think he had something to do with what happened to your dad?'

Ricky shrugged. 'Dunno, just wondering. I don't know,' his eyes flashed left then right. He squirmed and put a finger to his mouth to chew on a nail.

'Stay away from him, Ricks,' Ximena warned. 'The old dude's bad news.'

As if he didn't know! He tried to keep a distance, but the guy was like piles—always popping up uninvited.

'X-men,' Ricky lowered his voice even more, 'he's after me.' He bore into her eyes for understanding.

'Who is?' Ximena looked at him concerned, unable to ignore the hollowness in his cheeks and the purple circles under his eyes.

'Tukô,' Ricky whispered in a breath. 'And the others—'

'What? Who others?'

Ricky waved his arm out at the crowd. 'Take your pick. Any of them. The Chinese,' he lowered his voice further. 'Durog, the cops, all of them. They're after all of us—heck, maybe even the Moros are in on it. Hugo said when he went to the casino—for ransom money—they picked him up. It was me they were after—then, the other day—'

'Oh Rick,' she soothed him sadly. 'You need to get some rest, have you slept at all?'

He was biting his fingernail and shaking his leg, the entire pew was rocking from his twitch. 'What? Yeah, few minutes here and there,' he scanned the church. Ximena wasn't sure what—or whom—he was looking for.

'Promise me you'll rest after today? You need it, Rick. Your brain is on overdrive—'

'Listen,' his tone was suddenly meek, 'what have you heard about my dad?—I mean—in general.'

Caught off guard by her cousin's change of topic and demeanour, Ximena considered her reply, uncertain how honest she should be. Ricky clearly had enough on his mind.

Her uncle Freddie was—*infamous*—nothing at all like their grandfather had been.

Her uncle Freddie—always eager to pull a fast one—made enemies wherever he went.

Talk around town was that if you shook Freddie Castillo's hand, you'd lose four fingers.

People killed for less on these islands.

How do you tell that to a shameless man's son? Poor boy already felt like he was being followed.

Funny how little children really knew about their parents.

So many blanks you had to fill in for yourself.

'He was—quite a guy.'

* * *

Hugo was the last of the family to turn up at the church, filling the last two spaces in the front pews. He brought a date—a respectably dressed Rah-Rah Girl was draped over him.

The same one who was in Ricky's bed a week earlier.

Hardly surprised, Hugo's sister Merche smiled at him, then she cocked her head and winked at the Rah-Rah Girl on his arm.

Merche didn't know how the new couple met, but clearly, nothing was improbable in Manila.

These Spanish cousins were fresh meat for the city's sharks.

* * *

'Is it always like this?' Greg Parker was sitting with Javi Yrastegui by the musicians. They were on their fourth hymn to accompany the queue for communion. 'There's more people here than I've ever seen attend church in Boston.'

'Catholic country, Tito Greg,' Javi reminded him. 'This is—an event.'

'Yes, I see. I'm just amazed there are so many believers—for such a cosmopolitan city.'

'Who said they were all believers?' Javi winked. 'It's Manila. It's more important to be seen.'

Greg examined the congregation curious. It was, after all, his first time in the city of his husband's birth.

'Why aren't you with, Tito Julián?' Javi wondered.

'I asked him the same question,' Greg's brow furrowed in more than slight annoyance. 'He's not like this in Boston.'

Across the aisle, a sudden commotion. Through a side door, the president and his entourage were shuffling in.

#Durog was so late he missed most of the mass—*perfect timing*—if he himself was asked.

'Another thing I don't get,' Greg indicated the tardy president. 'How is that man the elected leader? You have Western ideals of democracy, and yet your people choose someone who rules like a dictator.'

'Welcome to The Islands,' Javi stated, with a wry smile.

* * *

Other than #Durog's disruptive late appearance, the service went off without a hitch. Just as Doña Alma had planned. A sober display of class and decorum that not even the looming rain dared disrupt.

There was music, there were tears, there was silence.

There was a heartfelt eulogy delivered by Don Rafa Mendoza.

The esteemed newspaper owner was an old friend of Don Federico and Doña Fatimah.

'Iko and Timah crossed oceans and continents—and found each other. They fought for freedom and built their castles on the ground. Despite their differences, their union was the strongest I've ever seen.

And this world—' Don Rafa was suddenly distracted by the hashtag president, who was seated near the podium.

#Durog seemed bored and was chewing something indiscreetly.

'—this world,' Don Rafa dared, 'is not as she had hoped to leave her children.'

He looked directly at the man who was their president—Durog hadn't blinked, still masticating whatever-it-was like a goat.

* * *

When the last of the eulogies was delivered, Ximena—being the reporter—spoke on behalf of the family. A few words to thank people for coming.

Her aunt Maca was expectedly unimpressed.

Seated in a front pew, Doña Maca Santos furiously flicked her foldable Spanish hand fan. (The sweat on her nape was sullying her brand-new diamond necklace.) She should've insisted Dito or Manny speak for the family. But one didn't argue when Alma made the call.

Beside Maca, Manny was swiping at the screen of his mobile phone.

As Ximena retook her seat next to Ricky, the musicians struck up a final hymn.

Alma shed quiet tears, with Andy—discreetly—holding her hand.

There was a part of Alma that wished she raised her children in Sombra. Maybe then, they wouldn't have moved away.

She wanted to wrap herself in the shadows of her mother.

All the while, Cova kept her head high. It had been decades since there were any tears left in her. Pain had seeped into every crevice of her skin like water. Frankly, she didn't know who she was without it.

She couldn't breathe, and just wanted to return to Spain.

As the music played, Julián shut his eyes and flicked through images of what-might-have-been. Twirling his mother's braided ring on his finger.

What if he stayed and took his place alongside his father? What if he came home instead of waiting for a green card? What if Tino had not died that afternoon?

Julián needed his parents to forgive him.

Some pews away, a Muslim statesman shared their grief without their knowledge. Paying respect to the departed in silent distance. Since his father died, Ibrahim—Adil's son—stayed in contact with his aunt Fatimah. But they told no one, and he was careful not to step across the aisle.

* * *

When the service ended, people rushed towards the family to offer their sympathies, but Cova noticed a woman to her left heading for the exit.

'Patti?'

Her old friend shook her hand like a stranger—'Condolences, Cova.'

'Where have you been all these years?' Cova was glad to see her familiar face.

'I can ask you the same question,' Patti replied, cooling herself with a woven hand fan of dried palm leaves. 'You simply—vanished.'

Cova took a breath and lifted her chin. 'I moved—we moved—to Spain. Better opportunities, you know how it is.'

'No, actually, I don't.' Patti smiled, almost icily.

Cova was surprised by the bitterness in her old friend's voice—this was not how she remembered her Sparkles partner.

'I could never leave The Islands,' Patti said with finality.

Cova gave her a slight smile. 'Uh, are you married? Do you have kids?'

Really?—Patti thought. Even the sophisticated Covadonga Castillo—who moved abroad—asked the same banal, insulting questions.

'I couldn't have children,' Patti slammed. 'Freddie's fault.'

There was just a touch of surprise on Cova's face.

'Didn't you know? I kept him—company—after you—disappeared. He fell in with my dad and the Rodríguezes, then I got pregnant, he panicked. Said he wouldn't leave his wife. So, he made me get an abortion—the asshole—oh, God rest his soul. It messed me up, I'm sure you can imagine.'

'I'm so sorry,' Cova didn't expect the epic narrative. 'I—I had no idea.'

'Well, at least there isn't a Castillo de Montijo bastard running around, no?'

Cova thought to end the conversation—but hoped to do so on a better note.

'Aren't you going to ask about my father?' Patti filled the awkward silence.

'Yes, of course,' Cova was grateful for the prompt. 'How is your father these days?'

'Dead,' Patti replied, dispassionate. 'Thanks to Freddie.'

Cova's breath caught in her throat.

'He and Manny padded an army contract, then pinned it on my father when they were caught. He was dishonoured. Worse thing you can do to a military man. He killed himself.' Patti recounted without emotion. Her hand tirelessly flicking her woven hand fan.

A tear rolled down Cova's cheek.

Patti checked the time on her watch. She was still wearing the digital Casio from her father.

She looked around and saw Durog Marasigan headed their way. 'I better go.'

Cova noticed the wordless exchange between her old friend and the repulsive president.

'He's been good to me,' Patti immediately declared. 'I met him in the province, after the abortion. He understood the suffering and pain of being violated like that. He became my friend, my protector. Told me he'd help me get justice from Freddie.'

They were approached by several armed men before Patti could finish.

'Madam, we have to leave.'

Patti nodded, then turned back to Cova. 'It was good to see you again, Coco. I only wish it were under different circumstances.'

And with that Patti Gálvez—more widely known as the president's mistress, Madam Marasigan—rejoined her escort.

* * *

Pepa couldn't believe she was at a mass with Durog and Madam— *What luck!*—he was known to never attend such religious customs.

The young maid didn't feel appropriately dressed to sit by the Castillos, but Núria insisted she stay near them at the front.

'Are you okay?' the soft-spoken Señorita Núria handed her a tissue. Pepa dabbed her eyes and nodded shyly. She was overwhelmed by a mix of emotions, uncertain how to navigate the currents.

As always, she found strength in the golden talisman in her pocket.

The Castillos felt like—*family*—and yet, nothing could be more foreign to her.

She looked down at the skirt and blouse that she had on, embarrassed that they were hand-me-downs from Núria. (She didn't otherwise have anything appropriate to wear.)

It would have been the perfect occasion for her nice pearl studs— the Yrasteguis gave all the maids a pair the previous Christmas. (Not their fault they didn't know her ears weren't pierced.)

Pepa remembered Doña Fatimah warmly—the old lady didn't speak much but was always kind. Even offered to send her back to school.

But Pepa preferred to work at Sombra—what could ever be better than life on the grand estate?

She never imagined that Doña Fatimah might die.

'Don't worry, Pepa,' Núria consoled the sobbing girl. 'Everything will be okay.'

Núria promised that Doña Alma wouldn't cast her out on the streets. A probability that Pepa had never considered.

* * *

As the church emptied, off to the side behind some pillars, Ricky was reunited with his godfathers. He hadn't seen the 'Chinese mafia'—as his sisters called them—since his childhood.

They each handed him an envelope with cash. Ricky supposed it was some unfamiliar Chinese custom.

Harrison Chong—aka Chongki, the reclusive Taiwanese billionaire—was the only one he recognised from a few photos in the media.

'My condolences,' Chongki handed him cash and—*a tiny melon?*

'It represents family,' his sharply dressed godfather said of the monk fruit.

Ricky continued scratching his arm and cocked his head. Behind him, he noticed a band of shifty men trying to blend into the crowd.

'You do know where the money is, yes?' his godfather's tone was clipped.

Ricky remained in silent confusion.

'How unfortunate,' Chongki pressed his lips into a smile. Ostensibly resigned.

He took back the monk fruit and crushed it.

'Fred insisted family ties were stronger here than in China, the bond between fathers and sons,' another toothless grin as he cracked the gourd. 'Guess he was being—*creative*. As always.'

Ricky wasn't thrilled to get a lecture on his father from a stranger, but his muddled brain couldn't formulate a response.

He stared blankly at Harrison Chong with his mouth hanging open. He began to cough as an altar boy walked past with a censer. The brass container still burned the last of the myrrh.

'So many ceremonies, you Catholic Islanders,' Chongki threw the crushed fruit on the ground. 'I still have that gold coin from your baptism—what a party, you Castillos.' He wiped his hands on a hankie and shook his head. 'Impressive. Your father said personalised coins were minted each time a child was born into the family. *Ha*, told me to sell it if I went broke,' he trailed back over his memories without a smile.

Ricky wasn't enjoying the reminiscence either.

Out of the corner of his eye, he thought he saw Tukô, but the figure slinked away before he could be certain. *Thank God*. Maybe he'd finally be left alone. With his father dead, what could anyone still want from him?

'So, what happens with the estate?' Chongki asked the question on everyone's mind.

'Uh, I don't know,' Ricky was truthful. 'That's up to my aunts, and I'm not privy to their discussions.'

He scratched his other arm and searched the church for his mother—his skin was burning, and mosquitoes were eating him alive.

There was a crack of thunder and a snap of lightning.

Ricky covered his ears and shut his eyes—it was time to go.

'Well, I'm glad I held on to that special coin of yours,' Harrison Chong patted Ricky's shoulder like a patronising uncle. '*Zàijiàn*, Federico the Third.'

Ricky stared slack-jawed as the tycoon melted into the throng. His gang of goons disappearing with him.

The church was crawling with important people and their bodyguards. Uniformed cops and a host of undercover security.

Men with weapons always made Ricky nervous. He looked around—certain he was in someone's crosshairs. He checked his pocket, desperate for another gram.

Joder—someone had slipped in a mobile phone.

A blinking text—'Tick-tock, I'll see you soon.'

This was not the way he envisioned saying goodbye to his family. With each one rushing off to somewhere else.

His mother unaware, his aunts impervious, his cousins undaunted by his fears.

No one seemed to see that ghosts were coming, and Aba's wasn't the only grave they marked.

'Hijo?'

He jumped as his mother grasped his arm.

'Mom,' he hugged her like a lifebuoy. 'There you are—it's time to get us home.'

Chapter 37

La Cuenta y la Deuda | **The Accounting and the Debt** | Ang Pagbilang at ang Utang

The house stood at the end of a long, serpentine drive carpeted in potholes and weeds. In patches, there were glimpses of cobbled granite and pebble wash, worn smooth and stained with age.

The trodden path was attended by a sorry phalanx of trees—colourless and balding—like disappointed ancestors trapped in eternal despondency.

Once magnificently verdant, the sprawling lawn gasped brown with lack of care.

A stagnant fountain sat squat at the entrance roundabout. Consumed by moss and a settlement of insects.

The whole ensemble barely whispered a breath of elegant days.

The masters of the house were no longer home.

Julián and Cova had returned to foreign shores. Alma reigned in her own manor. And Maca resettled in a government-funded penthouse palace.

In Sombra's back garden, by the chapel, the young maid Pepa tended to the remnants of the world they left behind.

She watered flowers, pulled up weeds, and uttered prayers while tracing the flourish of the letters on the tombstones.

'Fatimah de Castillo, beloved Aba.'

To her left: 'Federico Julián Castillo, querido de Montijo a Manila.'

The graves were sheltered by a wide molave, which over the years had grown hollow and strangled by vines.

In Pepa's home province, such trees became a storied banyan— colonised by spirits, a mystic portal to other realms.

She sat awhile on a stone bench to cool down, rubbing her golden talisman out of habit. It was a gift from the masters handed down her family. Received by her elders when her mother was born—it even had her name on it: 'Freidah Magpantay, daughter of Nena.'

'Pepa,' her great-grandfather Tining had once instructed, 'we must be grateful and accept the lot in life that we are given.'

Their lot in life was to serve those to whom God had given gold.

* * *

They hit him again, and as he gasped for air, the gold coin they had shoved down his throat sputtered out of his mouth. Flipping off his chin and rolling to the floor.

'Mga lecheng Castillo.'

Ricky recognised the speaker—a plain-clothes cop he'd previously encountered. He wondered where they got the keepsake from his christening.

'People are starving—and you mint your own useless coins. Entitled thieves!'

Ricky let the words—and targeted spit—wash over him. He'd lost all feeling by the third time he was flogged.

In a fog of pain, he thought he heard a gecko—*tick, tock*—was he back on the sub?

Or nauseous from loss of blood?

* * *

'You're late,' he coughed and spat a blood-orange glob into a saturated napkin.

'Bah, I am never late, Facundo,' the older man corrected. 'Lesser men simply fail to function at my pace.' He hobbled closer, patting down his suit of wrinkled linen. 'So—click, clack—to what do I owe the honour of being summoned?'

It was rare for the two most powerful men on the islands to meet. There wasn't a space large enough for their egos.

Other than their closest aides, they were alone in the safe room beneath the palace.

Durog Marasigan poured his enemy—erstwhile friend—a shot of brandy. The amber liquid shone gold through the presidential seal etched on the glass.

He handed it to his guest and waved him to a seat.

'As president—'

'For now, Facundo. You are president—for now. Click.' The guest pushed his green-tinted glasses up his nose. In the lighting, the gold rings on his fingers sparkled emerald.

'Are you threatening me?' Durog kept his voice low.

The guest laughed unreservedly. 'My boy—click, clack—I wouldn't bother.' He handed the brandy to an aide who sipped it in practiced motion. Clack, click.

'Gaddamit Eliseo, get those 'tang-inang dentures fixed! That clicking doesn't scare me.' Durog's fist trembled in anger.

Eliseo Salazar—aka Mang Eloy, aka Tukô—leaned back in his chair. 'You don't need me to frighten you, Facundo—you're all afraid of your own shadows.'

Still alive, Tukô's aide passed him back the drink.

Durog coughed. His chest rattling like a sack of stones.

'Wipe your mouth, Facundo,' Tukô said, unsympathetic. 'And stop acting like your life is near its end.' He flicked orange spit off his suit. 'People like us don't die—we're constantly reincarnated.'

Durog spat a wad of betel nut on to the floor.

'Look Eloy, truly, we're on the same side,' he stifled a cough. 'I'm—fixing—our mutual problems created by Freddie Castillo.' Another cough. 'For a small share of your market, I'll throw in Pip Rodríguez and ensure he's convicted of plunder. I'm tired of him, and I know you want payback for his parents' double crossing you.'

Unintrigued, Tukô kept silent.

Durog picked up a small brass bell. 'Shall we seal our agreement with a special game of pusoy dos—two hearts—for old times' sake?' He rang the bell without waiting for an answer.

A side door opened.

The hashtag leader nodded as a well-dressed man ushered in a bevy of naked Caucasian women. Each only wearing high-heeled shoes. The man pushed them forward with a slap on the bum.

As the women took turns kissing the president on the mouth, Tukô leered at their shivering, silicone-d bodies.

'Click, cluck, I'm impressed, Armando,' he smirked at the man who brought them in. 'I see your position in the power company has improved your pull with the ladies.'

Through the years, Armando 'Manny' Santos had learned when not to speak. It's how he moved past Mikey Reyes, straight to Durog.

Manny gave a slight nod and led the ladies out through another doorway.

A large television came on in the safe room.

On screen—in full high-definition colour—the women were seen entering a long, brightly-lit hallway. Part of a network of tunnels underneath the presidential palace.

The volume was raised on the TV as a whistle sounded. And a pair of rabid dogs was set loose on the ladies. Pusoy dos—two hearts.

Their bloodcurdling growls were the primal cry of perdition.

Watching in the safe room, the men wagered on who would survive the chase. The winner got to do whatever he wanted with any survivors.

The room filled with ferocious roars, punctuated by women's high-pitched shrieks and clicking heels. The syncopated frenzy of a ruthless flamenco.

Outside, as usual, a hail of bullets pierced the night like shooting stars.

* * *

Last Ricky Castillo remembered, he was at the speakeasy Armario. His head resting on a table when a burst of light crashed into his gloom.

A flood of boots—raining metal—stormed through the doorway.

Ricky's head spun at the onslaught of activity. Dizzied by pings and tiny sparks of lightning in the darkness.

He shut his eyes and failed to notice the fleeing bar staff.

'*Principe* Castillo!' A heavy hand yanked him by the hair. 'You're coming with us.'

When next he came to, someone had kicked him in the groin.

'Where is your father? And where is the stolen loot?'

In agony, Ricky spluttered to explain they had it wrong. He knew nothing. He'd done nothing. He was—nothing. A victim of his ignorance and inheritance.

They grabbed a blood-soaked fistful of his hair and pulled a burlap sack over his head.

Held flat on the ground, buckets of sewage were endlessly poured on his face.

Ricky always knew that at the end he would drown.

* * *

Legend says that as the Night's tail erupted in lead and steel, the ground roared and shook Dawn back into darkness.

In truth, Po'on Volcano thundered open and ashfall drenched Manila. Extinguishing colours and choking the air with sulphur.

Underground, the president recorded a message for later broadcast. His deal with The Lizard was signed in blood and gold.

'Fellow Islanders,' his post-eruption pronouncement began, 'in our time of need, who else can we turn to but family?'

Pepa listened to the speech on her mobile while tidying Ricky's room. It always smelled rancid, no matter how she cleaned.

She hadn't seen him in months but there was always laundry.

He was officially the lone Castillo still residing in Sombra. (His mother had not returned from Europe.)

In the last few weeks, Pepa noticed that things went missing—Ricky's TV, his computer, his old cameras. Then, items began to vanish from Sombra's salons: a Chinese vase, a Persian carpet, some ivory carvings. But it wasn't her place to question the absent señorito.

'Our great brothers in China are sending aid,' #Durog continued. 'There's a new world order—and many of us have Chinese blood. They will even help the Moros get all their villages on to the power grid.'

Pepa knew what it was like to have no power. She was raised in a bamboo hut on stilts without electricity.

'But you must behave and stop fighting me,' the president bleated. 'This isn't time for selfish inclinations—'

Pepa felt bad for her troubled señorito—she knew what it was like to be abandoned. Her grandmother Nena had died before she was born, and her teenaged mother left her in the care of her elders, Tining and Lydia.

They had since died—and Pepa was all alone.

* * *

Stuck in traffic, Núria listened to the same presidential proclamation in her car. She was headed to Sombra to drop off Pepa's groceries.

She made the same trip every week for the last six months.

The hashtag president announced the installation of checkpoints and a nationwide curfew. Reminding Núria of the era the Grown-Ups called 'The Challenges'.

She wondered how those in charge forgot that power was a social contract.

Sigh—if only the public wanted to break the pact.

* * *

'Thanks, Pepa. I'll see you next week,' Núria was rushing to get home before a looming downpour. As she got in her car, the young maid ran down the drive to open the gate.

When she pulled it back, there was a large package blocking the path to the street.

Had Señora Maca dropped off her laundry in haste?

Yes, the old dragon still came by for all sorts of chores.

'Pepa?' Núria stepped out of her car to check on the holdup, just as the sky shattered in pieces over the estate. Hardening in the places still coated with volcanic ash.

'Puñeta!' Núria squealed, dashing back to her car. Leaving Pepa in the rain to move the package.

On the radio, Durog was still declaiming: 'Those priests fuelling revolution are leftovers of white colonialism—like democracy. They serve no purpose in our Asian world. A strong leader—like me—will take care of you!'

He coughed and was forced to take a breath.

Núria stepped back out of her car to shield Pepa with an umbrella. The young maid was struggling to shift the oversized load. She failed to notice her heirloom talisman slip out of her uniform pocket.

'It's too heavy, Señorita—'

Núria caught a glimpse of the gold as it sank in the mud. She tried to retrieve it, unaware that she—and all her cousins—had a similar keepsake.

Pepa fell back in her flipflops as the floodwaters rose. She tripped over Núria, whose wind-blown umbrella got caught on the package.

Pulling on the implement, Núria—unintentionally—undid a corner of the cumbersome bundle. Releasing a shroud—a jumble—of lifeless flies.

As rain poured in sheets of concrete from the pallid heavens, Pepa scrambled over and carefully peeled back the tarp.

Under the sheet, Señorito Ricky stared blankly at the sky—his mouth wide open, with a golden token from his christening on his tongue.

Pepa made no sound as Núria shrieked beside her.

They were ignored by the gridlocked traffic on Marasigan Drive, the street formerly known as Calle Sombra.

A piece of cardboard was tacked on to Ricky's bloated, disfigured corpse.

On one side, in characters Pepa couldn't read: 'Rich is the man with no debts.'

On the other, in Filipino, below some sort of printed reptile: '*Bayad sa utang.*'

In payment of debt?

Pepa handed the soaking card to a horrified Núria, who was crumpled beside her, lapped by a rising tide—a foetid mix of rain and sludge and sewage.

Lost in the muck was Pepa's lucky medallion, imprinted with her mother's name, the Castillo crest and motto—written in a language she didn't understand.

'*La Familia Primero: Unida y Protegida*'

Family First: United and Protected.

* * *

Legend says that on the day the last Federico Castillo was found, raindrops went from pebbles to the size of stones. Then, a torrent of blazing boulders pounded on rooftops.

In the thunderous tempest, Sombra's shadows trembled and cobwebs shivered—while an army of lizards, the house over, scuttled down walls.

Somewhere, unseen, a lone bullfrog moaned to a chorus of geckos.

A singular dirge for the House on Calle Sombra.

'Dijeron que antiguamente
se fue la verdad al cielo;
tal la pusieron los hombres,
que desde entonces no ha vuelto.'

'They said that in ancient times
truth fled to heaven;
driven to do so by men,
it's not been heard of since.'

'Sabi nila noong unang panahon
tumakbo ang katotohanan sa langit;
dinahas ng sangkatauhan,
hindi na ito nagparamdam mula noon.'

*Highlighted by Doña Fatimah de Castillo in her copy of *La Dorotea* by Spanish writer Lope de Vega.

CLOSURE

Los Cabos Sueltos y los Restos | **Loose Ends and Leftovers** | Ang 'Di Natapos at ang Tiratira

One Year Later.

Babylon

In a language he was just beginning to understand, Sergio Pereira was asked what he was doing.

'*Mermão*, only taking a photo—beautiful view—'

'Better take it with your mind, *vei*—no geo-tagging. Put that away.'

Sergio did as told and put the mobile phone back in his shirt pocket.

It's not as if he was going to post the photo online, but he didn't want to upset these Friends-of-Friends either way. It was early days—he was just getting to know them.

The rough lean man walked to a corner table without another word, expecting Sergio to follow.

He waved one of the skimpily clad waitresses over and pulled back a chair. Sergio did the same, taking a guava from a bowl on the table as he sat down.

'Que, *mano*, what have you got for me?' the man—his contact—looked bored.

'Whatever you need, I can get,' Sergio took a bite of the immature fruit, hoping he looked nonchalant. It was the reply he was told to give when asked that question.

The man snorted, a combination laugh-and-sneer. He shook his head slowly, as if performing a mime. 'Like I haven't heard that before.'

'Look, I won't waste your time, we have people all over—sources and distributors,' Sergio lowered his voice and leaned forward, 'and we're expanding. You've heard of the New Silk Road, yes? We've got spotters all along that route—'

Bem, the contact, had no idea what Sergio meant, but he nodded, squinting his eyes to look smarter.

Sergio twitched as his pocket began to vibrate. 'Excuse me,' he rose without waiting for a reply, 'I need to take this call.'

He pulled his mobile out of his pocket and returned to the balcony. Sergio noticed several pairs of eyes following him.

He pressed the answer button.

'Joder, I've been trying to reach you for days—why are you only returning my calls now?'—careful to keep his voice low.

'It's hard with the time difference,' the line crackled.

'Where are you?' he worried the phones were bugged.

'Home, where else?'

A heavy silence. Then, 'Oye, can I come back now? What do you think?' he asked, earnest.

'Do you really want to be a dead man? Stay put, we don't need more trouble.'

'Easy for you to say, you're not the one living with puto rats,' he couldn't contain his frustration. 'It's disgusting, I'm serious. At least in the jungle it was—I don't know—fresher. Clean air, fresh food, unpolluted water. This has been—'

'Well, no one commanded you to go there—why did you pick that place?'

'Shitholes are the best hideouts when you're being chased, rule number one,' he explained. 'Unruly, lawless, and people are—shall we say—more easily swayed to do things for you because they need to be—resourceful—to survive.'

'And you couldn't have gone to—no sé—Colombia?' the voice echoed. The distance evident despite the cellular connection.

'*Un poco* cliché, no? Plus, the friends who helped me get out wanted to expand their market here—it's untapped, waiting to be mined. I pass for a local. Sort of. I'm still honing my translation skills, you know—Spanish—Portuguese, not too different.'

'If you say so. Bueno, what did you want?'

'I want to come home.' Sergio confessed.

'A million times, no. We've been over this—you're a dead man the minute you set foot here.'

Another loaded silence.

He took a breath—'I need money.'

'You always do, but you just said you're expanding on a growing market, or whatever. So I'm sure it's just a matter of time before things look up.'

'Please,' he stopped before saying her name—he feared the call being traced. Every week or so he changed his number. He was just grateful she still returned his calls.

So far.

'Please, I'm alone here—I missed Mom's funeral—my daughters aren't speaking to me—and my son—'

'Think of it this way—you're unencumbered. Isn't that what you always wanted?'

He said nothing. Not appreciating the sarcasm.

'Mira,' the long-distance caller again, 'I will find a way to send you some money, pero that's the last of it, okay? You can't imagine how much it costs to run this place, and I am keeping your bastard grandchild employed, remember? She's not the smartest of maids. This is what you get for sleeping with her grandmother in the first place. I mean, really, the cook's daughter, for God's sake. Your bastard child then begot another bastard—no surprise.'

'I know, I'm sorry. I can't thank you enough for helping,' he muttered meekly. 'So, they stopped battling you for it?'—he always changed the topic when he was uncomfortable.

The caller laughed. 'The house? What other choice do they have? I have signed papers.'

'But they're not real,' Sergio stated.

'Well, they look more real than your forgeries, idiota, and I didn't bandy them around to pay a debt.'

He had always discussed things with her—every business opportunity, every move—calculated and decided by his sister. She was always the smart one. The one time he hadn't consulted her, things went awry.

He would never make that mistake again.

'Listen,' his smart sister said, 'I'm declaring the company bankrupt. The others will think I'm doing them a favour. So, I can't keep sending you money. My husband can't afford to have his reputation besmirched by your shenanigans, not with—you-know-who—very, very, sick. Even his doctors in China can't help him.'

He had no idea that lunatic despot was ill.

Again, the line crackled. 'You've always been good at fending for yourself, so—fend for yourself. We've all had to.'

Then, she hung up.

He looked at the sun setting over Rio de Janeiro, wondering how he ended up in Babilonia. One of its most dangerous hillside neighbourhoods.

The views were breath-taking, but the homes were a hodgepodge of cinderblocks and cement. The streets were winding treacherous alleys, and the smells were nauseating.

On every corner—and there were many—guns and goons. That— and the backed-up sewage—reminded him of home.

He shouldn't complain, he knew that. At least, he was alive.

Which was more than he could say for his son.

He found out while he was in Sabah. Hiding in a wooden shack with friends of his father-in-law. Or rather, his former father-in-law.

He escaped, but his son was dead. Killed by any number of his enemies.

It was online. In the news. Gone viral. Another casualty of his sins.

He stood there for a moment, gazing out at Copacabana bejewelled by night lights against a softly bruised sky. All gold and pink and purple. A town embraced by its textured shadows.

No one knew him, which is why he chose this place.

He hated it.

The sticky breeze felt harsh on his skin, and he recalled a kinder wind.

There was a time when he had his own island. And his own chopper to take him to it from his city.

Once, a young boy playing in the sand took his photo, using a small instamatic camera that wasn't at risk of geo-tagging.

He loved that image.

His eyes blurred, welling with tears.

Coño—this was not the way to win over the leader of this Rio gang.

He wiped his face and put his cheap Chinese mobile back in his pocket. Then, he reached for another guava from a low hanging branch.

A gecko croaked—his heart stopped—*Tukô?*

He looked left—then right—he took a breath.

This was not how he envisioned living out his days.

He composed himself—just as his mother taught him—and returned to the mark at the table.

Acknowledgements

My eternal gratitude to the following for their immeasurable support during the production of this book:

Angela Casauay
Isabel Olondriz
Monica Olondriz
Anton Ortigas
Cristina Ortigas
Inés Ortigas
The Family of Danny Pangan
Danton Remoto
Silverlens Galleries: Isa Lorenzo and Rach Rillo
Corinne Goodrich & Michael Visconti
Katherine Visconti